GEORGE FOY

Tidal Race

Fontana/Collins

This book is dedicated to the people who helped, including Gerry and Merle Lynn Brown, Harry Trumbore, Harvey Klinger, Bill Strachan, Gerry Howard, Beverly Lewis Eames, Laura and Michael Baksa, Vicki and Iain Nasatir, Peter Dervis, Jane Vonnegut, Caleb and Pat Warren, Toby Eady, Lavinia Branca, Maria Teresa Train, Chester Crosby, Jr., Kip and Lee Gowans, Joe Amaral, Manny and Yoko Ax, Mark Cohen, Judy Cressy, Donna Levitan, Jacques Barzun, David J. Damkoehler, Dan Burke, Anne LeClaire, Sepp and Peg Dietzgen, Leonard Rodsham, E.P., A.A., C.W., C.S., and last but not least, my parents, my brother, Louis, and especially Ann and Skye.

First published in 1984 by
The Viking Press, New York as *Asia Rip*
First published by Fontana Books 1985
Second impression July 1986

Copyright © 1984 by George Foy

Made and printed in Great Britain by
William Collins Sons & Co. Ltd, Glasgow

PROLOGUE

The water was turning purple.

At first the man couldn't believe what he was seeing. His eyes were doing strange things; vision blurring then sharpening, fading and sometimes failing altogether as he sank into unconsciousness. Then he realized what was colouring the water.

Blood. The decks were soaked in it. Blood was seeping from the freeing ports of his trawler as she settled deeper into the waves. It was trickling gently down the scuppers towards his body as he lay sprawled against the wheelhouse astern.

Fascinated, he watched as each succeeding hiss of foam pushed a fraction of an inch further up the deck towards his useless legs. As it advanced, the dark water melded with the scarlet blood that was still pumping from the piercing wound in his abdomen.

His boat was taking almost as long to die as he was.

Blood was no longer spurting from the wounds in Tony's body, or Jed's. And for the first time he realized that the pathetic sobbing noises Dan had been making all night, all morning, had ceased. Dan was underwater now.

The sun's touch was almost hot. The man licked his parched lips and tried to feel his own body. The pain was bad but more terrible was the feeling of inner entropy, as if each part of his body, nerve by nerve, were losing touch with the whole.

It had taken hours for him to drag himself to where the radios were fastened. The longer-range sets had gone dead, shorted out by water in the engine room or deliberately sabotaged, but he was able to curl his fingers around the walkie-talkie at his side. He had to lift it out of the deepening water, although he no longer had the strength to speak into its mouthpiece any more, and the last message he had managed to tap out by squeezing the transmit button, on and off, had gone unanswered. But it was his last link to the real world. When he tried to raise the walkie-talkie he lost consciousness again.

He woke for the last time an hour later. Dan, Tony, and Jed had all vanished, drifted away in the ocean that now covered most of the deck. Blue water welled over the gunwales, but only a russet colour surrounded his chest.

The boat lurched and the freezing water crept towards his mouth. Cold had numbed the pain. He thought of his boat and his wife, the two things he most believed in. He thought of his father and the sea, the two things he had always struggled against. He had left the city to fight the sea instead of his father, yet both had beaten him in the end.

Then there was no time left for thought. A red cloud of anger exploded in his mind as the sea closed gently over his head.

CHAPTER ONE

The weather was much too fair for the *Marie S* to disappear.

Admittedly, what fishermen termed 'fair' on Nantucket Shoals would have sent mariners in most other parts of the world pounding for shelter, diesels at full tilt and radiotelephones pegged to the international marine distress frequency – just in case.

But these atmospheric conditions were better than good – they stood just short of miraculous for a tenth of November. Wind sighing gently, five to ten knots from the southwest, swells three to five feet. The sun struck reflections wherever it touched the water, and the sea was a dangerously inviting deep blue.

Visibility was five miles (sinking to three in haze), courtesy of a high-pressure zone from central Canada that had dropped in on New England like a kindly uncle, bringing gifts of clear skies and tales of distant prairies where air cooled quickly in the fall.

The crew of the sixty-five-foot fishing vessel *Sofia* was working the middle of Nantucket Shoals that November afternoon, setting a series of five longlines off Fishing Rip in a north–south pattern in fifteen fathoms of water. They were twenty miles southeast of Nantucket Island, fifty miles southeast of Cape Cod, off the southern corner of Massachusetts.

The gear had been dumped in the morning, two hours before the tide turned at midday. The turn of the tide was when codfish, haddock, and other groundfish *Sofia* was hunting got peckish and would take the sea-clam bait the longlines offered.

It was after four p.m., and they had been hauling gear for close to two hours.

The three men were working hard to take advantage of the good weather that had first come into the area on 8

November. The thermometer was barely touching forty-five degrees, but still sweat pearled and ran down their brows as the men coiled line and frenetically stowed fish.

They were not working fast enough for *Sofia*'s skipper.

Larsen hooked cod with a short gaff, heaving it into the gaping hatch of a fishhold midships at a rate young Billy, the deckhand, was finding hard to follow.

The skipper's legs were braced against the ship's roll, his large hands working fast and without fuss. His whole way of moving a tall, hunched body denoted impatience with anything that slowed progress between the last thing he'd done and the next thing he had to accomplish.

He had an uncompromising chin and a long, curved nose. His grey eyes were set at the end of two sprays of creases, deep wrinkles carved by sea glare. Lines that belied his thirty-three years.

His thick black hair was cut workmanlike short, permanently tousled. He wore patched khakis, a French Army shirt, and an Australian Army bush jacket. An ebony-handled sheath knife hung from his belt as if it had grown there. His drill trousers were rapidly turning the colour of cod blood.

Larsen shoved the last fish into the hold, shouted to his mate to hose down the deck, and climbed swiftly to the wheelhouse.

There was a reason for working fast at this time of year. This good weather was a freak. There was no way it could hold; it could, in fact, turn at any moment – as it had last November.

The crew of *Sofia* remembered last November vividly.

The weather then had run truer to Nantucket Shoals form, a string of low-pressure fronts keeping the fleet idle and losing money for a three-week stretch. Then had come a break – a continental high, like this one – and what boats had not been laid up or repossessed by the bank put out faster than kids at recess. But it was as if the sea had planned an ambush. A circular storm that was supposed to stay south of Hatteras sneaked up on Georges Bank. Larsen and *Sofia* found themselves battling a screaming madness of thirty-foot waves and hurricane-force winds that carried away their radar and the wheelhouse windows and vaporized two boats and five men from the Cape fleet as if they had never existed.

The first call came over *Sofia*'s VHF radio set, bolted to the buff steel deckhead of the wheelhouse.

'Fishing vessel *Sofia*, fishing vessel *Sofia*, *Sofia* this is *Pegasus*, *Pegasus*, Whisky Hotel X-ray 482, come in, *Sofia*.'

Tom Dryer, skipper of the fifty-foot Bruno-and-Stillman gillnetter *Pegasus*, always sounded like the goddamned Coast Guard on the radio.

Larsen was steaming westward for the next longline, a mile-long, quarter-inch-thick yellow nylon rope punctuated with baited hooks every nine feet, spread out and anchored flush with the ocean floor fifteen fathoms below. The anchors at each end of the rope were connected to buoys for recovery. The buoys consisted of tall, vertical floats topped with a radar reflector and flag. It was for one of these, bobbing and weaving in the distant swells, that Larsen was aiming.

One hand reached automatically for the VHF above his head, thumbed the transmit button, his eyes never quitting the next buoy.

'*Pegasus*, *Sofia*.'

'Switch'n'answer twenty-five Lars over.'

'Twenty-five.' The fisherman impatiently stabbed the digital channel selector from sixteen, the distress and call-up frequency, to channel twenty-five. Some skippers liked to anaesthetize the lonely hours out of sight of land by talking shop over the VHF. Larsen was not one of them.

'*Sofia*, *Pegasus*.'

'What is it, Tom?'

Dryer finally got sick of the Armed Forces Radio routine.

'Lars, I got a relay for you from Mallebarre pier: they wanna know if you've seen *Marie S*.'

'Nope.' The next longline buoy was 200 yards ahead, Larsen coming up on it obliquely so the ten-foot bamboo pole with its styrofoam floats and reflector would surge within easy reach on the starboard side. Larsen left the wheel for a moment, taking the VHF mike on its concertina cord with him, to look out a starboard wheelhouse window at the deck below.

Silva, the mate, was telling young Billy, the deckhand, what seemed to be an obscene joke, to judge by the thrusting gestures of his huge right hand. Billy was listening hard and looking unutterably bored, as usual.

Larsen pounded on the window with his knuckles, pointed forward, eyebrows hoisted sarcastically, as the two men looked up. They moved next to the hydraulic line hauler, still talking, ready to take the buoy and accompanying line as it came alongside. They'd done this a thousand times.

Billy would heave the buoy inboard, swing it on deck, break the quick-release shackles to disconnect the anchor line and pass it to Silva.

The mate would take the line, and loop its half-inch nylon around the hydraulic winch (or hauler) and engage the winch drive. The anchor line would start reeling in, and Billy would coil it clockwise into a plastic tub.

Three hundred feet later, the anchor would come inboard, with the south end of the longline itself. Silva would loop the yellow longline around the hauler drum and minutes later they would see if the fish had hit or not.

'Nope,' Larsen repeated. 'I know he usually fished Little Georges, Tom, or else sometimes around Asia Rip, but I'm . . . a little further north.'

'Yeah, well, I'm coming by Pollock Rip and I'm just relaying this to you,' Dryer said, 'but Joe Sciacca's wife called the Co-op and she's worried he's overdue. He was s'posed to call in at six p.m. yesterday on the single-sideband radio and he didn't. They've been trying to raise him all day on the single-sideband.

'He was due in this morning at the latest,' Dryer continued. 'He's s'posed to be fishing the southern shoals so you might be able to reach him . . . the Coast Guard said they'll send out search and rescue tomorrow morning if he hasn't come –'

There was a crackle of static. Another boat, over the horizon and just beyond the VHF's thirty-mile range, cut into the frequency in a garble of meaningless intonations.

Larsen listened while the static faded, thumbed the transmit, stepped back to the starboard side of the wheelhouse with his left hand on the wheel.

'*Pegasus*,' he called, 'stand by for a second, stand by.'

Hooking the mike back into its overhead slot, Larsen spun the wheel, slid the throttle control to slow as the swinging, dipping marker buoy minuetted closer to *Sofia*. A twist of rudder as the boat lost speed, a short burst of RPMs: a swell bunted the pole into Silva's waiting gaff hook, and the buoy was aboard, anchor line already around the hauler and throwing off a silvery shower of saltwater as 2000 pounds of hydraulic thrust started thrumming it from the depths.

Billy coiled expertly, gloves flashing in the sun as the cold, wet line came squirting off the hauler drum.

Larsen's eyes, fine-tuned by practice, had already picked up the next buoy marking the submerged line's northern end. He adjusted the throttle to dead slow while waiting for the rest of the line to come aboard, and swung his boat north towards the buoy. It was time to give the hauler a chance to catch up.

'*Pegasus*, *Pegasus*, this is *Sofia*.'

'Yeah, Lars, what happened to you?' Dryer must have been hanging breathlessly on to the radio. Without waiting for a reply he rambled on, 'Anyway, the guys at the pier told Joe's wife you were in the same rough area and she wanted you to call for him and get back to the pier on the double-sideband radio, and also tell the other boats in the area.'

'I can do that.'

Larsen's voice was steady, modulated to carry well on the tinny, low-tolerance wavelengths of marine radio. It did not betray the unease he felt when Dryer's message had started to come through.

Larsen came from a bloodline of Norwegian seamen, many of whom had disappeared at sea, deaths heralded by off-colour morsels of news like this.

'I can also head down there and have a look, if he doesn't answer,' Larsen said. 'Most likely, though, his electrics are just on the blink . . . Tell the pier I'd like to talk to Marie

– Joe's wife – on the double-sideband, get her to call me, to get a better idea of his last position.'

'Roger, Lars,' came the reply. 'I don't think she knows, though, but I'll tell her. All set?' As if Larsen had been the one to request assistance.

'Wait, Tom.' Larsen stepped over to the chart table and thought quickly. 'Tell the pier I'll be standing by on 2182 for Marie Sciacca. Also tell the boats down your way to do some calling, and I'll try to get hold of someone on Little Georges. *Sofia* Whisky Yankee Zulu 917, out.'

Larsen turned the radio volume down as *Pegasus* relayed his own message back to the Co-op. A thud on the afterdeck and a trawl anchor was aboard, the longline itself now spinning around the brass hauler drum. Too fast – the line was slanting aft as it led through rollers on the boat's rail and down into the bowels of the southeast swells. *Sofia*, shunted northward by a stern tide, was overshooting the longline spread on a north–south axis over the sea floor below her keel.

The skipper opened the window to tell Silva to speed up the hauler – more revolutions would catch up on the line the boat had overrun – but the mate was already boosting speed, the first brown-and-silver briskets of fish were glinting, deep inside the swells, and Larsen felt an atavistic excitement years of commercial fishing had not yet succeeded in quelling squeeze gently at his gut. The first ganging was vacant, but nine feet deeper the fat, striped sides of a large whale cod slowly twisted and turned, catching the sun's rays as the fish halfheartedly fought a rising hook.

It was a good set. There were few hooks where the bait had been taken by skate or dogfish or conch or crabs, and most of the good fish were the larger and more valuable 'steak' cod. They were getting almost forty cents a pound yesterday for those in New York's Fulton Market, not a great price, but the average steaker weighed in at around twenty-five pounds.

The rest of the fish were medium market cod and small cod or 'scrod', a haddock, some hake. On one hook there was the evil skin and buck teeth of a wolf fish: a 'trash' fish, worthless to sell but tasty to eat, if appearances didn't bother you.

The kid and the older mate worked well together, Silva

gaffing fish and sliding them aft as they came aboard, Billy coiling longline like one possessed: two quick coils and a twist of the wrist to secure the hook and leader, then lay it in a plastic tub symmetrically over the previous coil.

The end of the longline looped through the hauler. Then the anchor and buoy came aboard, and mate and deckhand went aft to gut the catch.

Shipboard routines of fishing. Engine roaring as the boat headed for the next longline, three miles eastward. Larsen checked the Loran automatic direction-finding co-ordinates on a chart that defined the next longline's exact position on a featureless blue plate of ocean. He compared those co-ordinates with his present position, plotted course and speed and correction for current.

Five boxes of steak cod at forty cents a pound, minus eight cents a pound for handling charges, came to –

Flick on the autopilot. Set the new course. Wait while the primitive feedback device gets a feel for compass heading and rudder and wave resistance, and finally steadies. Larsen adjusted the VHF's background control and began calling for the overdue vessel.

'*Marie S*, *Marie S*, this is *Sofia*, *Sofia*, come in Joe.'

With the transmit button released, the solitude of short-range ether crowded into the wheelhouse. Nothing lonelier than a radio call that went unanswered. The skipper waited one minute and called again, waited three minutes and tried a third time. Still no answer.

A reflexive glance around the horizon. Larsen noted with surprise that the sky was burning orange at the edges. Another hour and it would be twilight.

He moved over to the varnished chart table in the starboard after-quarter of the wheelhouse and switched on the double-sideband radiotelephone. Unlike the coastal-range VHF, the Northstar 850 was a space-age telecommunications machine that could talk to Istanbul if one wanted it to. Not having much business with Istanbul, offshore fishermen rarely used or even kept radio watch on the double-sideband radio except in emergencies. Some of them didn't even own one.

Joe Sciacca did. It was a good insurance policy in case something happened, fifty or a hundred miles out at sea.

The tuner was preset on 2182 kilohertz cycles, the international marine distress and call-up frequency. Larsen adjusted the 'squelch' to cut down background traffic from farther afield. Any local traffic on 2182 would now come in through the wheelhouse loudspeakers. He went back to calling on the VHF. *Sofia* thudded her way into the evening, rolling contentedly eastward at a steady twelve knots like a big-assed, long-legged hooker.

There had still been no answer to Larsen's intermittent transmissions on VHF when the second call came through, this time on the double-sideband.

'*Sécurité, sécurité, sécurité.*' The international code for a cautionary message, a second-class crisis at sea, an emergency-about-to-happen. The nasal tone coming over the double-sideband belonged to Dickie, manager of the Mallebarre Co-op.

'All vessels in the vicinity of Nantucket Shoals and western Georges Bank, this is Mallebarre Fishermen's Co-operative. Please advise if you have seen the side trawler *Marie S*, overdue since last night. The vessel was supposed to be on the south part of the Nantucket Shoals or on western Georges Bank and is now overdue . . . Vessel is painted dark green with white trim and a white wheelhouse aft. Her federal registration numbers are 576318. The US Coast Guard will be starting a search tomorrow. Please advise if you have seen this vessel.'

The message was repeated, then static rushed to fill the void as the Co-op's radiotelephone went off the air.

Larsen slowed his boat to half-speed. Outside the wheelhouse windows, sunset had been replaced by a deep purple twilight. It was almost dark.

He stood at the wheel, eyes watching the radar screen bolted next to the steering station. The Furuno radar was set for close-quarters work, its foraging microwaves sweeping everything within a half-mile radius into a cathode display screen. The aluminium radar reflector from a longline buoy stuck out on the screen, a yellow intrusion on the backdrop

14

of ocean.

Answers from vessels in the shipping lanes started to come through.

'Mallebarre Co-op, this is Nantucket Lightship. Negative sighting on this vessel.'

'Mallebarre Co-op, dis is *Tromsø Princess*.' The accent fitted the name. 'Ve are yust ten miles north of southern end of Great South Channel.' That would put them twenty-five miles southeast of *Sofia*. 'Ve have not seen de vessel you describe, only a stern trawler.'

'Mallebarre Co-op, this is *Shamrock*, Loran co-ordinates 2345–6789.'

'Mallebarre Co-op, this is the fishing vessel *Santa Caterina*.'

'We have not seen her.'

'We haven't seen any vessel like you describe.'

'Negative on that boat.'

Silva came up the companionway from the saloon below. The opening hatch threw a smell of black coffee and a splash of yellow light into the darkened wheelhouse.

'Shut the goddamn hatch, Long John, you've just shattered my night vision. You've got to dim the saloon lights before coming up.'

'Sorry, Captain, sir.' There was a chuckle in the back of the mate's throat.

'Your mother, Silva, you goddamn Portygee,' Larsen growled.

'Yuh muthah,' Silva agreed.

Silva shut the hatch and stood against the chart table, watching Larsen handle the wheel with one hand, searchlight control with the other. A tight, almost tactile beam of light shot out over the boat's starboard bow, skipped over swells and panned left, steadied on a dark shape rising up and down in the black waves 150 feet ahead.

A pressure that had been building in Larsen's brain for the past hour suddenly carried away the inhibition blocking it.

Larsen pulled the engine controls to neutral, gave her some starboard helm so *Sofia* would coast clear of the buoy, and swung around to face Silva.

'To *hell* with it!'

'What's up, doc?' The mate was impassive.

'Long John' Silva was a huge man, a little shorter than Larsen but built like an M-80 tank. He was forty years old, and looked thirty – or maybe sixty, in the fashion of many Cape Verdean descendants of West African slaves and their Portuguese captors. His face was the colour of mahogany, structured around a noble Roman nose and a thatch of black curls.

The calm oval eyes and thickened cheekbones hinted American Indian blood as well. Larsen knew Silva's mother had been part Wampanoag, a Cape Cod Indian of the Algonquin Federation.

'I want you to run her. Billy can work the hauler and just shove the trawl line aft instead of coiling. I'll clean the snarls up later.'

Silva said nothing, dug a stubby finger into the top pocket of a filthy padded green jumpsuit, plucked out a mashed pack of Pall Malls, and pinched a cigarette into his mouth. A cupped hand sprouted shadow and sulphur light. His eyes never left Larsen's face. Larsen would spit it out soon enough.

He spat it out then and there.

'Joe Sciacca's overdue. He was supposed to be on the southern shoals, he was supposed to get in last night or early this morning. He didn't call in and nobody's seen him.'

'Shit.' The mate bit the word out; the half-smile usually suspended under his nose was ironed out of existence. The curse was an insult to whatever fates might have the audacity to pull a trick on someone he knew.

The skipper stepped next to Silva and snapped on the red chart light as another fishing boat came on the air.

This one had seen the *Marie S* three days ago, outbound from Mallebarre, heading on a course that could have taken her anywhere. Useless information.

'So I think we should go 'n' search around Asia Rip,' Larsen said absently. 'Marie's supposed to call me but I bet that tight-lipped Guinea never even told her where he was going to fish, so nobody could find his honey holes.' Larsen's splayed fingers drew smooth ellipses on the chart spread over the mahogany. 'What I can't figure out is, nobody's seen him. If you and Billy can handle the last trawl yourselves, I'll plot out a search area . . . the Coast Guard's not going out till tomorrow.'

A lot could happen in twelve hours to a boat in trouble.

Larsen's face looked ghoulish in the evil sheen of chart light. Silva sucked hard on his cigarette, his eyes examining the white depths and blue-green shadows emulsified together on the chart in the nasty mixture that was Asia Rip.

'Shit,' Silva repeated. The word conveyed all the disgust the mate needed to communicate.

Planets glowed and stars pricked through the night. A freshening breeze blew away patches of haze. A half-moon floated belly up in the sky, dead and yellow, then sank slowly as the night progressed, painting longer blue shadows behind the anchor windlass and rails of the forward deck. The shadows changed shape entirely every time *Sofia* turned ninety degrees to run the next leg of the grid search.

They had been searching for four hours.

The fishing boat's movement would alter as they turned, going from a slow roll when the boat moved in line with the waves to a twisty patch as she took them up the rear.

Larsen normally enjoyed standing graveyard watch in the earliest hours of the morning. The night shut you in securely in your own little world of radio waves, sextant altitudes, and magnetic bearings. Dark and warm in the wheelhouse, you could lose your identity, count out elapsed time to the next course change like a mantra, hypnotize yourself with the rhythmic swing of the boat's prow, black against a starry horizon. The ship became mother, lover, spaceship, earth, life itself in the cold loneliness of the pinprick galaxies. But you knew the secrets of those galaxies, you could calculate the movements of Altair and Betelgeuse and Aldebaran with cube logarithms and sextant, you could correct for the earth's magnetic field with a simple addition. You could understand space and the meaninglessness of time.

But now there was a leaden feel to the darkness.

Somewhere out there could be the body of a friend, rolling gently over the white sand, flesh gone cyan and sagging from sea pressure, fiddler crabs getting at the eyes. What would Marie say to their as-yet unborn child?

'Full fathom five thy father lies . . .'

How many nights at sea like this in a private cosmos of compass light, how much to show for it but a quick grope of eternity?

An occasional murmur from the VHF or double-sideband sets.

The chart showed three parallel lines, five nautical miles apart, running between Asia Rip and Davis South Shoal. Each line ran roughly east and west, for eighteen to twenty-five miles, and connected at alternate ends with a five-mile dogleg running north to the next track.

A boat following the grid on the chart would find itself weaving a shuttle between two shoals. The shuttle track covered an area Larsen had known to be a favourite fishing ground of Sciacca's, a fact confirmed by Marie Sciacca when she called in via the Co-op's double-sideband at eight p.m.

Radiotelephones sometimes had trouble conveying words, let alone emotions, but Larsen had felt his own gut contract when he heard her vocal cords hum taut with pent-up fear. Latched up just behind the fear the grief waited to bust out.

Marie Sciacca was a good friend and the wife of a good friend, but her voice still brought back memories of what had seemed like four seasons of summer as Larsen became the lucky kid in high school who was 'going' with Marie Riley. Puppy love or not, there was an emotional minefield fenced off forever for the woman who eventually married Joe Sciacca.

The shuttle search pattern was not the most effective way of quartering a given sea area; the standard navy practice of covering three sides of a series of boxes was more thorough. But *Sofia* had been nearing the end of her trip when the call from *Pegasus* came through, and fuel was running low. Even so, they were covering an area of more than 400 square miles. At no point in the search area had Larsen been more than two and a half miles from a target – if there had been a target to spot, a disabled, anchored side trawler, or an inflatable life raft.

But there was no visual contact, and the radar, though ratcheted to its maximum thirty-six-mile range, had come up with nothing other than an empty oil drum of South American manufacture and a Liberian supertanker headed for Port Elizabeth, New Jersey.

The grid was almost complete.

Billy stood braced on the starboard side of the wheelhouse. He had taken off a salt-eaten bomber jacket in deference to the warmth of his station, revealing a lurid purple T-shirt with a punk-rock logo – two rotting skeletons and the words 'Necrophilia Stinks'.

Larsen looked up from his radar console, saw the boy's unlined face reflected in the mute pink glow of instruments.

Billy refused categorically to admit being serious about anything that could not come in loud over stereo headphones, Larsen mused, but he had become almost professional in the two years since he had dropped out of high school and come to work for Larsen.

'Be dawn pretty soon,' Billy said, noticing and evading Larsen's glance.

The skipper checked the chronometer. 'Another seventeen minutes, Billy, and that's it. Let's hope we have enough fuel.'

'It's a long swim home,' the deckhand agreed shortly.

Larsen read the recording depth sounder – *Sofia* had just come over an eleven-fathom bank. He checked his dead-reckoning position on the chart, the position where the boat should be given speed, course, and elapsed time. He compared that position with the charted location of the eleven-fathom bank. Finally he checked everything against the digital readout on his Loran. You couldn't always trust the Loran towards dawn, a time when solar radiation fried radio waves, but everything squared.

'I'll go wake up Long John and make some coffee; when he comes up you can turn in. Let me know when it's six o'clock.'

*

The saloon-cum-galley area of the *Sofia* was almost luxurious, for a commercial fishing boat.

There was carpeting, a tape player and stereo system, an L-shaped settee covered in green canvas cushions, three long bookshelves stuffed with everything from nautical almanacs to Bowditch's *Practical Navigator* to volumes of poetry by Charles Bukowski. There was also eight months' worth of *Penthouse* and a score of Louis L'Amour Westerns – Billy had done a term paper on his favourite novelist just before dropping out of Mallebarre High.

The bulkheads were painted a deep yellow. Running under three portholes on the starboard side of the cabin were the crew's nominees for Playmate of the Month. November's candidates featured two brunettes and a blonde, all with exceptional curves.

Under a book rack on the forward bulkhead there was only a framed photograph bolted to the panelling. It showed a deeply tanned woman lounging on a patio. The scene looked Mediterranean, light blue and bright white behind the dusty green of olive leaves. The woman was smiling at something off camera, neck slightly bent, long fingers cradling a tin cup.

The shipmate stove was lit and fenced in with a brass rail to keep you from falling against it in heavy seas. Altogether a pleasant, warm area to spend hours off watch.

By contrast, Silva's tiny cabin aft of the saloon smelled of fish intestines and old socks. All Larsen could see of his mate as he switched on the light to wake him was a half-naked woman with huge breasts tattooed on the relaxed brown muscle of the mate's forearm. The other arm carried a tattoo of Christ bleeding profusely on the Cross.

Larsen was pouring steaming coffee from a battered pot when the wheelhouse hatch slammed open.

'Lars!'

A background of garbled voices on a VHF turned too high. Larsen scalded himself as he slammed the pot down.

'It's the *Marie S*!' Billy's voice almost cracked, tough act forgotten. He liked Joe Sciacca.

Larsen bounded up the companionway and stood by the

VHF set. There was nothing but static again.

'He just called. It sounded like him, though – ' The kid's face had acquired wrinkles all of a sudden.

'Mallebarre . . . barre Co-op.' The transmission was scratchy, very faint and almost choked in static, but Larsen felt a surge of excitement as he recognized lilts that belonged in Joe's voice. '*Marie S* . . . Co-op . . .' Something unintelligible; then 'Hear me?'

Larsen had the overhead mike in his hand when the wavelengths changed note and transmission ceased.

'*Marie S*, *Marie S*, this is *Sofia*, *Sofia*, come in Joe.'

The fisherman repeated the call a minute later. Then again and three minutes later, again. 'Where the hell is he?' Relief pushed the words out angrily.

Billy said, 'Right at the limit of range,' and Larsen scowled impatiently at the obvious, then, took a breath, relaxed and grinned at his crew. Silva had come up while Larsen called and was doing his Inscrutable Indian Brave routine by the chart table.

The skipper spread his hands wide.

'Well, what the hell – the son of a bitch is still afloat, anyway.'

For the first time he could pick out a hint of grey yellow to the east, a subtle colour, like the tint in the cheeks of a drowning victim. The sun was coming up behind a bank of clouds that told of bad weather moving in.

'Let's go home,' Larsen said.

He could already taste his first drink over at Louis'.

CHAPTER TWO

The bar was a former rum-smuggling depot, hidden behind a neon Budweiser sign in the mid-Cape woods. It smelled of spilled beer and wasted lives and was composed of Naugahyde, linoleum, chrome, ceiling fans, and long, brown shadows.

Larsen thought Louis' the best bar on Cape Cod, but it didn't suit most of the Cape's social sandwich.

It did not suit the upper crust that lived on the southern and northern strands during summer, a world of lime green and yacht shoes whose idea of refinement was a good Dun and Bradstreet rating that could play tennis.

Nor did it suit the blue-haired retirees, lemming Rambler-drivers looking for a beach to die near. The 'blueheads' provided filling for the Cape sandwich, living in flimsy plywood condos on cheap pitch-pine land in the peninsula's centre, far from any saltwater.

But for the rest – the unemployed landscapers, carpenters, fishermen – it was a refuge, a place to get drunk, play pool, swap the same bedmates, winter in, winter out.

Larsen swirled his ice around with a finger. He had already been in Louis' long enough to sink two shots of ouzo.

He needed the liquor to eat through the leaden feeling in his gut.

It was five p.m., Wednesday, 11 November. Armistice Day. The *Sofia* had been in port for four hours and there was still no sign of Joe Sciacca, his crew, or the *Marie S*. The Coast Guard had been searching since the early hours of morning, without success. Joe had not taken refuge in any anchorage or harbours in the area. No other vessels had seen or heard from him or sighted any wreckage or flares.

Fish pier gossip said the *Marie* was a goner.

And now, as expected, the weather was taking a turn for the worse. They were predicting forty to sixty-knot winds for tomorrow, temperatures below freezing: a winter storm that would made searching difficult, if not impossible.

Two polished regulation shoes underpinning stiff blue trousers encroached on Larsen's downcast field of vision.

'Captain Larsen? Lieutenant Salett. US Coast Guard.'

The fisherman looked up at the intruder, the planes of his face showing quarries in the stark lighting.

Larsen did not overly admire the Coast Guard. Like many professionals, he thought US Coast Guard 'General Officers' were too often better at filling out forms and enforcing regulations than handling ships and seamen.

Grey eyes regarded the officer levelly for a good five seconds.

'Any news of *Marie S*?' A polite enquiry.

The lieutenant seemed hesitant. 'Uh, no.' Larsen's head sank again until his eyes were once more on Salett's shoes. The long, hooked nose wriggled, a certain mark of worry, or annoyance. So what did the guy want? Still, there were times any fisherman needed the Coast Guard. The way Joe Sciacca needed them now. Larsen dimmed his scowl into a neutral stare.

It was still his favourite bar.

Salett shuffled his shiny shoes. 'We wanted to ask you about the VHF message you said you heard from the *Marie S*.'

'We' included the entire Coast Guard, the federal government, the President, the Supreme Court, and every taxpayer in the USA, solidly phalanxed behind the officer standing in front of Larsen.

The lieutenant (j.g.) had a thin face, a pimpled forehead, a pug nose lifted high in the air in counterweight to the Vast Authority saddled on his shoulders. He spoke according to the *Manual on How to Deal with Civilians*. He had a protruding Adam's apple and an expression of having just stepped in dogshit.

Larsen waved at a stool. 'Go ahead. Drink?'

'No, thank you.' Salett did not actually say 'Not while I'm on duty', but his expression semaphored the message. He glanced disapprovingly at Mad Uuno Laavinen, the Finnish quahog poacher melted over Louis' thirty-foot bar under a huge fedora and painter's pants.

Uuno was trying to persuade Sarah Eldridge to go skinny-dipping with him at Lemuel's Pond. The Black Russians she was drinking would act as antifreeze, he argued. Sarah smiled.

Salett pulled up his stool and laid a shiny attaché case on the table, snapped it open, pulled out a form in triplicate, and laid it carefully on the attaché case.

'Your boat is *Sofia*, federal numbers MS 579109 RR?'

Larsen nodded assent, fingers suggestively spinning an empty shot glass. The lieutenant ignored the hint.

'You say you heard Captain, uh, Joseph Sciacca, call on the VHF radio at, uh, oh-five-thirty hours today. Well after he was overdue?'

'I didn't *say* I heard Joe Sciacca, I *heard* Joe Sciacca.'

'Yes, well.' Salett cleared his throat, swallowed. Larsen watched, fascinated despite himself, as the man's Adam's apple shot up to hit his chinline and dived down to his throat again.

'You realize that, in response to a request from Mallebarre Co-operative, we have had two H.3 search-and-rescue choppers from Otis Air Base searching the area since oh-eight-hundred hours this morning. In addition, the cutter *Cape Race* has been diverted to the scene. So far there has been no trace of the missing vessel.'

Salett continued, 'You know you were the only vessel to hear this transmission?'

Larsen frowned. 'I told Nantucket Coast Guard station everything I knew on the VHF, while I was coming in this morning.' He paused: 'The voice was definitely Sciacca's. The signal came in very faintly but I know him and his voice very well . . .'

'Yes,' said Salett. 'After you called in, we got in touch with Mallebarre Fishermen's Co-operative and uh – Marie R. Sciacca, the captain's wife, in Squibnocket. Luckily we did not cancel the search, in case *Marie S* was broken down or in some other kind of trouble . . .'

It was the j.g.'s turn to pause.

'Now, of course, we don't hold out much hope. If our

search did not locate them . . .'

'You're not going to cancel the search now?' Larsen asked suspiciously. That would be unlike the Coast Guard, for all its faults.

'No-o-o, not at the present time. Of course, there's no point in a chopper search after dark, especially with cloud cover coming in, and they may not be able to fly out tomorrow. They're predicting winds at the airfield of over fifty knots, even a possibility of icing conditions, but the cutter will stay out and it's possible to use the Goats, the HU Albatross planes. If the wind's in the right direction.'

Larsen suddenly realized there had to be some other point to this interview. The Coast Guard man was having trouble getting to it.

The lieutenant made eye contact and for once there was an inflection of humanity in his voice as he said, 'Marie S has been posted officially missing since oh-six-hundred hours yesterday morning. We – think there's little chance. That they would have survived, I mean.'

Larsen said, 'You don't believe I heard him on the VHF last night.' It was not a question.

Salett carefully shifted his attaché case. 'You said yourself it was a weak transmission.'

'I recognized his voice.' Then, 'Have you – has the search at least – concentrated on the area his boat would have been in, given the range of a VHF, and my position when I heard the transmission?'

The search had taken all those waters in, in addition to a wide swathe of sea between Mallebarre and Little Georges Bank. The lieutenant enunciated slowly, in laymen's language, ignoring the fact that Larsen would understand marine terminology: the manual on civilians was quite clear on this point.

There was another pause. This was it.

Salett sniffed, made ballpoint marks on his government form. He said, 'You were business partners, I believe?'

'We *are* friends,' Larsen replied, trying to conceal his irritation at the man's roundabout manner. 'We *are* going to get together in a business venture next spring.'

'May I ask what it is?'

'What?'

'The business venture,' Salett said.

'We are going to buy a refrigerated truck and market our catches directly to restaurants in New York, next spring . . . if it works, we're going to do it for other Cape boats – maybe.'

The Coast Guard man continued smoothly, 'Did Sciacca have enough money for that? Do you know,' and his face went sharper with the effort of couching it diplomatically, 'if he had any money troubles you might have been aware of? Any personal problems, perhaps?'

Larsen laughed incredulously. So this was the reason the Coast Guard had tracked him as far as Louis'.

He shifted his chair to look Salett full in the eye, measured out the words. 'You . . . don't seriously . . . suspect Joe Sciacca disappeared deliberately, do you? Because of money troubles? That the VHF message I heard was a hoax, something I invented to help him get away, perhaps?' He leaned forward perilously in the rickety chair.

'No, of course not,' the officer said, uncertainly. He looked young, distinctly uncomfortable, and still officially suspicious. 'But with the expense of search and rescue – we have to check out every angle, though . . .' The clichés of bureaucracy, brought out like talismans to justify the steamrolling of individual lives.

'Are you sure he – well, maybe he was under pressure from fish dealers in New York? Perhaps they didn't care for your scheme. He might have left just so –'

'Are you interrogating Marie Sciacca like this?' Larsen demanded. Salett looked blank. 'You'd better leave her out of your angles. You can accuse me of anything you like, but it's her husband that's missing, maybe dead.'

Larsen noticed he was trying to crush the shot glass, and relaxed his grip. 'And just for the record,' he said, 'Joe Sciacca would sooner spit on a consecrated Communion wafer than leave his wife, or run away.'

A runnel of sweat escaped Salett's hairline. 'Well, she said he had gotten threats.'

'Who?'

'Mrs Sciacca.'

'So you have been questioning her,' Larsen said easily. 'You bastards.'

'Listen, Larsen. You were involved in this so-called business deal. You would know if someone might want to –'

'Want to what?'

'We don't know. Obviously. Why were they threatening Sciacca? Don't tell me this is news to you!'

Larsen stared at him. 'I honestly don't know what in hell you are talking about. Threats? From who, for chrissakes?'

'She told us the New York fish dealers.'

The fisherman laughed. 'That's the most ridiculous thing I've ever heard. Marie would have told me. It must have been a joke, or something.'

'Well, could he have been frightened into disappearing?' Salett persisted.

'By what? I tell you, this is the first I've heard of any threats. And if you stand there making up crazy stories about why he might want to disappear, instead of doing your job, and the guy is out there, probably in a sinking boat, in trouble, with a storm coming up . . .' Larsen realized he was shouting. He drew a deep breath and looked away, up, at the ceiling fan rotating slowly overhead.

Don't get mad. The Coast Guard is Joe's only chance. When he spoke again, his voice was under control.

'I'm not even going to give you the courtesy of a reply to that bullshit. Pressure from New York? I have nothing more to say to you,' the fisherman said. 'So why don't you please go back out there and co-ordinate the search, or whatever it is you do?'

Interview over. Territory unfriendly. Mission accomplished, sir. But the natives refused civilization, sir.

The lieutenant hesitated, snapped his attaché case shut and stood up awkwardly, started to say something, hesitated again, then finally stated like a tape machine, 'We will keep the Co-op informed.' The Adam's apple bobbed again and he was gone.

Larsen still stared at the fan, thinking what chance Sciacca could possibly have if they discontinued the air search tomorrow.

The old phone booth at Louis' smelled of varnish and amaretto. Inside was a narrow seat where you could talk, safe and insulated, and peer out through twin glass rectangles into the brown and neon stage set of Louis'.

Larsen had taken refuge in the booth with a palmful of dimes. He had called Marie Sciacca twice – no answer. Then he dialled Sage O'Malley's number and left a message on the answering machine.

O'Malley lived down the dirt road from Larsen, near the salt marshes. He was a GI Bill PhD who supplemented his income by teaching political science at a Boston university. The bulk of his dollars came from designing ad campaigns part-time for a New York agency.

O'Malley owned a twin-engine Cessna that he used to commute to New York once or twice a week, and chartered out occasionally. He had few customers because he was considered dangerously insane by most of the 'normal' citizens of Mallebarre.

He would need to be insane to do what Larsen had in mind: take the Cessna up in the fifty-plus winds and below-freezing temperatures forecast for tomorrow and search 2000 square miles of ocean for the *Marie S*, or what was left of her.

The Coast Guard wasn't going to do it. Larsen knew Coast Guard habits well.

At sixty knots, the big H3 choppers could no longer engage their rotors to take off, and any icing at all would cancel helicopter search-and-rescue missions for the duration. The choppers' turbines were not shielded against ice. The USCG Goats might fly – if there was no crosswind. But according to Murphy's Law of Aviation there was always a crosswind. Joe Sciacca's fate would be sealed, unless O'Malley would get his plane up and search towards where the *Marie S* and her four-man crew might be drifting.

Larsen had to do something. If only for Marie's sake.

Dimple-faced kid Marie with the uninhibited smile, the curly locks and the big eyes that had been the first to wheel

Larsen's emotions over the brink of the cliff he had called, for want of a better term, love. Maybe it had been the real thing – Marie Riley was the first woman Larsen had ever made love with. Just the thought of touching her again made his pulse quicken.

Maybe that was why he had to do something to prove to Joe, Marie, himself, that he was not letting a friend die so he could have his woman back.

Larsen was trying Marie Sciacca's number for the third time when Eliza Blatchford walked into Louis'. When the fisherman saw her come in he misdialled the number and cursed, and hunkered his large frame into the booth to avoid detection.

The first time Larsen had got an eyeful of Eliza Blatchford he had caught a strong whiff of smoke. The way she moved – fast, trying to catch up to a moment that would always be just out of reach – hinted at desperation and ambulances. Her black jeans and black Yves Saint Laurent rollneck had only seemed to counterpoint the combustion inside.

The first time he saw her, in that pretentious bar-room three months ago, Larsen had known she would be taking others with her in the conflagration. He had moved closer to the group she was with, intrigued by the brittle drama of her movement. The drama was enhanced by a taut, slim body and three straight feet of reddish hair, flapping in her wake like the red pennant that signified dangerous cargo.

The view had got better. High cheekbones and a perfect chin framed a straight nose, a wide mouth, and large eyes. Too straight, too wide, too large: the face was just shy of beautiful, but the frenzied life in it would attract men long after they had tired of *Vogue* models of womanhood.

Larsen had had a little too much to drink and his words slurred faintly when he asked her to dance. A dumb move; the box was playing some lobotomized disco tune that precluded co-ordinated rhythm. The eyes had dampered right down, and her voice chilled as she refused.

The fisherman stood over her and played out the hackneyed charade: her name, whether she worked. She was a reporter for the Cape Cod *Sentinel*; she lived in Oystertown,

29

on the south side, she told him. Then she impatiently turned her back and shut him off where he stood.

Larsen had moved aside and slowly, regretfully surveyed the tight buttocks, the coltish legs. He looked up to find a pair of sea-green eyes staring into his. Two red spots were burning in her cheeks. A woman fully conscious that American society was dominated by males, and not 100 per cent pleased with the fact either.

'Fuck off, sailor,' she said pleasantly.

Was it that obvious he was a fisherman?

Larsen had returned the compliment, telling the bar that spoiled children weaned on the sweat of manservants should avoid frequenting establishments where they might be treated as women.

She had thrown a full shot of Remy in his face and Larsen had gallantly thrown a rum drink at her consort before being escorted, albeit in a dignified fashion, out of the establishment.

Larsen watched her now as she strode determinedly down the aisle at Louis', checking the tables. She asked Mad Uuno a question and he pointed at the phone booth.

She'd seen him.

This time she wore a pair of cheap, baggy, chemical/ biological-warfare pants, dyed purple, a green army-surplus sweater and a Halston harlequin cape. The pants and sweater together might have cost thirty dollars; the cape would have set Daddy back $500. But, Jesus, she could move well, right up to his lair. She knocked twice.

'Lars Larsen?' Was she embarrassed, were a couple of those summer freckles left stranded on a pale November face maybe a touch pinker? Larsen sighed, retrieved his dime, folded open the phone booth's doors and stood.

'What can I do for you, Ms Blatchford?' Distant, indifferent. Perfect tone.

'I'm . . . covering the disappearance of the *Marie S* for the *Sentinel*. I wanted to ask you a couple of questions.'

'I don't feel like talking about it right now,' the fisherman said heavily. 'Why don't you ask the Coast Guard?'

Behind her eyes a panther glanced briefly at the scene outside.

'I've asked the Coast Guard,' the woman said calmly. 'They gave me the usual Coast Guard runaround: "You'll have to talk to Coast Guard Search and Rescue, SAR, in Boston and it's after four p.m. so the public information officer, the PIO, has gone home but call back at eight tomorrow."' Her voice mimicked Coast Guard talk. '"The search will probably be called off tomorrow due to adverse weather conditions—"'

Larsen waved his hand impatiently. 'So what do you want from me?'

The woman paused. She had a felt-tip pen braced in her long fingers and it bent ever so slightly. She drew a breath and said, 'Look, Captain. I know we had words in that bar. You were loaded. If that makes it impossible for you to talk to me, that's your problem.'

Blatchford ran out of that breath and tried another gulp of oxygen, nitrogen, and tobacco smoke. She wasn't finished.

'But I am a professional and I have a job to do, distasteful as it may be,' she continued. 'And if you are any kind of professional in your own trade, you'll talk to me.'

Larsen went for the bait.

'Your job is to ask questions. What does my profession have to do with answering them?'

'You answer them so things like this don't happen again.'

Her words speeded up, gestures grew more nervous.

'They're already talking "ghost ship", down at the fish pier,' she said.

Larsen nodded. He'd heard that talk, too, as he unloaded his thirty boxes.

'Like the *Patricia Marie*. Like the *Captain Bill* . . .' Blatchford went on. 'But if you're any kind of seaman you'll know that seaworthy vessels don't just disappear for no good reason.'

Larsen folded his arms and threw his head back, banging it slightly on the booth.

Blatchford continued, 'So if I can get information on the disappearance, and write about it, maybe it won't happen again. Do you understand? Maybe some dipsomaniac

31

fisherman won't drop his anchor into the propeller and drift into a rock. Maybe he won't haul his trawl door right up through the hull in perfect weather. Then his superstitious friends won't start blaming the ghosts of the deep.' She rode on her heels, marking 'end of tirade', threw her shoulders back. Larsen noticed how her breasts quivered, just this side of perception. No bra. You could see the nipples. Christ! The fisherman levered his gaze away: he'd make the same mistake as last time if he wasn't careful.

'You seem to be quite an expert on disappearing boats,' Larsen commented, only slightly sarcastically. 'But still, Ms Blatchford, no one knows what really happened to the *Captain Bill* or the *Patricia Marie*. Or to the *Marie Celeste*, for that matter, or the *Waratah*, or the ten-odd oceangoing ships that vanish for no good reason every year.'

The journalist observed the fisherman with something close to pity. 'Strange things happen at sea?' she said, and her eyebrows added their own sarcastic postscript.

The phone rang behind Larsen. It was O'Malley.

'Just got in an' got the message, buddy. I'll come down and join you for a quick single malt?' His voice rasped loudly down the wire. He'd already had a start on the Scotch.

O'Malley was the only pilot Larsen knew who would fly the day after a good drink. He'd had a lot of experience on Navy Tomcats, Sage said, flying endless hung-over patrols over the Indian Ocean, but it was one facet of his friend's character the fisherman did consider nuts. Larsen himself would not allow serious drinking at sea. But now was not the time to bring up an old argument. Fresh or hung over, he needed O'Malley. Joe Sciacca needed O'Malley. Marie needed O'Malley.

'Head on down, boy. It's soul-destroying to drink alone.'

Larsen suddenly felt reluctant to put the phone down: it was a relief to turn his back on the woman, to talk to a friendly, relaxed voice. 'Before we get down to serious business, though – ' Larsen hesitated, suddenly acutely conscious of the magnitude of what he was about to ask the pilot. 'Listen, what I want to know is, could you take the

Cessna up in fifty-, sixty-knot winds? Possibly with icing conditions?'

O'Malley paused. Then he said, 'Why should I want to fly tomorrow? I've got a paper to finish for the *Poli Sci Review*, I have a cord of wood split, stacked, and dry as a bone, a good fireplace, and a case of German beer. And I don't feel like suicide – yet.' He made the connection himself. 'No word on your friend Sciacca?' The *Marie S* had been all over the evening news.

'Nothing,' Larsen said. 'And the Coast Guard probably won't fly a search tomorrow. In fact, they're half convinced he just decided to leave town.'

'And you think I could find what the professionals can't.' That was the second time in five minutes someone had started pontificating about alleged professionalism.

'I could put you in the right search area, anyway. You met Joe Sciacca, didn't you? Anyway' – time to stop babbling hysterically – 'what I'm getting at is, would it be possible at all? Because if so, I know where the currents could have swept him. It's possible if not likely the professionals missed him entirely. Not likely, but very possible – a life raft, wreckage –'

'A life raft is hard enough to spot from a hovering chopper, let alone a bucking, speeding Cessna,' O'Malley finished, mimicking Larsen's clipped speech. 'That is, assuming there's anything left afloat.'

'There has to be something left afloat.'

'Why?'

'Because I heard him on the VHF after he was overdue.'

'I know. I heard it on the news.'

'Okay. So if I heard him, he had to be afloat, even if the boat's swamped. Or even if he's only using the portable VHF from the life raft.'

'Then if he's afloat, why didn't the Coast Guard find him?' O'Malley asked, stubbornly.

'Come on, Sage. The Coast Guard's not infallible. Or else Joe was fishing in different areas than he fished normally, not the ones everyone was concentrating on near Asia Rip and Little Georges.'

Silence.

'Well, can you do it?'

Still no answer.

In the vacuum, Larsen remembered Salett's words and for a brief moment wondered if perhaps Joe had skipped town under some sort of pressure. After all, you never really knew what was going on in a man's mind until . . .

But it would not wash. Joe was too painfully moral. He had quit his father's fish business in New York because of some off-colour business practices sanctioned by his old man. He decided to fish instead, Sciacca said, because it was clean. That summed the guy up – clean. And he would never desert his wife.

'Can you?' Larsen insisted.

'Yeah, I could do it. If I could get into the air at all, and I can always get into the air – and I probably would get into the air.' The pilot was practically yelling. 'If. If I was earning Mau Mau rates for the Colombia nose-candy run. Or if somebody gave me another good reason for risking my life, which is extremely valuable to society as much for pinnacles yet unclimbed as for accomplishments past . . . the opportunity cost for the untimely death of O'Malley? Why –'

Larsen butted in. 'I'll rent the plane, you know. I want to come with you as spotter.'

'Uh-uh, that ain't good enough.'

'Looks like no one else is going to do it either.'

There was a hoarse silence on the other end. Then O'Malley said plaintively, 'Can't this wait till you buy me that drink you owe me?'

'Get down here. I'll buy the round.' The voice could be heard chirping astonished appreciation as Larsen hung up the receiver.

Blatchford had her shoulder to the side of the booth, leaning with ankles crossed, one ear halfway inside. As the fisherman came out she asked, 'Are you planning to organize your own search?' There was a notebook in one hand, a few chicken tracks of information already down.

Larsen snorted.

'Where'd you go to J-school? Langley, Virginia?'

'Are you implying I was eavesdropping?' she asked, incredulous. 'I didn't have to eavesdrop. Your voice was loud enough to carry halfway across the bar.'

'You listened to a conversation you were not intended to hear. If that's your idea of journalism —'

'My God. What do you know about journalism?' She was getting riled, and Larsen unexpectedly had to repress a grin at how speedily she went off the handle. He'd thought his own temper was bad.

But she was in full cry by now.

'You're like the rest, another self-important nonentity who believes a good newspaper is one that lets men play their own petty power politics in peace.'

Larsen wiped a fine drop of spittle ostentatiously from his cheek.

The woman spun furiously away from him. 'I believe in — in this job. But I can't report the news without pushing for it.' Was that a sniffle? Her face was half hidden behind a waterfall of reddish hair.

'Ms Blatchford.'

She swung halfway around.

She said, 'You, everybody else, even Sam, my editor, think good investigative reporting is out of place on a local weekly. Well, I disagree. I think a goddamn community weekly has more of a duty to investigate stuff like this than —'

He had to calm the woman down before they were slinging drinks at each other again.

'Okay, okay.' Larsen's psyche was feeding back a sneaky urge of sympathy for this twenty-seven- or twenty-eight-year-old cub reporter. It couldn't be that much fun writing copy about church garden parties and weekly ostomy society meetings. By the standards of Daddy's set she should have been writing for *Time* by now, not paying dues on a community weekly.

Probably couldn't write. He almost put a conciliatory hand on her shoulder, but restrained himself in the nick of time.

At that point the door to Louis' exploded open and Silva strode in. It had started drizzling and his oilskins were glistening fatly against the chrome enticements of the cigarette machine. The mate's eyes searched the bar, adjusted to its smoky haze, and found Larsen at the phone booth. He threw a gesture: 'Hey, Larsen!'

The bar had just got to quaking as Sarah Eldridge thumbed a quarter in the jukebox. A click and a whirr and Fats Domino was trying to push 'Blueberry Hill' past the distortion of ancient speakers. Yet tension came into the room with Silva's manner of entry and ears tuned out the background: '. . . thrill . . . on Blueberry Hill.'

Larsen waved Silva over. It would have to be something really urgent to pry the mate away from home two hours after they'd put the boat to bed.

'They just got another message from the *Marie S*. It's not voice, it's Morse code. But it's gotta be Joe, he identified himself.'

Blatchford was intently watching Silva, fingers subconsciously readying the notebook. There was no trace of tears or even melancholy on her mobile face. Had she been acting? Larsen wondered idly as his mind accepted Silva's news. Well, he didn't give a fuck. Not now, not ever, not if the sea was giving up something it had already claimed. He was back at his table, shrugging into the worn army jacket, throwing a ten-dollar bill on the table. 'Credit me, Louis,' he called. The ancient Cape Verdean nodded without looking up from his cribbage game.

Blatchford descended on Silva, but Larsen elbowed past her, pushed his mate out the door, then on impulse turned to the woman as she went the colour of boiled lobster in the entrance and said, 'Okay. You've got a point. I'll answer your questions, but not right now. I'll be at the fish pier, later. Or if not there, then at Harry's Canteen, on Ocean Street.'

He disappeared into the night. The woman looked after him for a full ten seconds and then stomped back into the bar.

CHAPTER THREE

When Larsen and Silva parked their trucks and entered Harry's Canteen half an hour later, there were a lot of people talking low over their coffee. Were it not for the time of day, this would not have been unusual. It was a popular place, the bran muffins steamy with the aroma of molasses, the coffee hot and strong.

But this was six-thirty on a Wednesday night, a time when Harry's customers, most of them fishermen, were usually home, sleeping if the weather looked good and they were going out again at three a.m., or playing Monopoly with the kids, chopping wood, getting drunk or doing other domestic activities they only had time for when storms were brewing. There was hardly a booth to be had.

Larsen and Silva found a table in the corner, left unattended because it was right next to a heat register that wafted a faint perfume of number-two heating oil. Agnes shoved menus in front of their noses. Larsen and Silva exchanged nods with a few neighbours. There were more nods than usual – almost everyone in the coffee shop was a fisherman. They shuffled the menus and ordered two coffees, black.

You could feel a tension in the room, an undercurrent hard to identify. The men were talking a half-tone lower than usual, as if there were something out there who might hear their words.

'Okay, Long John, lay it out,' Larsen said.

Silva blew on his coffee, then slurped noisily at the rim of his mug. 'Nantucket Coast Guard station at Brant Point started noticing clicks on VHF radio around one o'clock this afternoon.'

'Clicks?' said Larsen. 'What do you mean, clicks?'

'Just clicks,' Silva repeated. 'They didn't pay it any mind for a while. It was the kind of clicks you get when someone's keying the transmit button on a VHF, when there's a radio carrier wave going out but no voice getting carried. Know what I mean?'

Larsen nodded. Silva's hand stopped feeling up the ceramic mug and went for his cigarette packet in an automatic action: his eyes were still on the North Atlantic.

Cigarettes were Silva's one real weakness. He drank rarely, unnaturally so, Larsen thought, and venerated the saints, his two children and his curvy Azorean wife. Larsen had only known the mate to slip once since he had known him, and the short affair with a blonde schoolteacher had been conducted in a discreet, dignified Mediterranean manner. Dolores had not been told and had never found out, to Larsen's knowledge.

Silva expertly cracked the bottom corner of the pack on the index knuckle of his left hand and a staggered rank of Pall Malls rose above the foil.

'You mind?' Larsen towed one out with his fingernails and stuck it in his mouth. Silva said nothing but lit a match for both of them. The skipper always ended up back with the tobacco when there was emotional trouble: dying friends or departing lovers deposited tar on Larsen's lungs.

The mate continued, 'They must have had a genius on watch. The clicks clicked, know what I mean, and he realized he was gettin' a Mayday signal in Morse, three dots, three dashes, three dots: SOS. That was about as far as his Morse code went, so he went and got the duty officer.' Silva took a deep breath to settle the smoke nicely into his lungs.

'I don't remember the exact wording of the message. The Coast Guard gave a pretty detailed report to Jenny, at the Co-op office, which is how everybody' – Silva pumped smoke out now with every word – 'found out, but there was the Mayday signal, and then, spelled out in Morse, "*Marie S.*" The duty officer answered in voice, asking *Marie*'s position. There was no reply. "Who is calling?" the officer finally asked. The clicks spelled out "Sciacca".

'At this point the Coast Guard figured they had a hoax on their hands,' Silva sighed, 'so they asked him to prove it by giving his wife's birthday, Marie's birthday. Obviously they didn't know offhand if the date he replied with was the right one so then they asked for his Social Security number, which of course they didn't know either but they figured it would be easier to check.'

Silva continued, 'He spelled that out, too, but by the end of it he was fading. The officer started asking the regular questions – yeah, Agnes, gimme some hash and fried eggs and home fries – like "What condition is your vessel in? What was your last position?" But then all they heard was more Maydays, and something like, I don't remember exactly but something like "Mayday, my men are dying . . . Mayday: tell my wife." A couple more letters back, but they couldn't make sense of them.'

'Jesus Christ,' Larsen said.

'I know,' Silva replied quietly.

'Damn!' Larsen said, shaking his head in response to Agnes' demand for a food order. 'I'd hoped . . . how'd the answers come out?'

'What answers?'

'To the Coast Guard questions; the Social Security number, his wife's birthday?'

'They checked out.'

The tobacco tasted rough and sweet, nicotine giving Larsen's respiratory apparatus something to really chew on. The men at the next table were silent – you could almost see their ears twist with the effort of homing in on Silva's words. They'd heard the story earlier at the fish pier but the prurience of disaster made them relish it again, checking for salacious details.

It wasn't often you heard a ghost story that touched so close to home.

'For a while after that, I can't remember exactly what Jenny had down, you know they wouldn't even give her their report till Dickie went through Boston to get permission?' Silva shook his head in disgust, took another drag at the butt. 'Anyway, there was nothin' for a while.' The big mate paused. 'Then the clicks started up again, quite a bit stronger, and – this is weird, really weird.'

The mate's voice rose an eighth of an octave, his eyes were intent. 'They spelled out, "Can anybody see me?" Can anybody *see* me,' he repeated, 'as if *he* could see people.'

Larsen said nothing, but he thought there could be a dozen possible explanations for the use of those words, assuming the transmission did not come from some cruel hoaxer who had known Sciacca, who possibly held some kind of grudge.

Agnes put down a dish of steaming hash and eggs with the style customary to Harry's, thumping it on the Formica and skidding it across, to ram Silva's fork and knife and paper napkin.

Long John looked at his meal absently, as if waiting to be introduced. 'Well, the clicks were fading even faster this time. The last words they could spell out were garbled, the Coast Guard couldn't figure them out. Maybe a foreign word?' He took another gulp of coffee. 'It looked like some Portuguese word. LuGuercio – Luguercio – something like that. But spelled out twice, same spelling both times so it couldn't have been a mistake.' The mate suddenly realized he had come to the end of his story and picked up a fork.

Three tables away, Ben Crowell and Fat Maxie Sturtevant stood up to pay their check. Crowell was a thick forty-year-old with a pudgy face, usually half-shaven, that radiated a firm belief in the red-neck ethic. He owned the forty-five-foot gillnetter *Loligo*.

They moved towards the table Larsen and Silva were using. The skipper looked up and saw them coming and murmured to Silva, who raised his eyebrows expressively.

For the two gillnetters to sit down with Larsen and Silva was almost unthinkable. Mallebarre fishermen were a reclusive bunch who seldom mingled socially except in drunken brawls over women at Louis'. Occasionally, two or three would form friendships but as a rule they would cluster within their own small groups and vaguely discuss factors about which they could do nothing: weather, the price of fish at the Fulton Fish Market, and the price of diesel oil. Then they would go their solitary ways.

Sturtevant and Crowell did not belong to Larsen and Silva's professional kaffeeklatsch. Larsen did not like gillnetters to begin with.

The two gillnetters were standing bearishly in front of the

40

two seated men, waiting for their deviation from pattern to be recognized and accepted in light of attenuating circumstances.

All four fishermen grumbled the ritual 'Hayadoin''.

Small talk came first, the usual tribute to the Olympian deities of weather and fish prices, but the talk was plastered over a foundation of shared knowledge. Larsen knew there was only one reason for Crowell to be engaging in conversation with him, and Crowell knew he knew.

'I wanted to ask you about Joe Sciacca, Lars. You know I was friendly with him when we both fished Provincetown. Maxie here – you know Maxie – says you were the last to talk to him? By voice anyway . . . I guess you heard. He's still tapping out there?'

There was a strain to Crowell's voice that Larsen had never heard before.

'Yeah, I heard about the clicks . . . John here got the word at the Co-op. It's . . . strange.'

Crowell and Sturtevant simply stared at Larsen, expectantly.

'Well, when we heard him,' Larsen continued, 'it was yesterday morning around five-thirty, twenty-four hours after he was due back, almost.'

'How'd you know it was him?' Crowell was nervously fingering his fleshy face, trying to reshape the tissue and rebend his nose; all his attention was on Larsen. Sturtevant just stared at the coffee.

'I know his voice. It was his voice,' Larsen stated flatly, and Silva growled, 'We all recognized it,' in assent.

'I don't get it,' Crowell whined. 'What in hell do you think happened?'

'It's like the *Captain Bill*,' Sturtevant ventured timidly, still watching his coffee.

There was a skipped heartbeat of dead air.

'Well,' Larsen said, 'he obviously had radio problems. He always carried a portable VHF walkie-talkie in the wheelhouse: maybe his engine room was flooded and his batteries were knocked out, so all he had left was the portable set. It would explain why we could hear him and no one else:

that set only had a real short range.'

'And the walkie-talkie fucked up?'

Larsen shrugged. 'I guess. That would explain the clicks, anyway. The voice components shorted out, so he just hit the transmit key. It happens, Christ knows . . . and sometimes those clicks, when you hit the key, carry much further than the voice . . .'

'Maybe that's how come they could hear it in Nantucket,' Silva commented.

Crowell shifted in his seat and glared at Agnes, tried to bend his ear into a pretzel. 'I still don't see it. There's too many things that don't add up. I mean, if there'd been any kind of weather out there . . .' the gillnetter blustered on. 'I mean, if he could send by radio, he must have been afloat, so why didn't you or anybody find him? Even the Coast Guard? You're sure you heard him?'

Something in Crowell's voice hit a chord in Larsen's brain, and Larsen finally recognized the feeling that ran beneath the odd tones and body movements of the men in Harry's that night.

The feeling was fear – fear of the unknown.

It was part of living on the sea. A fear of whatever happened to the Provincetown dragger *Patricia Marie*, which disappeared in perfect weather in '76. Or to the *Captain Bill* in '79. Imagination rushed in to fill the factual vacuum: shapes in old-fashioned oilskins that boarded your ship in the midnight watches; ghost ships that came out of the fog to lead you to perdition on a lee shore.

There was nothing you could do about it when another boat vanished without a trace, leaving you holding your dread like the widow her babes. Nothing to do except invoke the old superstitions, carry a black knife, don't mention pigs or carry women passengers, and talk it out of your system with other men who knew the feeling.

Larsen, Silva, Sturtevant, and Crowell were still talking it out twenty minutes later when O'Malley came into the café, Eliza Blatchford bobbing in his wake.

O'Malley stood around 5′ 1″ in his socks and had the grace and girth of a stork. He sported a huge fan-shaped red beard, in which he stuck a battered pipe, usually unlit. One of the most annoying facets of an otherwise engaging individual was the fact that O'Malley's fluid speech was invariably punctuated by disgusting gurgling sounds from the pipe's core, a reeking sump of cold saliva and liquid nicotine.

Above the beard and thin shoulders two bright button eyes peered through a thick pair of horn-rims, trying to design a theory that would not only take into account what had come before but include, explain, and predict *you*.

O'Malley wore a neat short-back-and-sides haircut in the mistaken belief this would soothe his passengers, and a white three-piece suit with a red ascot at the neck. The effect was ruined by the inclusion of a leopard-skin shirt under the suit.

O'Malley strode over to the table and leaned towards Larsen.

Crowell and Sturtevant broke off their questioning and looked up with the condescending apprehension that sane people reserve for the whacked out. All the fishermen knew O'Malley: he flew for the Co-op during the dog days of summer, spotting swordfish among low swells when the giant fish liked to come up and snooze, gleaming on the surface like fat German tourists on Corfu, easy targets for boats equipped with a pulpit over the bow and a harpoon.

The pilot had a low, grating voice and a theatrical bent. He declaimed rather than spoke.

'And so, Captain Larsen, after having guzzled my whisky for months on end, pleading destitution, relying on my soft heart and well-stocked cellars, the one time I am offered a return favour you run like a dog to hide in this greasy spoon?' Right hand gesturing with the briar.

Crowell's face changed modes to express unalloyed dislike. He enjoyed the food at Harry's.

O'Malley swung around, almost braining Agnes with his long arms. The waitress's mouth was too full of Juicy Fruit to snarl at short notice but she glared at him in compensation.

'By the way, gentlemen, let me present Eliza Blatchford, a writer for the *Sentinel*, by whose good graces I managed to track you down from the ginmill where we were scheduled to meet. I suppose,' he continued as if he were making tea-party conversation, 'you know that the weather is going to hell in a handbasket.'

Eliza Blatchford needed no introduction to make her presence felt in the all-male assemblage. Larsen felt himself getting embarrassed as he noticed the number of eyes zeroed in on the rump of her Halston cape. 'Sailors' all, he thought, unliberated and unrepentant. She had a point: and yet, what more sincere form of compliment could you pay that perfect arc.

O'Malley threw himself lankily on to the one remaining stool, leaving the woman standing. Awkward. She still gripped the notebook in one hand. Her eyes found Larsen's and surprisingly she gave him a half-smile, half apologetic, half determined.

Larsen suddenly got a glimpse of a different person, altered by a simple play of cheek muscles the way a countryside became warm with the passing of a summer rain. He found himself grinning back and quickly returned to staring down at his coffee.

But O'Malley was leaning forward in his insistent professorial style towards the fisherman and saying, 'I'm serious, Larsen. I'm not sure even *I* can fly tomorrow, let alone the US Coast Guard.' Even when he was serious, the pilot affected a stage-Irish twist to his words. 'They're predicting some terrible winds and icing conditions. I've been thinking,' he said, then trailed off vaguely, not specifying what. Larsen wished he'd cut the accent.

He removed his horn-rims and polished them on Silva's crumpled napkin. Larsen saw it leave a slick across the lens. If O'Malley noticed the difference when he replaced the glasses, he didn't show it. 'But if you still want to go, and I think it's possible, I'll go. My only condition is that *she* come along.' He jerked a thumb at Eliza Blatchford, and Larsen suddenly understood the expression on the woman's face.

Gloating triumph. He should have known. O'Malley had always been a sucker for redheads, and this particular one had convinced him to go flying in a hurricane.

CHAPTER FOUR

The old pick-up jounced crossly in third gear as the road top switched from asphalt to dirt. Larsen fought the wheel with one hand, sipped a long-necked bottle of Rolling Rock beer ('brewed in our glass-lined tanks') with the other. He had bought the six-pack at the airport liquor store and already downed half of it.

The road wound through a thick second growth of stunted pine and oak, poison ivy, beach plum, and juniper, cut-rate vegetation well suited to sandy, acid soil. Occasionally there was a glimpse of salt marsh to the right, winking yellow, brown, and sometimes purple with the last blossoms of sea heather to adorn it before the snows came. As if the woods needed more decoration. The wind had dipped some, but it still sent carnivals of magenta maple leaves dancing through the air and piling in drifts on the road.

It was Thursday, one p.m., twenty-four hours after the last, coded Mayday from the *Marie S*.

The Coast Guard had duly cancelled its search, but O'Malley had managed to fly and it had been very rough – three hours of endless grey Atlantic and cloud wrack, being smacked about by the updraughts, downdraghts, and crosswinds of the strengthening storm.

And no sign of the *Marie S*, or her crew. Once Eliza Blatchford had spotted what looked like wreckage and they had gone low, 100 feet off the spume, to investigate, and a whirl of turbulence had knocked them downward, almost into the tormented sea. O'Malley only just pulled them out by pushing the Lycomings to full revs and standing the Cessna on its tail. Blatchford had paled, snapped at Larsen when he laughed, accused him of hiding fear by feigning cool.

On the way back the de-icer quit. The wind was so strong that O'Malley was actually flying the plane at a standstill when they landed in the airport parking area. They taxied in as they had taxied out, in the lee of a fuel truck conscripted to protect the control surfaces. Larsen had to throw his weight on the upwind wing to keep the plane from being flipped.

Trees thinned to accept a small clapboard house dressed in peeling paint and wedged to the side by a large vegetable garden. There were carvings of ancient Norse monsters roughed out along the eaves. The half-wrecked Ford station wagon usually parked on the verge was gone. Larsen's uncle was out, probably quaffing the first in a long series of schnapps at the Veterans Club down the road.

A curve, and the track became a white path of sea-clam shells, discarded when Larsen's crews shucked bait on the roadway. The wheel ruts ended abruptly in front of a yellow structure, a rambling series of cockeyed cubes and rectangles that had started out as a simple shingled shelter built around an eighteenth-century chimney. The house had since been added to – a square wing to the south, another tacked at right angles to that one, a crooked barn on the southeast corner, a tilted porch on the west – till it looked like it was, a study in architectural hindsight. There was an old skiff propped up beside the barn. A faint hint of smoke wreathed the chimney whenever the wind took a breather. Ole had kept the coal stove going.

Lars was nine and his brother Per twelve when their parents took a curve too fast to cope with ice on the road that Christmas Eve a long time ago. They had spun, rolled, and died in a flash of fire and ice. The fisherman could still remember standing outside the porch with his uncle's long arms around him and his brother. The deepness of that night sky still came back to him, as did the shimmer in the starlight: it was so cold it felt almost hot and the Milky Way sparkling looked like heat waves on a turnpike.

Uncle Ole had used clumsy clichés wafted on 100-proof breath to explain something children could never grasp: the concept of death was a sad and final thing that brought salty pillows, but it came down to their mother being gone to a long party and Pa no longer teaching them how to whittle in the evening.

46

That and a constant aloneness somewhere deeper than a night sky . . .

It had affected them, although Ole had laboured nobly as a surrogate parent, supplementing a meagre life-insurance settlement by doing odd electrical jobs and carving wooden birds for the tourist trade. He gave them friendship when they needed it and the strap of a belt when they got out of line, taking it out on a bottle rather than on him and Per when things grew too much for a bachelor's soul.

Maybe the loneliness had been good. Perhaps that was what had kicked both Lars and his brother out of the seasonal poverty cycle that trapped their schoolmates. Lars Larsen had become a relatively wealthy fisherman, but his brother was the one who had really escaped the Cape trap. Per Larsen, at thirty-six, was one of the youngest US Attorneys in the country.

Larsen unlatched the sagging barn door and braced himself as twelve Nubian goats butted out of the dark, bleating into his knees. He checked the barnyard with his nostrils: that not-too-musty tang of good alfalfa, the brown-sugar aroma of oats, the acid odour of a happy chicken coop, the healthy sharp smell of goatshit.

There was something out of sorts about the fowls, though. An unobtrusive hole had appeared in the chicken wire near one of the driftwood posts. One – two? No, one chicken gone, more feathers among the scattered corn. A smashed egg, the shell licked clean. Brother raccoon was back in town, after Larsen had sent half his clan into political exile twenty miles away, courtesy of a humane trap. As usual, the dog, Pariah, had deserted his post to chase sticks in the woods.

The fisherman snipped a loop of wire from an extra roll in the shed, wound it tightly across the hole twisted by the masked marauder, anchored it with ¾-inch staples. The sixth dead chicken in three weeks. Death just another arc in the circle of life. Joe was dead, so were his mate Dan Eldridge, and his two deckhands, Tony Falcaro and Jed – what was his name? He could never remember it and it bothered him now. But they were out of it, no more worries.

Larsen had done what he could to keep them around in a world that made little sense. The sea had them now and that made all the sense they'd ever need.

Inside the old house smelled of leather and books and a thousand late-night arguments. People who lived there had rubbed off on its walls, leaving a human residue of squabbles and laughter, harsh words and unspoken desires in the very feel of the wood.

The chimney was made of thick granite from the glacial excrement that was Cape Cod. The kitchen had been wrapped almost wholly around its hearth, creating a warm stomach for the house. A huge black coal stove held sway over the inner sanctum in a visual cacophony of cast-iron baffles and handles, flues and coal dust.

The aquavit had disappeared again, but there was a good cup of raki left. The fisherman took his mug and this week's *Sentinel* over to a farmhouse table, switched on the lamp, and sat on Disraeli, who let out a piercing kittenish shriek and tried to fly off the couch, landing in a heap of gravity, indignation, and long, tiger fur.

Larsen apologized to his cat.

The front page of the *Sentinel* featured its usual combination of trivia and scandal. There was a longish article by Eliza Blatchford that attempted to prove financial connection between interests trying to build a casino on a Mallebarre beach and a local councillor who thought that was a wonderful idea. The proof, Larsen thought, was inconclusive at best, but the woman could write well, though her style was perhaps a little too flowery, too obviously committed for good journalism.

Inside, under a headline that read, 'Doing It', was an account of how one menopausal town hall secretarybird had surprised a couple making passionate love in the Conservation Commission's restroom. Larsen grinned and put down the newspaper.

Another *Sentinel* article caught his eye. This one was from last summer, and Larsen had taped it up by the coal stove.

It featured a picture of Joe Sciacca in his kitchen, and one of Larsen looking moronically out of *Sofia*'s wheelhouse window. The headline read: '*Cape Fishermen to Try New Market Scheme*' and the subhead: '*Selling Fish Direct to NY Restaurants*.' The scheme. He remembered it, and it curdled his mood.

Larsen took his sheath knife and began to whittle rapidly at a piece of applewood he always carried in his pocket.

The scheme would die with Sciacca.

He and Joe had wanted to try in New York what some fishermen attempted locally in the summer season: cut out the middleman entirely and sell fish directly from the boat to high-priced restaurants in the city. Restaurants would buy the fish. Mallebarre fish was some of the best there was, mainly because smaller boats like *Sofia* and *Marie S*, unlike the large Gloucester or New Bedford draggers, could make easy one-, two-, or three-day trips to the best fishing grounds in the world and come back with produce that was a day or two old at the most. By selling fish directly they could clear three or four times what the Co-op got selling in bulk through Fulton.

But the plan relied on Joe.

Sciacca had been essential because when it came to the wholesale fish business in New York City he knew every in and out and string to pull. Although Joe had left the family business to go fishing, his father had been one of the top Fulton Market dealers. Joe had been very confident about shortcutting the rough-and-tumble dealing of the dingy dockside area in the shadow of Brooklyn Bridge.

Larsen put aside the applewood, dropped his knife into a sheath on his right hip, and went outside. One advantage of autumn was that cooling temperatures kept any beer left in the pick-up truck at a perfect degree of chill.

Beer in hand, he wandered through the back door and into the rain forest of paperbacks and rusted-out chunks of salvaged ships that was the study. Scuba diving for salvage was another team effort he and Sciacca had been good at. Just another activity he would probably forsake now, as he one day would give up on the little ideas and inventions that were going to make him filthy rich.

Like the toothbrush-cum-toothpaste gadget. The paste was contained in a squeezable handle and came out through soft plastic tubes in the brush. He was going to call it 'DecaDent'. Or the evil-smelling lotion that garbage bag companies would coat their products with to keep dogs and raccoons away (Pariah still wouldn't go in the basement, where he'd concocted the formula. Neither would anyone else.) Or the computerized cocktail machine. At least he had a prototype for that one, only because he had paid John Jacobs in New York to design and order the circuitry. The rest were all flyspeckled blueprints in the mechanical chaos of his workshop.

Larsen uncradled the hall phone and dialled Sciacca's number. The rings seemed even more eternal than last night.

Someone was answering this time – old Eunice Riley, the dragon of Larsen's high school days. Thrilled to hear his voice, her words were like the clear pearls of fluid that came when you squeezed a cobra's venom sacs – did she think her little girl would be necking with him at the drive-in again come spring? Marie was hysterical and sick all night and sedated and was sleeping. Would she tell her Larsen had called? Yeah. Yeah maybe, or yeah maybe not.

Then came a sound of Bakelite being muffled, distorted voices, Eunice yelling 'You shouldn't even be up!' and someone else was on the line.

'Lars!'

'Marie –'

'Lars, oh, Lars, where are they?'

He was not prepared for the grieving, pleading hopelessness in her voice.

'Marie, are you okay?'

'They said you heard him. Lars, what *happened* to him?'

'I don't know, but he could still be fine, you know: he could be broken down, be drifting way off the beaten track . . .' The silence of disbelief. 'He's got a life raft.'

'Lars, why didn't they find him then if he's out there?'

'It's a big ocean. He could be anywhere, you know.'

She was crying now. Her voice quavered as she said, 'I'm so frightened.'

'Do you want me to come over?'

In the background Eunice said, 'Hang up, sweetheart. Get some sleep.'

'Lars,' Marie took up, 'I think someone might have hurt him.'

Salett's words came back to the fisherman. Something about threats.

'What are you talking about? Who on earth would want to hurt Joe?'

'There was a man,' Marie said. 'A man who called a couple of times. Because of the plan you and Joe had.'

'When was this?'

'Last summer. After the article they did in the *National Fisherman*.'

'Why didn't you tell me?'

'Joe told me not to, he didn't want people talking about it, you know how people talk around here. He said it was nothing, just somebody who was jealous.'

'He was right,' Larsen said, not without a twinge of hurt feelings. In the old days Marie had told him everything.

'Marie,' came Eunice's screech, 'get some sleep!'

'It could have been the Organization.'

'What "Organization"?'

'The one that controls Fulton, that sets the price of fish.'

'Oh, come on, Marie. That's pure myth –'

'How the hell do you know?'

'Because it's typical, it's what everybody believes. Because they can't control the factors that affect their own lives.'

'Like Joe disappearing?'

'I'm sorry, I didn't mean that.'

'Someone there could have wanted to hurt him.'

'Marie, even Joe said that conspiracy stuff was all bullshit, and he knew Fulton better than anyone.'

'He never told me that.'

'He never talks about his old man, or Fulton, I'll bet not even to you. No one would want to hurt Joe, Marie. He's just overdue, he could easily show up safe tomorrow.'

'Oh, God. I know he's gone. I *know* that had something to do with –'

'Those threats were nonsense, Marie,' Larsen interrupted forcefully. Deluding herself would not help. 'You wouldn't believe how often people threaten other people. Because they can't *do* anything. I know for a fact that some people in Mallebarre would love to stop us trucking fish to New York. But they'd never mess with Joe.'

'Then where is he?'

It was his turn to be silent.

'Look, do you want me to come over?'

'Not now. Later.'

'She has to go to bed,' Eunice yelled, somewhere in the vicinity of the mouthpiece.

'She's right. I'll call you. And, Marie –'

'Yes.'

'Don't give up. Not yet.'

Sucking absently on his fifth beer, the fisherman wandered back out to the porch in front.

How had Joe Sciacca died? And who in the name of all the gods would want to do him harm? The idea was absurd.

The front of the house was cradled in twin arms of scrub oak, glowing shyly in the recessed November lighting. The long marsh swept in a gentle curve from house to harbour. You could see three miles across the harbour to the seven-mile-long barrier beach of dunes, white-pine copses, eel-grass, driftwood shacks, and beach plums known as Dead Neck. It was a visual feast of the most subtle flavours: a crowd of browns changing to olives and grey-greens or yellows as wind bent the salt-meadow grass, a clutch of blues deepening between ocean and harbour.

Larsen never tired of the view. But now, with the wind, it was getting cold enough to counteract even the combined effects of raki and beer. Larsen shivered and went back inside to escape the wilderness of sundown, old and new ghosts crowding in with the night.

Darkness came quickly. The temperature dived as the clouds departed and a high-pressure front moved in. A clatter of old Ford parts and perforated silencer and Ole Larsen was in the driveway, swinging around a dirt circle in front of the house and skidding to an unsteady halt inches away from the red pick-up's fender. Seconds later, Larsen's black dog crashed through the house, a loose assembly of tongue, floppy ears, hunger, and good nature, whose sole purpose in life was to chase sticks. An explosive mixture not tempered by brains.

Ole and Pariah found the big fisherman bent over a tangle of longline in the workshed, the little Jøtul stove glowing in a valiant effort to counteract the wind still whistling under loose shingles. A light bulb swung gently, turning the mundane jumble of rusty cans of paint, workbench, tools, spare oars, coils of line, and boxes of Mustad hooks into an alchemist's cave.

'You owe me forty-five dollars. *Ja*. I had to buy extra hay – the goatshed was almost flooded with the storm and rain.'

Larsen did not look up, crooked one recalcitrant loop through a second, and straightened out another three feet of line. 'It's in the drawer – the usual envelope.'

Ole stood by the Dutch doors that opened into the house proper, looking at his nephew. The old Norwegian was thin and stooped and had a strangely senile habit of scratching his crotch with his right hand every time he said '*ja*', which he did often because his English was not very good and the phrase gave him time to cast around for the next word.

But the blue eyes, ensconced among grey hair and huge eyebrows and a large, hooked, red nose, were very clear, and there were traces of affection in them that remained invisible among the singsong dynamics of his Scandinavian accent.

'You want something to eat?'

Larsen straightened a final tangle, glanced up. He stood and stretched.

'No thanks, old man. What I need is a drink.' Then, accusingly: 'You found the aquavit bottle again, dammit. It was gone from where I put it.'

Larsen kept the bottle hidden in his emergency bag, the same bag that contained his passport, a change of clothes, and a reserve of cash. But Ole wouldn't have found the other stuff: the gun and false papers were in a secret pocket.

The old man stood straighter. 'Yes – *ja*.' He scratched his crotch. 'Vot do you think? I work here for nothing? I fix people's toasters all day and feed the goats, *ja*, when you are away and vot kind of tanks for raising you like a son?' The blue eyes flashed like police lights.

Larsen smiled inwardly. They had this same battle every time he went out. Although it was Ole who insisted on keeping the goats, the old man did have a right to the liquor. The fisherman spread his hands palm outward towards his uncle, who by this time was scratching his crotch as if every flea in New England was attending a convention there. '*Ja! Skrekelig stug gut!*' the old man said. 'It is a Swede's trick to hide the aquavit.'

'Okay, *onkel*, okay. I just don't want to lose you.' Larsen stopped himself from putting a conciliatory hand on his uncle's shoulder. 'Your liver's like Swiss cheese already, the doctor said.'

Ole snorted, brushed off Larsen's hand, and stomped into the warmth of the living-room. Larsen yelled after him, 'I have to go to Rumbelly's. I'll buy you a nice cool beer?' He added, not quite loud enough for his uncle to hear, 'It'll take you a little longer to kill yourself that way.'

CHAPTER FIVE

Rumbelly's lay halfway between the harbour and the Route 28 mall.

Route 28 was a strip of fast-food joints, drive-ins, and fitness centres, an epitome of the commercial hell Cape Cod had become since the heavy tourist onslaught in the Kennedy years.

And if Route 28 was a hell, then Mallebarre Mall was its eighth circle, a huge sprawling wasteland of parking, glass, and greed designed solely to milk tourist dollars in the summer and survive off the sparse savings of those doomed to hang on through winter's bleakness. And now someone was trying his damnedest to open a casino nearby.

Ole Larsen hated the mall, and the downtown business district it had slowly invaded and conquered. He seldom went there, and did not want to now. Lars watched him in amusement as they drove. His uncle puffed harder on a cheap cheroot and became more and more sullen. His unshaven cheeks grew darker, more concave. The mall ruined the business of craftsmen, hyping Hong Kong imitations of Ole's painstakingly handcarved waterfowl.

'Why are we going to this place?' Ole snarled as Larsen slotted the pick-up into a vacant space in Rumbelly's parking lot.

The old Norwegian's face was curled in contempt. All around the pick-up were cars belonging to the upwardly mobile elite of Cape Cod: rising young lawyers, bankers, doctors, developers, undertakers, and car dealers, men who controlled the Cape's service economy. They drove sports Datsuns and middle-of-the-line BMWs, with the occasional sleek Mercedes 280 SL or studiously antique Packard thrown in. The old Chevy truck looked like a washerwoman among debutantes.

'I'm s'posed to meet O'Malley for a drink – come on.' Ole

sat disgusted, rooted to his crumbling leather seat, his feet trapped by used McDonald's wrappers, mooring line, and other flotsam on the Chevy floor.

'You're fine,' Larsen insisted impatiently. 'They'll let you in – you're not wearing jeans.' He pretended to appraise seriously Ole's garb. 'They might even let you out.'

Larsen himself had changed into a clean pair of khaki slacks, handtooled Western boots, one of his few remaining Turnbull & Asser shirts, and an Antartex leather coat. Play the game.

'Come on, *onkel*.' He shook his head, impatience giving way to affection for the old man. '*I'm* buying, remember?' Ole stayed put. Larsen shrugged, strode past the bouncer and through the door.

Rumbelly's was a converted nineteenth-century 'Captain's House'. Inside was a mixed cocktail of fake Lalique and real Lacoste, low-tar cigarette smoke and affected accents. Sears double knit and marital double cross at the bar. Larsen found O'Malley polishing his horn-rims at a round table wedged between the baby grand and a large and inaccurate model of a famed New York tea clipper.

'I brought Ole,' the fisherman said as he carefully slid his large frame into a couch seat, near the aisle to stretch his legs. 'I'm trying to keep him off the hard stuff and broaden his social horizons at the same time. He hasn't made up his mind whether to come in yet.'

'I don't blame him,' O'Malley replied darkly, scowling into a 'Cape Codder', vodka and cranberry juice. Sage was on the warpath and another speech was in the offing. 'Look at these savages,' he gestured at the assembled multitude. 'Laws, loopholes and martinis. That's it. The perfect amorality of the post-industrial communications state. Cheers.'

'I think I owe you a drink. That was an interesting flight, as the Chinese would say – ' Larsen tried to change the subject but O'Malley did not reply. He went back to staring at his drink and mumbling into his beard as if there were a mike in the collar of his corduroy three-piece, or the tiger-striped shirt below.

He kept sniffing in a suspicious fashion. Larsen knew that O'Malley snorted cocaine like it was going out of style.

Towards the entrance a wall of cashmere sweaters suddenly parted to allow an arthritic flow of cotton and cheap cheroot smoke. Ole had evaded the bouncer. The alert old eyes held a faint hint of panic, his right hand went to touch the crotch and then froze – this was not the kind of place where Ole Larsen could be himself. He found the table and wordlessly sat down. A baggy, grey cotton suit and a porkpie hat constituted Ole's usual attire. In this environment, he stuck out.

'And it's even worse when they shuck their one talent, of systems efficiency, and stand me up,' O'Malley complained. 'Me – an expert from New York in *advertising*, which is, to whit, dressing up those lines of communication so the victims they sell their retirement accounts to won't know what hit them. Make it all palatable. Incidentally,' O'Malley leaned forward, pipe gurgling, 'there's a guy you may want to meet.' The pilot removed the pipe from his beard and poked its chewed stem at a fat, jovial man with cold eyes. 'Next president of the Cape Cod Chartered Bank. Only forty-seven years old. Loves to fish: just the guy you want for a reefer truck loan.'

The waitress had finally noticed them. Larsen ordered a Dos Equis for his uncle, a refill for O'Malley, and a Mount Gay and tonic for himself. He shook his head. 'It's no go. I can't do it without Joe Sciacca.'

There was a peal of clear laughter in the front, the born-to-succeed tones of an East Coast Ivy Leaguer, and a fruit salad of incredibly livid colours came into a lounge not noted for its sartorial restraint to begin with. The colours were sported by four towheaded Anglo-Saxon men of the type that usually had beaten a fashionable retreat to Riverdale and Brookline by this time of year.

O'Malley had a theory that Americans wore unnatural colours in direct proportion to the size of their bank balance, the way African chiefs collected obese wives to prove how wealth made them independent of their impoverished environment. Measured by that yardstick, this group was filthy rich.

In the middle of the lime greens and plaids, like a strawberry crowning the chef's special dessert, was the long, flowing head of red hair that belonged to Eliza Blatchford.

Larsen groaned. His uncle looked at him speculatively, then went back to staring at the far wall. O'Malley smiled in appreciation. 'Ah, our erstwhile rear gunner. Seems you can't escape, Lars.'

The fisherman switched his gaze and gave his friend a long, controlled look. Their drinks arrived, whisked on to the table with the flourish of a professional waitress. Ole took his beer and metaphorically went to ground inside the frosty glass; O'Malley shifted on the couch to get a better view of Blatchford and her crowd; Larsen sank slightly into the cushion. The noise level had increased twofold since their arrival. He should have remembered this was where she hung out: their first shouting match had been in the next room.

A twist of her head and she had noticed them, hesitated, left the security of the bar, made a foray under the escort of a tall blond man wearing white pants punctuated by huge signal flags of royal blue, and a pink polo sweater. His face was straight out of F. Scott Fitzgerald. He had a thin nose and an expression of unsinkable boredom.

'Sage, Captain Larsen.' She was talking to the Great Gatsby, categorizing O'Malley as Valiant Pilot, Larsen as Bereaved Friend of the missing fisherman.

Gatsby nodded briefly, his eyes losing some fraction of their boredom when he was introduced to the half-shaved cheeks and total discomfort of Ole Larsen. A slight, well-bred lift of the lips: Gatsby's real name was something Whipple. Freddie?

She was sitting down. Freddie was reluctantly going to fetch their drinks, 'just for a while'. The deep-green eyes were looking at him, then at O'Malley. What was she babbling on about?

'The article's going to be out tomorrow.' There was still desperation hidden under the surface layers of those green waters, with an overlay of excitement: this apparently was action journalism. Ten years ago, she would have been trying to hitch a one-way ride on a Huey Cobra out of Danang or Khesanh. Now there was only a missing fishing boat. War of a different kind.

Blatchford made sounds about embarrassment, stepping into painful areas a second time, but she had a couple more questions, if Larsen wouldn't mind?

'I need to round it out, fill in the holes. I wanted to ask if you and Joe Sciacca were in business together?'

That was straightforward enough. She had been talking to Salett. Gentle probing. The finely carved lips took a genteel sip of a garish mixed drink.

Larsen wearily gave a synopsis of their marketing scheme.

Blatchford said, 'Someone, a source, claims the Coast Guard is wondering whether Sciacca might not have ditched his boat on purpose, and left town due to financial – money – pressures, or for other reasons, perhaps.'

Larsen had a brief, nightmare flash of a tired world where the same questions were repeated, over and over again, like a Levantine secret police interrogation. In five minutes Blatchford would go out of the room, and the hard man would come in with his rubber hoses and truncheons, with Salett directing the questioning from a nearby cell. Salett. Try as he might, Larsen could not quite repress the quick return of the fury he had felt when the Coast Guard lieutenant had broached that same subject yesterday.

The son of a bitch! Sciacca was dead! And the goddamn Coast Guard didn't even have the balls to fly out and look for him. But she was ploughing on regardless, mentioning something else now, and the fisherman went very still as he heard Blatchford say '. . . implied a possibility that he was involved in smuggling grass, or narcotics? Is that possible, do you think?'

O'Malley was looking steadily at him. Easy, Lars, he seemed to be saying. As if to defuse the situation with a mundane act, O'Malley took the pipe from his mouth, rapped it sharply upside down against an ashtray till the carbonized dottle shot out.

Larsen relaxed his grip on the table top. Paused. The anger bubbled like nitrogen to his brain, fizzled briefly, started to dissipate. That bastard Salett. He thought out his words.

'There is absolutely not one iota of a shadow of truth in that allegation.' Paused again, took a large swig of rum, looked straight at the journalist, making an effort not to slur his words.

'I suppose you got that from Salett, making up stories because the Coast Guard doesn't have the guts to do what we did this morning. Spreading the lies of others doesn't make you any less the liar.'

Maybe he was riding her too hard, Larsen thought. She was looking at him oddly, ready to detonate without a doubt.

Larsen waved a disparaging hand, took another gulp at his drink.

'I'm sorry. It's been a long couple of days. Can you see where that kind of accusation might get me upset?'

The girl just looked at him. Ole, seeming more miserable than ever, cleared his throat loudly, and finally said, 'My glass is empty, kid – you vant me to die of thirst?'

'Let's change the subject,' Larsen said, looking at Blatchford.

She said, 'I'm just trying to do my job, as always.'

'And you want some good quotes.'

'And I want some good quotes.'

The waitress came over and took their order. Larsen said lightly, '"Another storm brewing: I hear it sing i' the wind: yond same black cloud, yond huge one, looks like a foul bombard that would shed his liquor." You can quote that in the story if you like. We saw enough of it flying today. Speaking of liquor, incidentally –'

'"The sky it seems, would pour down stinking pitch, but that the sea – dashes the fire out."' The woman did not say 'checkmate' but her eyes showed a hint of it.

Larsen stared at her as Blatchford spoke the lines, her voice rising and falling with the immediate commitment of a born ham.

The woman's eyes, he was thankful to see, had lost their

interest in his lack of co-operation in answering questions. O'Malley was watching those eyes with an amused curiosity the fisherman shared. It wasn't every town-hall reporter who would call your bluff with an apt quote from the Bard.

'"I have suffer'd with those that I saw suffer,"' Larsen matched her slowly, more seriously as the full meaning of the remembered words seeped through his inebriation: '"A brave vessel who had, no doubt, some noble creatures in her, dash'd all to pieces. O, the cry did knock against my very heart. Poor souls, they perish'd."'

He was getting drunk, quite drunk, he realized.

'"Had I been any god of power,"' she cued in, '"I would have sunk the sea within the earth or e'er it should the good ship," umm, "so have swallowed and the fraughting souls within her . . ."'

The fisherman's eyes were locked with the woman's, and their small table was an oasis of silence brought about by the cadence of the lines and the unlikelihood of the setting.

It was to this frozen stage set that Freddie returned, leaned over the table, and started talking half softly and at length into Eliza Blatchford's ear.

He looked fed up. Through the Andover drawl Larsen caught the words 'local yokels' and 'fucking bore' and 'fishermen'. Blatchford was flipping her notebook closed, her face all of a sudden sterile, impassive. She started to utter conversational excuses, 'I'm sorry, we have to meet someone – I have to go –' Whipple's hand was caressing her neck with a familiarity the fisherman found disgusting. And they belonged together, same class, same clothes, you mingled with the populace when it suited your purpose but they would always lack the pedigree to count.

Larsen butted in, primed with rum, raki and beer, rounded on Blatchford's beau, wishing as he did so that he could suppress it, keep his feelings battened down and rely on the knowledge that people like Whipple were basically pathetic, but the guy had whispered loudly, so deliberately.

'What's the matter – too good for us local yokels?' Schoolyard talk, brainless machismo. All machismo covers up insecurity. The woman had that figured out. So what. He tried again. 'You underbrained product of institutionalized mediocrity: if you don't like us rubes, why don't you go back to Park Avenue, to Daddy's money?'

That scored. Blatchford's face had darkened and Whipple looked at her, brushed off her restraining arm and moved over to stand right next to Larsen's seat – inside the perimeter of defence every animal created for itself. An open act of hostility. The silence of a challenge thrown invaded Rumbelly's.

'You're an asshole.'

At least Larsen had no monopoly on schoolboy talk. The bar had stilled. The bouncer was elbowing his way through the crowd with two of Whipple's friends, O'Malley had taken off his glasses, and Ole was trying frantically to get out from behind the table. The inevitability of violence hung in the bar.

Whipple pushed Larsen back into the couch as the fisherman tried to rise. Larsen fell back, harder than he had to, hooked his left foot around Whipple's right heel, and pushed hard at Whipple's right knee with his other foot. The guy had the reflexes of a linebacker – twisted as he swayed, grabbed at the table and went down, bringing table, cloth, glasses, rum, beer, flowers with him. Larsen launched himself forward, landed with a knee fair in Freddie's kidney as Freddie tried to roll out of the way. A large hand had smacked the fisherman's ear and started to crook itself at his throat and Larsen had just time to smash his clenched fist into Whipple's exposed nose when eight pairs of hands dragged him off the floor and hustled him through a lake of pale faces to the door. A man on the phone in the lobby, O'Malley shouting with the manager, the word 'troublemaker' repeated: why did he always get into fights when he was too drunk to fight? The high-pitched tones of women, finally a rhythm of blue lights, and, shit – it was Slade and Harris, two of Mallebarre's 'dirty dozen', some of the more brutal and ignorant cops in a police force not renowned for its liberal, reformist attitude to law enforcement.

The ritual cracking of shoulder joints, the cold bite of

steel at his wrists, a slapping at the inside of pants legs, the chill of the outdoors. A fat elbow in the stomach as they jackknifed him into a cruiser idling at the kerb, another smack on the head just to remind him who was boss. He was alone in a cage at the back. Where was Whipple? Shaddup, asshole. And the same to you, officer, sir.

A kick as they shoved him up the steps of the large new brick police station recently built for no good reason with federal funds.

They took his sheath knife, wallet, and belt, and slammed the bars shut on another night in the tank, courtesy of the police department, Town of Mallebarre, Massachusetts, USA.

CHAPTER SIX

They came for him at nine in the morning, steps reverberating around the cold tiles of the clink. Bars rang as the lock twisted, the door swung open smoothly on well-oiled hinges.

The cop beckoned Larsen out of his triangular world of steel bed, monolithic toilet, sink. A new patrolman put the cuffs on him again. Down a bare corridor to the booking room, where they took the cuffs off. Why did this country detective sergeant have to wear his .38 police special in a James Bond quick-release holster? But Jimmy Ames had always been gun crazy. Larsen had decided long ago that his obsession must make up for a deep sexual deficiency. It was why Ames had joined the police force.

Ames was talking to a woman sitting on the customer side of the desk and Larsen's gut did a back flip through the haze of hangover as a pattern came through the glass: the angle of her head, glasses, the blonde hair, the pert nose as she looked towards him, the blue eyes, ringed like a raccoon's with exhaustion but still . . . 'Marie!'

Marie Riley Sciacca stood up, saying nothing. She wore a nicely tailored pair of grey slacks and a thick Icelandic sweater. She looked questioningly at the sergeant, who had rolled his beer belly into a comfortable chair behind the glassed-in counter.

The police radio jabbered stupidly in bursts of 'Easy 10 . . . Old Mill Road' . . . silence.

'Why do you still worry abut this deadbeat, Marie?' Jimmy Ames asked pleasantly. His tiny eyes flickered between the woman and Larsen.

'Leave it alone, Jim. Please.'

'Mr Hotshit Larsen with that fancy, fast boat nobody knows just how the hell he got. Mr Cool Larsen who went to Harvard.'

64

Another thing about Jimmy Ames; he had always lusted after Marie when they were in high school together.

A captain came into the room. The spiteful expression on Ames' plump face disappeared. In its stead Detective Sergeant Ames wore the look of tortured magnanimity common to cops the world over when you were leaving their control.

He pushed a tin tray containing Larsen's belt, sheath knife, and wallet towards the fisherman.

'No charges filed,' he said briefly. 'Protective custody. If the town had more bucks for it, we'd press charges. Next time, we will.' There was a click of an electronic latch. Larsen knew the cops would not press charges on that kind of offence on private property, and without independent plaintiffs. It was his good luck the manager of Rumbelly's wanted to avoid publicity and legal fees. Jimmy would have loved to book him.

He checked his wallet, but the money was all there, for a change.

The air outside was sweet and pure and bracing. It was totally inadequate to the task of washing away the prison smell of grape-soda disinfectant, vomit, and guilt. Sandwiched between layers of discomfort and insecurity induced by rum-sickness, the odour seemed to follow Larsen like a perfumed accusation.

Why hadn't they busted Whipple?

At the bottom of the police-station steps Larsen and Marie paused and turned towards each other: she took off the spectacles, laced her arms around Larsen's neck, butted her forehead into his shirt. The shirt was stained with blood. His? Freddie's? Then she was crying, the sobs ripping at her chest. The fisherman stroked her back awkwardly, conscious of his inability to say anything that would help, crushed with the weight of her grief, aware – and he hated himself for it – of how the slimness of her body balanced well with the slight bulge of her pregnancy. She'd always been the kind of woman who had no hips at fourteen, straight and athletic, but she was rounding out now with a vengeance.

Grief, hangover, and guilt for breakfast.

A little later, when Marie's tears had receded, they found a coffee shop by the bus station. She went to the ladies' room and washed while Larsen ordered coffees. Marie's face was a battleground when she came back but she managed a rueful smile.

'Lars. Always the same. I should have known I'd find you in the drunk tank.'

Larsen shrugged helplessly. 'How'd you know where to find me? I've been trying to reach you. I called again yesterday evening, but Eunice said you were passed out. I thought she might be lying.'

'I *was* passed out. I woke up at three this morning and tried to call you back. Your uncle answered and told me what happened so I came here to bail you out. But you didn't need bail. Lars – ' she looked imploringly at the fisherman – 'they're trying to be nice to me. My mother, the Co-op, the neighbours, the Coast Guard. Everybody. They've been telling *me* lies – '

'Marie – '

'No. Stop. Not you, too.' The tears were very close to the surface. 'My father was born here. His father was a fisherman. I know these things. I know Joe – is never – '

The tears finally took over. Larsen reached and covered her hands with his. A fat man in a white apron behind the counter looked at them curiously and went to read his newspaper in the farthest corner of the grill.

'I know Joe's dead now,' Marie snuffled at last, dragging her soaking blue eyes to meet Larsen's. 'I don't think I've ever cried so much in my whole life . . . I didn't tell you last night but I got a feeling last Wednesday. I can't explain it but oh, God! It felt like I had lost half my body out there – I was just scared before, scared to my wits' end, but then I *knew*.'

Larsen looked at her, feeling the death grip from her hands, struck dumb by the volume of sadness she was pouring out.

'But I have to know, Lars! And they won't tell me. They told me first when you heard him call. Then they started saying maybe you hadn't heard him call after all, the Coast Guard didn't think so.

'Then I heard mother screaming about some cruel hoax on the phone. They don't tell me: they just feed me Seconal and put me to bed because all I can do is cry, and cry and cry.' She started to sob again on cue, burying her face in the thick folds of the sweater. Her voice came up muffled.

'They told me this morning about finding the VHF antenna . . . I stopped by the Co-op. I couldn't believe Joe's boat wasn't there like it always is.'

'Marie – what do you mean, finding the VHF antenna?'

Those eyes again, behind a rampart of white wool. 'They found an antenna broken off, in the shipping lanes. An O'Hara dragger from Rockland found it floating . . . You didn't know?'

Larsen said, 'I went up in O'Malley's plane to look for Joe yesterday. I stopped by the Co-op to get the money from my last trip, but they didn't mention it.'

'They only found it yesterday afternoon. They said it's the kind Joe had.' A trembling hand wrenched loose from Larsen's, conveyed a sip of foul, lukewarm coffee to her lips.

Larsen asked, 'Did they tell you where they found it?'

It was the first tangible sign of Joe Sciacca. Not a garbled transmission, or weak jumps on a Coast Guard signal-strength meter, but a solid, unromantic, unghostly piece of tubular fibreglass. Assuming that it was indeed Joe's. Larsen felt a thrill of excitement. Marie was right: anything was better than not knowing.

Marie said, 'I'm not sure. I don't remember. The shipping lanes, off Nantucket, I think.' That could mean anywhere. She rambled on listlessly, thinking back, thinking of something else. At least there was no more talk about fantastic threats from mysterious strangers.

'Oh, no, they said more – I remember now, it was twenty-five or thirty-five miles northeast of the lightship. I remember now; it was twenty-five miles northeast of the Nantucket Lightship, not Nantucket,' she said.

Larsen said nothing, just looked at Marie. Twenty-five miles northeast of the lightship put the area where the antenna was discovered right next to Asia Rip – Sciacca's favourite fishing grounds, his favourite anchoring spot when waiting for a tide change or doing repairs or catching some sleep. Asia Rip, where the *Sofia* had searched and the Coast Guard choppers had searched two days ago and presumably were searching today. Marie hadn't made the connection, wasn't looking for connections, was only looking inward in a cry for help to try to fill the vacuum left inside by her husband's loss.

There was something else, though. Larsen had sensed it since Marie's first outburst. Something Marie was holding back, waiting for it to creep out of the space behind her eyes. She was silent now, playing with the cheap alloy coffee spoon, letting it click idly against the plastic coffee cup. She did not look at the fisherman. Her eyes were still gliding at low altitude above an ocean of tears.

'What are you thinking about?' Larsen asked gently, wondering if grief had made her baby act up more than usual. It was hard to be subtle through the pounding in his head, but he reached out and took her right hand back. 'There's something bothering you – beyond Joe's being missing.'

'What could possibly bother me beyond that?' No inflection of anger, a simple statement of fact. 'But I must know how. Tell me about the transmission.' There was still an incomprehensible note of urgency in her voice. If Joe was dead, if she'd really accepted the fact, how could the 'why' matter so much?

Larsen repeated his story. He went beyond the transmission, anxious that she should understand the finality. He explained the thinking behind his search around Asia Rip and Davis South Shoal. He outlined the area the Coast Guard had searched, and the reason he and O'Malley, and Blatchford, had risked their asses to expand the search on yesterday's flight. He explained how he had felt the first transmission was Sciacca's voice, the same way you could identify a person by the way he walked: a complex, subconscious matching of symmetries.

Marie was paler when he had finished.

'It doesn't make sense. It just doesn't make sense.' A pause.

'*Tell me how it could make sense, Lars!*'

So Larsen explained how it could make sense. He outlined how the *Marie S* might have hit a floating piece of wreckage and started enough of her planks to sink her. She could have sunk quickly at first, then slowed as the natural buoyancy of the wood hull asserted itself, as trapped air created little watertight chambers, as the pumps started to take hold, as Joe and his crew stuffed mattresses into the hole. They could have drifted around like that for a long time, batteries shorted out and the main radios inoperable but the portable VHF functioning. The portable VHF usually only had a twenty-mile range, so it might easily have been possible for the *Sofia* and no one else to hear it, since *Sofia* would have been the closest to Asia Rip. The small batteries in the portable VHF would eventually have weakened. The transmit circuitry might have shorted out so the voice component no longer functioned. Then, when the time came to inflate the life raft, they could have found the CO_2 canisters that inflated it inoperable, or the raft's nylon fabric damaged beyond repair. Men in survival suits would not last beyond six hours in water that cold and would eventually be swept out to sea.

Or, the *Marie S* could have been put out of commission by a collision. Or fire. Or any of a series of mishaps that routinely occurred at sea. It was only when there was no one left to explain the humdrum prelude to disaster that you heard talk of mysterious threats, Bermuda Triangles, *Captain Bills*.

Marie heard the fisherman out, her face taut. The fat man came over and began hinting about the amount of time they were tying up his table, so Larsen bought a cranberry muffin he did not want and another round of battery-acid coffee. Marie remained silent.

Finally she said, 'You remember last July when you and Joe decided finally to try that scheme together.' Larsen nodded, but she went on as if he hadn't understood. 'Bypassing Fulton, marketing fresh Cape Cod hook fish straight to New York restaurants? Buying a refrigerated truck . . .?'

'You're not going to talk about those "threats" again,' Larsen said in exasperation. Marie did not answer. She had

69

not heard. She was back in the soft summertime when Joe was alive and Larsen had spent his days ashore in the Sciaccas' kitchen or on their porch, weaving dreams out of thin air until one day they had actually formed a corporation to carry them out. He could remember the Italian's dark, handsome face: 'We'll give 'em the best, Lars baby. The best fish in the world!' Fingers smudging at the ideas he scribbled into *Marie*'s logbook. The logbook doubled as Joe Sciacca's family Bible. He used it to record major events of his life or notions that came to him on watch, as well as the usual Loran bearings and oil changes.

It was during that summer Larsen had finally spent enough time with Joe Sciacca to vanquish a lingering, instinctual jealousy and become friends with Marie's husband.

'Joe went down to New York for a couple of days in August,' Marie continued. 'He never used to tell me too much about it, but I gathered he went and talked to some restaurant people he knew. They were pretty excited, I guess. You know that. It was a good gimmick. They hadn't been getting very good fish from Fulton and you and Joe together could guarantee a good supply.'

'Marie –'

She didn't even look at him.

'Anyway, two days after that Gaetano called. Joe's father. I don't know if he ever told you,' Marie said, 'but Joe hated his father. He thought he was all kinds of crooked, he had tried to coerce Joe right through his childhood. Tricked him, lied to him and everything. They never talked. When there was anything to be said, I was the go-between. They stopped talking the night Joe refused to take over the family business.

'The night he called, Joe still wouldn't talk to him, so Gaetano gave me a message. I think the old man, cruel as he was, got lonely in his old age – Joe was his only son, his wife was dead. Anyway – ' She honked her nose into a sodden handkerchief. Larsen admired the way she kept her back frozen straight, refusing to succumb.

'He told me to tell Joe to give up on this marketing scheme.

I don't know if it was my imagination or what, but he sounded very sad and a little nervous. Maybe he knew he was dying.'

'Was that the "threat" you were talking about?' Larsen asked, careful to keep the sarcasm out of his voice.

'Sort of. Let me finish.'

Larsen gave up. If she wanted to believe in conspiracies, let her. Different people had different ways of short-circuiting stress.

Marie sighed and pushed at her coffee cup. 'Gaetano said the scheme was dangerous, he was messing up everybody's game. I asked him what that was supposed to mean and he just told me to repeat the message as I'd heard it. He was a rude old man.

'So I did. Joe got mad. He got so mad he went to the phone himself and started arguing with his father – mostly in English, but sometimes in Italian. Gaetano was born in Naples . . . Joe said he knew it was messing up the game and, not only did he not care, but that was half the point. It was time to clean it up, give fishermen their due. Fishermen were always getting cheated. This coffee is really putrid.'

'You ain't kidding.'

'If it worked, Joe said, and if people started imitating it, it would mean a whole new ball game. Without the scumbags, he said.

'The old man died a month later. Joe didn't go to the funeral, but one of his sisters came up later: Catherine, with her three kids. She delivered a letter from their father. It wasn't really a letter, just a couple of small pieces of paper, like stationery. I remember Joe reading it over the kitchen table and I asked him what it was. He seemed kind of excited. Was it a will, I asked him. He said no, it was a kind of insurance policy.'

Marie gave a half-smile. 'He's liberated in some ways, you know, he went to Fordham and everything, but he's Italian enough not to believe in telling women about business – ' Larsen thought a new spate of tears was coming on, but she bit her lip and said, ' – was, I guess. I'll have to get used to it. I'll have to get used to so much . . .'

'He never mentioned any of this to me,' Larsen said quickly.

'It figures,' she replied. 'He always was kind of ashamed of his old man. He's so straight, but it's funny, you know, they both look the same, the way they hold their head.'

'A week after the old man died, we got another phone call.'

The eyes were looking inward again.

'I was in the bathroom. Joe was out getting the new power take-off fixed. It never worked right. The phone rang in the hall. It sounded long distance and the man's voice was indistinct, muffled. He asked for Joe. I said Joe was out, I was – his wife.'

'"Tell him we want what Gaetano took from the man," he said. Just that. "What Gaetano took from the man." Then he said, "We want his insurance policy. Tell him to give it back to us and nobody gets hurt."'

Marie's voice was a small bird fluttering, lost in a new cage.

'He said that if he held on to it, or kept trying to blackmail him with it, just so Joe could set up his nickel-and-dime fish business, then somebody would get hurt.

'I finally asked him who he was, but all he said was, "You just tell your husband that, little lady." Then he hung up.'

Her eyes were wide, questioning, that pretty shade of cornflower. Larsen said, 'Do you want some cranberry muffins?'

'Don't try to coddle me, Lars! My mother tells me it's nothing, some guy who maybe owed Joe's father money. Or vice versa. But it's more than that. What could it mean?'

Anger was supposed to help with grief, Larsen thought, but this anger sprang from the well of sadness, drew strength directly from her loss. Larsen said, 'It doesn't make sense. Insurance policy? What Gaetano took from the man? What man?'

The woman said nothing, looked at him unflinchingly.

'Were they talking about what Joe's sister brought?' Push, push those tiny sparks of current through the spavined channels of his hung-over brain. Every synapse was a raised drawbridge. Maybe the fat man had some aspirin. Undoubtedly he would charge for it.

'I don't know,' Marie said.

'And what did that have to do with the marketing scheme?'

'I don't know,' Marie repeated. Her voice rose. 'I don't know, but I do know what that voice on the phone implied.' She leaned forward, and this time it was her hand that was doing the wrenching, her eyes were stabbing at his. 'And I know Joe disappeared on a fine, clear day and for no good reason. Lars, he may have been *murdered*!'

'That's extremely unlikely.' Sherlock Larsen at your service, ma'am, the butler had an alibi. It was an accident. QED. Aspirin!

'I want to know.' And the sadness was back again, translating through a flash of determination. 'I *have* to know. And if he was, I want the people who killed him caught!'

'Marie. He wasn't murdered.'

'How the hell do you know?' Her fist was clenched. She used it in small, definite movements to emphasize her point.

'What for?' Larsen said. 'Despite what you see on TV, people don't go knocking other people off for no good reason. If there was some kind of business foul-up, they would sue him, maybe even threaten him, but not kill him. Then they'd never get their money back. And even if, say, a loan shark was into Joe's father they might rough up Gaetano but they'd leave his son alone.'

Marie's face was set hard and stubborn as New England granite.

'All right,' Larsen said, 'who do you think wanted to murder him, Marie?'

'I *told* you, the Fulton Organization.'

'Oh, for God's sake!' he exploded. 'You know, making up murder stories isn't going to bring Joe back.' He regretted the words as soon as he'd uttered them, but she didn't react. Marie had always been an expert in using silence like an axe to chop at his ragged thoughts.

He sighed.

'Okay. Let's assume for the sake of argument – and only for the sake of argument, because it didn't happen – that Joe was murdered. How are you going to prove it? For chrissakes, how *was* he murdered, fifty or a hundred miles out at sea?

'There's no evidence,' he finished. 'Unless we find *Marie*, and she's gone.'

Marie's namesake leaned back. There was a triumphant gleam in her eyes. 'That's it, we'll have to find her.'

'What do you mean, "we"?' Larsen asked suspiciously. 'For chrissakes, the Coast Guard has been combing the ocean for two days! I've been combing the ocean for two days. What do you want? If there was anything floating out there, we'd have seen it.'

'Then you'll have to find it sunk.'

'Marie – ' Larsen's voice was despairing. He tried once more. 'You know what things are like out there, no matter how good the weather. One error doesn't kill you, nor the third oversight, but once things start going wrong they go all to hell at once and suddenly there's a hot oil pipe, and there's spare rags in the bilge, and then there's a fire, and the gasket you put off replacing in the main pump suddenly crumbles and you lose suction and someone misplaced the fire extinguisher and the life raft doesn't inflate and the radio's shorted out and then you are dead.'

'It's what happened to your grandfather, Marie.'

More strokes of silence.

'You'll have to find her sunk.'

'Impossible!'

'Don't yell. It is possible. I heard it in your voice.'

Larsen looked at her. Fifteen years and she could still read him like a goddamn book.

He gave up. 'All right. It's possible, if the antenna was found where you say it was, near Asia Rip. That could mean Joe – *maybe* – was on Asia Rip. If Joe was on Asia Rip, still afloat, and I did not spot him when I searched, it's just possible that the surf there, there's always a big swell on that rip, even when it's calm, would have shielded him from my radar, especially if for some reason or other he was only half afloat. Jesus, this is all speculation. Or, somehow or other, the *Marie* might have gone down around the Rip while they were fishing and . . .

'But the only chance I have in locating him,' Larsen mumbled, 'is if he was at anchor, because I know exactly where he used to drop the hook. And if he's not there, sweetheart, he could be anywhere within a five-hundred-square-mile area and no one, but no one, is going to find the boat unless some dragger fouls her in his net.'

'Then you'll look for him? At the anchorage, I mean? The next trip out?'

Only the Gods knew how tired he was.

'You know I will. Why even bother to ask?'

She smiled wanly. 'I don't know – you're the same old predictable Lars. You know,' the smile took on the pale richness of memory, a thin layer on an undercoat of sadness, 'you still drink a lot. Why do you do it?'

'To remind myself of the basic existentialist tension of life,' Larsen answered flippantly. 'To escape the curse of Prometheus. To forget about the Bomb.'

'The dumbest kid in my eleventh-grade lit. course could tell you existentialism was never intended as a blueprint for living. But it's a great way out for those who would rather never buckle down to anything. You're still a moral hobo, Lars.'

'And you, always the schoolteacher, Marie.'

'I just love you, Lars,' she said. 'Not in the old way, not like Joe. I just like to keep my friends.'

Funny how a woman you once loved could still get to you, the way an amputee got twinges from his lost limb.

'Well, you've got this friend, dammit. This will make the second goose chase in two days. Let's get out of here.'

They made their goodbyes outside the coffee shop. Marie melted into tears again, and Larsen felt the lump in his throat storm and almost breach the tired revetments of his eyes. He had not cried in twenty-five years.

As she turned to go he called, 'Wait.

'The last transmission. They received it in Nantucket at – a certain time on Wednesday.' He scavenged about in his mind for a phrase that would not hurt her. Impossible. It would hurt her forever. Only time would make it less relevant.

He asked, 'What time on Wednesday did you get that "feeling"?'

'That Joe was dead?' The cornflower eyes wilted slightly, and drew courage.

'In the afternoon,' she said. 'Maybe two, three?'

Larsen nodded, waved uncertainly, and turned away. The last clicks had come around one p.m. For whatever that was worth.

It was one hell of a Friday.

After meeting Marie, Larsen found a phone booth and called the National Weather Service on their commercial fishermen's line.

Time was stretched by the lingering, depressive influence of alcohol on the brain, and a thick tongue gave the day a taste of the mortuary.

The metallic, tape-recorded weather oracle was favourable, almost too propitious. Winds had been moderating steadily since yesterday evening and would continue moderating through the weekend. Decent weather.

They should have gone out today. If it hadn't been for Marie, they could have. He would have hired Caleb Lothrop as an extra hand and let Silva take *Sofia* out, and he would have turned in, strangled the hangover in a skein of sleep. Long John would be angry in his silent Portuguese way, always needing more virgin dollars to feed Moloch Bank and Trust as part of the eternal 15 per cent religion of his mortgage. Today was a day wasted, in Silva's book.

He called Long John. The mate was silent, and then grew uncharacteristically vocal and bitched about missing valuable fishing time, a coin of great scarcity value in November, and they made arrangements to leave at three on Saturday morning.

Saturday. The one advantage in skipping Friday was they could make a shorter trip of it. It was pointless to come back in before Sunday, since the New York market was closed all weekend and fish unloaded during that period would have to wait until Sunday evening to be trucked south. If they had gone out today, common sense would have dictated making a longer trip than usual out of it, and killing time offshore until Sunday morning. More time offshore meant more fish, but the hell with it. It was Larsen's boat. If Silva had sold his time to the bank, that was the mate's problem.

Larsen nursed his head gently down to the harbour. Overhead the rearguard squadrons of Canada geese were heading for their aquatic mobile-home parks in Florida. The harbour was bare of the gaudy pleasure boats that clothed it during summer.

A lot of the fishing boats had been hauled out as well, victims of low prices and autumn weather, and most of the remainder were at sea being productive. The Protestant ethic gave Larsen a small twinge in the lower guilt tract. He should have gone out today.

For the next few hours, Larsen spent time on the *Sofia*. A boat was a kind of woman, an old and hackneyed analogy but time did give it proof. You had to spend time with a boat to figure out her needs because there were always secondary drives that the very complexity of her nature hid from conscious speculation. So you sat down and let the subconscious percolate it out.

The fisherman stood at the quayside and his eyes once more caressed the boat, covering her as they would a lover: her deep waist, flared bow, the upturned transom that almost, but not quite, made her a double-ender, her fat tumblehome, the nicely proportioned pilothouse set a little forward of midships.

Then he went to sit in his leather pilot chair on the starboard side of the bridge, watching the gulls scrap and wheel in the frosty air outside, scribbling lists of stores that needed buying.

'You're a moral hobo, Lars.'

Larsen gently shook his head to clear the echoes. To no avail.

'You're content to dream up fantasies and make do in your own little world, and think up big plans. But when it's time to get up and do something about your fantasies, you're too lazy. Too afraid of rocking the boat.

'And then, when the outside world – the government, other people, me – don't match up to your dreams, you're surprised! And afraid . . .'

It had been in the fall, during the late '60s. They were in the Bilbao, a trendy coffee shop near Inman Square that served cappuccinos in terracotta cups to people who read foreign magazines without ever folding back the cover.

Marie had taken a rare weekend from her teacher's college in western Massachusetts to visit Larsen at Harvard.

They had split up for the last time at that café, Larsen yelling that he had already done something about his fantasies, he had left the rural ghetto he lived in though it would have been much more comfortable to stay and lobster with old Ben Lothrop through the recurrent heartbreaks of the Cape's economy, and if he thought Marie did not match his ideals than maybe it was she who had changed, not him.

High on Heidegger and a history major named Sandra, he had marched out of the café that morning to leave Marie in tears among croissant crumbs and spectacles peering shocked over mastheads of *Le Monde Diplomatique*.

But Marie had been right.

Larsen had, in fact, found the world less than perfect. He had tried to do something about it, forsaking a fascination with history to devote more and more time to planning antiwar rallies and helping to smuggle draft resisters to Canada. His grades had suffered. Nixon successfully internalized the Vietnam protest, Harvard withdrew half his scholarship, and Larsen decided his university was a nursery for the elite of corporate America that did not match his ideals.

Two years later, when May touched Mount Auburn Street with lilacs, Larsen had hopped a turboprop to Luxembourg and, eventually, the Mediterranean.

He stayed near its shores once he got there, drawn by the quality of light and laughter, living on *vin ordinaire* and soft cheese, talking rubbish to pretty guitar-strumming Australians on the steerage decks of ferryboats as they rolled from one chalky jewel set in wine-dark seas to the next.

Halfway through the summer he got a job as mate on

Artemis, a seventy-foot Southampton-built barquentine that sold charters to the very rich out of Piraeus, the harbour of Athens.

Rereading Greek history and mythology during long hours on watch, Larsen initiated himself into a personal religion that blended stellar navigation and the abiding presence and power of the Mediterranean gods.

That fall, *Artemis* was contracted to a team of West German archaeologists who were salvaging a wreck off the coast of Syria. The dipsomaniac South African who commanded her was fired and Larsen was promoted to captain.

The barquentine was to be based out of Beirut for the project. Larsen took her to a yard in the Lebanese capital to have her bottom checked and painted, and while the work was being done he spent a week sipping raki on the sunbaked patio of the St George's Hotel. There, watching the long brown limbs of those peculiarly Levantine women who seemed to recognize no particular nationality but to be distilled from some fertile upwelling of waters where Europe and Asia mingled, Larsen had met Joseph Stangerson.

Stangerson was a tall, slender Englishman in his early forties who looked like an 'Embassy chap', slicked his hair back with Paco Rabanne cologne, wore an ascot, and smoked Turkish cigarettes in a holder made of semi-precious stones. He was a weird crossbreeding of Oxford, Sandhurst, and the Katanga conflict, an East-of-Suez holdover with a cynicism that surpassed even Larsen's: no matter what they discussed there was always a quick joke at the back of Stangerson's eyes.

It was only later that Larsen had realized that joke was not with you but at you, fruit of a dearth that also spawned, somehow, a taste for physical danger and prepubescent girls.

Stangerson seemed to have nothing to do all day but read the gossip column in the Beirut *Daily Star* and solve the crosswords in the *Daily Telegraph*, so Larsen was not surprised when one evening the Englishman had offered him a job skippering a boat full of hashish from Lebanon to the United States of America.

At another time, Larsen might have considered the offer – 80,000 dollars was not to be sneezed at – but by then he had met Sofia Mavromikalis.

The ship's clock tolled six times.

It was late. He had to get diesel fuel for tomorrow's trip. *Sofia*'s GM engine reverberated loudly among the empty docks. Oil pressure and engine temperature were normal. Larsen went on deck to cast off all but a spring line linking the stern section of his vessel with the forward part of the pier. He ran the engine slow astern on hard starboard rudder, enough to lever the bow away from the bulkhead at which *Sofia* was moored, using the spring line as fulcrum. An outgoing tide took charge then, pushing *Sofia*'s bow further away from shore. He cast off the line and proceeded dead slow ahead to the fish pier, rocking ever so lightly in a ten-knot southwesterly wind.

There was still a black sense of loss hanging over the skipper: essence of Marie and Joe, hangover, memories and guilt. Larsen finished tying up, went below, and slumped on the settee in the friendly, unimposing company of a cold bottle of Rolling Rock while the drug addicts who ran the Co-op's fuel concession filled port and starboard tanks with black gold, diesel fuel, the devourer of profit margins. One day he would get that design for an efficient, sail-powered longliner off the drawing board and on to a boat-shop floor. *Mañana*. *Mañana* to that, and the fish-marketing project, too. *Mañana* to the wrecks he'd never have time to dive on, and all the other little schemes and inventions that were going to make his fortune some day and leave him free to do nothing but drink French champagne and carve seabirds out of valuable fruitwoods. At times like these you realized that time controlled you instead of the other way around. Controlled you and teased you and one day it was too late and you had nothing left but regrets and empty wishes.

The light was fading as Larsen locked the wheelhouse and stepped ashore. The fisherman was heading for a phone booth that lay caged in a circle of a yellow streetlight in the parking lot. Her number was in the book – what the hell was he *doing*?

A second, then a third and a fourth beer, had teamed up with the hangover and warped his usual behaviour patterns.

Ring. Pause. Ring. Pause. Ring. The seconds spent waiting for a phone to ring, one or one hundred or a thousand miles away, O'Malley maintained, were the only institutional time left for modern man to speculate on the meaning of life and social relationships. Every other moment was deliberately filled by television and *People* magazine and other sedatives.

'Hello?'

She had a low, breathless voice on the phone. Urgency.

'Miss Blatchford? This is Lars Larsen.'

Silence. 'Ms Blatchford?'

'Yes, Mr Larsen. What can I do for you?'

What in Hades *could* she do for him?

'I, um, wanted to apologize for last night.'

'Yes.'

'I think you realize that it was not entirely my fault. Your friend Whipple was deliberately insulting.'

'Words, words. You didn't have to knock him down, or punch him.'

'There's no point in this – '

'No. I agree,' she said.

'Look, I'm *sorry*! I shouldn't have got angry, but I did . . . Can't you accept an apology, at least recognize that it wasn't entirely my fault?' He had to control an unexpected urge to chuckle. It was pure soap-opera dialogue.

'All I recognize is that two pathetically unconscious examples of American male ego chose to insult each other in the most boring way possible in a bar-room and then beat the shit out of each other as a result. And for the oldest of reasons. Territory. Harem. Power.'

Larsen took a deep drag on the evening breeze and wished he'd avoided drinking those beers. What he needed now was sleep.

'Look, Ms Blatchford, I've apologized and I'm not going to continue saying I'm sorry.'

'Apologies come very cheap to the "Me" generation. Do what you want and apologize later.' Her voice sounded tired, no longer angry.

'What do you want me to do?' One last try. 'As a tangible token of how mortified I am, do you want me to offer you an unparalleled opportunity to continue your Pulitzer-winning quest for the truth behind the Mystery of the *Marie S*?' He'd have to soft-pedal the sarcasm.

'You're doing another search? The story's out already.' Yet there was a hint of interest in her tone.

'There's a chance – no more than that – I know what happened to her,' Larsen said. 'More to the point, I think I know where it might have happened.

'We're going out on a regular fishing trip tomorrow at three a.m. Sometime during the trip I'm going to do a sonar search of that area and if I find anything anomalous that could be the *Marie*, I'm going to dive on it. You seem to have, uh, unusual interest in this. If you're willing to sacrifice your weekend, you might have a real story.

'We'd be back on Sunday,' he added.

What in the name of all the gods was he doing? He owed her *nothing*! Male ego or no male ego, Whipple had provoked the roughhouse at Rumbelly's. In any case, she wasn't answering.

'Well – do you have to cover a planning board meeting or something?'

'It's not that, although I do work Saturdays, but – I shall have to get my editor to approve my taking tomorrow off. He's not as keen – he's not all that interested. Although I do have a comp. day coming. And I have an appointment tomorrow night.'

'Suit yourself.'

'Wait.' Interest returned to her voice. 'Can't we leave it so that you can expect me if you see me?'

'It's not quite that simple. I'll have to get extra stores if you come.'

'I'll bring my own food if I come.' She mentioned a twenty-four-hour supermarket in Hyannis.

Larsen said, 'Don't bring any fish. We don't eat it when

we're gutting cod all day. And if you're not here by three a.m., Ms Blatchford, we'll be gone. I'm not immolating a good tide on the altar of your indecision.'

'Aye, aye, Captain, sorr.' Humour had made the reruns in the head of Eliza Blatchford.

'And Captain Larsen . . .'

'Yes, Ms Blatchford.'

'Nothing. You're sure we'd be back on Sunday?'

'I want to get Monday's prices.'

'Well,' she said. 'I might see you.'

Larsen depressed the phone lever, slipped another dime in and phoned Billy's mother's number. He needed Billy to get the supplies; he couldn't face the supermarket's neon risks, the homicidal housewives with their sharp elbows. Most of all he needed to tumble fully clothed into his huge, oaken, horsehair-stuffed bed and sleep his way back to a world where he could prevent himself beforehand from committing acts as perverse as inviting Eliza Blatchford on a weekend trip on to the North Atlantic.

Perhaps it was his Lutheran sense of penance prescribing self-mortification . . .

There was one other task to accomplish before he could seek oblivion.

If the ocean were a gambling casino, the odds against finding the *Marie* would make even a Vegas syndicate man feel a little embarrassed – they gave the house too good a break. But if by some fluke he did find a wreck, Larsen would have to have his diving equipment ready to see if it really was the *Marie*. That meant regulators to check, scuba tanks to fill, gear to assemble.

God, his head hurt.

CHAPTER SEVEN

Once the initial shock was over and Larsen had hurled his clanging, battered German alarm clock against the wall to still the ringing, being awake at two a.m. was almost enjoyable.

The hangover was mostly gone and Disraeli was delighted to have Larsen's schedule coincide with his nocturnal prowling hours. The kitten followed Larsen down the narrow stairs into the kitchen and began doing Tai Chi exercises on a hooked rug. Pariah gave the boss a required three tail wags and went back to dreaming of a land where all rabbits were slow and sticks could throw themselves.

This was limbo time. The whole world seemed asleep except for the people who were dancing, or making love, or giving birth or dying. They and the cops and the short-order cooks at the all-night joints with Kent ashes drooping into hash browns, and the fishermen. Storm troopers of the night, the cold-eyed elite of darkness.

Larsen fed cat and coal stove, put the coffee pot on the fire, switched on NOAA weather radio, and staggered out to hump tubs of clam meats and his scuba gear into the back of his pick-up.

It was cold and almost still, but the wind never retreated completely from the salt marsh; it always left some scouts and sentinels, some stray cat's-paws as lookouts to keep an eye on the human enemy.

Three a.m. on the ship's clock. Mallebarre was inhabited only by the shadows behind streetlamps, the feverish regrets of insomniacs – and fishermen. Pat Elliot's scalloper had come in last night. Her decklights and running lights were on and the hum of her generator sang harmony to *Sofia*'s. Elliot had already unloaded and was heading back out on the same tide: they would have company eastbound.

They had buried the fishhold in an avalanche of fresh chipped ice at the fish pier and gone back to the bulkhead to wait. No sign of Eliza Blatchford.

Long John had given Larsen a very long and vinegary look when he was informed of the possibility of having a woman on board. Larsen had challenged his mate's unverbalized opinion and Silva had held his peace.

There were two possibilities, Larsen decided. Silva thought Larsen was sweet on the journalist, and disapproved, or he shared the common superstition that women were extremely dangerous cargo on a boat. Either belief was myth, Larsen repeated to himself. Women could and did cause trouble on a boat, but only for the most mundane of reasons. And Larsen was too old a hand at emotional poker to confuse admiration for a pair of well-turned buttocks with infatuation, let alone love.

In any case it was irrelevant. There was a roar as Larsen's pressure on the key combined with a half inch of throttle to start the engine. Silva and Billy went to cast off, Billy unlooping the mooring lines from shoreside bollards and Silva hauling them inboard.

But the feeling of freedom when a boat finally severed itself from shore was lost. A swathe of headlights swung down Ocean Street at high speed and swerved into the fish-pier parking area. Eliza Blatchford popped out of what Larsen was surprised to note was a battered, rusty VW with a tarp over its side window and the rear fender bent to hell. It was a Cape Cod car, the kind that populated the roadways in small folksongs of rust and oil leaks and holey silencers throughout the winter, only to be submerged come Memorial Day in a flood of new four-square Subarus owned by summer people.

He would have thought she'd drive a BMW, like the rest.

She saw the running lights and waved dramatically, reached behind and pulled out a small travelling carry-all and three brown supermarket bags. Silva glanced moodily up at the wheelhouse windows, Larsen shrugged and gave the boat a little forward throttle and port rudder, reversed with starboard helm, then forward again to turn her 180 degrees and slick her alongside the fish pier. Eggshells for bumpers, delicate as a brain surgeon. His father would have been proud.

The tide was almost slack. He had no trouble keeping her alongside as Silva took the woman's carry-all and then manhandled the shopping bags aboard. As he gripped the third one and pulled it off the pier there was a rip and a cascade of veggies fell from the bottom into Mallebarre Harbour.

Cries from Blatchford, growls from Silva, but she jumped aboard quite gracefully. Larsen gunned the diesel and pointed *Sofia*'s bow south to the harbour entrance.

Blatchford came up to the wheelhouse as Larsen was starting to thread the channel through the outer bar.

The outer bar was what set Mallebarre fishermen apart from their counterparts in relatively deep-water ports like Hyannis or Provincetown. Two grim miles of shoals, seabirds, mists, and pastel-shaded mirages: millions of tons of virgin white sand, scoured and shifted and stirred around daily by the powerful tidal currents that raced in and out of Mallebarre Bay and around the outer Cape. When a winter blizzard blew from anywhere but the western quadrant, the huge combers and bitter wind combined to shift thousands of tons of that sand, steam-shovelling it 100 yards or half a mile away.

Every fisherman in Mallebarre had at one time or another felt fear grip his stomach like a wolftrap as he came over the outer bar in rough weather and saw, all around him, as far as the eye could reach, nothing but evil combers and the light green of shallows. Closer acquaintance with that pretty green colour could only signify sinking for your boat and death for yourself.

Larsen tried to explain some of this to the woman as he followed, on radar, the path marked by movable longline buoys which the fishermen themselves shifted daily or weekly as the channel changed.

When he lapsed silent she said nothing. In fact, she had said nothing but hello since coming up the companionway, causing the skipper to talk in pure self-defence.

Larsen wondered again what wormlike subconscious had

made him invite a woman into the most explosive situation possible for people who didn't get along – a small vessel in the open ocean.

'I can see how that would make fishermen feel different. The camaraderie of the sea, I suppose.'

Her words rang hollowly ironic in the green cavern of instrument lights. Larsen just snorted as he turned his boat ten degrees to starboard, heading her straight as a steeplechaser for the next blip on the radar screen. A course of eighty-five degrees magnetic from this seventh buoy meant the channel hadn't shifted much since the last storm. Then again, it had been a westerly blow.

'Why do you laugh?' She buttered her words with irritation.

Larsen looked at her directly for the first time. She had her hair in a long ponytail and the binnacle light dug shadows around her cheeks. She wore a thick black rollneck sweater and jeans and sneakers: no-nonsense clothing that contradicted the quick flash of rubies on a Schlumberger bracelet as she moved her hands.

'I laughed, Ms Blatchford, because there is no such thing as the camaraderie of the sea among fishermen.'

'Re-ally?'

Larsen could imagine the lifted eyebrows. The bar's easternmost combers were coming into view, flashing molars in the purple night on both sides of number-eight buoy. He steered for the gap between them, close to the jury-rigged navigational mark. Due east, near enough. He could relax once they had left this one behind.

Blatchford, moving between the starboard door and the control panel to get a better look at Larsen, said in her brittle tone, 'Can you explain that? I would think the very fact that you have spent so much time searching for Sciacca's boat would contradict what you just said.'

So Larsen explained.

The camaraderie of the sea, the idea that everyone on boats belonged to the same seagoing country club, did not apply to commercial fishermen. Any fisherman would do his level best to help a vessel in distress because the next time it might be his life that wanted saving. But living 100 miles out on an ocean that did not give a flea fart whether you survived or drowned, you got used to the fact that only your own wits would wrest a living from the beast. You accepted that no one, most likely, would be around to help out if you failed, and men other than your crew became irrelevant to the task.

No one knew, the fisherman ended, if the North Atlantic made men solitary, or if it simply attracted only those able to rely on themselves. It did not seem to make much difference.

Larsen shut up. The endlessness of the night horizon was playing its usual philosophical tricks. What did it matter, anyway, what fishermen thought or did? They were all social misfits, in an anachronistic industry. And what did Eliza Blatchford, journalist, care?

Her voice came softly. 'It really burns you, doesn't it?'

'It no longer matters to me, Ms Blatchford. I've lived with it. It has its positive points.'

'Like letting you aestivate comfortably in your shell. Providing you with an excuse not to get too serious about life.'

He wasn't going to let her rile him tonight. Maybe it was the horizon.

'I'm comfortable.'

'Captain Larsen?'

'At your service, ma'am.'

She moved again, sliding off the pilot seat. Larsen hadn't even noticed her climb into it. The brittle edge to her words was harder, more evident as she said, 'Where am I supposed to sleep? In your bunk?'

'Didn't Long John – my mate, the big guy who helped you – didn't he show you?'

'No. I have a feeling I'm not very welcome on this trip – or maybe welcome but for all the wrong reasons.'

On the *QE 2* they hired suave multilingual pursers whose sole job was to take care of difficult passengers.

Larsen checked the horizon a final time. Number-eight buoy had just exited stage left. No ships or lights, only stars and planets. No moon as yet. The autopilot had settled in nicely, compensating for the boat's tendency to yaw towards Mexico. Dead on.

'Come on, Ms Blatchford. I'll show you.'

Sofia's sleeping accommodation on the deck below the wheelhouse consisted of one stateroom aft, separated by a panelled companionway from a head that included shower, sink, and toilet. The midships saloon and galley took up all *Sofia*'s considerable beam, while forward there were another two cabins also separated by a companionway, a collision bulkhead, and finally a stowage area in the forepeak.

Other fishermen, envious of the comfort of *Sofia*'s accommodations, not to mention her looks and speed, called her 'Larsen's yacht'. The fact that *Sofia* was one of the highliners, the stars, of the Mallebarre fleet did not in any way diminish their envy.

Larsen led the woman to the forward, portside cabin and opened the door. He bowed sardonically, and waved her in. ''Ere yer are, Countess. Yer own private, personal cabin, wiv lock'n' bolt on the inside. Ring fer the steward if yer need anyfing. We'll be in Port Soid in a week.'

She stepped over the coaming and looked at the neatly turned down Hudson Bay blankets, the louvred mahogany door, the carpeting, the polished brass porthole, the reading lamp by the bed.

'I – uh – I didn't mean to imply . . .'

'The hell you didn't, Ms Blatchford, but don't worry about it. Sweet dreams.'

The hell with her and her implications. Larsen went topside.

The 'PR' buoy that *Sofia* was heading for had just shown up on the horizon, winking its short–long flashes as friendly as any buoy that showed up on course, on time.

Larsen edged over to the chart table to correct his next compass course for the drift imparted by tidal currents when the hatch behind him opened, letting in a flash of light.

'Shut the goddamn light, Long John.'

'It's – me.'

Larsen swivelled as he heard Blatchford speak. She stood half in, half out of the hatch. He waited, parallel course rulers stiff in his left hand, pencil in the right.

The woman finished her climb up the stairs, shutting the hatch gingerly. She stepped across to stand by the winch controls. Her hair gleamed in a backwash of starlight.

'I couldn't sleep and I . . .' She seemed to chew her words carefully. 'I think I owe you an apology.'

'What for?' Larsen kept his tone indifferent. If he wore such an obvious shell, he might as well use it.

'For implying that I was invited along as a sex object.'

'It's okay.'

'No, it's not. I make fast assumptions – they're usually the most correct but I also get upset easily, and between those two . . . character traits I often find myself in hot water.'

'I'd say it's not an unfair assumption to make, for a male ego like mine.'

'I'm sorry.'

'Funnily enough, though, you were right.'

She shifted her weight to brace the small of her back against the winch panel. The swell had intensified slightly: they were getting beyond the shelter of Monomoy Point.

'What was I right about?'

'There's another pilot's seat here, hooked by the door.'

'I'm okay.'

'You were right about male egos, in general.'

'I'm surprised to hear you admit it,' she said, with a flash of the old fire.

'Ms Blatchford, I was passionately debating whether it was sexist not to allow women to stand in the frontline of a peace march and get their eyes seared by Mace and their asses kicked in by National Guardsmen when you were still deciding how to clothe your Barbie dolls. I'm fully conscious of how powerful male ego is.'

Larsen got up from the chart table and paced to the other side of the wheelhouse and back, instinctively checking for traffic. Away to the east were the range lights of a container ship in the traffic lanes. Three miles astern he could make out the green and red and white ziggurat of running lights on Pat Elliot's scalloper, following them to sea. Engine

90

RPM, temperature, oil pressure okay. All quiet on the eastern front.

'Maybe I should also apologize for last night?' she asked the hydraulic pressure gauge.

'For Freddie?'

'Who?'

'Freddie. Your preppie friend.'

'Oh, you mean Fergie.' There was a ghost of a chuckle behind the shadow.

'Ferguson Blakely Whipple the Third, believe it or not,' she added.

'The same Whipples with half of AT&T in their portfolio and the big estate in Cotacheset?'

'The same.'

'If you don't mind my asking, what do you see in the guy?'

'I saw enough in him to be engaged to him for two years.'

'But not any more.'

'No, not any more.'

Larsen kept quiet. After a moment, the woman went on thoughtfully, 'You know, it's interesting the way a certain political system – also economic system – can condition people to belong to a class. They're conditioned and so they want nothing but to remain in that class. Fergie is a case in point. He is 100 per cent, Department of Agriculture approved, Grade A American Ruling Class. Andover, Dartmouth, Columbia Law School. A caricature, almost.' She was looking up at the horizon now, her movements stilled. She continued, 'He is very intelligent, doing very well in a successful Wall Street law firm. And completely unaware of how massive and unalterable his blinkers are. The blinkers he was born into. Do you understand what I'm saying?'

'And where does that leave you, Ms Blatchford?'

'The same place it leaves you. Trapped behind walls built by my particular corner of the system that nurtured me . . .'

'Do you ever try to see over those walls?' he asked, sharply. 'Look past the ivied bricks to the outside world? See that landscapers, or derelicts, or kings, or cabbages, for that matter, all have something valid to offer despite their environmental conditioning? Do you see, for that matter,' he went on, 'how much it suits kings for the cabbages to remain in their vegetable state?'

'And you, Captain Larsen?' The discussion was honing the edge of her tone until it was becoming sharp enough to hurt.

'I try hard enough. Hard enough to realize that I can see beyond those walls, to an extent. Hard enough to realize I'll never be entirely free of them except, sometimes, intellectually.'

He was finding it easier to hold his own anger in check with her. Maybe he was past trying to impress her in the automatic sexual way. So it should not have surprised him when her anger vanished in the next words.

'It's going to be a long trip, Captain Larsen.' She sighed. 'Why don't you call me Eliza?'

Diesel stilled, generator off, batteries charged, the fishing vessel rocked to the ocean's beat, anchored in the night inside Davis Bank and east of Great Rip.

Blatchford had put up a fuss when Larsen told her they were going to spend the first day fishing but had settled down to the extent of bringing them coffee all afternoon as they worked and even preparing dinner, vegetarian style.

'What is this?' Billy asked cautiously as the woman ladled out servings of what looked like green-and-red gruel with a wedge of greenish-yellow pie. Filling was running out faster than crust could keep up with it.

They were seated primly at the saloon table, lined up around the settee like a Catholic family at Sunday dinner, everyone still wearing filthy boiler suits, but Billy, Larsen noted with shock, had actually combed his hair and put on a clean Bahamas shirt, with pictures of palm trees and conch shells, underneath his. A woman's influence on a man's world.

'Ratatouille Niçoise, otherwise known as vegetable mush. And cheese-and-broccoli quiche.' Billy looked as if he wished he hadn't asked.

Silva said nothing, staring moodily at his plate. He'd been sullen all trip.

92

The deckhand tasted the food, warily. His fork hovered in suspended judgement, then came in for a cautious landing on the ratatouille.

'The quiche isn't all the way done,' the woman said uncertainly, 'but I hope it tastes all right.' She sat down and set the example by starting to carve big chunks out of her pie.

Silva stood up, edged past Billy and over to the fridge, took another beer, and went aft to the cabin he was sharing with Larsen this trip. He left his plate untouched.

'What's eating him?' Larsen asked Billy. 'He's been in a lousy mood since yesterday. Is it because we cut Friday?'

Billy shook a pair of full cheeks. 'Family problems.' A swallow. 'He drove me home the other day. We stopped by Betty Lou's on the way.'

Betty Lou was the blonde schoolteacher. It appeared that Silva was not as adept at handling extramarital affairs as he seemed. They were easy to start, hard to control, like a war, or a brush fire.

The woman said, 'What makes you think you can find the *Marie S* in one day just like that? She could be anywhere, right? You said that when we went up to search for him on the plane . . .'

Larsen was busy selecting mood music. He found a Champion Jack Dupree tape, slotted it into the cassette deck, and the strains of 'Walkin' Blues' began to distort seconds into slow rhythms.

He said, 'I don't think we can find the *Marie*. I think there's maybe one chance in twenty,' he continued, 'unless, for some reason, she went down while she was anchored, the way we are now.'

'I don't understand. Can you elaborate?' Blatchford asked, in her best press-conference voice.

Larsen elaborated. 'I don't know if you know, but a New Bedford dragger picked up a VHF antenna, same make as the *Marie*'s, around twenty-five miles northeast of Nantucket Light. They found it Wednesday evening.'

'I heard that,' she said.

'Well, the currents in that area are tidal, and they run strongest along a north–south axis. They also run at weaker

93

velocities in other directions, shifting clockwise, through a twelve-hour cycle, high, low, high.

'An object found floating in those waters would tend to cover an elliptical path that would bring it back roughly where it started from, all other things being equal.'

The journalist was scratching at her notebook again, eyes narrowed in concentration. Her flaming hair was tucked back in a workmanlike bun.

'But all other things are never equal out here. For one thing, the wind. For another thing, the waves that the wind creates. Both have been from the southwest since Wednesday, which was the earliest the *Marie* could have sunk, assuming the transmission we did hear was Sciacca, which we all think it was . . .

'They stayed southwesterly, then they shifted around to the north and west as the storm came through, but the overall trend would have pushed that ellipse gently towards the northeast, at a fraction of a knot per hour. If you assume the *Marie* went to the bottom and the antenna broke off simultaneously, sometime Wednesday afternoon,' the skipper's nose wriggled in concentration, 'and if you ascribe an approximate speed of, say, point two knots per hour for a light, drifting piece of fibreglass, you'd have that antenna covering, roughly, four or five nautical miles to the northwest over the period of time involved.' He should have been a prof, Larsen thought.

He paused, took a huge swig of his beer. 'I could show you better on the chart . . . Understand this is all speculation. The effect of wind, wave, storm, tides, and so on is all very approximate, there's a huge margin of error. And the antenna may not have been the *Marie*'s at all.

'But it just so happens,' Larsen continued, 'that if you backtrack four or five miles to the southwest from the point where the antenna was found you find yourself virtually on top of Asia Rip. And the inside of Asia Rip, between the Rip and Phelps Bank, is a nice patch of hard white sand and gravel bottom that was Joe Sciacca's favourite anchoring grounds. His favourite in this area. I used to anchor with him there myself, once in a while.'

94

Eliza Blatchford was intent on the hieroglyphics in her notebook. Larsen said to Billy, who was yawning over Louis L'Amour on the settee, 'Why don't you go up and play lookout now, *hombre*? Radar watch. I'll clean up.' He looked at Blatchford. 'I very much doubt we'll find her. I'd never bet in poker on a hand like that, and I'm a good poker player.'

Out beyond the portholes, a seabird called as if in its sleep, an eerie sound that cut through the background murmur of Atlantic surf.

Eliza said sharply, 'You could have told me that before I came.'

'I did,' the fisherman replied.

CHAPTER EIGHT

They found the *Marie S* in thirty fathoms of water at 8.35 Sunday morning.

At 5.30 a.m. they had winched up anchor and headed southward, towards the intersecting Loran bearings that marked Sciacca's anchoring grounds. Thrumming steadily along as the sea mimicked a lightening sky, Larsen marked out another search pattern on the largest-scale chart he could find that included Asia Rip.

The search grid proved almost superfluous.

Joe Sciacca anchored inside Asia Rip because the shoal, which ran approximately north-northeast to south-southwest, afforded some shelter from swells pushing up from the south. The long bulges of water would spill their guts on the shallow ground in a welter of white blood. They would mount up high over the sandbar but leave a vessel anchored on the other side in relative peace. Asia Rip also offered protection from large merchant vessels trying to cut corners around Nantucket Island on the Boston–New York route.

More than one huge freighter or tanker, under home-office pressure to make time and manned by less-than-qualified officers, had missed a small blip on his radar screen and almost run down fishing vessels anchored well outside the shipping lanes.

Any merchantman trying to include the three fathoms of Asia Rip on his shortcut would find it the last shortcut he would ever take.

Larsen started his search from the northernmost point at which Asia Rip offered protection, ran west to Fishing Rip, and turned east again on a course that took the tidal currents into account. He kept his hands on the wheel, his eyes on the compass, and a chart clipped to the control panel beneath the wheelhouse windows and the chronometer that would signal when it was time to turn around.

Silva, sullen and glassy-eyed from lack of sleep, watched the sidescan sonar graph as its tiny needle etched out sand waves and contours on the ocean floor.

'Wanna tell me about it, John Boy?' Larsen asked once.

The mate had eaten little of Billy's fried breakfast, just smoked Pall Malls and swallowed strong coffee, far gone in an emotional badlands. He snarled some incomprehensible answer.

Larsen knew it would come out, later rather than sooner.

On the third dogleg, Silva grunted, 'We got something.'

Larsen automatically looked up at the winking Loran position-finder above his head and jotted down co-ordinates on the edge of the clipboard: 16217, 13860. He waited one minute and spun the wheel, bringing *Sofia* around 180 degrees, until she was heading the way she had come, and ran her for two minutes.

'Nothin',' Silva said. 'We must have just caught the edge of it. Whatever "it" was.' Larsen repeated the drill, aiming a little to the northward of their previous track as he turned the boat around again.

'There it is.'

Larsen flicked the autopilot to 'on' and checked the sidescan sonar. There were two spikes, showing an object that stuck up twenty feet off the ocean floor.

It was in the wrong position for the only wreck on Asia Rip that was marked on the chart.

He flicked the autopilot off and went back to the wheel.

'John, why don't you and Billy rig up a grappling line, use one of the trawl anchors for a grappling hook, and fifty fathoms of anchor line with one of the reflecting buoys? Leave enough slack so I can back her when it catches, and then we can drop the buoy and anchor. We can dive –'

The mate interrupted, 'You want to dive on this? It's thirty fathoms deep.'

'How else are we going to tell if it's a wreck or new shoal or a sand wave or a dead whale?'

'It's too sudden for a sand wave. It drops off too quick.'

'You've dived deeper than that many times. So have I – '

There was a crash behind them. The two men turned to see Blatchford bent over in the hatchway with two mugs of hot coffee in her hands, a third splashed on the deck. Silva did a fair imitation of an old lame grizzly bear in need of three root canals and slammed out the portside door.

'Sorry . . .' She looked chagrined.

'We found something, Eliza,' Larsen said.

It proved a great deal harder to hook the wreck than to pick it up on sonar.

They made five passes over the Loran position, scoring hits with the sidescan on four occasions before the line flaked out on *Sofia*'s afterdeck jerked, and started uncoiling like a mamba. The splayed flukes of the grappling anchor, 180 feet below, had snagged on something.

Billy shouted and moved fast to unhook the line from the port bollard, while Larsen put the engine into reverse as quickly as three-to-one ratio-reduction gears would mesh.

Then the buoy was floating placidly in clean swells, *Sofia* rocking beside it.

'If only everything was this easy,' the fisherman commented to Eliza Blatchford, who was gazing at the spikes on the sonar chart that marked what was below. She was very close. There was a faint whiff of honeysuckle and when her elbow brushed his, Larsen's brain recorded another spike coming off the cardiac rhythm.

No way. Not her.

'John,' he moved suddenly to the open portside window, 'stand by the anchor winch and get her ready to drop. I'll tell you when.'

He moved the boat slowly to a position fifty feet away from the buoy in the direction of tidal flow. Silva unlatched the devil's claw, a hook-and-chain arrangement that secured the anchor chain itself, and looked up at the wheelhouse, gloved hands ready on the winch's brakewheel.

Larsen nodded. The anchor splashed and its chain rattled out in a cloud of rust and desiccated bottom mud. Larsen went below to break out the diving gear from the forepeak.

There was a section of corkboard glued on the starboard bulkhead next to the head, where *Sofia*'s crew pinned dirty postcards, tide tables, and reminders and notices that did not belong in the ship's log. Part of the corkboard was reserved for excerpts from the US Navy Diving Manual decompression tables, graphs showing the amount of time a diver could spend on the bottom or at varying depths before swimming to the surface. There were also graphs showing the quantities of pressurized air a diver would suck out of an air tank at different depths, and the corresponding amount of time he or she could spend at that depth.

Blatchford was taking notes again as Larsen and Silva finished planning their dive. Silva had not been as friendly with Sciacca as the skipper, but he had known him as a colleague and the debts of that association had apparently outweighed his earlier reluctance to dive.

That, plus the fact that a real diver did not let another diver go down alone to any significant depth. Silva was a real diver.

Blatchford said, 'I've dived before, in the Bahamas.' She had her head crooked over her notebook. The men were absorbed and took no notice.

'Thirty fathoms, one hundred eighty feet. We'll have all of five minutes to go down there, see if it is the *Marie* and snoop around there if it is. That's five minutes maximum if we want a zero-decompression dive. I sure as hell don't want to fuck around with decompression if we can help it.'

Silva nodded firmly. The greater the depth, the longer the diving time, the more compressed air a diver was forced to breathe to keep his internal pressure up in counteraction to the increased pressure of seawater he swam in. The more air he took in, the more nitrogen and oxygen went fizzing into his bloodstream.

No problems on the way down. On the way back up, the compressed air you breathed would expand as seawater pressure lessened. No trouble with the oxygen component, as long as you did not hold your breath and explode your lungs: surplus oxygen simply bled from your system, leaving as it came.

The nitrogen, however, could not be vented from the

bloodstream as quickly as it was assimilated, so you had to ascend much slower than you went down, to give it time to dissipate. The deeper and longer you stayed underwater, the slower you came up.

If you came up too fast, the trapped gas started to fizz like soda, expanding in your veins and arteries, lodging in joints or in your brain or alongside vital nervous links. Severe pain was the usual result: convulsions, paralysis, and death could follow in severe cases.

Most divers tried hard to avoid staying under long enough or deep enough to have to make decompression stops, precisely timed pauses on the way up that allowed a surplus of nitrogen to dissipate naturally.

The skipper said, 'If we do have to stay under longer, we have to do nine minutes total decompression stops.'

'That's nuts,' Silva said.

Larsen agreed. 'We start going back up inside five minutes, *Marie* or no *Marie*. The tides are okay right now; it should be less than half a knot by the time we go overboard.'

Blatchford asked, 'Can I come?'

For once Silva laughed, shook his head out the door and went to the stern deck. The woman reddened.

Larsen said, 'You know how to dive?'

'I told you, but you weren't listening. I've dived a lot, in the Bahamas.'

'You've dived a lot, in the Bahamas,' Larsen repeated wonderingly. 'How deep?'

'Sixty, seventy feet, sometimes.'

'Eliza, this isn't the Bahamas. For one thing, you remember when I tested the water temperature yesterday? Codfish like it between thirty and forty degrees Fahrenheit. It was Cod Heaven down there, thirty-five degrees in twenty fathoms. Even in drysuits, that's cold. The exposed body loses fifteen times more heat in water than in air: the suit doesn't entirely negate that effect.

'And it's the Atlantic, not the Caribbean,' Larsen went on. 'Murky as well as cold. Currents. On top of it all, this is a no-safety-margin dive, a bounce dive we call it: no time for trouble, not enough air for real trouble. All we have are single tanks: if me or Silva runs into problems, we won't have enough air to face them without coming up too fast. And if you've dived before, you know what that means.'

She just looked at him. Spoiled rotten, he decided, not for the first time, until she nodded.

'Silva was a Navy diver, and I've done a lot of deep dives before. And we're a good team.'

'It's okay,' she said. 'I thought I'd ask.'

'We should get going,' Larsen said.

The skipper and mate wore long underwear and thick socks, blue jeans and wool sweaters as they wrestled into their Swedish-made drysuits: neoprene body suits that totally insulated the wearer from surrounding water and included hood, boots, and gloves to make the arrangement complete. There was even a valve to bleed air inside the suit for insulation and buoyancy.

There was also a valve to bleed air out, in case the suit suddenly acquired too much positive buoyancy and the diver started shooting towards the surface like a Trident missile.

Billy helped the men on with their single tanks, buckled over the belly. Regulator, breathing hose, air indicator, and mouthpiece topped the tanks. Life vest, knife, flippers. Partial face masks would mean numb cheeks and chins later, but full face masks were an expensive luxury Larsen did not own.

Adjust wrist, neck, and ankle seals. Strap flippers and weight belt, and loop the powerful underwater flashlight to the right wrist. Larsen finally added a depth gauge and stopwatch next to his waterproof, pressure-proof Rolex. He looked at Silva, a clumsy, rubberized alien from inner space, who was already standing by the rope ladder leading overboard. Larsen took one end of the thin heaving line Billy would pay out as they dived, an emergency umbilical cord to the boat, and clicked the stopwatch.

They clambered up to stand on the gunwale for a moment, then flipped into the cold ocean. They swam next to the surface till they reached the buoy and arrowed downward.

As they followed the buoy past 100 feet, Larsen realized

he had lied to Eliza. The water was unusually cold for this time of year, and there were fewer plankton and other microscopic organisms to impede vision: as a result they had excellent visibility for these waters. At this depth all colours had been filtered into a sinister dull green, but you could still see the darker blotch of *Sofia*'s hull above them.

A five-foot sand shark, toothy but harmless, cruised by just inside their field of vision.

Silva was slightly ahead, finning himself along vigorously. You could not see bottom yet: the green just deepened around their single frame of reference, the long arc of line that led to the anchor below and whatever it was hooked on. A thin pencil beam of white light zipped out ahead of the mate: Silva had switched on his flashlight and the 130,000 candlepower flicked around as the mate kicked.

In the introversion of the depths you listened to nothing but your own thoughts and the click and bubble of your regulator.

Larsen checked his stopwatch: one minute into the dive. The depth gauge read 130 feet. They were still swimming fast, exhausting correspondingly more air to feed their pumping muscles. Larsen forced himself to breathe more deeply, evenly, in time with, even slower than the silver platelets of bubbles fanning across his path from Silva's mouthpiece below. Pretty little dishes of mercury-bright water. Diving was fun at this depth – you felt good.

A sheen, lighter than the surrounding universe and then –

A shadow, a hump, a patch of solid green colour. With angular, man-made lines, not the organic curves of sea things. The shape of a hull, maybe.

Breathe easy, deep, regular: one hippopotamus, two hippopotamuses. Hippopotami?

One minute, thirty-five seconds. It was cold. Larsen bled some more air into his drysuit.

A bow and a stern emerged, resolved and showed the hull was tilted slightly over on the portside. The box near the stern was a wheelhouse and midships was a fishhold hatch. Shadows became a mast with a strange cloud at the top and

Larsen felt an eerie thrill: he had never seen a sea creature with such long, dancing, Salome arms. A huge head with corrupt, dark blotches around the face, ugly as sin and not half so tempting.

The mate had seen it, too. His flashlight beam tracked right and pinned itself to the thing, which foreshortened into a cloud of monofilament netting: the remains of a gillnet, lightweight nylon twine come loose from its moorings and drifting forever with the tide, condemned by its weights to wander around the ocean floor catching fish no one would ever pick up. Fishermen called it 'ghostfishing'. The dark splotches were dead fish.

Divers everywhere hated and feared such gillnets; loose on the ocean floor, they were almost invisible until they had wrapped themselves around an arm or leg and made an unbreakable appointment for you with the devil.

The wreck was an eastern dragger, like the *Marie S.* Twenty feet above the mast Larsen switched on his own light and caught up with Silva. He gripped the mate's elbow and had to control an almost irresistible urge to guffaw as the big man jerked in surprise. Larsen chewed his teeth deep into the insides of his cheek till he could taste the musty tang of blood in his mouth. The impulse to laugh receded and was replaced by the same treacherous feeling of well-being.

If you discounted the primary perils of diving in an environment you couldn't breathe at six times the ordinary pressure of air, that feeling of well-being was the single most dangerous factor a diver had to contend with at significant depths.

Nitrogen narcosis. Rapture of the deeps. Nitrogen was more than half-brothers with the medical anaesthetic known as nitrous oxide, or laughing gas. Another effect of nitrogen being concentrated in the blood was to get you drunk at a rate defined by 'Martini's Law': every fifty feet of added depth was equal to chugging a dry Beefeater's martini on an empty stomach. Without olive.

At 180 feet they each had had almost four martinis apiece. Enough to get even Mad Uuno Laavinen more than halfway looped. Enough to get them busted for drunken driving if they got behind the wheel of a car.

As Silva watched, Larsen slowly pointed his flashlight at the stern of the wreck, an exaggerated signpost. Silva nodded, just as slowly. Larsen giggled into the rubber flavour of his mouthpiece.

Two minutes.

They finned gently towards the wreck. The skipper's flashlight reintroduced colours: green hull paint, grey decks, white superstructure. The *Marie*, it had to be the *Marie*. The inflatable life raft was still strapped to its cradle.

A mop of Codium seaweed – 'Sputnik weed', the oyster fishermen called it, because it had come from nowhere to carry away their oysters while Khrushchev was pounding shoes in the UN and so they associated it with the Red menace – had already fastened itself to the gunwale railing. There was a sea anemone on the fishhold hatch and a starfish on the heat exchanger under the bilge; sand had drifted and piled against the keel.

Apart from that, it was as if you could paddle slowly into the wheelhouse, start the diesel, and run her back to the surface the way she had come.

Three minutes, thirty seconds.

The fantail unrolled in a tight ribbon of light. The letters marched suspensefully out: *S* space space *e, i, r, a, M*, and underneath, the home port she would never see again, *Mallebarre*.

Joe's boat. A motel for ghosts. The portside of the hull looked intact, also.

Larsen checked the air gauge hanging at his left hip. They had used a third of their air.

The dory was still lashed upside down behind the wheelhouse. A dogfish, a kind of toothless shark that made the life of any longliner hell during the summer months by taking all the bait on his lines, flicked itself quickly out the open wheelhouse door.

The door closed gently.

Current, Larsen had to remind himself. The same slow tide he was finning against.

Three minutes, fifty-five seconds.

104

To stay well within the safety limits, they should head back up now.

Silva was still behind him. Larsen handed him the emergency line, pointed again to indicate what he was going to do, subdued an impulse to somersault and barrel roll like a seal, and kicked hard towards the door. It was strange how the latch had clicked, and how extraordinary a mundane act like turning the door handle seemed at 180 feet.

Larsen pulled himself inside. The wheelhouse was normal, except for a couple of wood fiddles, removable lips that kept objects from sliding off tables in heavy seas, and a wooden stool, all swaying in slow motion on the deckhead ceiling instead of on the deck. He looked behind the door and saw four survival suits, bulky rubber body suits like his drysuit that were made to keep a man afloat and warm in case of emergency. Three of them were still hooked and looked grotesquely human in their rubber stillness. The fourth had some trapped air in the legs and was doing a spiderman act above his head.

There was a Poisson distribution of heavier-than-water gear scattered around the deck. Binoculars, half-rolled charts, coffee cups.

Five minutes, fifty-five seconds.

It was time to head on up. Yippee!

Larsen jackknifed and hauled himself swiftly through the wheelhouse door, tapping his knee on the way out. He swung his flashlight around.

No emergency line. No Silva.

He kicked upwards, clearing the top of the wheelhouse with its frozen radar and the shattered stub of a VHF antenna.

The grappling anchor had hooked itself into one of the seawater freeing ports on the starboard side of the *Marie S*. Still no Silva – you could see nothing beyond the bow of the fishing boat.

Cold fear gripped Larsen's stomach, magnified and sharpened by the drunkenness. Where the fuck *was* he?

Seven minutes, thirty seconds.

They were into decompression time now, with maybe just

enough air to do a decompression stop – if they went up *now*.

The fisherman gripped his flashlight with both hands and slowly, deliberately played the light again in an arc around the sunken vessel. Nothing but dull, sick, green murk; the grappling line; *Marie*'s anchor line leading forward into vacuum. The darkside of a wet moon. A grey shark swam fast out of sight.

Except that sharks had only one tail fin.

Larsen launched himself forward. The bubbles burst loudly, richly, extravagantly out of his mouthpiece as he scissored in huge kicks in Silva's direction. The stupid son of a goddamn whore was heading uptide, towards deeper water.

The fucking *idiot*! The jibbering Neanderthal flatulent meathead. He'd fucking *kill* him! Rip his mouthpiece out and *laugh* as the moron *drowned*! Serve the bastard *right*!

Ten minutes, forty seconds.

Larsen checked his Rolex more diligently than a delayed commuter.

Silva was paddling idly next to the sand, flashlight drifting by the waist. Slowly, contentedly, he did a back flip.

Larsen was on top of him. He grabbed the mate's weight belt and pulled. There was a huge burst of bubbles and Silva's mouthpiece came loose. The man's eyes looked at him placidly.

Savagely Larsen pushed the purge button and jammed the foaming mouthpiece back into Silva's lips until he felt the teeth open and accept the rubber grip. *Idiot!* Larsen had to fight an urge to stab the son of a bitch with his saw-toothed diving knife. The bastard deserved far, far worse.

No. Do the emergency signal. Hand strangling his own throat. Point upward. Kick. Drag Silva along, downtide towards the *Sofia*, using his wrist compass for orientation. Bleed a little air out to compensate for decrease in pressure. At least the mate was breathing regularly, relaxed, though he wasn't kicking either.

Thirteen minutes, thirty seconds.

They were well into decompression time, and they had to spend a minimum of three minutes going up. Well, that was no problem, dragging Silva like this, except that now Silva was towing him and he wasn't even kicking. They were rising almost as fast as their own exhaled bubbles. Christ! The Cape Verdean had forgotten to bleed air from his drysuit and it was expanding, imparting more and more buoyancy as the depth decreased till they would both pop out of the water like rockets. Rockets with the bends, and maybe bubbles of expanding gas in their brain to boot.

Air embolism. Death, or worse, like total paralysis.

Larsen pulled the mate towards him and cracked the vent valve on the left breast of Silva's suit. A cloud of shining bubbles drifted upward slowly, then faster and faster as the two men slowed in their rise to the surface.

To the right, a thin line appeared out of the murk. Thank God: the emergency cord, curving away with the tide.

Silva was doing his own kicking now, but breathing quicker, more shallowly. Larsen could feel the effects of nitrogen narcosis wear off, leaving in their stead a black cesspool of depression. The choice of bends or drowning was not a pleasant one, but they had run out of air and it was time for choosing.

He forced his brain to remember the decompression tables, and felt a queasy dread when the digits clicked through to their inevitable sum. They needed a grand total of twenty-four minutes of air to be safe, four more than they had. The air in their tanks was supposed to last twenty minutes total, including the two minutes in the reserve. Enough for the short dive they had originally planned, but not sufficient to take them through the nine minutes of decompression they needed.

They could have fudged an extra half minute on the bottom with a quick stop at twenty feet, but they had stayed at 180 feet much too long for fudging, and anyway they had gone even deeper than that, used up much more air at a greater depth playing hide-and-go-seek on the bottom.

He looked at the air gauge. The needle was nudging the red zone. He was almost into reserve already.

They had no options left.

Larsen pointed to Silva's vent valve, opened his own. The

mate was lucid again and a twin stream of bubbles headed
for the silver light overhead.

They would have to stay under as long as they could, and
when the air gave out they would surface and more than
likely double up screaming on the deck of the *Sofia*, if they
made it that far.

The nearest decompression chamber was in Boston, one
hundred and fifty miles away. Try to breathe slow, slow.

Seventeen minutes.

Larsen became conscious of strain on his lungs. It was
getting harder to breathe. He reached behind his neck and
opened the reserve tank lever. Three minutes' worth of air
left. Not enough, nowhere near enough. They had to stay
down for eight.

More light. The mate reached behind his head and opened
his own reserve.

Twenty-five feet. Larsen pulled at his partner's belt. He
indicated his watch, then grabbed hold of the emergency line
they had been following. Spreading three fingers out to
reduce friction on the rope, both men floated gently up until
the depth gauge read twenty feet, and stopped.

They waited. Silva was hanging on to the line and Larsen
became conscious of strain on his chest again. No reserve this
time. No Seventh Cavalry in this movie.

Only eighteen and a half minutes.

Might as well take a shortcut. They floated up to ten feet,
stopped, wanted to keep going. Stick it out. Suck. Harder.
The chest hurt. Hold it a little longer. Just a little longer,
chest muscles trembling. The air was virtually gone.

Twenty-one minutes, almost.

Larsen found himself thinking of topside, of a cloud of red
hair and a pair of intelligent eyes smiling underneath and a
pert nose and a wide smile, bending over him. Bad luck on
a boat.

Twenty-two minutes, thirty seconds.

Could he suck out one more breath? If he dragged any
harder he would be vacuuming aluminium from the inside
of the tank.

Another five minutes to go.

Dreamily Larsen put his fist on the mate's weight belt to make sure he didn't float any higher, suck, hold the air, watch the depth gauge past the stars, expel the hair, the red hair, and that was all she wrote, nothing but stars and bubbles and when was the last time he had seen bubbles from around Silva's mouthpiece: he couldn't even find the stopwatch but they had still at least four vital minutes left as Larsen pulled the CO_2 release toggle on Silva's safety vest and blew out the last couple of lonely molecules of air that remained in his own lungs. He punched a fist hard into Silva's chest to expel whatever was in his lungs, then the mate ballooned towards the surface, head lolling.

Larsen pulled his own safety toggle and rushed upward, his mouth opened and salt water inside but mixed with air, harsh, sweet, succulent air, vintage Krug champagne air mingling with the sea to choke him as he drowned, coughed, retched, puked, and finally breathed.

Silva's head was dunking back into the waves as the skipper dog-paddled him sluggishly towards the fishing boat anchored only twenty-five feet away. The anxious white faces of Billy and the girl looked like helpless clown masks caught on the nether side of comedy, but Billy had thrown a line and then himself overboard, knotting the hemp around Silva's chest and clambering back up the pilot's ladder.

Larsen gained purchase on the rope ladder and heaved at his mate's weight belt as Billy and Blatchford hauled at the line. John Silva flopped loosely over the rail and Billy eased him on to the deck, slipping off his tank and harness as he did so.

Larsen managed to drag himself up the rope ladder and dropped clumsily to his knees. He unbuckled his weight belt, shrugged off the tank, it rang emptily on the steel deck, and crawled over to where Eliza Blatchford was unzipping Silva's suit, putting her finger on the mate's throat while Billy stuck his fingers behind the man's tongue and then gave him mouth to mouth.

Snow-pale face under the African tan.

Deep regular exhalations into the throat. Larsen watched, bunched up stiff and ridiculous in the drysuit, feeling helpless as a baby and thinking: Don't die, Johnny. You're an ally against the loneliness. They're too hard to come by, too easy to lose.

The sun beat down, all light and no heat.

The mate's chest rose every time Billy blew, then suddenly heaved of its own accord and a smelly belch of salt water and bile and black coffee welled out of Silva's sagging face.

Billy rolled him over quickly. Silva coughed and retched, gagged and breathed. Larsen just lay there, exhausted, waiting for the first knife stabs to tell him the bends had finally come to call.

CHAPTER NINE

Ten hours later, Larsen's knee had contracted a case of arthritis, where he had slammed it coming out of *Marie*'s wheelhouse. It was too painful to be the result of a mere knock, and he knew that what nitrogen had fizzed in his blood had probably concentrated around a small contusion in the joint.

But he counted himself extremely lucky, because that was as far as the bends had gone. Silva was even luckier: he had, as yet, no symptoms at all. The bends could strike as late as twenty-four hours after a dive but they almost always showed up within sixty minutes.

Perhaps they had not spent as much time at 180 feet as Larsen had thought. Susceptibility to the bends was, in any case, a variable . . .

The skipper had ordered his mate to take a long rest after recovering from his near-drowning but an hour later the Cape Verdean was on his feet again, pale, weak and restless, his dark mood blackened by embarrassment at the mistakes he had made below.

They had reset trawls after the dive, and hauled them over slack tide. *Sofia* was loping home at a steady ten knots. The informal rituals of a small fishing vessel put the Cape Verdean at the wheel for evening watch.

Billy, Lars, and Eliza were sitting in the saloon. Larsen was drinking a beer, the woman had poured herself a Grand Marnier, and Billy was rolling a joint, the single marijuana cigarette the skipper allowed him when his watch was over.

'Crazy fuckin' Portygee,' Billy said. The constant use of obscenity allowed him to speak sensibly while remaining true to his punk persona. The persona had dressed him in a new T-shirt that featured a group called Aborted Foetus.

'He didn't sleep a fuckin' wink last night, he didn't eat his breakfast except for a half slice of toast, he drank his usual fuckin' gallons of coffee,' Billy continued, lighting up the spliff in a fog of sweet grey smoke.

'I should have noticed,' Larsen commented disgustedly. 'Plus he was smoking more than usual, and on top of it he had at least four beers the night before. That smells like Jamaican.'

'It's Haitian. It's no fuckin' wonder he got narcosis,' Billy added for the tenth time. 'He's just lucky he ain't bent. Or dead.'

Blatchford was on a silent stage again. The morning's excitement had injected liberal amounts of pure adrenalin into her system and she had reacted quickly to help Silva. As the adrenalin wore off she turned pale, then subdued. She had slept most of the afternoon.

Billy stood up and stretched. 'I'm turning in.'

Larsen said, 'He should spit out what in hell is bothering him.'

'He will,' Billy answered. 'You know him. But I tell you it's that fuckin' woman.'

With a grin at Blatchford and a dragon-puff of smoke, the deckhand disappeared aft.

The journalist was sipping slowly, reflectively, eyeing the portrait bolted to the forward bulkhead.

'Is her name Sofia?'

'The first.'

'Wife?'

'Almost. Fiancée. Like you and Freddie. Sorry, Fergie.'

'Still around?'

'No.'

'*Si direbbe una Siciliana*,' she said in a disinterested sort of way.

'Clever of you to know Italian,' Larsen sneered, 'but no, she was Greek.'

Greek to the core, Larsen reflected to himself: although George Mavromikalis' daughter had spent most of her adolescence attending school in California so she was American in all the obvious ways, she had remained Greek in all the ways that counted.

She had appeared at the end of the refit week by the St

112

George's pool, five days after he first met Stangerson, and it was as if Larsen was suddenly chosen to provide a little sport for the top dogs lolling in togas on Olympus, getting stoned on nectar and ambrosia and giggling at all the funny mortals.

He had as much choice in the matter as that. She had a neck like a swan, a classic Greek nose, and two big dark eyes that fused into Larsen's the first time he looked at her.

'Don't get yourself hooked by that bitch,' Stangerson had warned him. 'That kind is nothing but trouble.'

She had come to study archaeology at the American University of Beirut. Her father owned banks in Patras, Athens and Thessalonica, as well as a minority interest in a fleet of bulk cargo ships. But for one glorious month, she chucked her family and obligations while the Germans prepared their expedition, and they had made Lebanon one vast, doom-ridden trysting ground.

Thirty days of hedonism, of figs, wine, and dancing amid the portents, of water skiing while Israeli Phantoms shrieked overhead. A month of feasts in hot valleys and lovemaking at dawn in a small stone cottage they kept in the mountains above Beirut. A time made sweeter by the feeling it could all end tomorrow, a feeling shared by those they knew: clothes merchants, spies, arms smugglers and artists who kept the hungry eyes at bay with parties, and more parties . . .

At the end of the month Sofia Mavromikalis had returned to college, but when spring came Larsen signed her on to the *Artemis* as cook and commissaire. They headed back to Piraeus for the first charter of the season. She took him to meet her parents.

Larsen's first meeting with Mavromikalis, a fierce, moustachioed tycoon with a villa dwarfed only by his temper, had gone badly. The tycoon came from Mani, a peninsula that stuck out of the Peloponnese like a finger obscenely pointed at everyone, a region noted for its piracy and an unquenchable thirst for Turkish blood. Quite apart from this hereditary xenophobia, George Mavromikalis had climbed too far and too fast to spend much time with mere mariners. When he had to spend time with them in the course of business, they were masters of 80,000-ton grain carriers, flying the Greek flag. George had made that clear to Sofia.

But Sofia was Greek. Confronted with a negative blessing on her choice of mate, she had cursed her father, kissed her mother, and stomped out of the villa.

They spent two months on *Artemis*, shepherding first the Germans, then a series of Californian movie people around the eastern Mediterranean and running off when they could be alone together in the clearest landscapes in the world.

It was in Delphi, capital of that clarity, shrine to Apollo, home of the oracle, that they had decided to get married, right after hearing that old man Mavromikalis had pulled strings and managed to have Larsen fired from his job as skipper of *Artemis*.

And it was on Parnassus, Delphi's sacred mountain, overlooking the crossroads where an unknowing Oedipus stabbed his father, just as the oracle predicted, that a speeding Mercedes truck had knocked Sofia's little Fiat into a ravine while the shimmering rocks and crystalline sky looked on the pyre without blinking, as if they'd known this would happen, all along.

Star-crossed.

Larsen had returned earlier to Piraeus to collect back pay. When he was told the news he went mad. So mad he forgot what he did during one whole day. Mad enough to spend a night sitting by the blackened wreckage of the little car. Mad enough to knock down George Mavromikalis when Sofia's father pulled a knife on him at the funeral. Too mad to weep.

When he had regained his senses Larsen flew to Beirut and accepted Stangerson's offer. The Englishman had smiled when he saw Larsen as if he, too, had known this would happen, all along.

'You don't want to talk about her.'

Blatchford pulled out a pack of Camels, nervously jerked one into her mouth, and lit it with a gold lighter.

'I forgot you smoked,' the skipper commented. Sofia had smoked as well – Gitanes.

The only reply was tobacco fumes.

'Have you decided what did happen to *Marie*?' she said at last.

'We've already gone over it four or five times,' Larsen said, 'and I'm no nearer to figuring it out.'

Give her a break, Larsen, he thought to himself, and relented. Collated his thoughts.

'Me 'n Silva saw no damage below the waterline,' he said, 'though there might have been some near her keel, where she was resting on her portside. She definitely wasn't in a collision, or the damage would have been obvious. I saw nothing in the cabin. I was in too much of a hurry.

'So it could have been a hole near her port keel from floating wreckage, maybe, or a fire in the engine room. But that begs the question of where the men are.'

There was no point Larsen could fathom in telling the journalist about Marie's suspicions. Conspiracy theories based on circumstantial evidence sounded like just what they were, especially when dragged into print by reporters.

He flipped his empty beer can towards the galley sink, got up, picked it off the deck, and took another out of the fridge.

'How about a shot of ouzo?' he offered.

She said, 'You drink a lot, don't you?'

Larsen laughed. Marie first, and now Eliza.

Then again, he thought, maybe she meant it as a compliment. In an area like Cape Cod where booze was a major local anaesthetic for the winter blues it was a toss-up whether such a comment rated as slur or accolade.

The eyes were looking directly at him, the desperate quality back behind them. Larsen realized at that moment it had been toned down, second layer since she had come aboard *Sofia*. Until this afternoon.

'Lars – this isn't a patronizing question.'

'What isn't?' he asked warily.

'What do you fear?'

'Fear?'

'Yeah. What is it that turns your bowels to water and your spine to mush?'

The prospect of a pretentious philosophical conversation

115

right after visiting a friend's grave, the skipper thought. He didn't say it.

'You want the truth?'

'Why not?' Opal earrings jangled as she drew on her Camel. For the first time the fisherman noticed that a thin corona of indigo surrounded her pupils like a beach around a volcanic lake.

Larsen drew the pack across and lit one himself.

He said, 'You know, you have a lot of nerve asking for the truth – Jesus Christ! People rely mostly on camouflage and white lies to get through their day. And even what they would call true varies with circumstances and the hour and what they had for lunch. After that quiche last night . . .' he shook his head. He pretended to ruminate, cheeks playing games with the harsh smoke.

'It isn't airplanes and it's not the bends,' she interjected, 'I'm not talking about a superficial definition, but what is it that could happen to you and your life that really, truly scares the living shit out of you? Do you understand?'

'A serious question?'

'A serious question.'

He made an effort and really thought about it. The tape had come to an end. The living cracks of a boat in a seaway stood out of the background noise. Finally he said slowly, 'I guess what I dread the most is winding up like everybody else, forced to do something I don't want to do. Forced by lack of money, lack of power, or by malignant gods, it doesn't make much difference . . . forced to get some office job when fish prices go all to hell, or when the gillnetters and the big draggers fish everything out . . .' He rambled on, 'They make you slot into the dependency trap, do the jobs the big banks dictate, and you do it willingly because of the material perks, and because the system in all its subliminal subtlety sort of brainwashes you into wanting those perks, cars, and houses and Toro mowers, and also because the job itself leaves you with zero time to think about your own life, one way or another . . .'

He pulled hard at the cigarette, and a quarter inch of tobacco and paper glowed and became ash.

116

'I think there's something you could call "subconscious cultural imperialism" that keeps ordinary people ignorant and unmotivated. They want colour TVs instead of an education, and all so the GMs of this world have a ready labour pool they can hire or fire at will.'

Larsen smiled at Blatchford. 'That's what you get for asking a serious question.' But she was paying attention.

'I guess what I like about fishing,' he continued after a further pause, 'is that it's still in a medieval state of grace. It's historically been a small, unimportant artisan industry in a nation of meat-eaters. Individuals mostly, in unsafe and outdated boats. People fishing because that's what they *want* to do. It's changing now, unfortunately: big companies and consortiums of lawyers are investing in large, efficient trawlers, paying cheap labour by the hour, turning it into factory work . . . but maybe they'll drive the price even lower and wipe out fish stocks and go broke on their huge fuel bills, and then maybe we'll have a go at it again.

'Medieval people were dirt poor and ignorant, but they had the *time* to think themselves into the Renaissance.'

The silence of doubt.

'Well, it *is* medieval,' he said defensively, 'the whole fishing industry.'

She was staring into the Grand Marnier as if scrying its amber glints, her eyes obscured by a wave of hair, long fingers tracing designs in spilled liquid. The diesel thudded tribal reassurances. She brushed her hair with an impatient gesture.

'You know a friend of mine did an article about fish prices. It's pretty good; I'll send it to you.' She was talking through a fog. 'What I fear is the opposite,' she said at last. 'I'm scared to death I will be prevented from doing the things I want to do. Doing some good, in-depth reporting that newspapers don't seem to want these days, or writing fiction for that matter, or a book. Surviving doing only those things, not hack work.'

'It sounds exactly the same as my, uh, fear.'

'It's fundamentally different.' She put the second word on a syllabic rack, stretching it till the phonemes screamed for clemency. Larsen twisted his knee delicately.

117

He waited for her to explain what had promoted this Cambridge coffee-house conversation, but all she said was, 'So. You're running, I'm fighting. Tell me, why did a Cape Cod fisherman learn *The Tempest* by heart?'

'Now you *are* being patronizing.'

She frowned. 'You're right, I suppose, though it would be surprising in anyone.'

'I studied it. I was going to be a Shakespearian scholar once,' Larsen said lightly, 'in college. It was my favourite play, maybe because it reminded me of the Cape. I was going to write a take-off on it, casting Prospero and all the Milanese as summer tourists, and Ariel and Caliban as local yokels.

'All the Milanese,' he added, 'would have worn clothes like Ferguson Whipple.'

She giggled. Then her background reasserted itself.

'You . . . went to college?'

'Uh-huh.'

'Where?'

'Harvard, of course,' he said lightly.

'Sure.'

'How come *you* know it by heart?' he countered.

'I played Miranda once,' she replied. 'In college. I was a drama major. I was going to be an actress before I realized I was getting too upset about the roles I played, I took them too personally.' Her words ran into one another. 'So I'd cover up my own involvement and I'd come off as a complete ham.'

J. B. Hutto took up an old Big Mama Thornton tune. Blatchford was looking miserable now, staring at the smoke.

'When will we be back in Mallebarre?' she asked abruptly.

'Another four hours, there's a storm coming up. I kept my promise. You'll be back Sunday.'

'I've enjoyed this trip, apart from the professional side of things. It helps to get out of range of shore and all your usual preoccupations for a while.'

The red hair was back over her eyes, protecting emotional flanks. Almost roughly she added, 'Let's see each other again, Lars, okay?'

And Larsen tried unsuccessfully to rationalize the strange twist of pleasure he felt at her words.

Larsen was cramming splintered ice into the last of thirty-one boxes of gutted seafood and thinking pleasantly of the payday 3720 pounds of fresh cod would bring, no matter what the price, when Dickie eeled out of his office and into the Co-op's working area.

It was a black night, and the southeast wind had started singing after dusk. The old wood building balancing precariously on the fish pier felt normal, as if it would collapse at any moment in a welter of flaking white paint and rotten fish boxes, chipped ice and ancient pink sales slips.

'Larsen!' The Co-op manager crooked a well-manicured finger.

Sometimes when Larsen got sick of his home turf he imagined everybody on Cape Cod, himself included, as looking alike, related to the same giant family of Protestant New England worms. Dickie Sears was the wormiest of the bunch, a slick worm dressed in polyester suits. But he was good with the books. Maybe too good.

Dickie said, 'You called Joe Sciacca's wife yet? She's been calling every five minutes to find out if you're in.' And I am not a receptionist, his tone implied. 'You didn't get the message? She keeps saying it's urgent.'

Larsen asked, 'You gotta dime, Dickie?' as he walked to the pay phone next to the fish scales.

'Sorry.' The manager made a pretence of patting his jacket pockets and darted back into the office. No wonder his wife had left Dickie for Eben Hallett, Larsen thought uncharitably, finally locating a quarter in the inner pocket of his boiler suit. Eben couldn't add two and two, but at least he wasn't cheap.

She answered on the second ring and her voice sent a little man with cold feet doing a reel on Larsen's vertebrae.

'Marie? Are you okay?'

'*Lars!* I'm so glad you called. I've been trying to reach you!'

'What's wrong? You could have got hold of me like before, on the Co-op's radio . . .'

'No, I couldn't. I didn't want them to know. Lars, he called again!'

119

'Who?'

'That man, the one who threatened me the first time. You know, on the phone. It was the same one.'

'The one you told me about, who wanted the "insurance"?'

'Yes.'

'What did he say?'

'Oh, God.' She was close to tears, her crying ducts constantly primed since the day a husband had gone overdue. In this case the grief was mixed with terror.

He could feel it.

'The same thing. He said "the man" wanted the insurance policy. He said I would have to find it right away and give it to someone called Laparensa or something, or, he said, I might get hurt. Those were his words –'

'Was it the same voice?' Larsen interrupted to quell the hysteria rising in her voice.

'I think so – it was long distance again, sort of fuzzy. Lars, what do I do? He ordered me – *ordered* me – to look through my own house for it and give it to this Laparensa or Laparensi, or whatever. He said he'd call again to find out. And I did, I've looked everywhere, Lars, all through Joe's stuff but I can't find anything about insurance, or anything like that note Joe got from Catherine.

'I've even gone through all his old boxes of junk in the tool shed, God I wish he were here, he'd know what to do!'

She rambled on distractedly, 'And Lars, I can't sleep and the doctor wants to give me a shot and I'm worried about what this is doing to the baby. She . . . it's kicking more and more and I get sick worse and worse in the morning, it's not normal . . .'

'Marie . . .'

'Lars, will you do something for me?'

'Marie –'

'Lars, will you go to New York for me? He said that man, Laparensa, he was in New York. Will you please go to him and tell him I haven't got it?'

'Marie, listen. I think you should go to the police.'

'*No!*'

120

'Why not?'

'They didn't believe me. I called them last night and they said to call the phone company and report it and they would send someone around tomorrow. Tomorrow! What would I tell them anyway? Someone I don't know is threatening me over something I know nothing about that belonged to my husband who has just disappeared? Did you find her, Lars?'

'Yes, I did.'

Marie Sciacca marched the words out at gunpoint.

'Did you find him?'

'No. There was no one aboard. She was sunk out at Asia Rip, still anchored as I thought she might be. I went down.

'The life raft was still there,' he continued, 'and so were all the survival suits. I didn't have much time to look around, but she was undamaged, as far as I could tell.'

'So they did! They murdered him! They took him away and *killed* him! Oh, my sweet Jesus.' The control came back, tattered. 'Please, please, Lars, go down and tell them I don't have what they want. It's the only way they'll stop, I know it. I don't care for me, I just don't care, but it's the baby, I want it to live, it's all I have left of me and Joe. You don't understand . . .'

But he did understand, Larsen thought; she was completely deluding herself. Sorrow had taken the path of least resistance and created responsibility for Joe's death, just as witch doctors cured pain by claiming someone put a curse on you. Responsibility implied accountability, accountability implied revenge and this gave Marie a course of action to follow that would further attenuate her grief. The only trouble with that theory was Marie wasn't talking about revenge any more.

'Listen, Marie. Listen to me. Nobody killed Joe. Any number of things could have happened to his boat; a rogue wave, a fire – '

'Damn you! *You* listen to *me*! Someone is threatening *me*! About something my husband has, and he disappears without reason! You think it's coincidence? And the phone calls – '

'No one killed Joe, Marie. Why don't I call this guy in New York, okay?'

'He's not in the phone book. I asked Information.'

'Tell you what I'll do,' Larsen said. 'I'll talk to Per about it. The barometer's doing a swan dive and I don't think we'll be going out for a couple of days. I'll visit him tomorrow if we don't go out, okay?'

'Please, Lars,' she spoke low and intensely, 'get hold of these people. I don't want them to be punished, it won't bring him back. I just want my baby safe, okay?'

She hung up.

CHAPTER TEN

The office of the United States Attorney for Massachusetts was located in downtown Boston, on the eleventh floor of the Post Office Building, an appendage to the complex of state and federal bureaucracy known as Government Centre. The centre's dozen adjoining office blocks, a vast benign tumour of armoured concrete and elevators, sunless patios and tiered parking lots, stood in architectural and political contrast to the tiny Georgian sketch of Faneuil Hall next door where a gaggle of town-meeting Demostheneses had once defied the might of the British Empire.

The eleventh floor should have commanded a panoramic view of the Hub, but its views were obscured by the taller edifices of State Street banks that alone took precedence over the New England prefecture of the information state – bastion of a larger and more insidious empire.

Larsen had not seen his brother since last Christmas. Almost a year. He wore a clean, pressed Pierre Cardin suit, which had been all the rage on Saint-Germain ten years ago. A brace of Cerberean secretaries outflanked him as soon as he stepped off the elevator and into the US Attorney's offices. Something – the remnants of a deep-water tan, a hint of physical preparedness in the large hands, the lack of an attaché case – cued the two women: this man did not have the codes; he was an interloper.

He waited in one of the fake Danish-modern armchairs in the reception area and leafed through the *New England Law Review*.

A Harvard Law School prof described the political tendencies that supposedly led the courts to reinterpret laws so broadly as to, in effect, be making and enforcing statutes, thus usurping functions that should have been left to Congress and the President. More heretofores and inasmuches, but that was the gist of the article. Government by judiciary.

So what else was new? Larsen thought. In a country as vast, rich, and complex as the United States of America, the judicial system offered the only sure and direct accountability for any individual American who could afford such a luxury. What else was he going to do? Cable the White House? Write his congressman? Picket Washington?

It was a far cry from the stormy and personal meetings in Faneuil Hall. Per had picked a profession with a future. And to judge by what he'd said last Christmas, he was going to use it as a stepping-stone to higher things.

Per Larsen strode around the corner, sharply creased trouser legs slicing the air conditioning. Lars got up and the brothers hugged each other, awkwardly affectionate.

'Lars.'

'Per.' The lawyer had been christened with the Norwegian version but had Americanized his given name to Peter in law school.

'Over this way. Would you like some coffee? Peggy, two cups of black coffee when you have a minute.'

A small, plain woman with Trotsky eyeglasses forsook her IBM Selectric at his command.

Peter Larsen's office had a picture window the size of a Texas swimming pool and a long, oiled desk on which the Dallas Cowboy cheerleaders, pom-poms and all, could have stood without disturbing the stack of legal briefs neatly piled on one end. Cotton clouds packed the city skyscrapers like fragile china. In the foreground of the harbour, between a pair of banks, you could see a knot of men on the deck of a replica of an eighteenth-century barque. They were busy chucking empty crates marked TEA into Boston harbour, dragging them back on deck with ropes, listlessly recreating patriotic mythology for Nipponese tourists.

Diplomas hung on the silent walls; a plush couch with a coffee table, a photo of Patty and the two kids and their suburban lawn. Commendations. Plaques. Not a trace of Per's origins, no pictures of Uncle Ole or Lars or his dead parents.

'You've never been up here, have you?' Peter asked his brother, knowing the answer.

Lars shook his head, smiling and thinking that they never saw each other as much as they used to. Hell, they'd seen more of each other when Per was at Georgetown.

The lawyer echoed his thoughts.

'We don't see enough of each other, little brother. Here . . .' He walked over to the desk and spun the leather chair. 'Try this out. See what it feels like to be the US Attorney for the entire Commonwealth of Massachusetts.'

The fisherman complied, knowing his brother was half joking.

Family and a demanding profession were the usual wedge that loosened old ties, tragedy the knot that bound them back. They had been unusually close when they were kids but it was normal, Lars told himself, that Per should now carry an air of distraction that showed his mind was on more important matters.

According to the law of bureaucratic status a man was as powerful as his office seat was comfortable. By that yardstick Per Larsen wielded a good deal of clout. His sibling spun himself around and landed his Western boots hard on the desk top.

Per smiled, letting the challenge pass. The lawyer had a charcoal-grey three-piece suit fitted neatly to disguise his paunch, shiny shoes and horn-rim glasses, the Precambrian ridge of his father's nose, a shock of brown hair, and pepper-and-salt sideburns. Fastidious and aggressive.

They traded the inconsequences that reaffirmed kinship ties. The coffee came.

Lars said wonderingly, 'You know, I've been thinking. You really did what we swore to each other.'

'You mean the pact?'

'The pact. To get out of the Cape trap – to become powerful or rich enough so we wouldn't be forced to stay half poor, with half a job like everyone else. And not motivated enough to escape it either, to cross the bridge. You have really done it.'

Per said, 'You're not doing too badly yourself: you've got a $300,000 boat, you even have the ancestral manse now.

You make a damn good living.' He crossed his legs elegantly, picked a shred of lint off his pants.

'When fish prices are high,' Larsen answered.

'Someday you'll have to tell me how you bought that beautiful boat free and clear,' the lawyer smiled engagingly. 'Incidentally, I made up my mind about what we were talking about last Christmas. I'm going to run for Frank Smith's Congressional seat when he runs for the Senate next year. I've got his endorsement. You're one of the first to know, don't tell anyone till it's official.'

The phone buzzed deferentially. Per Larsen picked it up and listened for ten seconds and said, 'Hold them till ten-thirty.'

He rehooked the receiver and made a face. 'I'm really sorry, Lars. It's a busy day. If you'd given me a longer lead time we could have had lunch but – ' he gestured vaguely. 'You said you wanted to see me about something?'

'Yeah, that's okay.' Lars dismissed the apology with his own hand wave. He hadn't given his brother much notice, so if he felt rushed it was his own fault. 'And I'm glad you're running, Per, you'll do well . . . this state could certainly use a decent politician. You know our councillor's still taking payoffs . . . ?'

Silence. His brother had transmuted into professionalism. Lars got up and paced to the end of the office, ordering his thoughts.

'You remember Marie Riley, don't you?'

'Of course.' The preoccupied look was still there but her name had brought back a surface slick of nostalgia to Per's eyes for a moment. They had all been at school together.

Lars outlined the circumstances surrounding the loss of the *Marie S*, the threats to Joe Sciacca and his wife, the demands for an insurance policy stolen from a man who might or might not be called 'Laparensa' or 'Laparensi'. Skipping over details to save time he summed up locating the wreck and the fact that there was no apparent damage to the *Marie S*.

The lawyer stared out over Boston as his brother talked, watching the first raindrops splat against the glass. His hands

126

were dug in behind pinstriped pockets, listening hard, professionally – a good lawyer.

When the fisherman had ended the attorney sat down at his desk, plucking with two fingers at the skin of his forehead. It was a sign of concentration Lars knew of old.

Finally he said, 'Who does Marie Riley think is at the bottom of this?'

'Organized crime, naturally. The Fulton Organization. It's a fisherman's myth, a sort of organized-crime cartel at Fulton Fish Market that everybody says runs the fresh fish racket on the East Coast . . . They even say it has links with the New York Families.'

Lars paused, expecting a reaction that did not come. 'I tried to tell her it was probably someone he or his father owed money to,' he continued, 'or any number of sordid scenarios, but there's nothing to point to the Organization.' Lars snorted to demonstrate scorn. 'Joe Sciacca's old man probably had something on his creditor that prevented him from collecting while he was alive, as simple as that. But there's the folklore, Christ knows, and the Italian names. Marie's convinced, of course.'

Per Larsen picked up a phone and said, 'Tom? Pete Larsen. Listen, call up the computer, and see if the organized crime files, East Coast, that's right, list someone with the surname of Laparensa?' He spelled it, raised his eyebrows at the fisherman for confirmation, got a shrug in return. 'Laparensi? Try different spellings. Probably New York. Okay? Soon. I'm in my office for another five minutes.'

He leaned back and exhaled deeply, noisily puffing his cheeks.

'It's an incredible story. It's certainly incredible that you found the boat as you did. That was a nice piece of seamanship. Right inside Asia Rip, huh? Way out. And, you know, Marie might even be right.

'But it's so unlikely, Lars. The Fulton Organization. Organized crime. I mean, what is organized crime? The New York Families? The Cosa Nostra? The Black Hand? The Unione Siciliano?'

127

The United States Attorney for Massachusetts laughed a showman's laugh, a jury-impressing laugh, reciting at full tilt. 'The Jewish syndicates in Jersey, the Cubans in Miami, the Chicanos of Nuestra Familia in L.A.? The Aryan Brotherhood? Pappy's black numbers runners in Harlem? Giuldini right down there in the North End? Mazzie and the Genoveses, or is it the Gambinos in Worcester, let's see, the Lebanese boys in Salem, the Portuguese in Fall River, and the Tongs in Chinatown . . .'

Per shook his head sorrowfully.

'Oh, traditional organized crime exists all right, Lars. Some of it even still has links with the old *padrones* in Palermo. But in the main it's just a bunch of old ethnic diehards who remember when Italians, or Jews, or Orientals were still third-class citizens and don't speaka de English too good.

'Plus a bunch of punks, thugs of every age, race, and description who do the work for the vice and gambling and drug rings that exist in virtually every city in the world. Even in totalitarian places, like Moscow.

'Real organized crime though,' the US Attorney leaned forward, 'is as legal as the Chase Manhattan Bank. The sons of the old Moustache Petes went to Yale and Stanford and Harvard Business School. They came home to Brooklyn, Miami, Buffalo, or Chicago and took all those lovely tax-free greenbacks and invested them. They bought hotel chains, designer-jean companies and movie studios, restaurants, trucking firms, car-hire firms. They purchased ranches in Arizona and honeymoon resorts in the Poconos. They bought Wall Street brokerage houses and became business consultants. You talk about organized crime, you're talking about 30,000 corporations! That's what organized crime is today.

'One thing mobsters don't do, though,' Per plucked at his forehead again, 'is go around knocking off Cape Cod fishermen who by some quantum leap of the imagination might be deemed to be in their way. They'd be far more likely to sue him in Superior Court – but indirectly, through about four buffer levels of attorneys.'

128

Lars Larsen nodded glumly. 'I know. I tried to tell –'

The phone burred. The lawyer flicked it to his ear, listened, put it down without speaking, and wrote two neat lines on a piece of white notepaper.

'You know,' the US Attorney continued as if his brother had not spoken, 'the myth exists for several reasons. One, law-abiding people enjoy it: it gives them an easy framework to explain why they can't control their own lives, why they can't even *understand* their lack of control. Crime, drugs, pollution: it's all organized crime. City government doing something you don't like? They've been paid off by the syndicate. Your company loses out on a contract? The New York Families strong-armed the unions. And you can never disprove the myth because *everybody's* been paid off. The cops, the judges, the politicians. Very convenient.

'The second reason is that both organized crime and its opponents right here in the Justice Department have a vested interest in seeing that the myth remains alive and well. Mobsters like it because the few people who really are connected can scare the shit out of people because everybody thinks they're ruthless and omnipotent. You know, Marlon Brando in *The Godfather*. And the organized-crime strike forces, the FBI and so on, like it for the simple reason that the more organized crime is perceived to be a threat, the more money is allocated to combat that threat.'

There was a knock at the door that opened to reveal another pinstriped man clutching legal papers. He made a show of being embarrassed at interrupting.

Per Larsen made a show of being disturbed. He glanced at his watch and smoothed his hair and stood up so easily that the abruptness of his movement was almost lost on the fisherman.

'I'm late already . . . an appointment I forgot, darn it.'

That was hogwash. Per Larsen had the most phenomenal recall his brother had ever known.

'Look,' Per said, 'why don't you come visit us in Brookline in a couple of weeks? Patty and the kids would love to see you.' He steered his brother to the door. 'I'll be back from

Washington on Tuesday. I'm sorry, Lars, but you caught me on a bad day.

'Peggy,' he called, 'will you show my brother out, please? No, wait.' His voice lowered. 'What to do about Marie Riley. I'll have a tracer put on all calls to her phone, it's in the book, right? This month and, uh, the next few weeks if she gets any more threats. Okay? Unofficially. A favour, so don't spread the word. And don't mention what I told you earlier. Anyway, when we know whom we're dealing with in Marie's case, we'll take it from there.'

'Per,' his brother said, half desperately, half firmly – where had his boyhood playmate gone? 'I know. Just one more minute, okay? Marie wants me to go to New York and contact this Laparensa guy somehow and tell him she doesn't have whatever it is he wants. I said I'd ask what you thought.'

The lawyer shook his head, wearily. 'It's insane, of course. She must be very distraught.' He glanced at his brother, thinking of something else, looked again.

'You're not seriously thinking of going? I mean, even if you could find this Laparensa guy, even if it's the same one, why should he believe you? And you could get hurt.'

'I thought you said . . .'

'Lars, you never know. My God, you're really considering it. Listen, just forget it.'

'I sure don't want to. Go, I mean. But she's so desperate.'

Peter Larsen was getting angry. The younger lawyer stood impatiently, fidgeting and swaying from one Brooks Brothers tasselled moccasin to the other.

'You know what, I think you've already decided to go. I think you're still sweet on her. God,' he said again, his irritation deflating as quickly as it had blown up, 'you and your women, Lars.' He shook his head, torn between disgust and affection, then punched his brother hard on the biceps. 'And you never could get used to the fact that this is an unbalanced world, kid brother.' He put an arm around him and walked towards the exit. 'I remember you plotting to kill or maim that guy who ran over Meatdog, you remember, when we were kids . . . You can't go around like a paranoid avenger any more, wreaking revenge on people who you think have hurt you, or your buddies. We only have to pick up the pieces.'

He sighed and pulled a folded slip of paper out of his waistcoat pocket, the same notepaper he took phone messages on. 'This is the full name of a Jack Parensi in New York. It's the closest the computer came up with. You do *not* know where you got this info. I have to remind you that there is no clear evidence of Parensi being directly linked to organized crime, but it's all you'll have to go on. Watch your back. And call me in a week or so.'

Lars Larsen found himself outside the closed door at the end of a long, hushed corridor. The plain woman with the Trotsky glasses was looking at him suspiciously, ready and waiting to deliver him to the outside world.

He went quietly.

CHAPTER ELEVEN

So maybe he *was* still sweet on Marie Riley, Larsen thought disgustedly as the Manhattan skyline exploded into view over the Bronx Expressway and through the windshield of the Chevy. How else could he explain what he was doing?

The old truck groaned and clanked as it smashed into a six-inch pothole at sixty mph. A 727 whistled overhead on its way to La Guardia.

All to ease the mind of a woman he had been infatuated with in high school. It was crazy. Five hours of Howard Johnson's coffee and AM radio pap in a 1958 Detroit gas guzzler to look up a man with a name that might be similar to one mentioned in connection with some insignificant and sleazy business deal involving a dead man he had never met.

Don Quixote in a pick-up truck.

So he would check out Parensi, and perhaps he would talk to a few more people he knew, and this would mark the final payoff of the debt he owed Marie and Joe. There were too many other things he wanted to do before he got too old to do anything.

The abode of Jack Parensi was listed as 351 Mickel Street in Queens. In the days when Larsen came to New York fairly frequently he had always used Manhattan as a reference point and he did so now, negotiating the vast steel *tagliatelle* of the Triborough Bridge and heading down Franklin D. Roosevelt Drive in mid-afternoon traffic to the Queensborough Bridge.

As always the city rushed in on Larsen like a psychedelic drug, coloured noises, solid smells and smelly touch, a roller coaster of sensory impressions and the freedom that came with knowing that everything you were or wanted had a hard cash price in New York.

It was a marketplace town. Except that the markets were imperfect, and imperfect marketplaces everywhere became dominated by Mafiosi of one kind or another, the organized cartels that determined who and what was bought and sold in artwork and books . . . and, according to Marie, fish.

He filled the gas tank again on the Queens side of the bridge.

When he had finally picked his way through the underpasses and fire escapes, the wrecked Buicks and high cheekbones of south Queens, Mickel Street proved to be an Italian oasis in a desert of neighbourhoods sacrificed so other people could go to and from other places at as high a speed as possible. Just east and west, huge expressways cut shadows and roared as they fed the island of the Manhattoes with nine-to-five pilgrims.

Rows of shoulder-to-shoulder houses, neat and fussed over, stood clothed in grimy colour. A Mom and Pop store on the corner.

The sidewalk near number 351 benefited from the last rays of a setting sun, and some sweatshirted ten-year-olds were lobbing a football around in the light. Larsen parked by a hydrant, walked to the stoop of a two-storey vinyl-sided white house with a Virgin Mary in its postage-stamp garden. Plastic strings of worry beads served as curtains. He rang the bell.

The beads shivered. The kids had stopped throwing the football and were watching him curiously. The fisherman could feel stares sticking out of his back like Apache arrows shot from the windows up and down the street.

'Yes?' A woman's voice full of foreign intonations and the porcupine suspicions of the city dweller. 'Who is it?'

'Is Mr Parensi in?'

'What do you want?'

'I wanted to talk to Mr Parensi. I have a message . . . from a friend of his in Massachusetts.'

'Who are you?'

'My name is Larsen.'

There was a silence, then footsteps, then the noise of locks being opened, fat clicks three times in succession. A short, muscular man in a frown and vest stood at the door. A scared Barbara Fritchie head looked out from somewhere beyond his armpit.

'Whaddya want?' the man said.

'I have a message for Jack Parensi.'

'Mr Parensi died four months ago. Who are you?'

That figured, Larsen thought. The only consistent thing about this whole business was that it lacked consistency.

'Are you his son?'

'Lodger. He got no sons. What's yer name again?'

'Larsen. Lars Larsen, I had a message from a friend of his in Massachusetts. Joseph Sciacca.'

Barbara Fritchie shook her grey head. Uncontrollably. Parkinson's disease, Larsen thought.

'Does that mean anything to you?'

The woman's head shook even harder, her voice screeched, too loud. 'He don't have a friend in Ma—ssa-chusetts. I don't know him.'

The vest said politely, 'Scram, asshole,' the door slammed and the plastic beads stirred again.

Larsen got back into his truck and negotiated the gauntlet of suspicious stares and plastic Virgins until he was on a major artery heading to the heart of Babylon.

It was hardly surprising. The Justice Department relied on confidential sources, and those sources could never be completely up-to-date or accurate or comprehensive. In any case, Jack Parensi, alleged small-time mobster, recently deceased, could not have been involved in the threats made to Marie Sciacca.

He had arranged to do a few more checks. It seemed hopeless now but he might as well do them, since he was here, and then he would head for home with a clear conscience and the knowledge that his instincts were right and Marie was wrong and there was nothing more in her suspicions than the normal coincidences of living that tragedy and hindsight alone made significant.

Why did sunset always breed doubts? Because the night brought peril to cave-dwelling ancestors?

He could, of course, be totally wrong, acting like one of those suburban drivers on a freeway who convinced themselves that the guy lying prone in a ditch was probably sleeping or drunk, it was much more likely after all, and they'd be late for cocktails if they stopped and all those *boring* statements to make . . .

So he would contact Fritzy Vogel. And he'd get in touch with the academic O'Malley had told him about on the phone last night, when he had called to put his friend in the picture – and ask his advice.

Go, O'Malley had said. Might as well put your mind at ease.

After that there was no more he could do, and he could go back to fishing, and when the weather really socked in he would start working on a patent prototype for the computerized chart machines, and maybe DecaDent. He would do some serious carving on the new batch of applewood he got last month.

Larsen recrossed the Queensborough Bridge and headed downtown. The Commuter was heading the other way and he had little trouble finding a parking place on Twenty-third Street by Seventh Avenue and checking into the brick nostalgia of the Chelsea Hotel.

Larsen was fond of the Chelsea because of its scrollwork fire escapes, its ornate shabbiness, and because, like some Left Bank hotels in Paris, it still nurtured a community of nighthawks who rented their rooms by the month and traded cups of sugar, ounces of grass, and artsy-fartsy remarks on the top floor.

Back when he'd worked for Stangerson, Larsen had stayed there fairly regularly.

Many of the nighthawks had changed into the androgynous neo-punkers of New York's nouveau riche New Wave, but that was also par for the course. Change was the only constant in their world.

The lobby was crammed with cheap carpeting and mediocre abstracts whose creators might one day achieve fame if they catered to the right people in the art Mafia. The surrounding neighbourhood was a mishmash of office supply warehouses, cheap Chinese restaurants, and artists' lofts.

He checked in and found his room, lay down on the bed, and tried to call Fritzy Vogel. When he touched the phone his hand met a slimy coating of Vaseline. He went to fetch a towel, refusing to speculate on what sexual antics by previous tenants would have involved coating a Western Electric receiver with petroleum jelly.

To Larsen's amazement, Fritzy Vogel was still at the same number. Even more surprising, he was in the first time the fisherman called.

'*Mish 'ma oul*, it's not possible!' Fritzy exclaimed ostentatiously in Arabic when he found out who it was. 'Lars baby, I haven't seen you in years!'

'I like to keep in touch with old friends, Fritzy, and I haven't been in town recently. I see you haven't forgotten your Arabic.'

'I heard you'd retired to the country for good, buddy.'

Larsen hated being called 'buddy'.

'That's right. Have you got time for a drink tonight?'

'I should do that. Leave the rat race . . .' Fritzy commented, unoriginal and insincere. 'I'm sorry, Larsy, I'm booked up solid.' His voice lowered. 'I gotta take this model to Xenon, you know how it is, she's been bugging me for weeks to go out with her, take her to dinner.' Larsen could imagine the flashy smile at the other end. Fritzy ate models for breakfast.

'Well, what about now? You got ten minutes? I have a favour to ask you.'

'Sure, Larsy, any time, you know that, but today's really bad, man, bad.'

'You owe me, my friend. I'm sorry to put it that way but this will take you a maximum of ten minutes.'

There was a sigh at the other end.

'You're right, man, you're right. *W'Allah*. Where are you?'

'Twenty-third Street. West Side.'

'Shit, I'm really tight for time, buddy. Can't we make it tomorrow?'

'Why don't I meet you near where you live? If you're still living at the same place?'

'Yeah, well. Where?'

Larsen thought quickly. He'd never been out on the town

136

with Vogel, not in New York, but Fritzy must surely know Chez Jean, it was right around the corner from him.

He suggested it to Fritzy. 'It's on Sixty-ninth and Madison and they serve real raki.'

'I know it. How soon can you be here?'

'Half an hour?'

'I'll be there, Lars baby. No more than ten minutes, okay?'

'Ciao.'

Lars grinned as he hung up the phone. Not only had he caught Fritzy at home, probably in bed with another emaciated clotheshorse, but he'd actually nailed him down for this evening.

The gods were smiling, for a change.

The fisherman took the Lexington Avenue subway north to Sixty-eighth Street and walked over to Chez Jean, a sidewalk bar decorated in the regulation wall mirrors, brass counters, and prints of Napoleonic battles that proved this establishment served truly French cuisine, although the owner was Tunisian.

But the lamb was good and he did serve real raki.

Fritzy was sitting at a corner table under the Battle of Wagram, reading the *Village Voice* and sipping a Scotch. He had the same easy smile, the styled hair, the beautifully cut suit; the same eyes that never quite held yours. And an art deco tie. His clothes screamed 'hip millionaire' and their statement agreed with most of the other duds in the restaurant. Which made sense because as long as Larsen had known Vogel, Fritzy had always dressed the part he was playing and the part usually suited the surroundings.

Larsen ordered his raki and sat down.

'Long time, Captain Larsen.'

'Long time, Fritzy.'

They clinked glasses in the Arabic manner, each trying to dip his glass lower than the other's in deference to a respected guest. Fritzy was from Sonoma but he had lived for years in Lebanon and still affected Levantine behaviour.

They traded small talk while Larsen looked over the women who paraded in and out of the swinging doors of Chez

Jean. The bar was still trendy, the women some of the most gorgeous in New York, heiresses and actresses and corrupt/ innocent young things who wanted to be heiresses and actresses. The women were so beautiful you could forgive them all the narcissism and the posturing. Larsen forgave them.

'What did you want to ask me, Lars baby?'

'Last night I heard you were still in the business, Fritzy.'

Vogel's eyes flickered, and he paused before admitting, 'Yeah, sure. Sometimes.'

'I assume you people still deal with the NY Families,' Larsen asked.

'Sometimes.'

'Like always. What I want from you is simple, a little information. Just check out a couple of names for me. A friend of mine has been getting the squeeze from these names, and he thinks they're from New York, probably from one or two of the families. I kind of doubt it myself, but I promised I'd check.'

'I don't know too many connected guys, you know that.'

'Do what you can, okay? And we'll consider the debt paid.'

Larsen wrote the names on a cocktail napkin and slid them across the table.

'Laparensa. Parensi. Same guy, right? LuGuercio. I don't know them offhand. Any idea who they work for?'

'No,' Larsen said. 'But they might be – probably are – involved with fresh fish marketing in some way.'

Fritzy looked up sharply, his eyes seeming to focus for the first time through the sham bonhomie he adopted to hide a genuine intelligence.

'Fulton Fish Market?'

'Fulton, maybe.'

Fritzy shook his head. 'Man, I owe you this, but I tell you that's playing with fire. Fulton is fucking tough. That's a real motherfuckin' dirty group, buddy.'

A little more shrewdness peeked through. And a sharp concern under the swarthy complexion.

'What's so bad about Fulton?' Larsen asked.

'Ho-o-o boy. What's so bad about Fulton? Man, they're all enforcers. Every fuckin' one of them. I mean that place is *controlled*. They got everybody there by the balls, and you cross 'em they don't even wait to think about hurting you.'

'Who's "they"?'

'Who the hell do you think?'

Larsen had to strain his ears to hear. Jean was screaming into a telephone: 'Do we have bluefish? Yes, we have bluefish, we have red fish, we have pink fish, we have yellow fish, we have purple fish but we don't take reservations, Madame. Goodbye!' All this talk of seafood . . .

'You mean the fish dealers down there really are – belong to – the Organization?'

Fritzy looked around at the neighbouring tables, automatically. He caught the bartender's eye and raised his fingers for another round.

'Jesus, where have you been? I thought you were a fisherman. Don't you guys sell fish over there?'

'Well, you know how it is. Everybody says they're organized crime, and nobody has a shred of proof. Once in a while the *National Fisherman* does an article about how prices are fixed, by some kind of criminal cartel, presumably, but they never prove anything. Except circumstantially: I even had a friend of mine who used to work there and he said that was all bullshit.'

'What the fuck do you expect him to say? He would be in it, too.'

'He left it and went fishing.'

'Doesn't matter.' Fritzy took a slug of his new drink. 'Those guys are Sicilian. Well, Sicilian or Jewish. A couple of Moonies, Koreans. But either way, Sicilian or Jewish, there's no tighter families in the world. Once you been a smart fella, you don't talk about family business to *anybody*. Anybody. Whether you agree with it or not.'

Larsen said, 'Omerta?'

'Omerta, that's TV bullshit,' Fritzy snorted. 'It's not Omerta, it's family business. Whether you like it or not, you don't talk about it. It's not legal or illegal, it's just that outsiders are outsiders, and insiders are – have relatives, brothers and uncles and cousins, in the family business. It's – ' he shrugged helplessly, 'it's just family. I know a few of these guys, I can't put it any better than that.

'Look.' Fritzy glanced at the gold Rolex Cellini on his wrist. 'Jesus Christ, I gotta go.' He finished the second Scotch, ice cubes clinking. 'Lars baby, I'll look into it, although I don't like it. I'll ask around, because of what I owe you.'

For the second time that evening Fritzy's eyes stopped roaming around and looked at Larsen. 'But after this I consider the debt repaid, buddy. No more free favours for you. Fair enough?'

'Fair enough,' Larsen agreed. 'When do I call you?'

'Try me tomorrow, although I don't think I'll have anything that quickly.'

The same city shark smile switched back on as he stood up. 'It was great to see you again, Larsy baby. Seriously. Call me up ahead of time next time you come to town, and we'll get together and really do it up.' He slid towards the door. 'Okay? Like we did in Beirut.'

'Fritzy,' Larsen called as the man was vanishing behind a crowd of young jetsetters flashing South African gold and Bahamian tans against the bar. 'Say hello to Stangerson for me,' Larsen said.

Fritzy Vogel paused, then he smiled and winked and was gone. Still the same old Fritzy Vogel.

Perhaps if he had stayed in the business, Larsen would have become like Fritzy, too, another piece of international jetsam, pockets full of cash and eyes full of deals. He had grown to like the smuggling life, while recognizing the toll it took in nerves and sweat . . .

Once Larsen found himself looking down the three-inch barrel of a Colombian patrol-boat cannon. His sloop had been impounded for two hours, and he and his crew were pistol-whipped and thrown in irons until the payoff, which had disappeared at the rank of colonel, finally made it to the brigadier level.

And in another instance, helping out as a favour on the caïque run from Jounieh, Larsen's boat was caught in a

140

crossfire between motor launches belonging to two rival Maronite fiefdoms. Larsen got clear by firing back with the Lee Enfield he always brought with him on smuggling parties, but during the firefight, one of Stangerson's boats was badly mauled by antitank rockets. When she started to burn, Larsen pushed his dumpy vessel back into the thick of the fray to haul off her crew.

That was when he first met Fritzy Vogel, and that was when he should have learned never to trust Joseph Stangerson. Vogel's coaster, which Stangerson had told him was full of hashish, knocked the pilothouse off Larsen's old caïque when the coaster's cargo of artillery shells blew ten minutes later.

It was during that period Larsen first prepared his escape bag, a canvas duffel bag containing a change of clothes, 100 feet of Manila line, shaving and tool kits. He had the bag sewn up in a Damascus suq and paid extra for a false bottom in one end. Under the false flap he kept a German automatic pistol, a 7.5 Heckler and Koch P7 with palm-actioned cocking mechanism, ammunition, a Swiss passport with his face and a different name, as well as 10,000 clean American dollars.

Larsen upended his drink and noticed, two tables down, a brunette with legs like a symphony being serenaded by a stockbroker with a gold American Express card.

He'd have dinner here, he decided. There was a new Fellini movie playing on Lexington later, and around three a.m. the Fulton Fish Market would be opening for business.

He pulled out the *Boston World* article Eliza had promised him on *Sofia* and duly delivered the next morning. It was an interview with a fisheries economist from a New England university. Six paragraphs were underlined in the middle.

'Fish prices are determined largely by Fulton Fish Market because it is far and away the largest fresh fish buyer in North America,' Jameson explained. 'They do respond to the laws of supply and demand, but not so that you'd notice.'

What relationship fish prices had with supply and demand, Jameson said, went hand in hand with the weather.

141

'In good weather, lots of boats go out and you have a good supply so the price fishermen get for fish drops like a rock.

'In bad weather, no one goes out, and there's no fish.' But Jameson stated that poor supply did not push prices up as quickly or as far as when they went down.

'It is this differential that ensures the consumer always pays from three to four times what the fisherman gets,' he said. 'What he pays, within a certain range, is always high: what the fisherman gets is always low. It's the dealer who makes a very good profit.'

Jameson said that in most cases dealers will vary what they charge up and down the market, giving each other breaks, staying friendly. 'In this way they ensure they will always have a steady supply of fresh fish to either sell or buy. But this is not the whole story . . .'

It probably wasn't the whole story, Larsen reflected, but no newspaper article he had ever seen had even attempted to find out what the whole story was.

He signalled the waiter and ordered another raki. Eliza Blatchford would feel at home sitting at this table, he thought. He found himself wishing she was. Then his thoughts turned to Marie and he felt guilty again.

Fulton Fish Market at four a.m. on a freezing November day was a vast cavern of night and sky under the rude Gothic steel structure of the Brooklyn Bridge. The cavern was patrolled by a biting wind and lit by the glow of fires crackling in oil barrels. A plywood sign announced that the market would shortly be transferred, at the expense of the taxpayers of New York in particular and the United States in general, to a sanitary facility one block away as part of the ongoing conversion of South Street into a tourist trap, but for now it lay as it always had, in a squalor and smoke Herman Melville would have recognized.

On one side of South Street was a concrete warehouse with long columns of iron pillars dividing the rows of fishmongers. Bare lights polarized the market into white and black. Yellow windows in a second-storey bridge shielded countinghouses where bosses could look down on the floor below. Under the warehouse the East River oozed silent, cold and thick with rat corpses and purple chemicals. Over it stood the dark girders of the Franklin D. Roosevelt Drive.

Row upon row of older brick warehouses took up the street's other side, disappearing into recesses of plaster and dirt and wheezy steam heat, subdivided into stalls that displayed names like Lucci Fish Company and R&A Wholesale Fish Dealers Inc. Here and there were former speakeasies, broken windows boarded up and ancient bars groaning under the weight of espresso coffees and shots of sambuca and prosciutto-and-cheese sandwiches. The taverns were full of men in thick jackets wearing the long curved box hook of their trade: ten-inch-deep steel hooks, with a wood handle set across the top and the point honed to an evil sharpness. The hooks were used for loading fish or dragging boxes and were snagged over a leather patch on the shoulder when not in use.

The market sprawled like a drunk into the cobblestones and potholes of South Street, filling the night with shouts, arguments, the roar of trucks reversing, and fish.

Fish everywhere. Windowpane flounder and yellowtail, fluke, and sundabs; pink Gulf shrimp and blue Maine lobster; skate and dogfish and squid and octopus; hake and cusk, cod and scrod and haddock and pollock; bleeding carcasses of mako shark, tuna and swordfish; catfish, ocean perch and wolf fish; eel and crab and redfish and red snapper; halibut and mackerel and porgy and whitebait; scup and bluefish and striped bass; conch and quahogs, softshells, mussels and oysters.

Wherever you turned your head, fish were frozen slimy and cold in the grimaces of death: on scales, on tables, in ice or under the knife, and in boxes.

Their smell mingled with the smoke of diesel exhaust to create a perfume that should have enhanced the studiously nautical atmosphere of the South Street Seaport Museum lying close alongside.

But the people next door probably didn't like it, Larsen reflected as he dug his frozen hands deeper into his pockets and continued ambling through the bustle of the marketplace. Anyone who took beautiful old fishing schooners and four-masted barques, pickled them, and charged admission like the Cairo Museum to view the mummies would probably puke at the real stench of an ocean.

He walked like a sightseer, a tourist in nondescript khakis and army jacket warmed by the shot of sambuca he had bought earlier at a tavern down the road.

There seemed to be two categories of workers: older men with pasta stomachs and grizzled faces who prodded the fish with gloved hands and wrote figures down in notebooks: and younger, muscular types, with black moustaches and gold chains on the neck and hands. They wore long rubber boots and work trousers, patched down vests, rubber gloves, wool caps, and the regulation jacket and hook. All wore the closed faces of initiates.

He finally located the Sciacca Fish Company. A fat man in his early forties was finishing a hot dog while two cohorts hooked boxes of cod into a panel truck marked Le Franc Comtois French Restaurant.

'Laparensi around?' he asked casually, watching his own breath condense in the cold.

'Who?' The chubby cheeks spat out shrapnel of frankfurter and bun.

'Laparensi? Or Laparensa?'

The man shook his head and returned to his hot dog.

'He doesn't work here?' Larsen indicated the Sciacca sign.

'I told you, I never heard of him.'

'Mr Sciacca around?'

The cheeks stopped in mid-chew. 'You got business here or sumpin?'

It might be better not to insist, Larsen thought. 'Nope,' he said.

Without much hope, the fisherman walked on and began buttonholing people at random.

'I was interested in a job, hauling or cutting fish,' he told an older type in a cloth cap and thick spectacles who was supervising the disembarkment of a shipment of Nova Scotia haddock for the Pierce Fish Company.

144

The man squinted at him with one eye. Openly hostile.

'No jobs. We don't cut fish.' A huge shoulder cut him off finally.

'Do you know who does?'

The man turned around, irritated. 'Go bother somebody else. We don't cut fish. Other side of the road, but it's all union.'

'Do you know a guy called Laparensa?' Larsen asked, but the man walked off, shaking his head.

Two stalls down, at the Zangara Fish Company, Larsen stopped a man of about his own age, curly black hair, moustache.

'Do you know where I can find a guy called Laparensa?' Larsen asked. Then, in a flash of inspiration, 'Or Mr LuGuercio? They told me those guys could help me with a job here. I'm a fish cutter . . .' he ended lamely as the man just looked at him without a spark of recognition greeting the two names that were all he had to go on. He shook his head.

'There's no jobs around here, pal.' Zangara the younger put his hook into a box of flounder and dragged it thirty feet away.

Obviously the open, warm-hearted hospitality of southern Italy was not passed on genetically to the second or third generations, or maybe it simply withered on the vine in these cold and foreign climes.

On the other side of the road Larsen tried a beautifully subtle trick question on a Korean fish hauler, only to be treated to a free demonstration of Oriental indifference. The fisherman decided to change tactics.

'I gotta truck up the road,' he told a grey-haired man with a hook and a rubber apron and a stogie growing mushy in the quirk of his mouth, 'and it's s'posed to go to,' he pretended to consult a scrap of paper, 'the LuGuercio Company, or Mr Laparensa, or Parensi?'

The man looked at him steadily for a moment and said, 'I been watchin' you going around here. You're not union, and all the truckers are union. We don't want none of you trash night dealers from New Bedford around, asshole, so whydun you fuck off before you get hurt?'

145

'I don't know what you're talking –'

'David! Johnny!' the man yelled into the back of the building.

Larsen fucked off, in a crowd of men unloading whitefish for the Meier Fish Wholesale Company. The man's eyebrows followed him as he turned a corner. He was getting chilled, and the windows of one of the market bars burned with friendly invitation.

The guy had been bluffing, that much was plain. What in hell was a night dealer?

The tavern was jammed, what gaps there were filled with smoke and noise. But he managed to find a stool at the bar and order a sambuca and coffee.

A young man with a hook and jacket tiredly filled the gap at his side. He asked for a beer and a grilled cheese sandwich, and Larsen noticed he was served immediately. He stood still and hunched, a cigarette hanging off a short moustache and wisping smoke into drooping eyes. The ash was one-inch long and growing.

There was a TV over the bar showing a talk show, the kind that aired at four in the morning.

The coffee and sambuca came. Larsen drained the sweet, sticky shot, and sipped the coffee slowly. He took out the pack of Gitanes he had bought earlier at Chez Jean and lit one. He didn't have to feign fatigue, or being buzzed after five rakis, a bottle of Bordeaux, and two sambucas.

'You seen LuGuercio around? Or Laparensi?' he asked the man who had just arrived.

There was no reaction at first. Then the man slowly raised a scarred right hand to remove the cigarette. He airlifted the ash smoothly over to an ashtray and it fell, seemingly of its own accord.

He turned to look at Larsen and gave the first friendly smile the fisherman had got that night.

'Huh?'

Larsen repeated his question.

'Never heard of 'im, Mac. Parensi? No. But you might find the Guercio in here tomorrow, earlier than this, though.'

Jackpot! The fisherman nodded as if that was exactly the

answer he'd expected, paid his bill, bought his neighbour a drink at the same time, and headed into the darkness for his truck and the Chelsea and bed. He had time for four or five hours' sleep before his next appointment.

CHAPTER TWELVE

The appointment with Samuel Shapiro, former professor of sociology at New York University, proved something of a letdown. O'Malley's old prof lived on Duke Ellington Boulevard, on the third floor of a building once owned by the King of Jazz. The boulevard itself was a short strip of 106th Street that ended abruptly under the hindquarters of a bronze general on horseback. The general saluted with doffed hat the icy blasts and occasional snow flurries coming in his direction from the Hudson River.

Shapiro himself was stooped under the weight of a plantation of cottony hair that sent tendrils over his eyes, under his collar, and into the lesser bushes of his eyebrows. His face was a study in contour ploughing, the furrows raised by seventy-five years of living.

He was dressed in a faded plaid smoking jacket and looked through a pair of granny spectacles, the picture of amiable senility. One of the best social historians in the country, O'Malley had said. A genuine expert on organized crime.

'Don't mind the cats,' the old man muttered as he led the way past a pair of mullioned windows that looked out over the grey breadth of the river to deserted warehouses and housing estates on the Jersey side.

But you couldn't help but mind the cats. They were everywhere: on the sagging couch and among the remains of last night's dinner, on the bookshelves and on the rug; there were five on the heater and two on the ancient Victrola, and decaying cans of cat food lay wherever books were not stacked. The smell of old tomes and cat litter was pervasive.

'Sit, sit down. Coffee?' He disappeared into a musty kitchen. His voice remained, surprisingly strong: 'Now I remember. You wanted to ask me about organized crime in New York. Everybody wants to ask me about organized crime in New York,' he complained.

148

The coffee was drinkable but Shapiro had never heard of the two names Larsen was interested in.

'The names,' he said vaguely. 'I did my original research fifteen years ago, when the Sicilian Families were sparring, the Gambinos were rounding on the Colombo-Bonanno people, maybe four or five articles since that time . . . Joey Gallo was trying to organize the Blacks in Harlem into an independent family. A neat trick . . . I could maybe have helped you then,' he went on, 'but now, I hear just a little, here and there, I have some friends still. I never heard of those names, though. Do you have any idea who they might work for?'

'Not really. I think they might be connected with the fish industry,' Larsen said.

'Fascinating, fascinating,' said Shapiro, sliding wrinkled hands behind the cushions of his couch. 'Now where on earth . . .'

Larsen watched as the old man dithered shortsightedly and finally located a crumpled pack of Chesterfields under the rump of a Persian. The cat said 'Rowr' and expressed his frustration by cuffing a young tiger who was sitting, a little dazed from the altitude, on three weeks' worth of the Sunday *New York Times*.

'The fresh fish industry is interesting because, don't you see, the Italian organized crime family in New York is still a recognizable descendant of pre-Garibaldi Italy,' Shapiro intoned.

The professor built thunderheads of tobacco smoke, leaned over the coffee table and with trembling hands stroked a pregnant grey. Larsen squirmed impatiently. It was like being at university again.

'Yes, they started with the *gabellotti*, sort of enforcers for the big feudal landlords in eastern Sicily, who would extort taxes from the peasants, and they became a force in their own right, mediating between the two . . . almost parallel development here, in fact, don't you see, as middlemen between the Anglo-Saxons who ran government and the destitute, powerless immigrants from northern Italy. More coffee? No?'

149

The professor lit another Chesterfield from the butt of his previous one.

'Don't you see, that's why a fish market, Fulton Fish Market especially, is so perfect for any kind of criminal group that makes money by restraint of trade: because in marketing a fresh product that becomes bad, valueless in three, four days – especially a product where the supply is so variable because of weather, don't you see – you have to be able to trust the people you deal with. To overcome those bottlenecks . . . to give you a regular supply of fresh, good produce you have to know people's names, faces. They give you a good supply, when they don't have much, you buy fish even when you don't need it in times of plenty. It works both ways . . . you deal by word of mouth. And cash only, of course . . .

'Which is why I think the Organization took control of Fulton so easily, years ago.' Shapiro was almost purring his delight at having an audience again. 'There was no paperwork, just one big marketplace . . . personal deals, backed by personal threats. Middlemen. They give protection, they get a percentage from all the dealers, they help set the price when it gets too low, everybody makes a good living . . . tax-free.'

Larsen had stopped fidgeting.

'It's interesting to note that the first real organized crime in New York City started around Rosanna's Vegetable Market, also on the Lower East Side . . . are you sure you don't want more coffee?'

'Yes, I'm sure, thanks. You mean the Fulton Organization really exists – it really sets the price of fish here?'

'No, not always,' Shapiro replied. 'Only when it gets too low, or too high, because there's too much or too little fish: they like to keep it above a floor price. They can pay the fishermen less, but *they* always make the same percentage. But things are much better organized now, I hear, since the old days. It's a sort of neutral ground for the Organization and all the five New York Families – the Gambinos, the Colombos, the Luccheses, the Genoveses, the Bonannos, though Funzi Tieri is trying to take over the Bonannos. It's not just Sicilians, either: half the groups are Jewish and lately they did a deal and you have the Koreans in on the act . . . the whole shebang is what they call "The Organization". Now, I've heard, you have the Neapolitans from the Camorra and even the Corsicans trying to get in as well . . .

'But that's all rumour, naturally,' the old man went on. 'The Justice Department did another investigation recently and couldn't prove anything.

'Would you like – oh, no, of course.'

There was more in the same vein, but Larsen was becoming nauseated by the vicious fumes of tobacco and cat litter, hypnotized by the scholastic drone.

He made his excuses and left to revive himself on fresh fruit juice in a Cuban café around the corner. He called Fritzy from a phone booth next door: Vogel was apologetic but he hadn't had time to quiz any sources about Larsen's names.

It was good just to sit and lean on the café counter, isolated in a sea of Cubans, rabbis and Columbia students, Blacks and Puerto Ricans, and rest for a while.

It was going to be another long night.

At three-thirty next morning, Larsen was seated at the same corner of the Fulton Street bar, nursing a sambuca and coffee and looking at the swirling crowd of patrons, wondering which of them might be the mysterious LuGuercio.

At three-forty-five he was still waiting for someone to sit next to him so he could open a conversation naturally, when his moustachioed acquaintance from the previous night blew in with a cloud of sleet and three other market men in patched jackets with hooks on their shoulders.

The man with the moustache and the dangling cigarette finally recognized him and came over. He put a hand on Larsen's shoulder, looked closer to make sure, and asked, 'Aren't you the guy was lookin' for LuGuercio?'

Larsen said, 'Yeah, that's right.'

'If you wanna wait 'til I'm finished with my break, I'll show you where he works.'

The man went back to his crowd and his beers. Two of his companions ritualistically stood mugs upside down on their lips and left. Finally the young one beckoned to Larsen and headed out the door.

The wind was blowing hard and cold. Fulton Street was a gallery of woodcuts, carved out in black and sepia.

The man walked slowly eastward and waited for Larsen to catch up. He turned right, down a narrow cobbled alley that paralleled South Street. The alley was inhabited by garbage and lumpen cats, trucks and brick warehouses. The warehouses formed the back of fish houses on the block's other side.

There were three squares of solid orange light and a clatter of dishes behind one particularly mangy stoop – a restaurant with no sign – but Larsen's companion walked past the door impatiently, now leading the fisherman steadily northward. Ahead, the prehistoric mass of Brooklyn Bridge lay in a state of tensioned shadow. None of the streetlights worked around here, and Larsen had to pick his way carefully among the rotting fish, boxes, and upended garbage cans.

Larsen's companion was ten feet ahead of him when he suddenly turned and stood in the middle of the sidewalk and threw his cigarette into the gutter.

Larsen could not help but notice that the man's hook was no longer hanging on his shoulder and was in his right hand. The curved point was turned in Larsen's direction and it glinted twice as the man swung the hook slowly, back and forth.

A garbage can clattered behind the fisherman.

Larsen spun around. Two, three dark shapes were coming out of the shadows in front of the lighted warehouse. A fourth was loping swiftly around a parked van across the street. All of them had hooks, and all of them were swinging them slowly, suggestively, horizontally in front of them.

The fisherman stopped and waited five seconds, hoping there might be some mistake.

'What does this mean?' he asked loudly, twisting his head to address the man who had led him here. He kept his back towards the warehouse wall nearest him.

The man said nothing, but a glint of stainless steel, reappearing regularly, demonstrated that he hadn't suddenly had a change of heart.

'If you want money, boys, you can have it,' Larsen said, backing slowly towards the wall to protect his rear. At least he had flattened the tremor in his voice. There was something unbelievably sinister and inhuman in the slow assurance of his attackers, in their total silence, in the medieval tools they were armed with.

Somehow he didn't think money was what they were really interested in but –

'Here.' Larsen put his hands in his back pockets and drew out his wallet with the left hand. He flipped it ten feet away. It hit the boots of the man on the cobblestones, who didn't even bother looking at it. The man stood between two parked Cadillacs and swung his hook: he had a good sense of rhythm. His breath came slow and even, white steam and a gleam of unwinking eyes behind it.

A slow shiver drag-raced up Larsen's spine. Son of a bitch! What did these guys want?

They had all stopped. One or two of the hooks had stilled. They seemed to be waiting for something. The man on his left mumbled a phrase to his lapel. Ten, twenty seconds passed, eternities that Larsen used to ease further backwards and check the terrain behind him: two garbage cans, a stack of empty fish boxes, and a brick wall. Fifteen feet to his left, a railing and stairs led to the warehouse cellar.

Larsen's heart was beating a drum solo. He forced himself to breathe deeply, as if he were diving. He kept his right hand in his hip pocket after flipping the wallet out. Now he gently loosened his knife in the scabbard where it lay, flat against his right thigh.

There was a sigh of big Detroit tyres and a black Lincoln Continental purred into view, on the bridge end of the street. It took the curve and froze their tight group in its headlights, then stopped, silently, next to the man who was still ignoring Larsen's hard-earned cash.

The car was a half-mile long and had smoked windows. One of the rear ones hissed open.

Larsen caught a glimpse of a thick head and a pair of wide glasses – there was something odd about their cant – and a mane of grey hair.

The glasses nodded. The window hissed shut. The limo whispered down the street, a great black manta ray, and disappeared at the next corner in a red wink of brake lights.

That person had not been a member of the Larsen Benevolent Society (Lars Larsen, president, treasurer, sole adherent), but Larsen somehow felt incredibly lonely when the Lincoln disappeared.

As if a spell had been broken, the hooks started moving in. They were all swinging again, slowly. It had started flurrying, Larsen noticed, his brain wishing desperately it were somewhere else where it mattered what the weather was doing.

They were five feet away when the fisherman whipped his right hand in front of him and lunged with knife extended towards the man at his right.

The man jumped back, spreading his arms and hook clear of Larsen's swishing blade, and the fisherman twisted immediately, back to the wall, to face the rest of his attackers.

They had shifted positions towards him as he moved – there was a whole frame of action Larsen had missed when he lunged – but now they stopped, one of them taking a step back. And waited. Waited patiently. They had all the time in the world.

Larsen mimicked the slow swing of their hooks with his knife, thumb flat on the blade, keeping his own eyes on the occasional flash of theirs. Once or twice he flipped the knife from his right hand to his left. 'Keep your eyes on theirs, keep your eyes *off* their hands,' Jorge had taught him long ago. Jorge had been good with a knife but it had not done him any good because Jorge had been cut in two by automatic rifle fire in a Barranquilla slum.

The man on the cobblestones took a step towards him. A slow hiss came from his lips, the small sign of concentration made by an expert faced with a problem that had just become a little more complex.

Desperation had compressed Larsen's fear into a cold resolve. It translated into muscles ready to whip at the slightest command from nerve endings. He was ready.

Without taking his eyes from their faces he put his knifeless right hand back to the trash barrel directly behind him and arced it hard, dipping his left shoulder, overhead towards the hissing lips. Larsen saw him put his hook up in self-defence and then the fisherman hurled himself again towards the man on his right, trying to wound him and get past before the rest could touch him. He threw himself low, but the man had the reflexes of a cat and slipped sideways.

The split-second chance had gone. Larsen braked, his right foot skidded on the wet concrete, and as he whirled around there was a burning, brutal pain in his left shoulder. His left leg found purchase on an uneven paving stone and he roared, pushing back towards the main group of attackers, tissues tearing as he dragged the hook from the first man's grasp. His knife sliced across a gloved hand, there was a gasp, and they were all back in their old positions, chests heaving, ready for the next movement in this lethal saraband.

Larsen plucked the hook from his shoulder and the world swam. He couldn't let them know but the pain was becoming numb and warm. He could feel the blood flooding, if it was an artery he'd be dead inside a minute. His only chance was to move now . . .

But the man on his extreme right had decided to take the initiative and he threw himself low at Larsen. The fisherman kicked the stacked fish boxes in his direction, threw the hook at the next man. There was a fist on his jacket but he tore himself free and charged the man on the cobblestones. The man was spinning left and swinging his hook down, but Larsen threw himself inside it, into the man's chest, and the hook ripped his jacket. Larsen jerked his elbow and drove the knife deep into the exposed armpit. The man screamed as Larsen tried to dislodge the blade from the joint where it had lodged but cartilage had seized up over the steel and then he was under and past, kicking the knifed man into his friends behind him. A hand seized his jacket, tore loose.

Larsen staggered, recovered, and started sprinting across the street, pounding down, away from the bridge, his assailants close behind and to the side. He had to get back to the truck, take a left down South Street, but they were cutting him off to the left.

As he came to the curve a huge tractor-trailer loomed five feet away, twin horns blasting and air brakes hissing. Larsen skidded in the slush and the front wheels missed his feet by inches. From his prone position he could see a hook four feet behind and two more sets of wheels went by his head. The truck was a Mack, an eighteen-wheeler, which meant he could roll, and he *rolled* under the screeching bulk of the truck, rolled fast, and the shoulder felt like it had been ripped right off. The huge rear wheels were heading straight for his crotch; he arched upward and his hand met a brace on the underside of the trailer and he was bouncing under the truck, his heels maybe five inches from the rear set of wheels.

Then the truck stopped and Larsen was rolling again, running in a sea of pain that was far from the hunting calls behind him.

But the men were near, outflanking him to the left once more, and he had to turn right up South Street, away from his pick-up, under the FDR Drive. Ahead of him were the black river and two bowsprits piercing the night, *Peking* and *Wavertree*. South Street Seaport. There were shouts in all directions now.

Like a wounded rat, his only instinct was to go to ground.

He crossed South Street in a sprint, threading girders and shadows and huge cubes of armoured concrete next to the wharf, and climbed under the pilings where the wire fence that cordoned off the windjammers met the river. He swung himself around and under the barbed wire, left shoulder ripping, and staggered to his feet on the other side of the fence, gasping for breath, eyes shut tight against the pain. His right hand was warm and sticky where it tried to squeeze the wound closed. Fighting a sudden nausea, he jogged down the wharf to the second gangplank of the *Peking*.

The four-masted barque lay brown and huge, her masts

reaching into the orange glow of the Gotham sky. As he swung himself outboard of the gangplank to get around a padlocked gate, there was another yell coming from down the wharf. He jumped on to the deck of the windjammer.

She was all of 500 feet long and dark as the grave, with a bridge-cum-charthouse midships, forward of where he stood. There was no point in going aft, towards the dead end of the pier and river, so he climbed to the bridge deck, crouching low behind the charthouse, down to the foredeck and under the covered fo'c'sle deck. One glance at the bowsprit told him he could never hope to climb out its length and drop on to the street below without breaking his fool neck. That left the mooring hawsers.

Maybe the wound wasn't so deep. It didn't hurt so much now. And he was still alive, so it had missed the artery.

The massive, six-inch starboard hawser ran through a fairlead, a hole through the bow maybe one and a half feet wide. Not enough room.

The shouts were muted now; dogs closing in for the kill didn't bark when they had the quarry within jowl range. They were all on the *Peking*. There *had* to be enough room through the fairlead. There was no one on the wharf, his one line of escape – if he could cram himself through. He squiggled his legs into the hole, one ankle around the hawser. His hips caught, then bruised clear, his shoulder exploding in pain as he tried to corkscrew his torso around the hawser and through the steel lips of the fairlead. Then he was free and sliding swiftly down the mooring rope, hands burning – too swiftly – as he reached the bottom of the loop and the hawser soared again towards the wharf. His left shoulder had no strength left, and when it went his right could no longer bear the weight. His fingers clung long enough to let him ease into the East River with only a low splash.

From then on, it was almost easy. The freezing water was like a tonic, making his lungs seize up and anaesthetizing his shoulder. The tide pushed him gently northward under the wharf's blackness. He fended himself off huge, oily timbers and tried not to think about scurrying noises in the dark. The rats here probably grew to the size of Dobermans.

There was a tint of light and then a raft, the dark bulk of an old Gloucester fishing schooner tied up alongside. Painfully Larsen clambered on to the raft and crawled up the gangplank to wharf level. A flashlight was winking on the *Peking*, but there was no one he could see on the wharf. He squelched swiftly across to the fence and swung himself underneath for the second time that night. He could no longer feel his shoulder; the water had turned his muscles into nerveless lumps. He jogged clumsily northward, in the shadows of the elevated highway, keeping parked cars between himself and clumps of working fishmongers, to where he had parked the truck.

It took him almost a minute to insert his key in the ignition, so violently was he trembling from the bite of the East River. Pain returned as he shivered, becoming a vast ache that gripped his entire left side. Then the key was in and the engine running. He was still losing blood but first he had to get out of here, out of enemy territory: he could tend to the shoulder later. He put the parking lights on and accelerated around the first right-hand curve.

He almost smashed into the truck that was being moved to block the street deliberately. It was almost at right angles, but the driver was still reversing to fill a final gap when Larsen hit the brakes. A man directing the truck backward pulled something out of his jacket and the fisherman aimed the Chevy straight at him, roared in first gear behind the reversing tractor-trailer and up the sidewalk, knocking the man into a wall, smashing scaffolding and grazing a streetlight.

He turned right up Front Street, the same goddamned street he had been attacked on ten minutes or hours ago, jammed the accelerator down as headlights swerved into view behind him, and accelerated through a stop sign: there was the bridge and the road simply ended, one way back towards the market. He twisted the old Chevy left up the one-way street, away from Fulton, shock absorbers pumping, resisting the cobblestones. Dover Street. He roared up an incline, and through a red light at forty miles per hour, streets empty at this hour of the morning. It was too tight a turn but there was another ramp ahead he could take. He jammed the Chevy upwards. There was a vicious loop as the ramp came around 180 degrees, skidding around sky views of modern buildings, Pace University, the Gothic gingerbread of City Hall. He downshifted, braked, and accelerated as the loop untwisted, and then he was following a string of circus lights high, high, over the East River, over the Brooklyn Bridge and into Brooklyn at seventy miles per hour.

Headlights crested the bridge in the rearview mirror just when he thought he'd lost them. The bridge was about to metamorphose into a highway, and he knew he could never outrun a car on the three-lane. There were buildings, towers ahead: the Watchtower, a sign read four-fifty-eight, and the Department of Irrelevant Trivia in Larsen's brain came up with Jehovah's Witnesses, the Holy Rollers who had bought up half of this part of Brooklyn. He swung right (CADMAN PLZ. read the sign), through a red light, across a double-barrelled thoroughfare, and then bore left, trying to find the crazy streets where he could get lost and evade pursuit. The headlights swerved in line behind him and gained rapidly. Never any cops around when you needed them.

The fisherman took the next right, much too quickly this time. The rear of the pick-up skidded on the wet asphalt and slammed into a parked car. He trod on the gas, went across a stop sign, and right across the bows of a sanitation truck that blew its horn in outrage. Larsen prayed silently there was no crumpled metal from the crash jagging into his rear wheel.

He was in a pretty, quiet, residential neighbourhood – turn-of-the-century townhouses, sculpted balconies, little oak trees, brick and ivory. The Hotel St George, where one might safely park a maiden aunt. Rows of sleeping Volvos and Buicks. The headlights were 100 yards behind him.

The next ten minutes faded into a mad newsreel for the fisherman, a Movietone nightmare in black and white. He was shaking and sweating from the cold and loss of blood, his shoulder screamed every time he had to steer with his left arm so he could use his right for the gear lever.

159

A left, townhouses, left again, florists and Chinese food, a right, a green light for a change, and the enemy was riding right on his tail and trying to pass him over the broad avenue. He swerved into their path and then they were careering down another peaceful one-way street. A right again, thank God he had filled the gas tank yesterday, and the headlights were kissing his bumper. He suddenly jammed on the brakes, skidding, but they were ready for him, the bumpers crunched only briefly. He mashed the gas pedal once more but they kept slowing inexplicably and the wind started whistling through two new stars in his windshield and rear window. He kept his head low, pushed the old truck right: PUERTO RICO LIBRE! a spray-painted sign read, PSPR, and there were a pair of parking lights ahead – someone was pulling out of a space. Larsen leaned on his horn and accelerated wildly and as he passed the early bird he checked his window optimistically and yes! the car was pulling out in front of his pursuers.

He could hear the crash as he bore left on Van Brunt Street. For the first time he noticed that he had left the professional suburbs and entered a blitzed neighbourhood of rubble and bunkers.

He had lost them. The pain returned.

One eye danced back to his rearview mirror, as, 400 yards behind now, one headlight appeared. He skidded right at the next intersection and jammed his foot down as far as it would go. The old V-6 howled as if it had been fed nitroglycerine intravenously and shot straight towards a plaza that marked the end of the street.

The plaza had toll gates and huge storklike cranes that read UMS. Larsen braked, skidding on the fresh coat of snow. RED HOOK MARINE TERMINAL, a sign read.

He stamped on the accelerator again and swerved right; thirty, fifty miles per hour, there was a curve, a row of parked containers, the road became a track between two chain fences, and . . . a dead end. His headlights picked up a wire gate, but he was going much too fast and only had time to read CITY OF NEW YORK DEPARTMENT OF ENVIRONMENTAL SERVICES WATER TABLE TESTING before his brakes locked and the Chevy rammed through the gate, chain links screaming, and slid on the wet gravel into a wooden bulkhead that lay across the track like a wall. Larsen's head hit the wheel, and the truck dipped slightly forward, Larsen looked up in time to see the section of bulkhead he had carried away fall lazily forward into a fifty-foot-wide, twenty-foot-deep hole a corpse's length ahead of the truck's front wheels. A hole whose bottom was black, oily, salt water.

There was hope yet.

Taking care to keep the truck's wheels straight, he advanced the Chevy slowly, slowly to the very lip of the hole, then reversed it back the way he had come, carefully following his own tyre marks. At the end of the fence he pulled off to one side, behind the containers, switched off his lights and put on the parking brakes.

It took him precious seconds but he managed to find a scrap of plywood with which he scraped away, one-handed, the tyre marks he had made by reversing off the track through the slush. He got back in the truck, his hand groped through darkness.

It was as he'd hoped. There was a full, cold bottle of Rolling Rock in the glove compartment. He ripped the top off with his teeth and to hell with the tooth enamel. It foamed into his lap and he drank deeply, dehydrated, watching the single headlight waver around the terminal plaza. The snow was falling faster now, already turning the city into a horizontal lamination, a vanilla-and-chocolate layer cake. His tracks would be hard to miss.

They were the only new ones on the fresh snow.

The headlight found the tracks, picked up speed and flashed by Larsen as he waited and shivered and swallowed beer in the dark truck. A Buick or Dodge sedan, late model, New York plates. People in front and back. The red brake lights showed as they spotted the shattered fence.

Larsen inched the Chevy into the roadway and followed in first gear.

The car slowed further as its driver saw the tracks leading straight towards the broken bulkhead, and beyond towards nothing. The car came to within five feet of the hole and would have stopped, but Larsen rammed his truck into the rear fender and pushed it as fast as his lowest gear would run, engine racing. The reverse lights came on and their tyres spun; there was a flash, illuminating at least two heads in the back seat and another star appeared high in the Chevy's windshield. But then it was too late, they just couldn't match a '58 Chevy in sheer weight and cylinder-head acreage – the tail lights lifted, etched a parabola skyward and disappeared. A huge gout of black water rose to obscure the fairyland of towers across the harbour.

The fisherman put the parking brakes on again and got out to peer cautiously over the lip of the hole. His knees were trembling only very, very slightly. Then he went and fetched the rope that lived in the Chevy's bed, wrapped it around a piece of bulkhead, and threw the bitter end after the sinking car. Somebody might need it, but it was unlikely.

He got back in, turned the truck around and headed back into the grimness of Red Hook. If he found his way to Route 278, and then Route 678 northbound, he would eventually hit the New England Thruway, and from there to home was a straight shot.

He'd had just about enough of the Big Apple.

CHAPTER THIRTEEN

In Cos Cob, Connecticut, Larsen almost drove into the Mianus River.

He had taken Route 1 to avoid tolls on the New England Thruway because, with the exception of seven dollars and change secreted in his pockets, all his money had been in the wallet he had foolishly offered to his assailants and left in the slush of Front Street. He had already spent two dollars of that on tolls between Brooklyn and Route 1 and he would have to husband the rest: the Chevy would be thirsty for gasoline before the Massachusetts border. If he could even last that long . . .

Larsen felt as if someone else were driving the pick-up, as if the events of the past night had happened to another Larsen, a strange individual with a good right arm who was totally dominated by his useless left shoulder. The real Larsen lived on a distant planet of nausea, exhaustion, and pain.

But it was both Larsens that started to doze at the wheel, almost driving off a bridge over a narrow stream in a small town near Greenwich. He ran up the sidewalk and grazed the bridge railing before consciousness returned in a burst of adrenalin.

He'd have to take a break soon. The sun was rising, an orange disc flitting from billboard to billboard as he headed obsessively east. Follow the bouncing ball. Fly Delta to Florida, Eat Another Billion Big Macs, Buy More Unessential Products, Support Connecticut's Arms Industry. He must be free of pursuit now, at least.

Larsen finally turned off near a thin brook in Westport, and got lost for ten minutes in a development before he found a field offering easy access to the watercourse. The overnight snow had melted and the brook was chuckling merrily over its run-off.

163

Blood had congealed thickly on his shirt and jacket. The fisherman's vision blurred as he ripped at the shirt, and he could feel the world going dark. Clots of dried blood flaked like old paint. He swayed and fell to his knees in icy moss by the stream. Cars on the highway muttered by, uncaring.

The wound was a disgusting purple mouth still seeping blood. The hook had gone under the deltoid muscle behind his shoulder joint, slashing fibre and probably a ligament or two, its curved shape angling it back into the body. He couldn't tell if it had gone deep enough to hit a bone. It had missed his axillary artery, anyway – not by much, if he remembered his anatomy.

Using his good hand, Larsen painstakingly lined up two granite rocks so they would provide a funnel for the south wind and filled the gap between them with dry twigs, leaves culled from the underbrush, and a back copy of the *Sentinel* he had found in the truck. It took three matches but the flames started licking shyly at the tinder.

He set some water heating in one of the many tin cans littering the riverbank. The fire was anaemic. It would take a good half hour but the water it boiled should be free of tetanus and polio and typhoid and all the other aquatic side effects of sedentary civilization.

Yelling only helped a little bit when he poured the scalding water over the wound. Agony seemed to have a colour all of its own. Scrubbing the flesh with a piece of his shirt didn't feel very good either, and when the clotted blood had been washed off he could see the red sergeant's stripes of infection crossing his skin. The hook had probably been covered with rotten fish juices.

Perhaps he should have gone back to recuperate at the Chelsea. Or called the cops. But instinct had warned Larsen that if the people after him could roust out the manpower to cordon off Fulton Fish Market at the drop of a hook, they could also put out a city-wide alert for the fisherman or his truck. And people like that collected tame police detectives like postage stamps.

Yet he had to rest, sleep. How much blood had he contributed to the pavements of New York – a pint? A quart?

A lot. His raging thirst was testimony to the fact. He charred his lips draining the last warm water from the tin.

Larsen reversed the truck on to the field's verge, near a copse of maples, and lay down in the front seat with a tarpaulin to swaddle him.

He dozed fitfully at first, hampered by the pain, tortured by a recurrent need for water. The sound of the brook nearby was overwhelmingly lush.

Around three-thirty in the afternoon he got up to boil another can of water. A matron behind the wheel of a passing Datsun station wagon gazed at him suspiciously while he struggled to coax flames. His shoulder seemed glued stiff.

He fell asleep again around four-thirty. The next thing he knew night had fallen. It was eleven-thirty. He had slept in the front seat for several hours and his spine felt like a corkscrew. And he was shaking from cold. He started up the Chevy and pointed the headlight – only one of them worked after the encounter with the New York Department of Environmental Services bulkhead – back at Route 1.

The fever that had been playing hide and seek with him since Westport really hit between New London and New Haven. In the absence of clear thinking it only reinforced Larsen's obsession with heading back to Mallebarre. Getting home seemed the only answer to questions raised by the Fulton incident. It wouldn't answer the questions but it would give him time . . . to think . . . and he had to think.

Those guys at the fish market hadn't been interested in playing games with the tourist; they hadn't even been interested in scaring the daylights out of him or lifting his wallet. Nor had they wanted to just rough him up, hook him around a little for fun. There was a feeling to their movements that had spelled out a kill, and there had been none of the verbal insults and other messages that indicated the fisherman would still be alive afterwards to appreciate a lesson.

And those weren't BB-gun holes in the windshield, either: they looked more like .38 calibre. Not a howitzer shell, but lethal enough.

But *why*? Larsen asked himself as the shopping malls and

intervening trees rolled by, as the headlight metered out highway lines, the gas indicator sank steadily towards 'E' and the sweat began to stand to attention on his forehead.

Why kill *him*? Fulton might be rough but it couldn't be so rough that a stranger asking questions got rubbed out within twenty-four hours. Hadn't Shapiro mentioned an investigation by the Feds? Yet he couldn't recall anyone going around wasting FBI agents on the seven o'clock news. Perhaps they only stuck hooks into civilians.

But why *kill* him? Unless they had a specific reason.

Of course, they couldn't possibly have known why he was at Fulton, or his connection with Marie Sciacca – could they? And even if they did, Fulton was a world apart from the lazy miseries of Cape Cod. His friends with the hooks might not be bursting with the milk of human kindness but they would not bother a Cape Cod fisherman simply because of something his father might have done . . . or his friend's father . . .

Larsen swung off the highway at the next Howard Johnson's. Next to him under a parking-area spotlight was an olive-green Rambler with Maine 'Vacationland' plates and a rear seat full of dirty workclothes and beer bottles. The HoJo's was a wasteland at this hour, but as Larsen weaved into the lobby to use a toilet he passed a group of humanoid groundhogs with old lumbershirts and unshaven cheeks. Without much hope of results, their leader was carrying a sign that read, 'Please help us get back to Maine.'

On his way out Larsen stopped and addressed the lead groundhog.

'I can take you as far as Providence, or New Bedford,' he said with the easy familiarity of the drunk or hallucinating, 'if you help me with the driving and with the gas. Only need four, five bucks.'

After a couple of seconds, the head groundhog said, 'Ayuh.' He looked around at the three other critters for opinions. They exchanged ideas telepathically. He looked back at Larsen. The fisherman could almost swear to seeing his whiskers twitch.

'We only got nine dollars between us, we could mebbe

give you three or four . . . yuh drunk?'

Larsen said, 'I don't feel so hot, I have a fever. That's why I want you to drive.'

Larsen's remaining five dollars, and five dollars from the Maine critters, would buy just enough gas and oil to get the Chevy back to Mallebarre.

Two of the men hunkered down in the pick-up bed, under the tarp. Larsen sank gratefully in front, wedged in the crook of door and seat as the lead groundhog took the wheel. The moan of wind across the window became an endless Gypsy serenade, and highway lights flickering across his eyelids kept resolving into an indistinct face with red hair and eyes like a deep pool under a Greek island.

And then they would change and become a huge steel hook in the hands of a groundhog the size of a cargo crane, a veritable King Kong among groundhogs that kept repeating, 'Ayuh? Ayuh?'

And then they would be the red-haired woman again. It was almost like TV.

He slept fitfully through the rest of Connecticut. Somewhere in Rhode Island the truck stopped and one of the groundhogs got out, fumbled among the undergrowth with a flashlight and picked up some leaves, which he ground into a paste with beer they had brought along and folded into a not-too-dirty bandanna. He forced Larsen to take off his jacket and applied the compress to Larsen's wound.

'Thoroughwort,' he said, in answer to Larsen's protesting mumbles. 'Good fuh yuh.'

Near New Bedford they tried to persuade the delirious fisherman to go to a local hospital. When Larsen refused, stubbornly insisting he had to get back to Cape Cod at all costs, the chief groundhog and his lieutenant mumbled among themselves, and exchanged short sentences with the critters in back.

Then they drove the truck through Marion and Wareham and over the Sagamore Bridge on to the Cape, and the Mid-Cape Highway. While Larsen dozed they followed hospital signs to Hyannis and hustled the fisherman into the bright modern creditworthiness of Cape Cod Hospital's emergency room at six that morning.

'No!' Larsen remembered shouting when he realized where he was, but for once there was a good-looking nurse with strong hands, and a smooth teenage MD with a needle who wanted him to count backwards, as if he could ever count forwards at this point.

There was a long space after that when the times he was woken, touched, rolled over by people dressed in white appeared less real than when he had to combat the hook-wielding rodents in order to rescue a princess who was imprisoned in a warehouse hidden beneath a river. Sometimes she was blonde, sometimes a redhead, but always a princess. Certainly the adventure serial, although on occasion terrifying, was more pleasant than the disturbances, the forced washing, the injections.

When Larsen finally achieved a relative consciousness there was an ancient stranger tearing harsh breaths out of a respirator four feet away from him. He was imprisoned beneath the starch of hospital sheets, and Uncle Ole was standing in the silent company of a saline drip that ended in a needle in Larsen's wrist.

Larsen felt weak and hot and queasy in the stomach, but he wasn't sure if it was the infection in his shoulder or his pathological hatred of hospitals with their cleanly sandwiched odours of disinfectant and mucus. Sterile prisons run by secret police of the AMA, with its implied interest in keeping you around the wards as long as possible.

Ole was dressed in his patched flannel suit and he was clutching a copy of *Better Homes and Gardens*, the only reading material around. A small flask of schnapps bulged from his jacket pocket.

'Vot the hell you been up to, boy?' Ole said gruffly, the way he used to when his nephew had been caught throwing snowballs at cars, but there was real concern in the set of his eyes.

'Dey find your truck this morning in Plymouth. Someone borrowed it. *Ja*. Dey left a note to say tanks . . . I thought you vas in New York! Fer gosh sakes!'

So the groundhogs had gotten a jump on their long hitch home. More power to them.

The sun was giving the cranberry bogs outside a good scrub, cleaning the air till the bogs sparkled scarlet.

'How long have I been here?'

'You came in yesterday.'

'Then it's – Friday already?' The old man nodded.

'Get the nurse, Ole. Let's get this thing out of my arm. I want to go back to the house. And then, oh Christ, I have to see Marie. And then I want to sleep for a week, in my own bed.'

He gave an apologetic look to the unconscious man dying beside them. 'Let's get out of this damned place. *Nurse!*' He noticed the bell push next to his head and rang it.

The nurse protested and went to get the doctor and the doctor refused categorically and finally made him sign a form when Larsen threatened to sue the hospital for false imprisonment. He had to wait while the nurse delivered the balance of a course of tetracycline pills, and then submit to interrogation by the credit department, which seemed to equate existence as a human with possession of a driver's licence.

But finally he was out, and half an hour later he was home slugging a shot of Ole's aquavit for strength. Over the old man's protests he took Ole's station wagon and drove the six miles to Marie's house. He wanted to see her and tell her what had happened. He wanted to tell her in person. Then maybe everyone would leave him be and let him sleep.

She was alone, watching the soap operas. She looked much fatter and even more tired. The morning sickness had been worse than usual.

Larsen told her briefly what had happened, how the contact had been a dead end and how his Fulton enquiries had ended in violence. Marie was predictably horrified, but Larsen pleaded illness and left before she could start crying murder again. His strength was ebbing, and he headed home and passed out on the couch in the living-room with the salt marsh peeking at him through a window.

As he slept, the accumulated doses of tetracycline did their

169

trick. The unreal technicolours of fever mixed into more natural tones.

Larsen slept through the rest of the day.

When he awoke it was twilight and Ole was teaching someone with a river of red hair down her back how to use the drink-mixing machine, God help him; every time Ole used it he managed to blow all the fuses.

Larsen thought for a moment that the fever dreams had returned.

She was wearing tight jeans that did wonders for her ass and a very loose black sweater that did nothing at all for her small breasts.

'Ask it to make a rum toddy,' Larsen called from his supine position on the couch. His voice sounded faint and remote to his own ears; his head was still a little light. But that sensation-stretching phase had passed and Larsen could feel from the stickiness of his own body and the moistness of his blankets that the fever had broken as he slept.

'It's only a second-level program,' Larsen continued as they turned to look at him, 'so you have to specify rum, dark, one shot, to water, hot, two shots, and add your own lemon juice, sugar. But it will work. All the buttons are there. Just don't let Ole push them all at once.' He paused for breath, still weak.

Blatchford walked over and looked at him.

'What the hell have you been up to, Larsen?'

'I went to New York, I got mugged,' Larsen grinned up at her. 'Country boy goes to the big city and gets rolled. Old story.'

'It's a little more complex than that, from what your uncle's been saying.'

Larsen looked over to where Ole was studiously pouring himself a shot of Aalborg.

'You been shooting off your mouth again, Ole? What do you know about it anyway?'

'I tell her vat you been yellin' about it in your sleep all night and all day, when you vere sick,' Ole shouted, his half-shaven face suddenly angry. 'You fool kid. How you go about asking questions on vat is not your business? How Joe

170

Sciacca has been murdered? You never tell me, *ja*, but you never said it was a secret either.'

She sat down on his precious Nain rug in a manner so smooth and graceful it seemed as if the long legs had coiled themselves independently like cobras.

'You never told me about the threats to Sciacca, or about these Italian names,' Eliza Blatchford said. 'Or that Marie Sciacca thinks her husband was murdered!'

'For chrissakes, man,' Larsen yelled furiously at Ole. 'You want all this in the papers? You want me to look like a complete idiot?'

The old man stomped out of the room, slamming the door.

'Lars,' she said.

The green eyes were looking unprofessional.

'I won't write about this if you don't want me to. I promise. He was simply angry and concerned for you, and it all spilled out.'

'What all spilled out? What are you doing here anyway?' Larsen refused to be mollified.

'I called to see if you were around, I wanted to ask you something, and Ole told me what had happened. So I came over after work. That's a horrible wound . . . I watched your uncle change it. While you slept,' she continued. 'He's better than a doctor.'

'He was a volunteer in the Winter War, in Finland, in '39,' Larsen said. 'He saw plenty of wounds then.'

'I thought he was Norwegian.'

'He was, but he volunteered. He fought with the Finnish ski commandos – the Sissi Joukkeet, they were called – against the Russians. That's his rifle,' the fisherman added, pointing to the mantelpiece. 'It's a Krag-Jorgensen. He can hit a fly at fifty yards with that thing. I've seen him do it.'

'You say that proudly,' the woman said.

'He might as well be my father. Did you mean what you said about not writing about – what happened to me at Fulton, about Marie's crazy theories?'

'I meant it. I'm involved – a little beyond just the journalistic side,' she said. 'I mean, I've spent a lot of time,' she finished lamely.

Larsen thought for a moment.

'Well, I'd like to talk about it,' he admitted. 'I've been dreaming about it, with the fever, to the point where I'm not sure what is real and what isn't any more. The rum toddy's ready,' he said, hearing the click. 'Let me –'

'I'll get it.'

'Then if you're ready to promise you won't write about it,' Larsen said, 'I'd like to talk this over. I'll sort it out in my own mind.'

So Larsen talked. As he talked and sipped hot rum the strength came back to his voice, and he sat up on the couch. The shoulder still hurt but he found that he could now move his arm within a forty-five-degree arc on either side of the perpendicular. Perhaps the wound was not as deep as he'd thought.

Eliza Blatchford sat quietly on the rug as he talked. She listened well, like Per Larsen, and presumably for the same professional reasons: journalists, like good lawyers, were fundamentally investigators, and the primary art of investigation was to make people talk, and then listen hard to what they said. Her eyes would flick occasionally from Larsen's face, storing a question or recording a fact for later. She gave short, quick nods of encouragement, asked an occasional fast question.

But she'd said she wouldn't write about it. What made that so important: the implied lack of professional self-interest?

As the fisherman went back over the facts for the fourth time in six days, the questions posed by the facts, the vast gaps between those facts sifted and settled themselves in Larsen's mind until he found he could evaluate the problems more clearly and explain them more simply than he had with his brother or O'Malley.

Finally Blatchford said, 'Let me see if I've got it straight. Sciacca is warned off the fish project. By his old man. Then he gets threats. His vessel sinks and disappears in calm weather. A mysterious radio transmission mentions this LuGuercio. We find his boat, sunk but with no detectable damage. Right so far?'

'Damn,' Larsen interrupted, 'I still haven't told the Coast

172

Guard we found it! She's still officially listed missing. Did you write your story yet?'

'It's coming out on Monday. Now, where was I?' Blatchford continued.

'When we found the boat.'

'Oh. Right. Then there's another threat, right? Sciacca's friend, that's you, goes to Fulton where Sciacca's father worked, and starts asking for LuGuercio and another name mentioned in connection with the threats. Sorry if I sound like a wire dispatch . . . The next night some fish market people try to kill him – you. Right?'

'It sounds incredibly circumstantial,' Larsen said.

'I don't think so,' she retorted. 'As Al Capone said, "Once is coincidence, twice is something else, three times is enemy action."'

'But look at the holes,' Larsen objected. 'One, if someone did kill Sciacca, how did they do it, in the middle of an ocean, when no one knew exactly where he was to begin with? Two, why kill him at all if they really wanted to get their "insurance policy" back? Three, why would anyone want to kill me at Fulton? How the hell would they know who I was?'

'You're missing one thing.'

'What?'

'LuGuercio. The name in the transmission. The fellow you met at Fulton Fish Market knew him. There's a connection there.'

'I didn't miss that,' Larsen countered, 'but I don't know for certain that he did know him. He said he knew LuGuercio, then he led me out to the meat hooks like a long pig to the abattoir because I thought he knew where LuGuercio was. But it might have been a trick.'

'But if he didn't know who he was, why try to kill you?'

'It just doesn't add up, Eliza. It's too loose.'

She was looking at him as if he were a difficult squiggle of trigonometry to be solved. It made him uncomfortable.

'What?' he said.

'I think you just pretend to be dumb sometimes, so you don't have to deal with people.'

'Sez you.'

'You know, I think you're forcing yourself to believe it's all coincidence. I think you're afraid of the consequences if Sciacca was murdered.'

Larsen snorted derisively, then lay back on the couch.

'Oh, I still don't mean physically afraid,' she said, her eyes looking even more bottomless. She had her leg bent in front of her, her forearm on the knee and her chin on the forearm. 'I mean afraid to get trapped into some involved situation where you might be forced to come out of your little world and commit yourself to something. Like finding out who killed your friend, Joe Sciacca.'

'Come *on*,' the fisherman exclaimed. 'You'd never print a story with facts as tenuous as those. No responsible journalist would.'

'No. But I sure as hell would start checking it out.'

'What're the police for?' he asked petulantly.

'There isn't enough evidence for the police. They have to justify their expenses to the council, or the state, and without either more facts, or a more visible threat, they cannot, and will not, do anything. I know them.'

'And you know me so well?' Larsen asked angrily, turning on his side to observe her better.

'No – but it fits what you yourself told me.'

'What did I tell you?'

'That you fear being tied down and forced to do something you don't want to do. Forced by powerful circumstances that remain beyond your control.'

'Bull – *shit*!' Larsen stated, full in her face, deliberately, but he was thinking back: was he really fooling himself? Did the weight of evidence really point so decisively to murder? The inconclusiveness of the facts was matched only by the number of pieces of suggestive evidence. They were still going in circles.

'Lars. I think you're proving my point. I think there is something in you that you try to hide, to repress, when you get angry like that.'

'Jesus Christ. A fucking pop psychiatrist. And what, pray, are you hiding, Eliza Blatchford, when you fly off the handle, as I have known you to do, every so often?'

174

She had the same trick as Marie had, of looking straight in your eyes, a little sadly, and remaining silent, to score a point. It was very effective at a range of one foot.

A rebuttal suggested itself naturally.

Larsen leaned over on his right elbow and kissed her briefly, hard and full on the lips.

Her lips did not respond, but neither did she turn away.

'What was that for?'

'It's something I've been wanting to do for a while now.' It was only as the words came out that he knew them to be true.

'Why?'

'Don't you ever stop asking questions?'

'Should I?' she said, echoing the Jewish joke.

'I don't understand it.'

She looked at him steadily.

'You don't understand it?' she repeated.

Then she leaned forward and kissed him.

'What was that for?' he mimicked.

'I'm not sure. Perhaps I'm becoming a little infatuated with you.'

'Why don't we stop playing games and say what we mean to say?'

'I suppose you expect me to come right out and admit that I love you? It's not true.'

'That's not what I meant.'

Larsen pulled her towards him, bringing furious protest from the nerves in his shoulder. Her hair smelled of honeysuckle and her lips were softer than a pillow's dream.

Larsen looked at Eliza Blatchford and they both chuckled, a little incredulous, as if someone had told them a quaint but impossible tale.

'Let's let things take their course.'

She watched him, doubtful again.

'Stop arguing,' he explained.

'Okay.'

'Will you stay for dinner?' he asked in mock formality.

'Depends on what you have to offer.'

They ate baked beans with hot brown bread, fried cod

cheeks and tongues, and home-made goat cheese courtesy of Ole, who had taken one look at the situation and disappeared in the direction of the VFW bar. They washed it down with chilled Sancerre and a background of Big Mama Thornton.

She claimed to like the blues, she said she enjoyed smoky white wine. It might even be true.

A warm feeling like internal bleeding started to sneak up around Larsen's stomach, spreading upward and downward.

Afterwards the fisherman showed her his house. The old brasswork he had salvaged from the wreck of the *Portland*. The armchair made of driftwood. The sail-powered longliner plans and the blueprints for a computerized chart scanner that would store nautical data and update them by radio-telephone. The scoter duck Ole had carved, the scoter that almost breathed, and the stormy petrel he could not quite coax into movement from the cherrywood it was born of.

'You're wrong,' she exclaimed. 'It's flying. It's beautiful.' She seemed to mean it, which proved she was either a great actress or a lousy critic.

It might have been the wine, or perhaps the same warm feeling that was flowing through Larsen was spilling over into the woman.

They went back to the living-room, hand in hand like two high school kids and sat as close as possible, watching the flames oxidize beach wood into blue and green, recreating Stone Age necessities.

They kissed again. He could barely feel his shoulder now. The strength of another, longer kiss flowed from lips to neck and down their arms. The fisherman's hands grasped her waist and followed the tense curve of her buttocks. They were locked into each other's curves and the softness between her thighs met the hardness between his. The strength increased and the fire burned hotter and more distant at the same time.

Larsen unpeeled her sweater and the T-shirt she wore underneath.

He had trouble pulling the clothes over her shoulder with one hand. He snagged her hair in a twist of wool, overbalancing trying to free it, put his weight on the bad arm and toppled over like a dressmaker's dummy. Very romantic. They both tried to remain serious and both ended up laughing.

The essential ridiculousness of sex arose against passion, but retreated in the face of overwhelming odds. His eyes drank in every detail of her body as if it was unveiling secret messages of instantaneous truth that only he could decipher.

She was breathing rough, watching the fire. Her neck was arched, making dark hollows under her collarbone.

They were both naked and lying on the rug, past the stage of practical indignities. Being melted by the fire. They moved slightly as by some untraceable alchemy of movement she pulled him down, the valley resisting, deepening and then accepting him into her. The final riddle was solved. She moaned softly as they began moving, deeper and more in tune with a single song, thrusting the rhythm. The flames worked and he reached deep into her body, filling its every space, turning into a molten pool . . .

He tried to slow the reaction and then she caught up with him again, softer and harder and quicker and quicker, his own hoarse mutterings merging with her low cries until they were being poured together in a crucible of passion, liquid and movement fusing at the ultimate centigrade and they were forged into one tension as they climaxed, almost together.

He thought she called his name and she thought he called hers.

The feeling was still there, later, as they lay cocooned in a down quilt on Larsen's bed, watching frost rise on the marsh. She was turned towards the window and the fisherman was fitted deeply into her waist and knees. Far away a police siren howled, a mechanical coyote.

'It's hard to grasp this,' she mumbled.

'What?' he grunted, trying not to disturb the feeling. His shoulder was hurting again but pain had not risen back to the first stage of consciousness.

'You and me, like this. We fought so hard against it: it seems unreal. And then with all the mystery around *Marie*,' she went on. 'It's a fantasy within a dream.'

'Reality's relative, 'man,' Larsen said facetiously, a

fake acid-head whine to his voice. 'Turn away for, like, a moment of space-time, and events have already realigned themselves—'

'It makes sense,' she continued sleepily. 'I don't usually do this. Hop into bed, I mean. First date, so to speak. But suddenly it changed, seemed totally inevitable . . . One of my ancestors was a witch,' she mumbled. 'Maybe I knew it would happen.'

'Bet you say that to every guy you sleep with.'

Beyond the marsh, the wind was whipping up whitecaps in the dark. Her breathing became a little longer and more even. Eliza Blatchford had gone to sleep.

The phone pried him loose from his own dreams at midnight, letting the wonder flow back in with annoyance at being disturbed. He padded naked to the phone in the study. Calls at this hour should mean trouble but they usually meant O'Malley had found a good party.

It was O'Malley.

It wasn't a party.

'Lars. You're back.'

'Yeah, Sage. What is it?'

'What happened with Marie?' There was a diamond-hard quality to his voice.

'Marie? Marie Riley? Nothing. What do you mean what happened?'

'You don't know?'

'What do you mean, I don't know? I don't know *what*? What's the matter with her?'

'She's dead, Lars. Lars?'

'*Dead*? *Marie*? Oh, no – no, man. *How*?'

'You didn't do it,' O'Malley said with certainty.

'What the fuck are you talking about, I didn't *do* it?' he cried angrily. 'What happened to her?'

'Listen. The cops think you killed her. Her house was burning and the firemen found her. She'd been stabbed – with your knife. And the neighbours said you were over there around the time she must have been killed. They only just identified the knife. It's your sheath knife.'

Larsen let the horror run its course through him so as to

let logic jump it from behind. He could hear O'Malley repeating his name, Lars, Lars, are you there, but he let the emotions run through him and then felt his own instinct for survival catch and hold and start assessing the situation.

Marie! Kindness. Grief would follow later, when there was time.

'Sage?'

'Are you okay?'

'Sage. This is a frame-up.'

'I guess it has to –'

'No. You listen. You remember my telling you about Marie's theories, about the threats?'

'Lars, you have to –'

'Wait a minute. I got back from New York last night. I mean, two days ago, now. Someone tried to kill me in New York at the Fulton Fish Market. I told you they want something of Joe's, something connected with his father. I still don't know what. But they must have made the connection between Joe and Marie and me. And I lost my knife down there, when they ambushed me. It's a frame-up.'

'You'd better tell the cops all this, right away.'

'I wonder how thorough they were,' Larsen mused.

'Lars. They'll be there any minute: you should forestall them.'

'How come they're not here yet? How do you know all this before they've even got here?'

'I keep trying to tell you: there's a police cruiser in front of my house, blocking the road. It's Scotty Lynch. I know him. I was doing some toot and finishing some writing when he pulled up.'

'Get on with it,' Larsen snarled.

'I asked him and he told me all about it. Poor security. They know you're at home and they're just waiting for the Staties to back 'em up. They don't like to tackle anything bigger than old ladies by themselves. But if you go yourself, to the police station, it'll help you later.'

'No. I'm getting out of here.'

'Lars! Shit, man. Listen to –'

Larsen used his pain and rage to rip the phone violently from its jack.

There was a movement behind him. He turned. Eliza Blatchford was standing at the doorway, pale and naked.

'What is it, Lars? I heard you talking . . . is it bad news?'

'Oh, Eliza,' he said. The despair in his voice made her come over next to him.

'They've killed Marie.'

'They've killed –'

'Marie. Joe Sciacca's wife.'

'Oh, my God.'

'And they used my knife. The one I lost at Fulton. The police are coming over right now. They said – they must have done it right after I was there.'

'Who was that?'

'O'Malley.'

Larsen strode past her and down the stairs. A couple of embers looked at him with orange eyes. He grabbed his pants, and went back to the bedroom. She was still standing in the doorjamb, hugging herself against the cold. He threw on socks and woollen underwear.

'What are you doing?'

'Putting my clothes on.'

'You know what I mean.'

He came over to her, buttoning his shirt.

'I'm going to leave. Fight back. The only way I know how. I'm not waiting for them to come and throw me in the slammer for two weeks while they figure out I didn't do it. *If* they figure it out. Somebody has been way ahead of me on this, way ahead of Marie and Joe, too, all along.'

'You're not going to give yourself up?' she interrupted.

'No, I'm going to hide out for a while.'

Her whiteness bled tension into the room.

'You're running away again,' she stated flatly. Her voice was noncommittal. The contrast with the warmth that had been there before made her tone cruel.

He was dressed now, taking a thick wool sweater and black parka from the clothes locker. Fat leather ski gloves. A woollen watch cap. Finally he reached into the depths of the cupboard and pulled out a small duffel bag – his escape bag. He'd never had to use it before.

She was shivering in front of him.

'I want to know. Please tell me.'

'What?' He did a rapid checklist of items he would need. The tetracycline. He tested his shoulder: it ached, dull but manageable. He was still lightheaded, a little weak, fever on the way out. He'd need the pills. Christ, they'd be here any time now.

'On whatever there is between us – on whatever there could be – tell me if you really killed her.'

He froze.

'How can you even begin to think that? You must know how I feel about her.'

'Most murders are between people who loved each other once. The fact that you're running makes me think you did this.'

'Eliza,' he said. His voice was desperate. 'If you don't believe me I don't know if it matters what I do. I swear to you on everything I am, on everything your instinct tells you I am, good and bad, that I did not kill Marie. You *know* it, deep inside.'

'I had a feeling of death about this right from the beginning,' she said. 'Oh, why didn't I listen to myself?'

The horror was coming back in her words.

Unsanctioned murder was the ultimate act separating man the social animal from the society that gave him expression. And separation was the ultimate penalty: whether in exile, or jail, or death.

Innocent or guilty, society was putting him beyond the pale tonight and that terrible loneliness became complete at the thought of losing Eliza if she did not believe him. Eliza Blatchford. Only yesterday he would have laughed. The sadness and the wonder.

'Think, Eliza. Think!' he urged. 'Look at how it was done. Look at it like a journalist. Think of what you know about me. Ask O'Malley, Silva, anybody. But don't kill what we may have found. I feel like –'

Far away, the sirens yelped.

He hefted the bag in his hands, bent to kiss her statue. Was that a small response?

'I'll be back.'

He remembered to take the tetracycline from the kitchen table. The back door slammed and he was inside the night, smelling it like a fox would, becoming part of it. Cold.

He had sworn he would never do this again. Never!

He allowed himself a final, luxurious squirt of self-pity, let it change to anger, and ran lightly towards the salt marsh, eyes in tune with the dark. In jail he would have been helpless, trapped, at their mercy. Here he could meet the enemy on equal terms, in the secret ways.

He headed straight for the ocean.

CHAPTER FOURTEEN

No starlight penetrated the low cloud cover. Deep in the salt marsh, he could see only by interpreting the gradations of purple and black, each hue denoting a different distance between his eye and the object perceived.

The fisherman's boots crunched through thickets of cat-tails and sea heather on the borders of the marsh, through the long rustle of Spartina grass, then mud, eelgrass, and mussel shells crackled underfoot as he approached the deep channels that sucked and soothed and made the sea linger when it came and went with the tides.

Larsen knew every creek and island and sandbank of the marsh. In the old days the wetland had been the core of life for Mallebarre, providing fodder for livestock, grass for insulating houses, game and fish for food, and compost for gardens. It contained natural slipways to build, and harbours to shelter, the sailing ships that carried produce to Boston or left to fish the shoals off Cape Cod. Some of the fastest clipper ships of the last century had been built on a marsh like this one, a few miles down the coast in Dennis.

Now it was treated as a wasteland. Few people ventured near it except to dig for clams. Federal laws prevented building there so even the real estate developers ignored it, except when they could term it 'ocean view' or 'access to water' for houses they were selling nearby. Only a few kids who lived next door regularly explored its treacherous mudflats and quicksands, and Larsen knew the marsh better than any of them. He had fished it since he was a child, warding off the loneliness of an orphan by foraging for the raw materials of eel stew, or deep-fried whitebait and cold boiled crablegs, or razor-clam chowder, sea-robin-wing fritters and blue-mussel pie and all the other delicacies no one else bothered with.

Jules Island. The Stoneyard. Phillis Island. Heading west

and north, guided by the sodium-pink glow of the town on clouds behind him, skirting ripe tidal creeks when he could and fording them in numb feet, boots and socks laced around his neck when he could not, he would come to the dunes of Dead Neck Beach. Even if the the police Alsatians followed his scent through the Spartina, they would surely lose him when he went down the intertidal zone of the ocean beach. The tide was rising and would cover his tracks within a half hour.

Once he looked back towards the spit of land that sheltered his house, his home his father had bought and built on, but the drizzle that had just resumed obscured all detail and he could see nothing but four lighted windows. Three more than when he had left.

Eliza!

A guided tour through heaven and hell within six hours.

The woman would have no trouble convincing them that she had nothing to do with the murder. She had been at the newspaper all day. But Larsen had to grit his teeth when he thought of the indignities they would subject her to.

'Just *good* friends, huh, Ms Blatchford? He mention anything when you were in the *sack* together? You good in bed, Ms Blatchford?'

In the bored and unimaginative gestalt of the Mallebarre cop, there was room for only guilty and innocent, virgin and whore.

After the hard man–soft man questioning, the trick statements, the insinuations, would she still accord him the benefit of doubt he had felt in her lips?

She had to. If she had felt the force of the new reality that brought them together as he had, she would at least give him a chance. The contrast between the opiate of infatuation and the depressive effects of social ostracism was too harsh – even for rich summer kids.

When he started slithering his way up the dunes that separated Dead Neck barrier beach from the marsh, he realized how much of his strength had gone with the fever. He was not tired, yet. But there was mushiness under the muscle fibre where there should have been a solid feeling of force in reserve. The bag weighed only fifteen pounds but it was starting to drag at his fingers.

Far behind him some dogs began to bark.

He plunged down the seaward side of a dune, scattering a herd of deer that had been feeding in a copse of white pines. They disappeared like wraiths in the soft needles. A driftwood shack lay silent and black on stilts in the sand. The O'Malleys' shack, he remembered with shock. Summer barbecues and greenhead flies. The smell of coconut tanning lotion and the taste of soda pop.

Sage's parents had treated him like a member of the family. They would be reading about the murder in tomorrow's headlines. He climbed hard up the next bank of dunes to put the thought out of his head, submerge it in his pounding heart and straining lungs. At the crest of the dunes, the Atlantic spoke gruffly to his ears, whitecaps grabbed at his eyes, and he breathed the ocean's rich smell.

The sea was a familiar refuge, but he could not turn to it tonight. *Sofia* lay too far down the coast, probably under police guard. He turned away from his boat, westward, down the beach and towards the continent.

He spent an hour dodging waves on the sand, then plunged along the mud canyon sides of a tidal creek, heading inland, away from the ocean as town-owned land gave way to burning windows on the beachfront. The universal signal of home lights in the darkness only underlined his outlaw isolation: lights were now a finger pointing. Larsen slipped carefully under a culvert leading beneath Route 6A. He'd evaded the dogs long enough. He struck out across wet meadowland.

Using side roads, diving into soaking undergrowth when headlights split the darkness, he finally hit the railroad tracks.

Once, long ago, Larsen remembered getting off the train in West Barnstable with his family. The little pagoda station had seemed carved in snow. The train had huffed white stream, the conductor had a pot-belly and a turnip watch. He invited you through a silver door and the world had been a magical bustle of laughs and frost and red-and-green Christmas lights.

Then the New York, New Haven and Hartford Railroad had stopped the passenger trains, bankruptcy had stopped the New Haven, Penn Central had absorbed the system, and the government had absorbed Penn Central. Now only the odd freight, humping lumber for developments, used the rusted tracks and rotting, weed-covered sleepers. Washington had taken over the railroads but its heart was in the highways. The old sinews of a younger America grew older gracefully among the gravel and louseworts.

One day the inevitable suburbanization of Cape Cod would put it within the grasp of Boston's subway-commuter train system and the right-of-way would be fenced off. But for the present, the deserted railroad tracks still provided a clear path westward.

In Barnstable, Larsen had to skirt the floodlit area of 'The Hill', where a county jail nudged brick and barbed-wire elbows at the tracks. And farther towards Sandwich the railroad line left county woodland and began to weave in and out of too many backyards, not all of them belonging to summer folk.

Larsen left the track and struck out again cross-country towards the electric power lines, rejoining the woods. The power lines paralleled the Mid-Cape Highway, two swathes feeding Cape Cod with its electrotouristic lifeblood.

The bag grew heavier as Larsen slunk across the twin macadam ribbons of highway, across the service road and over Discovery Hill. His socks were soaking in muddy seawater, his hands and face were raw from constant collisions with pitch-pine needles and maple twigs. Twice he tripped over fallen trees and sprawled full length, crying out as his shoulder jerked. There was an occasional growl as a truck coasted down the highway at Shoot Flying Hill. A Howard Johnson's now decorated the ridge that Puritan refugees had used as a navigation marker.

His breath was coming in short bursts and sweat had returned from the pain in his side when a lightening in the bushy darkness at last defined the cleared firebreak at the foot of Com Electric's power pylons marching to the canal substation. Another two and a half, three miles to the canal. He stopped to change into dry socks and down another tetracycline tablet and then pushed on down the eroded, scrub-ridden strip below the towering totems to consumer power.

Far away in the direction from which he had come, a helicopter stuttered and threw around whiskers of light in the drizzle.

From here on in, the high-tension wires would be crossing the combined Army, Coast Guard, and Air Force bases of Otis and Camp Edwards. The old man who presently occupied the White House had been steadily bloating the military budget in the face of perceived menace from old men in the Kremlin, but Larsen devoutly hoped it did not as yet extend to Jeep patrols on power lines.

It was four a.m. and still dark when he finally stood on the bluffs overlooking the Cape Cod canal.

Behind him, caged transformers hummed love songs to the pylons. In front of him the canal lay inside the hills that cradled it, hills made of excavated earth and now covered with pine trees, bait shops, and motels. The electric wires themselves swooped from a very tall pylon on the hill on his side to a very tall pylon on a hill on the other and then disappeared into Plymouth County.

The canal stank of military geometry. It was paralleled by a concrete service road on each side, and its banks were sheathed in rock and gravel. Its black 200-yard breadth was picked out by arc lights, and radar scanners placed at intervals along its length told the US Army Corps of Engineers headquarters in Buzzards Bay exactly what was happening on its every square inch.

The Army Corps had built this waterway during the worst years of the Depression, partly to provide work for the many unemployed in New England. Because it was a strategic ship route, amputating the peninsula neatly from the mainland and providing an alternative to the long and dangerous trip around Nantucket Shoals, the Corps operated and maintained it now.

The canal and the two massive hunks of suspended grey-painted steel that spanned it were a symbol of Cape Cod's isolation in the off-season. Natives who thrived on that isolation referred to trips to Boston or even Plymouth as 'going over the bridge', and disliked doing so. Many became anxious as soon as they had crossed to foreign territory – the serious cases avoided it altogether.

To those on the wrong side of both water and the law, the canal and its two public bridges symbolized something other than isolation. If the bridges were blocked, or watched, the Cape became one long trap to which the canal was the tripping mechanism. Larsen knew there was no way you could swim that strong tide in late November.

Larsen slid and jumped to the bottom of the bluffs, crossed the Bourne–Sandwich road and cut through trees and bushes to the railroad tracks that ran along a service road to the canal. These tracks were a continuation of the line he had quit earlier when it had started to detour through Sandwich. Once again he adopted the stride length that would keep him stepping easily from sleeper to sleeper in the darkness. Telephone poles along the gravel bed pegged his progress.

Ahead a flow of streetlights arced into the air and back on to the continent: the Sagamore Bridge, built 1933–1935 and also operated and maintained by the Army Corps. The Cape side of the Bourne Bridge landed in a roundabout three miles from here. The Upper Cape barracks of the Massachusetts State Police lay by the roundabout. It was a simple matter to shut both spans within minutes. He could find out if they were guarded by simply climbing up the bluff to bridge level and peering around the sign that told would-be suiciders to call a number in Hyannis. 'Depressed?' . . .

He wouldn't even have to make the climb. As the fisherman strode methodically nearer, a glow of parking lights could be seen to outline a State Police cruiser, waiting with headlights doused just over the bridge's arch, in a position where it would be invisible to anyone driving from the Cape side. Larsen could see it through the seppuku-prevention fence. Reflexes melted him into the shadows of a bush, then he continued, slowly, hunching where there were gaps in the strip of woodland that separated the tracks from canal and bridge.

He'd never known the bridges to be watched before.

The railroad line ran in a black tunnel under the bridge abutments, continued northward towards Sandwich boat basin and the power plant, then took a slow curve to the east, towards Mallebarre. Larsen left the tracks at that point, to squat well hidden from arc lights and scanners.

If the bridges were closed, there was only one way off the Cape.

He threw a branch in the canal and it moved southwest. The tide was on the ebb. He knew from the tables that it would not change here, near the waterway's eastern end, for another three hours, well after sun-up.

Decisions were easy when choices were scarce.

Larsen followed the tracks towards the power plant. The primitive bulk of oil tanks, generator housings, transformers, pylons, and smokestack loomed threateningly above. Once past them, he turned left at the first level crossing, towards the harbour.

She was a converted schooner, canoe bowed, fifty feet, tender, half-rotten and beat to hell, and Knut Nilson loved her. Larsen slipped quietly from the dock to the scalloper's deck, borrowing darkness from shadows. He checked the wheelhouse but the door was padlocked. No one aboard. He headed forward to unlash the dinghy stowed forward, paused, and came back to the wheelhouse.

Four humanoid shapes grouped behind Knut's barometer had given him a better idea. With a silent apology to the fat Dane – one of the Cape's best fishermen – Larsen pried open a window Knut could only keep shut with a wedge of wood and crawled inside.

Twenty minutes later Larsen half slipped, half waded into the canal's deep tide, holding the escape bag above his head. He was far enough seaward of Sandwich basin to be invisible from the plant. The canal entrance light only caught his figure once every six seconds, and the smash of waves on the jetty's nether side drowned what little noise he made.

The survival suit was thick and warm, and covered his

whole body except the eyes. It kept him afloat, even with his arms uplifted, and made him feel huge, but even so the fierce tide took the fisherman in its grip and spun him around into the salty blackness as if he were a chip of balsa wood.

Its power was awesome. Larsen kicked as fast as he could inside the thick neoprene, but he was only thirty feet out by the time he was swirled back up the canal, past the lights of the Coast Guard office, the fish freezer, the power plant.

He kicked harder. He was getting nowhere. There was a series of huge 'dolphins' downstream, thick pilings used for mooring tankers, that he did not wish to collide with at five or six knots.

Ahead, the Sagamore Bridge reached out of the night in a leap of roadlights. Still in the same place, four parking lights bore witness to police vigilance: a car was stopped at the checkpoint.

Then the dolphins shot past, five feet away, water creaming around their corded timbers. A back eddy pushed him out towards the middle of the canal as he passed under the bridge.

Maybe they would have looked down to spot Knut's white fibreglass dinghy, Larsen thought as he drifted silently under its huge mass, kicking stubbornly for the canal's other shore, but the radar scanners would never spot a dark head drifting by on an ebony current.

Larsen touched bottom three miles down.

He clambered up the rock escarpment, took off the survival suit, weighted it with stones, and let it drift into the night before setting off once again on foot.

It was eight a.m. and as light as it got on an overcast day just this side of Thanksgiving. The rain had stopped.

Larsen had trekked from his landing point back to where the power lines jumped the canal, and he resumed his hike westward across from where it had first been interrupted by the waterway.

Half a mile of deep glens, wild oak, and cedar growth later, he came to a triangle of cut brush that ended in a typical New England grade C roadway of bumps and potholes accentuated by asphalt. The fisherman's compass showed it running roughly east and west.

Back to civilization. He headed west, away from the sunrise, past a pipeline station and a sheep farm. It had got colder with the dawn, somehow, and his shoulder ached. Dead leaves skirled across the roadway in a freshening wind.

At a quarter to nine he strode into Bill's Variety Store, a low, concrete, cinderblock affair of the type that both blighted and served every excuse for a crossroads in America, keeping the surrounding citizenry supplied with menthol cigarettes and chocolates, pretzels and *TV Guides* and other wholesome things. Bill's advertised 'ICE: cube and blocks', 'PINBALL', and 'Telephone' to the congregated bungalows nearby.

He could call Eliza at work. It was Saturday, but she worked Saturdays, he knew. Calls coming into Ole's or Silva's phone might easily be traced, but a newspaper received hundreds of calls a day and they'd have no way of knowing which was his.

If she didn't tell them.

The public phone was slung on the concrete walls; telephone numbers were scrawled at random around it. One read: State Police, 759-4488. He got change from Bill and dialled the *Sentinel*'s number.

'My God!' she whispered in a shocked voice. 'You!'

'Me.'

'Are you all right?' Her voice sank even lower. Larsen could imagine other ears listening in the newsroom. He heard a typewriter clacking in the background.

'Where are you?'

Larsen tried to talk as normally as he could, slurring the syllables just a little to make them unintelligible to Bill.

'I can't really talk but I need to know something.'

'What?'

'Eliza, will you give me help? Today? On the basis of what I promised you?'

The typewriter clattered on.

'If you can't,' he continued insincerely, 'I'll understand. But I want you to tell me, yes or no, now '

He felt like he was talking to dead air: her silence was more than an absence of words.

'Eliza, I have to do this my way. I have to be able to prove I didn't do it. Well, okay, maybe not, maybe I'm wrong. Tell me, you must be working on the story: has some new evidence come to light that points to someone else? Or was the frame as comprehensive as I thought it might be?'

He took the continuing silence as confirmation. Then she said, 'I'm not working on the story. Sam's furious. He says I'm too involved already. He's spiked my whole story about finding the wreck of the *Marie*. You might have cost me my job,' she added bitterly.

'Am I right?' he insisted.

'Your uncle swore up and down you didn't do it, and I told Ames – the detective – what you told me, but – '

'Ames? Did you say Ames?'

'Yes.'

'Great.'

'What?'

'Nothing.'

'Well, anyway,' she went on, 'you're right. There's no alibi for you, and no indications of its being anyone else. As if that proves anything. I mean, if you were the murderer, it would be a cute ploy to convince me that the more facts point to you, the more likely it's a frame-up.' Her voice sounded sad; there was a knot of fatalism in the grain of it, a knot of 'I knew this would happen'. After all, what else could you expect from a local yokel?

'If I was that cute, do you think I'd leave my knife lying around?'

'Oh, brother.'

'Eliza, do you believe me? Did you check it out, logically like a reporter, as I asked you to?'

'I checked it out. I went to the cops this morning with Gary, who's doing the story. Sam *loved* that.'

The telephone asked Larsen to sacrifice another dollar-fifty to Ma Bell. They waited as the coins were digested in a series of metallic gurgles.

'Will you help me?'

'Why me? Why not ask your friend O'Malley? Or the mate on your boat?'

'Because you're the one I really want to believe that I'm telling the truth.'

'And their home phones might be tapped,' she said sarcastically.

'And their phones might be tapped. But I still want you to believe me. More than anyone.'

'Horseshit.' She did some deep breathing and came to a decision, largely, Larsen thought, just to get him off the phone.

'All right. But after this you're on your own. What do you want me to do?'

Eliza Blatchford had worked up a pressure head of fury by the time she met the fisherman late that afternoon. She got out of her rented Ford and slammed the door hard enough to make the small car cringe and rock on its springs.

Larsen had told her he would meet her at the Bay Café in Buzzards Bay at three p.m. on the dot. He got the café's number from a local phone directory, and at three p.m. paged her at the café from a public phone booth at the crossroads near Bill's. He told her to meet him at Bill's at three-thirty.

He watched the crossroads carefully from the phone booth as she flashed by in a streak of blue and chrome. At three-thirty he called Bill's, asked for a distraught-looking redhead, and told her he was at the crossroads.

There were no Staties, no town police cars to block off the intersection leading to Bill's. She had not told the cops, and she had not, as far as he could tell, been followed.

'If you don't trust me, why ask for my help?' she yelled at him. Her freckles burned red with emotion.

'You don't trust me either, Eliza,' he said sadly.

She looked around disbelievingly at the grey intersection, the tacky plastic gas station-cum-convenience shop next door, at her own presence. She was a long way from Chapin School. The eyes flashed like welding torches but they still struck the same sparks against his own.

193

'You look wonderful.'

'Shove it.' The Chapin faculty would have died. 'Why *should* I trust someone who runs away from a murder rap, and then claims he didn't do it!' she yelled.

Larsen repeated his promises as he drove her to the Plymouth and Brockton Street Railway bus terminal at Buzzards Bay. She glowered, silently now, the whole way. As they pulled up to the combination of greasy spoon and news-stand that doubled as the bus station, she said 'Lars' in a hard voice.

'It's only because we fucked together that I'm doing this,' she continued. 'I just can't bring myself to believe that my sexual antennae were so out of tune. I can't believe that infatuation was so out of line. It's my sense of reality I'm trying to save, to believe in,' she babbled. 'It's pure egoism that's making me break the law like this.'

She got out and tried to break the door again, then motioned for Larsen to lower the window.

'I guess I *must* believe you,' she said. 'Take care of yourself. But you have to stop running sometime. If I don't hear from you within a week I'm telling the cops what I did. You'd better figure something out by then.'

'You'd be aiding and abetting,' Larsen called after her. 'It's a felony.' Then he put the car in gear and drove away. He tried not to look in the rearview mirror at the bus terminal as he stopped at a red light and rolled the window back up.

He was unsuccessful.

CHAPTER FIFTEEN

Larsen was filling the rental car with gasoline at a service station on Broadway in Cambridge, Massachusetts, when the AM radio changed his plans for driving to Canada.

It came at the tail end of a newscast designed to provide background to commercials for stereo tape decks and force-fed turkeys. The announcer's first words after the commercial break catapulted Larsen's stomach into his craw.

'State Police have a new lead in a brutal murder on Cape Cod. Police investigators now believe that fisherman Larry Larsen, suspected of knifing thirty-two-year-old Marie' – the announcer stumbled – 'uh, Skiassa, yesterday in the town of Mallebarre may have escaped the scene in a rented car.

'The murdered woman was three months pregnant at the time of her death. Police say her house was set on fire immediately after the fatal stabbing yesterday afternoon. Firemen responding to an alarm found the body in the burning house.

'Skiassa's husband was lost at sea and presumed drowned when his fishing vessel disappeared last week. The murdered woman was a former high school sweetheart of Larsen's.'

The insinuations continued. 'News radio KZH has learned from federal sources that the US Drug Enforcement Administration has also expressed an interest in the missing fisherman.

'State Police have asked motorists to be on the lookout for a rented blue Ford Escort, licence number 636 CDA. Police ask that you do not attempt to interfere with or contact the driver of this vehicle in any way as he is considered armed and extremely dangerous. Anyone seeing this car should contact State Police immediately. Do you have problems keeping those pumpkin-pie stains off your dentures?'

When the news bulletin first came on, Larsen turned the

volume low and checked behind him. The attendant was busy doing a jig and slapping his gloved hands together to keep warm and probably couldn't hear the radio playing inside his small glass cubicle. A large, muscled woman in a soiled Exxon boiler suit was eating macaroni salad with a plastic spoon from a plastic bowl and didn't look up once. Maybe it was a different station.

He'd have to ditch the car now. The pump gagged on gasoline fumes, stopping automatically. Larsen gave the pimply kid a twenty-dollar bill and resisted the impulse to take off. He had to act normally, fade into the background, not draw attention to himself by leaving sixteen-dollar tips to filling station attendants.

The kid brought his change. Larsen nosed into Broadway, turning back towards the centre of Cambridge. He cruised into the comfortable streets between Broadway and Massachusetts Avenue where grad students and classical musicians, associate professors and museum curators raked dead leaves into piles beside their angled Victorian houses. School was in, and there were no legal parking spaces between the maples of Frith Street.

He, the illegal one, had at all costs to stay legal. He had more luck on Dana Street. He took a pair of boatman's pliers out of his bag, unbolted the licence plate from the car, and walked around the block. He picked up an old VW van with a faded 'Dukakis for Governor' sticker and a flat tyre. Unlike the bolts on the new Ford, these were rusted solid, and even with pliers it took ten minutes to remove the van's plates. Once he had to dodge around the car to avoid a pair of jogging students. They were women, plain enough to be Cliffies.

But when he had finished he had an innocent licence plate to fasten to the wanted car's rear bumper. He threw away the hot plate.

He walked around slowly in the evening, one eye out for Cambridge police, collar turned against the chill as much as against identification. The cold seemed to have dried up the rain – now it felt like snow. Somewhere in his bowels a black worm wriggled and munched on his insides, leaving only an emptiness where before there had been substance.

Eliza Blatchford must have turned him in to the State Police. She had not given him the seven days she had promised, she hadn't given him the chance to prove his innocence and salvage her sense of reality, her pride in judging people. Pah! The memory of her eyes, her profile, sharpened in his mind to reveal the cutting edge of beauty.

A phone booth across the street beckoned, one of the old kind, with folding glass doors that kept your whole body out of the wind.

This was tapping deep into childhood, Larsen thought as he groped for a dime. But in the old days he didn't have to dial information to get Per's number.

'Hi?'

It was one of the kids. His voice came ragged, pure and soft into a world that seemed all dark and dirty.

'Jason?'

'Hi.'

'It's Lars, Jason. Your Uncle Lars. How you doing?'

'Hi?'

'Can you get your dad, Jason?'

'I'm going to be a turkey in our Thanksgiving play.'

'That's good – can you get your dad, Jason?'

'My – dad?'

'Yes; your dad.'

The phone crashed, and Jason's small voice said, 'It's Uncle Lars.' A minute passed, then another, and Patty Larsen came on, her own tones more country club than usual.

'Hello, Lars. Peter can't come to the phone right now. He said –'

'Patty, it's really urgent, I have to talk to him.'

'I'm sorry: he said to call this number and he can talk to you later.'

'Patty, please.'

A pause. 'Where are you?'

'Let me talk to my brother!'

'I'm sorry . . . you have to understand, Lars. After what you did – think of the position you put him in.'

'But that's just it – I didn't do anything!'

197

'He says to turn yourself in, first.'

'And the number?'

'It's the State Police office.'

Larsen hung up.

Ten minutes, twenty minutes, striding the streets of Cambridge, his shoulder beginning to protest every pace. The neighbourhoods changed, Portuguese, Italian, student. He bought a quart of Appleton's rum at a Jamaican-owned package store and sent a tetracycline tablet south with a draught of the fiery liquid. It seemed to deaden some of the shoulder pain and dissolve the last tightness in his throat.

Eliza, and now Per.

He did not consciously seek out the student streets by Inman Square, but familiar details occasionally registered until with a jolt he stopped in front of a varnished wood sign swaying in the bitter breeze.

Bilbao Coffee House.

The lump in his throat came back. Marie would have trusted him, Marie would have known. But Marie was dead, and if he, Larsen, hadn't been so bloody stubborn, blind, stupid, lazy – too lazy, too afraid to pry his ass out of the easy, comfortable routine, the fishing, drinking, dreaming, sleeping rural rut he had melted into, too afraid to look at the clues, the signs, even for a woman he had loved –

They had shifted the tables around and added ferns, but that was the corner they had once filled with unhappiness towards one another.

'*You call it independence, preserving your freedom. But it's cowardice.*'

But what could he do now? He found himself arguing with the memory of a dead woman, his face numb against the cold and yellow light that streamed from the Bilbao's windows. The frame was too perfect – every piece of evidence pointed straight at him. And he couldn't prove his innocence from Walpole prison.

'*It's really self-pity. It's weakness, Lars.*'

He could go the route they used to take draft resisters, he thought defensively. North through Maine. This far from the Cape he might, with great care and a couple of underground-railroad tricks, risk the bus. Then, the abandoned cabin they once used as a safehouse. Nathan's trail across the border. Once in Canada he could hide under his fake passport until the heat had died down and the short memory of the media had replaced his face with others.

'*Why should I trust someone who runs away from a murder rap?*'

Other faces blurred behind condensation were staring at him. How long had he stood there? He couldn't feel his cheeks any more and it was beginning to rain. He picked up his bag and walked down the street, stiffly.

Bus or car?

Lazy.

North or south?

Afraid.

The shame came burning like rum at his gut, but in the end it was common anger that made him take the most desperate route of all.

CHAPTER SIXTEEN

Shelby Street, East Boston.

Dollar Bill's Quality Used Cars/30-Day Guarantee still flew the plastic pennants, still asked no questions when Larsen put down $695 in cash for a green '71 Chevy Impala with temporary dealer plates and a rusted fender. Bill pretended to be entirely preoccupied with the Red Sox draft choices and a case of pastrami-cheap-cigar-and-coffee heartburn.

He sat there, looking like an overweight, undermoraled Airedale while Larsen signed the sales form and the title transfer and the state tax form and the excise tax slip with an assumed name. He said something about returning the dealer plates, without much conviction. Larsen took the keys and drove away into the smelly night.

The price was high but it represented – for a few hours, at least – anonymity. As he accelerated away Larsen gratefully discarded the cheap horn-rim shades he had bought at a nearby drugstore, and dragged from around his gums the slimy wads of rolled newsprint he had wedged there to fatten his jowls. He grimaced as he licked the sores they had caused. He had not shaved since New York and soon his beard would be long enough to dispense with this masque altogether.

At nine-fifteen p.m. he reached the Sagamore roundabout, where a State Police cruiser still hunkered on the mainland side of the Sagamore Bridge. Larsen drove slowly around the roundabout, watching as a car started climbing the span from the mainland side. There was a brief sparkle of blue and white, a flashlight pointing to the trooper's boots. The car stopped.

Larsen took the southbound road that paralleled the canal, driving past a hillock that marked the spot where he had thrown Knut's survival suit back into the tide. He could not repeat that trick this time: Sandwich basin was the only harbour and it lay on the other side.

He reminded himself to send Nilson some cash, anonymously. Same story on the Bourne Bridge. There were two cruisers there, 69ed in profile behind the suicide fence. At least no one would be taking the final plunge tonight, Larsen thought. He knew at least four kids from school, whipsawed between alcoholism and winter unemployment, who had taken that way out. The easy way.

Behind the Bourne Bridge, vaguely etched in the haze of lights that marked the town of Buzzards Bay, lay the railroad bridge. The hard way.

Of all the symbols that marked Cape Cod's estrangement from the mainland, the railroad bridge – the third, forgotten bridge across the canal – was Larsen's favourite: two huge, wrought-iron towers, complete with latticework, little cabins with windows, and capped with fairytale pointed hats with huge steel balls set shining at their top. Between the towers was a movable span with a set of railroad tracks. The span was lowered electrically to mate with tracks on either side when a train was due. The rest of the time it hung in mid-air, impassable, a final feudal redoubt for the vanished railroad barons of America.

A fantasy bridge. You could almost imagine little railroad gnomes with long beards and sleeper spikes living in the towers, hiding from the cars and tourists. At nine-thirty p.m. no trains were expected and the span was up.

Larsen's original plan was to climb the 200 feet of wet ironwork to the raised railroad span, walk across the span, and clamber down one of the Capeside towers. From a distance, the bridge had always seemed a sort of adult jungle gym. The elfin towers extracted any hint of seriousness from the climb.

Up close, the latticework still appeared intricate enough to provide easy handholds and footholds up the towers to the span level. But now problems became apparent. The first section of webbing to the top of frames bracing the tower from the landward side was uncomfortably close to live electric lines that powered the bridge's lift engines.

The latticework of the towers looked negotiable, except for three sections where horizontal main beams were riveted into the webbed columns that stood on each corner of the square hollow towers. The beams and girders had been fastened together with large steel gusset plates that completely covered the latticework for what looked like seven or eight feet. In that space, a man climbing the tower would have to haul himself up by two smallish drainage holes spaced three feet apart from each other.

All with one shoulder that would not take much abuse.

Finally, the fisherman's eyes picked out a glow of light in one of the tower cabins on the other side of the canal. Night light? Or Army guard? He would have to climb around and behind those windows on his way down, assuming he made it that far.

On the other hand, it was almost ten p.m. The darkness would last another seven, eight hours – all the time in the world. He could take it easy, take his time around the difficult bits.

The fisherman opened his pack and took out a coil of Manila rope. A quick double bowline turned his travelling bag into a backpack, and he stuffed the rest of the line back into the bag.

He followed an aluminium walkway next to the tracks as far as the tower – twenty feet ahead the tracks stopped abruptly where the water coiled and gushed, black and cold below. He deliberately ignored the sinking feeling that had oppressed his gut since the first sight of those gusset plates and began climbing. There was no alternative.

Almost immediately he wished he'd risked another route. The latticework was not horizontal but fastened in diagonal Xs between vertical joists in the tower corners. The narrow valley of the X pinched the sole of his boots at every step.

And it was starting to drizzle again, an insidious rain that permeated everything.

But his shoulder was the worst. It had stiffened badly since Cambridge, so that he could not raise his left arm over his head. So the left forearm had to clinch his body upright, next to the tower at waist level, while his right arm groped for the next handhold, and his left foot felt for the next X. The bullwork of fishing had given Larsen strong arm and shoulder muscles but his good right shoulder was already beginning to feel the strain.

Ten feet up Larsen stopped and painfully shrugged off his travel bag. He had maybe one and a half feet of clearance between the bare electric wires and the tower's support frames. He inched up one more step and gingerly pushed the bag over his head to rest in the cleft of an X above. He twisted his knees sideways to flatten haunches and torso against the tower, notched his left toes in the next foothold, and, calf muscles quivering, straightened his body. His chest was through with an inch to spare.

He brought his right foot up to the same hold as his left, let the right foot take his body weight as the left found the next X, and repeated the manoeuvre. His upper foot was slipping; he couldn't jerk upward as instinct prompted him or he would push himself into the wires. He heaved with his right shoulder and for a second time the load came off his feet entirely and he swung, arcing backwards from the wire, a mere inch away. He could almost feel the searing explosion of backlogged protons, then his right foot grabbed again and he lifted his hips up and out of danger. Two more steps and his feet were clear of the electricity lines.

Larsen rested for ten seconds, as long as he dared, then looped the bag around his right shoulder, and climbed again. Right hand, right foot. Left hand, left foot. Pause. Start again. Moisture was at last penetrating the thick leather ski gloves. Cold. The first gusset plate was just above him, the hole in it three feet from the nearest handhold.

No time to think or philosophize about the danger involved. Holding on with his left arm, he brought his torso as high up the plate as he dared, ignored the pain and reached with his right. Securing a firm grip on the lowest curve of the first drainage hole, he hauled himself up till his feet were wedged in the last space in the latticework below the plate. His waist was now at hole level. There was barely enough room for both hands to hook into the steel circle. Don't think of the drop. No more handholds, only the second hole above his head, so high above him he could not use his left arm at all when he pulled himself up to it. His whole weight would be on the one arm as he hung jackknifed over the canal, trying to find the lower circle with his foot.

The wind wept and tugged at his jacket.

He stretched his body upward, groped with his right hand, managed to crook his fingers in the lip of the upper hole.

Larsen's face, pressed flat against the steel plate, had a fly's eye view of a large rivet one inch away. His breath was coming in gasps. He let go with his left hand, bringing his body slowly up, up, to a level where he could arch his waist and fold his knees, scrabble with the toes of his boots, higher, higher. Then his toes found an opening. One final heave and his waist was at the level of the upper circle. Now he could bind his body to the tower with the left hand and, letting go with the right, reach for the top of the gusset plate. No problem. His right shoulder was holding up, for now. He repeated the procedure and the shoulder only grumbled a little when he finally got his whole body on the latticework again.

The canal looked as if it were miles below, inviting in its promise of peace: *don't look down!*

Another thirty feet to the next plate, the last on this tower. Larsen climbed as far as the plate, rested for a minute, a wingless bug on an iron wall. Then he began the same routine. Right hand, heave, grab with painful left, body aching to tumble outward, end over end into the uninvolved tide, jerk up the right arm to the next hold, quickly to relieve the worsening ache in his left side.

When he heaved again he suddenly found that his right glove had picked up a smear of greasy dirt on the inside of the last drainage hole. Before he had time to accept the implications, his fingers had slipped out of the upper hole and he was falling, falling the 150 lethal feet to the canal through high-voltage wires. The black water would be like cement from this height. As he began the long drop an instinct for survival tore through the pain inhibition and his left hand, still anchored in the lower circle, bent his wounded shoulder through the vertical, holding fast to the lower hold just long enough for his greasy right hand to grip, his entire body hanging once again from his hands, swaying from the three feet of free fall. But his right hand was slipping again and though he hooked his fingers into steel claws he doubted the left would hold after his right went – 'Marie,' he found himself gasping, then his feet notched into a pair of crossed girders and relieved the stress. It was only then that he caught breath and yelled, hard enough to rasp his voice pipe, hard enough to cut through the red haze of a pain that offered unconsciousness like a Christmas present.

After another minute the trembling subsided and his heart rate dipped below 100 beats a second. He carefully wiped the grease from his gloved fingers, reblanked his mind and inched upward again. There was no more time to spare for repose, no time for thought. His right shoulder could take another minute of this punishment, no more. He made it over the next, and last, gusset plate inside five minutes, and stepped methodically higher, to span level. He twisted his feet and his right arm around the corner pillars and swung on to the crossbeam, then crawled on all fours to the handrail on the elevated span. He pulled himself across to an aluminium gangplank that served as a walkway when the span was in the down position. His knees were under control now, but his shoulder throbbed.

He sauntered across the walkway on the raised span, as unconcerned as if he were strolling down Main Street. The aircraft warning beacons on top of each tower suffused him periodically in a pink haze of light. If the US Army could see him, it was too bad. But they'd be fools to look, because only a fool would attempt what he had done.

A kind of desperate elation coursed through his body as he walked. It was, he knew, a classic reaction to near death, the nerves having tightened to the breaking point as they awaited the absolute finish of everything: then the reprieve, the biological joy of knowing those nerves had another chance at sending messages. Just being alive was enough for now. It was more than Marie had, or Joe. His fever was returning; he was sweating and his knees were trembling. He swallowed another tetracycline with gulps of rum, and suddenly realized that alcohol was undoubtedly countering the antibiotic's effects. Against all instinct and upbringing he heaved the warm sun of Jamaica, as alchemized by the Appleton's company, over the bridge railing into the night.

Joe would have approved. Joe never drank much himself – too busy scrawling plans in his logbook. The image of his friend scratching at the logbook on his kitchen table came unbidden into Larsen's overheated brain. The logbook. Where Joe kept his most important papers. Where else would he keep the 'insurance policy'? At last things were falling into place.

Before beginning the climb down, Larsen broke out the Manila line and cut off three ten-foot sections, put double knots into the three strands at two-foot intervals, and hung them from his belt.

When he got to the first gusset plate, he fastened one ten-foot length to a crosspiece with a bowline, let it dangle, and then slid from knot to knot, braking the descent with feet, knees, and right fist, until he was back among the easy footholds of the latticework lower down.

Holding on awkwardly with his left hand, he threw the slack Manila back overhead until, on the third try, the coils went through the latticework on top of the plate and hung inside the framework of girders. Virtually impossible to detect from the ground. He went through the same motions over the second plate.

Then he was at cabin level. The lights from the grimy windows below seemed brighter now, but they were brightest at the southern corner of the tower. That was different, Larsen realized. Surely they had shone at the northern end when he first checked out the bridge from the other side of the canal. Someone was inside.

Luckily, the cabin rested on crossbeams riveted to the *inside* of the tower's four columns. The stairway leading from cabin to track level was too close to the doors and windows to use, but he could probably continue his path down the outside section of column without much fear of detection.

He stepped gently, easily down the latticework. At eye level he noticed a shadow playing on the dingy walls and controls inside – a small movement. He kept going. His head was about to sink below window level when he realized that he could see clear through the cabin to a window on the other side. In that grimy glasswork was the reflection of a tubby man in an orange jacket. The person was hidden from view by an electric panel. He was reading a magazine. Larsen kept going. No one but the Army kept guard from inside a lighted room.

Long John Silva's abode overlooked a small pond in Mashpee, a town divided between the wealthy, white, 'planned community' of New Seabury on the coast and the poverty-stricken black, Indian, and Cape Verdean community inland.

The Wampanoag Indian tribal council was continually suing to regain some of the land the Indians had sold to a Rhode Island corporation that owned New Seabury. The recurrent legal range wars kept real estate prices depressed in Mashpee. Four years ago Silva had managed to acquire several acres of undeveloped woods at a good price with the help of Moloch Bank and Trust.

Larsen approached Silva's ranch house around the other side of the pond. An owl hooted and branches waved threatening claws. He waded through banks of their brittle leaves, guided by white windows and the black tunnel of trail.

It had taken Larsen two days and a night to walk here, following the railroad tracks and power lines, living on checkerberries, tetracycline, and rainwater. He had spent one day by a tiny campfire, sleeping off his high temperature. Now fever had been replaced by the lightheadedness of hunger.

If Silva's truck had not been there he would have turned back: the weather seemed decent enough for the mate to have taken *Sofia* out, and he didn't know Dolores well enough to trust her: she occupied that odd social no-man's-land that men reserve for the wives of friends. But the long-range forecast might be different, probably was. He could see the green cab, the plywood sideboards in back. Dolores' car was absent.

A bluish-grey light held sway over the picture window in

the den. Larsen could see his mate slouched in an armchair, watching TV with no company other than six-packs of beer and a half-empty bottle of Wild Turkey. Something had happened to his sober, serious mate, one-beer-a-night Silva. Very odd. Silva was fully dressed, but watching him at home from the shadows of stripped winter bush was like catching a glimpse of red-polka-dot underpants at a cocktail party. Homo Domesticus Americanus, totally defenceless in his mortgaged keep.

Larsen went up and knocked on the picture window. Silva looked shocked when he recognized him through the reflection. There was almost a quality of fear to his movements when he stood, a trifle unsteadily, and hesitated. The hesitation hurt. Then he waved towards the kitchen door.

If Silva called the cops, Larsen would have no time left to run. Larsen measured the seconds but the door opened too quickly to include a phone call.

'Hello, John.'

'Larsen.'

'Can I come in?'

The mate hesitated once more, then stood aside. Larsen caught a strong whiff of Budweiser and old garbage as he passed Silva in the doorway. The sink was piled high with dishes. Toy trucks, spaceships, and Barbie dolls littered the floor. And newspapers.

'Local Fisherman in Murder Hunt.'

'Police See Drugs Link to Mallebarre Murder.'

'Search Continues for Murder Suspect.'

He had become something of a celebrity.

Larsen walked to the side of the kitchen away from the shouting newsprint.

'Where's Dolores?' he asked.

'With her mother. She took the kids.'

'Betty Lou?' Larsen queried sympathetically. Silva just looked at him, standing next to the closed door as if wondering whether to block his escape.

'Looks like both our lives are in a mess, Long John.'

'What the hell do you want here, Lars? Where the fuck have you been?'

Larsen did not answer immediately, but hitched his hip on to the kitchen counter in a move that put him deeper into Silva's psychological territory. A difficult move: he had to position his right cheek between half a stale pizza and a plateful of ancient angel food cake. Then he gave Silva a summary of events of the last few days.

'John, do you believe this?' Larsen finished, waving at the newspapers and knowing the answer. 'Do you believe I killed her?'

Silva made a gesture of dismissal with a can of Budweiser.

'Maybe – no – I don't think so, anyway.' His face was shut. 'But what the hell are you *doing*? Why did you run away? Well, if you really want to know, that makes me think you did it, know what I mean? Now you're back, though, I guess I don't know.'

'You, of all people, should know how I felt about Marie.'

'Sure, sure,' the mate said, crossing to the fridge. 'Beer?'

Not a sign of acceptance, but an automatic, Mediterranean act of hospitality.

'No thanks.'

'Yeah,' the mate continued in a frozen voice. 'But people get upset, do things without meaning to. You might have wanted to go out with her again, sleep with her, man – now Joe was dead. It's natural, anybody can get all excited and frustrated. She slaps you, you hit her back,' the big hands paddled the air, 'she starts callin' you names, and before you know it she's dead. My God, I almost beat the shit out of Dolores last week: I didn't, but I felt –'

'John.'

' – like just beatin' her senseless. I think you should go to the cops and –'

'John!'

' – give yourself up.'

'Listen to me!' Larsen shouted, slipping off the counter. 'Think about me, think of what you know about me.' This approach hadn't worked with Eliza, Larsen thought as he said the words, but then she hadn't known him like Long John. 'Would I lose my temper like that? Would I kill Marie

Riley, of all people? For chrissakes, would I do it with my own *knife*?'

'Why didn't you turn yourself in? They would have listened to you – your brother's a district attorney.'

'My brother – my brother has changed, somehow. He's become a government man. He wouldn't listen.'

'Maybe once you had turned yourself in –'

'Fuck!' Larsen yelled, wishing all his friends could take him on trust, on all the subliminal bits of information about a person that made up the inner level of logic known as intuition. It really hurt, dammit. 'I'm so sick of this.' He punched his fist into the wall so hard the knuckles cracked. 'First Eliza Blatchford turns me in, then my best friends don't believe me! Didn't O'Malley *tell* you what went down in New York? He said *he* believed me.'

'She couldn't have turned you in.'

'Screw her. Do you believe *me*, what I say?'

Silva swigged some beer.

'Do you?'

'Why did you come back?'

'I don't really know.'

'And what's New York got to do with this? Just because you got mugged –'

'I got mugged by Fulton people, Long John! I left my knife there! The same knife they used on Marie.'

Silva just looked at him over the rim of a Bud can.

'I did some thinking on the way back here.' Larsen rationed the words out, deliberate. 'It came to me when I was trying to climb the – never mind. But I didn't know why I was coming back at that point, except that I missed Marie like crazy and I wanted to do something to whoever killed her.'

Larsen paced up the kitchen, skirting a toy crane.

'She used to accuse me of running away from life, Long John, you know that? And I thought she was full of shit. And now, here I was: I had refused to believe her when she told me she was being threatened, I acted condescending, right?'

He was pacing faster.

'And then they killed her. Just like that. Marie. She was

so innocent, so – kind. She was pregnant, goddammit! And just because they rigged it to make it look like I'd done it, I ran away.'

'Well,' Silva said, 'you would have just gone into the slammer. You always said you'd kill yourself before going to the slammer.'

'That's irrelevant. I loved the woman. Maybe not still in the old way – oh, I imagined maybe I did, in a lazy sort of way, she knew that about me, too, damn her – until Eliza came along, and I realized it wasn't the same, but it was stronger than just, you know, falling in love with somebody. It was, I don't know, deep and strong as the tides, a kind of friendship and trust.'

'Slow down, man. You're making me nervous.'

Larsen walked over to the table, pulled out a Pall Mall, lit it with hands that shook imperceptibly, then leaned against the wall.

'Anyway. That's why I came back. But I started thinking on the way. I really had no idea what the fuck I was going to do. And I suddenly had a flash about where that piece of paper, that insurance policy Marie was talking about, was.'

'You think that's why they killed her?' Silva asked.

'Her, and maybe Joe, too.'

'They killed Joe, on his boat, on Asia Rip, and then they killed his wife and burned her house on the offchance they would find that insurance policy or whatever that Joe got from his father?'

Cold disbelief still stiffened Long John Silva's vocal cords.

Larsen shrugged. 'It would have to be some sick kind of animal to do that, just on the offchance. Or else, the "insurance policy" would have to be real dynamite to scare them that badly. Marie suggested Joe was using it to force them into letting us try the direct-sale scheme. But I can't think of any other reason.'

'So you find the piece of paper – what are you going to do then?'

'I find the "insurance policy" the New York people are looking for, and do a deal with whoever ordered Marie killed: Marie's killer for that piece of paper. Or at least

211

proof someone else did it.'

'Uh-huh. You don't care if they killed Marie. You just want the police off your ass.'

Larsen felt the anger come back, like boiling vomit, but he swallowed it down.

'I care, John. I care. But first things first, man. I can't do anything about the sonsabitches while people like you think *I* killed Marie.'

'How you gonna find it? The insurance policy?'

'I think it's on the *Marie S*. In his logbook.'

Silva nodded. 'He kept everything there. Even his birth certificate. But where's the logbook? I mean, how do you know –'

'I'm pretty sure I saw it in the wheelhouse when we dived on the *Marie*, just before you got narcosis. I saw something with the right shape, anyway.'

'You want to go back and dive on it? Count me out, man.' But there was the idea of a smile on Silva's lips as he said it.

'I'll dive on it alone.'

The mate walked carefully over to the refrigerator, leaned against it as if he truly needed the support. But when he spoke again, the ice in his voice had broken.

'Okay, okay, Lars. Man, I'm sorry. But this on top of Dolores, I don't know what to think any more. Plus, you know they're sayin' the federal drug people are investigating you? 'Course *I* know that's bullshit.' He threw the half-empty beer in the sink, came over and grabbed Larsen's hand. 'Sorry, skipper. We go find that logbook, pal, we go tell the New York boys, then we go to the cops, okay?'

He looked hard into Larsen's eyes. His own were very bloodshot, and his breath was rancid.

Larsen filled his lungs, slowly, from the side of his mouth. 'Okay, as soon as I know that it's going to work, that someone else takes the rap.'

'Fair enough.' Larsen had passed a test of sorts. 'You want something to eat? I got seven different kinds of TV dinners. Turkey, Salisbury steak, chicken cutlets – what's the matter?'

'What did you mean, she couldn't have turned me in?'

212

'The journalist? She couldn't have, because she got busted for helpin' you, renting that car. It was in the papers, even in her own paper as a matter of fact.' Silva chuckled, opened a flat, frozen pack of pork and mashed potatoes and sweet sauce, licking his thumb when it slipped into the sauce. 'Her father come down 'n' got her out on bail. Rich people. You sure you don't want some of this?'

It was typical of Long John that the fact he was aiding and abetting Larsen and risking the same penalties as Eliza simply did not cross his mind once he had decided to trust Larsen again.

It was eight p.m. but Larsen felt like the sun was rising on some inside horizon.

'Call her up for me, Long John.'

'Her?'

'Yeah. In case her phone's bugged.'

'My own phone's making funny noises, know what I mean?' Silva said, tapping the side of his nose significantly.

'Jesus. Well, don't say who you are, pretend you're a friend. Just to see if she's there. The number's in the book. I'll go knock on her window.'

'My God, Captain, you really are sweet on that broad. You poor son of a bitch. You don't even want to stay and eat my home cooking?'

Silva called and exchanged impersonalities with the unemployed waitress who shared her rented house.

'She says she's at her father's for dinner.'

'Thanks, okay.' Larsen made leaving movements, edging closer to the door. 'Let's plan to leave tomorrow night.'

Silva said, 'It's not going to be easy. I mean, the barometer's okay, but I think they've got somebody watching the boat.'

Larsen whistled, in some awe of the measures taken against him. 'At night, too?'

'I don't know. There've been cops walking along the bulkhead, checking when I've gone down there in the daytime. They've never done that, even when someone was ripping off electronics from the boats last summer. And someone was using a pair of binoculars from the point.'

'When was this?'

'Two, three days ago.'

'Have they tried to stop you from going out?'

'Nope,' Silva said, 'but I didn't try. You never told me.'

'You know it's your boat to run, whenever I'm away.'

'Yeah, well, then there was . . . this whole Dolores thing. I've made up my mind: I've got to get her back, I'm not seein' Betty Lou again.'

Larsen thought for a moment. 'I don't know what choice I have, *hombre*. Maybe they've given up by now. Maybe they were just making sure I wasn't on the boat. I have to dive on it,' he added.

'Don't worry – I meant to tell you,' Silva said. 'They came with a warrant and searched her, the next day.'

'Maybe they've given up by now. Anyway, I have no option. I have to risk it.'

Larsen outlined the steps Silva would have to take while he stayed in hiding: fill up with fuel, buy supplies, more lube oil, take the boat to her mooring as if putting her away for a time, and rent two sets of double scuba tanks. No bait, ice, or Billy: there would be no fishing this trip.

'Leave the dinghy at the usual float. We'll use one from the yard.'

'Where are you going?'

'To get another diving partner, chicken,' Larsen said, helping himself to the stale pizza to eat on the way.

'Your mother, Larsen.'

'Yuh muthah.'

Larsen got the Blatchfords' address from the phone book while Silva popped another beer. Munching pepperoni, Larsen went back into the cold.

Oyster Island was a millionaire's beach colony you reached by crossing a causeway and obtaining clearance at a manned checkpoint.

The Island, however, remained an island. Larsen nosed the boatyard's dinghy deep into the eelgrass of Schooner Cove, on the east side of Oyster Island. There were few lights shining in the expensively spaced summer mansions that

214

lined the bayside. He shipped oars and oarlocks, blew on his frozen fingers, and hauled the boat a little higher in the grass.

The Blatchford house was a huge, rambling, shingled monster, built by Victorian capitalists for Edwardian domestic staffs. The maids would have an entire wing and there would be space above the garage for the downstairs elite, butler and chauffeur, just down the privet hedge from the laundry house where gardeners could flirt with scullery maids before the house guests called for minted tea with their croquet.

The grounds were sculpted in the old style, with yew trees that had once been carved to resemble roosters, cracked marble fountains, and peeling gazebos. Here and there, behind a hedge or between a pair of dogwoods, a classical bust made believe this was all Italian opera, commedia dell'arte, Goldoni farce.

Or *Romeo and Juliet*, thought Larsen, hiding behind a rhododendron that had been dead for years, watching an orange window where Eliza was sitting amid a forest of oaken wainscoting. '*Deny thy father, refuse thy name* – ' The wainscoting, like the rest of the house, looked in need of some repair.

She was sitting immobile. A shadow within the room used her lack of movement as a focus around which to spin a series of gesticulations and pacings.

A woman came through the door. It was a face familiar from the village. She put a plate of sandwiches and a glass next to Eliza. The shadow stopped until the door closed again.

At one point, Norton W. Blatchford came and stared sightlessly out the window, moving his lips off and on. A nondescript figure in houndstooth business clothes, with a hint of fat at the throat and waistline, more than a hint of tension in the angle of his shoulders and neck.

Half an hour later, it began to sleet. Ten minutes after that Eliza stood and left the room. A table light next door came on, then went off. She was standing in the room again, looking very small and slim and with her back straight as a dragoon in the blurred window. She moved her lips, tossed

215

her hair like nailing a flag to the mast, and disappeared.

The fisherman had to cross some exposed lawn to find her again in a second-floor window, behind a small porch at the far end of the house. She was pacing alone. This end of the hacienda was brick, but the heavy ivy that almost covered the wall would never support his weight.

To the left, however, was a greenhouse that reached halfway up to a dormer roof over the first floor. The wooden gutters looked old but massive, and a dark windowsill right over the greenhouse would give him a leg up in between.

By the time he'd reached the porch and clambered over the railing she was seated at a small rolltop desk, writing almost as furiously as she was puffing a Camel Light. His knock slewed the woman to face him as if he'd slapped her, pale around huge eyes, pen lifted to write words on thin air. She sat for a minute looking fear in the face and then crossed swiftly to the porch door, unbolted it, dragged against a warped frame, and leaned out, eyes tuning to the darkness.

They stared at each other for twenty seconds till her growing night vision confirmed her suspicions. 'Larsen,' she hissed. 'Goddammit, why don't you leave me alone?' Then, 'You'd better get in here.'

He came in shaking sleet from his forehead. The room was hot. He peeled off his parka. Books, perfume bottles, more books, blue and white watercolours, a picture of Whipple, her father, her mother, someone else – a brother perhaps.

She rebolted the door and drew the curtains, picked up her cigarette with hands that trembled, delicate. But she leaned with studied nonchalance against the doorjamb.

'So you came back.' He nodded superfluously. 'Like a thief in the night. Why?'

'I decided to stop running, as you recommended. And I want to ask you a question.'

'What?'

'Did you turn me in? Did you tell the State Police about the rent-a-car?'

She shook her head. 'No.

'It was pure, lousy, bad luck,' she went on. 'The Staties knew you'd evaded their dragnet. They knew you hadn't

216

taken your truck or your boat, so they checked all the automobile-rental places, and the Mallebarre detective, Ames, recognized my name. They came for me at the paper.'

Jimmy Ames, Larsen thought. Old school grudges died hard.

She was staring at the wall, cheeks flushed with the memory, smoke dribbling now like lifeblood from her lips.

'I've lost my job. I went to jail. My father posted bail: five thousand dollars for aiding and abetting a fugitive. He is, naturally, absolutely furious.' She mimicked, "What will the golf club think, after all?" The fact that I'm not married is reprehensible enough.' She looked at him again.

'Incidentally, if he finds you here, he'll call the cops. So now, Larsen,' she said bitterly, '*now* what do you want from me? I'm not sure what I have left to give.'

She repeated the question ten minutes later, when he thought he'd explained what he wanted.

'Why do you need me? Anyway, I have to report to the state DA's office every week. My father's lawyer thinks he can easily get me off on probation. You know, foolish young girl swayed by dashing scoundrel, juries eat that sort of thing right up, they've seen it all on the soaps.' Humiliation, acidlike, corroded the words even as they fell from her lips. 'I've given you my job, I'm not going to the jailhouse again for you, I can't come and dive with you on that wreck.'

'We'll come back in ample time for you to report.'

'No, Larsen! No! I've got to separate myself from you.'

She mashed out her cigarette with a short, violent stabbing movement, like stamping on a tarantula.

'You might be in danger,' he said.

'I saw that movie.' She threw jagged glances at him, openly mocking.

Larsen picked up a volume – *The Oblivion Seekers*, by Isabelle Eberhardt – and turned it in his hands.

He said, 'If you still believe what you told me – about having too much of yourself invested in my good character –'

'Don't put words in my mouth. You're misquoting me.'

'Let me rephrase that. If you still have anything invested

in – your own belief in my honesty, then you have to believe someone else framed me.'

She did not nod.

He put down the book.

'Now *you* come on, Eliza! Look at the facts. If someone did murder once, or twice, to find this insurance policy, they'll do it again. For some reason, they're not prepared to take the slightest chance of its being found.' His fist tapped the wall gently in rhythm with the inductions. 'Chances are they killed Joe. I did not accept that until recently. They killed Marie because she was connected to Joe and they framed me because I was connected to Marie: can't you see where you might be vulnerable? You're the next link up the chain.'

'That is entirely predicated on whether my intuitions were right about you, lover boy.' Her cynical tone mocked the endearment. She looked far out the window into the rain.

'You're thinking that whenever one human kills another without a reason that is accepted by his, or her, society, there is always a neighbour, or parent, or lover to say "Oh, not our Bobby! I don't believe it! He was always such a good boy!"' Larsen found himself pacing back and forth, and forced himself to stand still. She kept counting the raindrops on the porch.

'But it wasn't their human intuition that was at fault, Eliza,' he continued softly. 'It was their energy. Most people don't have the time or desire to really think about anyone who does not belong to their family. Husband, wife, or kid. If they took the time, they would always find the sign that denotes a murderer.'

'The mark of Cain?'

'No, more the mark of Son of Sam, or John Hinckley, or Richard Speck. A deep hurt that cut him off from people long before he went to high school. I don't have it. I respect your intuition enough to know you know that.'

'You seem amazingly well versed in the subject of murderers.'

'I've known a few. But you can see the signs, almost as

218

deep, in ex-cons who've done a lot of time, or sometimes in army conscripts. The mark of the cut-off.'

'Since you bring it up, Larsen,' she said, swinging around to face him and folding her arms, 'there's something in you, okay, maybe not in your eyes but in what you say and what you don't, that cuts you off from me and from others. Your past, for example. You're a Cape Cod fisherman who indulges in long-winded philosophizing, who quotes Shakespeare verbatim. A simple yeoman type who always keeps a suitcase at hand ready to escape from the cops.' She snorted. 'An innocent skipper the Drug Enforcement Administration seems very interested in.'

'If you come to Asia Rip with me, I'll answer every question you have on the subject of my shadowy past. I give you my word.'

She flicked on the green high beams.

'Can't you see where I'm scared? If you're not what I think, but just an unbelievably fluent liar, I'd be heading out to sea with a murderer who last week knifed a pregnant woman.'

'And if what I tell you is the truth? You'd sit here waiting for them.'

'Who?'

He motioned her to silence. There were footsteps in the hallway, a knock.

'Eliza?' A woman's voice.

'What is it?'

'Dinner.'

'Coming.'

The feet clumped away.

'I have to go down to dinner. I have to think. No – stay here. Read,' she whispered, picking up her cigarettes and closing the door behind her.

He picked up a book and stretched out on the bed.

An hour later Eliza Blatchford shook him awake.

'Okay, Larsen,' she said without preliminary. 'I have to report to the court tomorrow at nine a.m., then I have a week. I'm flying on instruments alone. But if that son of a bitch is right about you,' she jerked a thumb violently downward, 'then I'd rather be wrong.' Her voice broke on the last three words.

'I'm not going back to being a New York deb for anybody.'

She opened a cupboard and began piling papers and paintings and jewellery boxes and summer frocks on the floor.

'Your father . . .'

'Threw me out of the house, the family, the *Social Register*, the lot. Get out, Larsen. I'm sorry. Leave me alone. When do you want me to meet you?'

Light from the lamp glanced brightly off her cheek.

'Let's make it three a.m. tomorrow night, like last time.'

'Please leave.'

'Meet you at the boatyard, this time.'

'*Please*. Leave. Okay.'

It seemed that all he did these days was leave precipitately; you'd think he'd be getting good at doing it with dignity by now. He grabbed his jacket but it was hard to depart gracefully over a porch railing.

CHAPTER SEVENTEEN

The sky was crying gently into the Atlantic as they rowed to the side of *Sofia* that lay away from the sleeping town.

Before starting the engine Larsen went below and opened a valve that had lain concealed and closed since *Sofia* had been built eight years ago. He checked the oil and went back topside. Silva let slip the heavy mooring line, and they drifted silently with tide and wind. Then Larsen started the diesel. *Sofia* smoothed seaward, a lean dark shadow that showed no lights and made no sound. The odd fogbank or patch of heavier rain further obscured the boat as she left harbour.

Long John blew into the wheelhouse, shoving into Eliza Blatchford at her accustomed perch by the winch controls. 'The exhaust! The cooling system's not working, Larsen.'

Larsen said, 'I can't hear anything.'

'That's what I mean! There's nothing coming out of the exhaust stack. She'll burn, man.'

'Relax, relax,' Larsen said. 'It's an underwater bypass system. Instead of going up the stack, the exhaust, and most of the noise, goes down a through-the-hull fitting, and escapes underwater.'

Silva said accusingly, 'There's only one use for that.' He came up to Larsen's side and thrust his jaw at the skipper. 'You son of a bitch! You *are* a smuggler! That's why they're interested in you.'

'Relax, Long John,' Larsen repeated. 'I've never used this boat for smuggling. I give you my word. The underwater bypass was just a precaution, in case I was forced to, but – ' He looked at them both, their faces stiffening in disbelief. It was happening again and he shouted, 'Stop! Listen. Why don't both of you relax?' He continued in an easier voice: 'And let me tell you a little story. It's the story I promised you, Eliza, Long John only knows bits of it. And it happened nearly a decade ago. The statute of limitations expired a few years back so the DEA's interest, I'm afraid, is purely academic . . .'

Steering automatically, Larsen started to talk.

It had been easy work. Stangerson fronted as a yacht broker. Every spring he arranged for a rendezvous between one of his newest acquisitions (usually a large fibreglass ketch or sloop) and a caïque, generally off the Lebanese ports of Jounieh or Jubayl. The caïque's crew were Maronites, moustachioed brigands who wore Kalashnikov or old Sterling submachine guns the way American kids sported high school rings. They tossed aboard a couple of tons of resinated marijuana, dramatic, talking in whispers, for all the world as if the Lebanese police were not fully aware of the deal and lying home in bed counting pounds instead of sheep. The marijuana was grown and processed by relatives or clansmen of the brigands in their Christian strongholds north in the mountains or across the Bekaa.

Stangerson's yacht would be stocked with four months' worth of food, fuel, and water. With the cargo aboard, Larsen stood off for Gilbraltar, reaching to the south of Crete and Malta, then northward around Ras el Tib and west through the Pillars of Hercules to the Atlantic. Never touching land or territorial waters, wearing a false name, a fake waterline, and a flag of convenience, Larsen's boat would shape a course south along the Moroccan coast to the northeast trades, west for three weeks to the longitude of Bermuda, and then northward until he finally made landfall on Nantucket Island.

Landfall day was chosen in or near June and the ketch, now flying US colours, would blend in easily with the myriad pleasure craft milling around Nantucket Sound or Cape Cod Bay. She would then put in to tie up at a dock – always the same dock, in Buzzards Bay, as if she'd just come in from a lazy weekend of cruising.

Larsen demanded and Stangerson granted him control of the operations side. He ran it his way, avoiding the pitfalls that often trapped the easy-money smugglers.

222

He rented a lonely waterfront house near Padanaram (paying by monthly cheques, never cash, using fake identification) and arranged for a couple of trustworthy contacts to use it normally, on a year-round basis. When he brought in the ketch they left the cargo untouched for ten days, and then transshipped it, suitcase by sail bag, into the house during daylight hours, as if stripping the yacht for winter. The cargo was removed a full month later, masqueraded as furniture, to points unknown. Larsen did not want to know. The moving van always made a trip back in the spring, bearing empty furniture boxes. The neighbours never caught on.

Larsen brought cash with him to pay his own contacts. He left the high-finance middlemen, front men, cutouts and payoffs to Stangerson.

During the first year Larsen had the rest of the fall, winter, and spring to sail back to Marseille, Cannes, and finally Taormina, and sell the boat.

Later, as Stangerson's operation grew, his American clients arranged for a South American run, and Larsen had to sneak in a winter trip, bringing grass and cocaine north. There were only two cargoes Larsen told the Englishman he would never touch: heroin and arms. But by then Stangerson had other men who would.

When the boat was at its final destination Larsen would return to Beirut to cauterize the Mavromikalis wounds with raki instead of rum, watching the country slowly collapse under rockets and internal stress.

Three years and six smuggling runs after the first trip, a ketch Larsen was taking north from Cartagena hit a floating log and developed a crack in the rudder housing, soaking some of her cargo in seawater. The pumps were able to cope with the leak but Larsen's crew was hard put to cope with the smell of kosher pickles emanating from the soaked bales of cocaine.

It took a while, but Larsen eventually remembered that while pickling liquid – acetic anhydride – played no part in the precipitation of cocaine hydrochloride, it did fulfil a vital function in converting raw morphine base into heroin.

223

While his crew looked on sceptically, Larsen slashed open bag after bag of nose candy until he came on the core of the cargo: 200 kilograms of white Thai heroin that had been flown in on one of the new routes, from the poppy fields controlled by the Ninety-third Kuomintang Independent Division on the Thailand–Laos border, to Uruguay.

It was Larsen's last trip. He dumped the horse, delivered the balance of the cargo, paid off his crew, and abandoned the yacht in Saint Barts. It was time to create an entirely different life for himself, and now he had the means.

Larsen grabbed his escape bag, flew to Beirut, collected cash from various safe-deposit boxes, and left for America the same day.

There he paid off the mortgages on his parents' old farm and used the cold months to design a fishing boat that would combine the seaworthiness of a double ender, the comfort of a charter yacht, and the versatility of a stern trawler. He came up with a design that he commissioned a Down East boatyard to realize in steel and welding rod. He bought his uncle a clutch of goats. He swore by every god on Olympus, when he came home to the Cape, that he would never ever return to smuggling if he could possibly help it.

But he always kept the escape bag close at hand, just in case.

And when his boat came off the ways he christened her *Sofia*, labelling the bottle in which his emotions had been corked since that split-second accident in Delphi, labelling it like an old wine that had travelled so well and so far you could never quite bring yourself to unstopper the bottle.

He finished the story an hour later.

For a while, the discovery that Larsen had been a professional hashish smuggler left the woman and the mate with little to say. Silva played with the radar, Eliza tried unsuccessfully to blow smoke rings. Maybe it was just wishful thinking but Larsen could detect in John and Eliza no pockets of the superficial morality that equated life as a functioning social animal with blind obedience to each of a nation's written laws.

224

The unwritten laws were more important, and in the 1980s the smoking of cannabis had become so widespread as to put the marijuana smuggler a fair way towards the unwritten status of folk hero.

Silva, the skipper observed, seemed torn between two emotions: hurt feelings, in that Larsen had not trusted his friend enough to confide in him, and awe at the amount of money Larsen must have cleared. Blatchford obviously considered that being a hashish smuggler was small beer compared to the possibility that he was a cold-blooded murderer of pregnant women.

She had really left Chapin far behind this week. And being a woman, she seemed more interested in the lady of the piece, Sofia Mavromikalis.

They found the *Marie* on sonar at ten o'clock and hooked a grappling anchor into the wreck on their fourth try.

By ten-forty-five, Larsen and Blatchford had dived and spotted the wreck visually. Silva had changed his mind and volunteered for the dive, but the skipper insisted on keeping an experienced hand on board *Sofia*.

Swimming down the grappling line was an eerie déjà vu for Larsen.

He had told Eliza to shackle the safety line to her weight belt, and they both held one end of a buddy line that would keep each in constant awareness of the other. He watched her carefully, but she was not breathing too quickly. Her eyes seemed alert and her movements as sharp as they could be underwater. Not bad for a ten-fathom Bahamas amateur.

They reached the roof of the pilothouse, and Larsen grasped the radar scanner to keep himself from drifting off with the tidal current. He motioned to his companion to do the same, gesturing twice, emphatically, to make sure she understood to stay in position.

They each had double tanks, more than enough air to decompress adequately on the way up, but he wasn't in the mood to conduct another chase after a drunk diver.

Then he entered the wheelhouse. He remembered glimpsing something of the same shape as a logbook, in the

225

space on the wheelhouse deck below the wheel and engine controls, but sand drifting through the door had accreted into a small bank against the forward end. He scooped sand and gravel away with his mittened hands, watching the debris cloud the white beam of his flashlight. A small crab scuttled away; a mussel had fastened its byssus to the rudder chains. *Marie* was becoming a sea thing.

Then he saw a corner of something black and rectangular. He pulled it free of the wall-to-wall carpet of sand. Sodden, leather, heavy bond, embossed, it was Joe's logbook. Eureka!

Larsen laid it down again, back under the wheel, pulled himself around to face towards the stern, and pushed down the companionway to the lower deck. A dogfish scooted in panic, a lobster waved hypnotically. He was breathing harder, and he forced himself to slow the bubbles. The engine-room hatch was open.

He checked the engine block but there was no sign of strange convulsions to show that the diesel had been running when she went down, taking in water through the air intake and twisting into metal pudding when the pistons tried to compress brine instead of gas.

Even here weed had penetrated, grabbing globules of loose grease from the engine-room water. It was totally irrational to think that the clammy, rotten fingers of Joe or one of his men would fasten around his throat but he fully expected something like – he played the flashlight around quickly.

Cut it *out*!

There was still no one home. Everything looked oddly normal, ready to run. Oil cans lashed, even a bundle of cotton waste jammed behind the electric control panel where Joe used to stash it. He turned to leave, and slowly turned back to the hoses.

The hose to the seawater suction.

Marie S had a primary saltwater cooling system, like *Sofia*. The hose stuck out from behind the Jabsco water pump like a severed artery instead of being clamped tight and intact on the pump valve. It had been cut cleanly with a knife. And the intake valve that connected the hose to the ocean was open.

They could have done the same with the other through-hull fittings, to the head, or the wash-down pump. She would have taken a long time to sink, water spurting through two-inch intakes, but she would have gone down eventually. As, in fact, she had.

He had already spent five minutes on the wreck: they would have to do nine minutes of decompression time. He headed topside, torquing his body through the angles of the wreck, stuffing the logbook into the mesh bag at his belt on the way, dreading what he would find outside the wheelhouse, but she was still there, eyes flashing ivory in the light of her own underwater flashlight.

In fact, she refused to budge, despite his repeated thumbjerks upward. She kept pointing with her neoprene mitten at the wheelhouse roof, at a spot, just below the lip of the wooden roof, that she had pinned with a beam of light. A weird shellfish, probably. It was a hell of a time for nature-watching. He pulled himself next to her, looking closer.

Not shellfish, but three jagged holes drilled into the planking at a shallow angle. Three holes of maybe nine-millimetre diameter. There was a glint of lead at the bottom of one of the holes. Bullets. If Eliza had not been perched right on top of them, she would never have seen them.

Bullet holes.

It would have been like the history books, and therefore totally unexpected. A vessel coming in at night, slow, from downwind. The whole crew would have been asleep when they boarded, with the possible exception of one hand on anchor watch, not expecting any kind of traffic inside the Rip.

Then the men came swarming over the side with knives and automatic pistols. They would have gone straight to the wheelhouse, busted in on the unsuspecting lookout as he sat in the captain's chair, warm and uncomprehending. They would have stormed into the sleeping quarters, rounding up Joe and his crew and leaving blood on the decks when anyone resisted.

227

Someone had resisted, though, breaking for topside only to be cut down by covering fire from the vessel alongside, bullets that had left a mark on the wheelhouse roof.

The crew could have been herded into a compact group amidships and gunned down in cold blood, left huddled to be swept away by tidal currents when the *Marie S* finally went down.

Only Joe Sciacca had survived his wounds long enough to send a Mayday after the pirates had left. A dying man on his dying boat, his only long-range radios put out of commission by water rising in the engine room. So he had crawled over to where the portable VHF was stored. Perhaps it had been Joe, not the radio, who had been too weak to use voice at the end, squandering the last seconds of vital force to tap out a message for his wife . . .

They could ruminate over the implications later.

Larsen thumped Eliza's arm with his flashlight, and they started upwards.

They were beginning the second phase of their decompression, six minutes at ten feet, when Larsen first became aware of the thrumming in his ears.

At first the noise only played back-up to the click-gush rhythm of their regulators. Larsen nudged Eliza and pointed to his ear, and the disembodied eyes behind the face mask nodded. She had heard it, too.

Then the thrumming began to impose its own rhythm as it grew louder, a pounding beat like tribal drums but with an inhuman depth to it that suggested something mechanical was building the sound out of wavelengths below the human range.

There was only one thing it could be: a ship. A ship approaching rapidly and much too close to be anywhere near the shipping lanes. A single-screw vessel that was not the *Sofia* because Larsen's boat was where she was supposed to be and her propeller was still, not thrashing the water into circular torture, creating the waves of pressure that were now pounding against their eardrums.

They could see *Sofia*'s hull crunching into the waves,

228

making silver whorls whenever she rolled, forty feet away.

One minute of decompression time left and they could break for the surface. It had to be a large ship, larger than the biggest New Bedford or Gloucester draggers; only the ten-, fifteen- or twenty-foot-diameter wheel of a cargo ship could make that noise.

Thirty seconds, twenty seconds. Eliza was watching him with wide eyes, watching him watch his Rolex. He jerked a thumb upwards. They broke surface in the foam of a shattered wave. The next swell lifted him up into a seaman's nightmare.

The tide was on the flow and *Sofia*, tethered to her anchor, was heading into the northbound current. Her stern was towards Larsen.

A half mile to the southwest, a cargo ship was heading out of a rain squall, driving straight for the anchored fishing boat at something close to full speed. It was a grey coastal freighter with rust-streaked sides, white superstructure, a jumble of antennae on the bridge and its loading mast forward. The kind of ship that had been doing the world's maritime donkey work for 100 years. Her speed lifted thin wedges of red bottom paint slowly out of the swells as she rolled. The bridge windows stared blind at her collision geodesic with *Sofia*. The stranger's radar rotated, stupidly. There was no name, nothing to identify her on the bows.

A hand knurled his shoulder. Eliza had seen it too. Larsen unhooked the mesh bag with the logbook, shoved it and his flashlight into the woman's arms and struck out crazily for his boat, foam creaming over his head every time he kicked himself over a wave. A flare shot into the grey sky from *Sofia*'s port bridge wing and drifted overhead under a small parachute, searing orange. Silva, keeping watch in the wheelhouse, must have spotted the coaster as she emerged from the squall line. *Sofia*'s horn sounded five times in the international emergency signal. The signal was repeated twice, battering the air as the freighter's prop was battering the water. Larsen and Eliza, swimming in and out of both environments, were living in a world of supercharged sound. And to that cacophony a new thump of underwater exhaust suddenly added counterpoint. Silva had started *Sofia's* diesel.

Then Larsen was at the ladder slung over the starboard side, hauling himself over the gunwale. He jettisoned his heavy tanks into the open dive locker, tore off his flippers, and raced for the wheelhouse.

At this range, the coaster's bows looked like a federal office building. In the minute and a half it had taken him to get into the wheelhouse, she must have halved the distance between them. The fishing boat's engine was clearing its throat in idle. Through the wheelhouse window Larsen saw Silva on the foredeck diving at the anchor winch, whipping off the devil's claws and throwing his weight on the brake wheel. Even now Larsen had time to admire the mate's seamanship and co-ordination, but he was still late, far too late.

Ahead the ship had become a cliff, and Larsen realized that the cliff was heading on a perfect course to take the coaster safely through a narrow gap between Asia Rip and Phelps Bank. This was no *Argo Merchant*, with inexperienced officers and a faulty RDF putting her aground by accident. The chances of that ship being on this heading by coincidence were a thousand to one against, which meant there was an expert seaman in full control, which meant he had to be on watch, on the bridge in such treacherous waters, which implied that if he was on a collision course with *Sofia* it was because he wanted to be.

As if to confirm this deduction a movement stitched a link between two reflections in the starboard window of the stranger's bridge. The bridge window gave the ship an appearance of wearing dark glasses, the mirror kind that hid the eyes of thugs.

Sofia's anchor chain started shooting out in a cloud of rust. Silva was throwing the forward hatch open, presumably in order to climb down to the chain locker and open a shackle that fastened the end of 200 fathoms of anchor chain to a ringbolt on the keel, but he would never have time, and if he did it would be useless; the freighter was towering only 100 yards away. A door opened on the portside of the bridge, and a figure with dark hair and an officer's cap came on to the bridge wing.

The sound of the freighter's engines was loud in the air now, and the crushed water from its prop slapped at *Sofia*'s hull. Larsen threw open a window to warn the mate but Silva had already realized he would never, ever loose the moused shackle before they hit, and was popping back up the forward hatch. Larsen waited another second that seemed like an hour. Every detail of the freighter was clear, blocking out the clouds; the rust on her hawsepipe, the outline of a name painted over in grey, the Roman numerals marking fifteen feet of draught on the bow. The scimitar edge of the bow was splitting water fifty yards away and heading for a point a little forward of *Sofia*'s midships section when Larsen threw *Sofia*'s diesel into full-reverse, hard-port rudder to try to pull her clear of the coaster. The anchor chain rattled louder as the diesel engaged, the boat jumped and began sliding backwards. But the coaster was changing course a fraction to compensate.

They were never going to make it.

A welter of white water appeared at the freighter's sides. She had her engine astern, too, but it would make no difference; the captain was merely trying to lessen the damage to his own ship as he tore Larsen's apart. The fisherman watched the murder of his boat inside a hollowness of shock. There was absolutely nothing he could do.

Then the two vessels collided in a crash and screech of torn metal. The freighter's bow ripped into *Sofia* just forward of the wheelhouse, canting the fishing boat violently over on her starboard side. The impact threw Larsen bodily to the portside deck. It was then that he remembered Eliza. He had seen her climbing over the gunwale. She must be on the afterdeck. He had lost track of Silva when he came out of the forward hatch. A fine shipmaster he was.

He let himself roll to the starboard side of the wheelhouse and out the opened door. The freighter's forefoot was grinding up *Sofia*'s side like an icebreaker. He could feel it forcing the smaller fishing vessel lower and lower in the water. Her starboard side was almost under; then a swell climbed aboard in a triumphant hiss. Larsen slipped and fell against the rail of the wheelhouse wing and saw above the sky a brainless expanse of evil, hostile steel, paint, a porthole. The freighter was pawing, gnawing at his helpless craft. *Sofia* would roll over and die any moment with the grey beast on top of her, slashing at her exposed stomach.

Larsen dragged himself aft down the steps to the flooded afterdeck. Tubs of gear had shifted to the starboard side, now lying under three feet of water, but the woman had vanished.

'Eliza!' he shouted desperately. Surely she hadn't gone below? He slipped again on the illogical cant of the deck, and fell into seawater, feeling himself dragged below the surface. He rose, twisted his hips over the gunwale, and hesitated.

He couldn't leave his boat now, with every other member of his crew unaccounted for, though they had undoubtedly either jumped or been thrown overboard by the impact.

He realized he had been cavorting madly around with twenty-five-odd pounds of lead weight fastened to his waist, almost unfastened the safety buckle, then thought better of it. *Sofia*'s list was worsening and Larsen let himself tumble and slip deep down the sides of his capsizing vessel, deeper, beneath the water.

The crash of *Sofia*'s prop, still in full astern, suddenly picked him up and flung him bodily forward, into the path of the oncoming freighter, ripping the left sleeve of his drysuit on a barnacle. He dived as far as he could, head cuffed back and forth by the converging washes of both ships' propellers, and then he kicked himself even lower, down, down, his lungs bursting, muscles demanding more oxygen. He had to come up. His time sense was distorted by the altered consciousness of danger, but the freighter must have ploughed over his ship by now, killing *Sofia* and Eliza and Silva as it would soon kill himself.

When he broke surface, gasping for air, he had been pushed twenty feet ahead of his boat. *Sofia* was back on an even keel, sinking fast by the bow. The freighter had stove in the steel hull next to the collision bulkhead, and there were not enough watertight compartments left to keep her afloat. Her foredeck was already lapping seawater. There was no

232

sign of life in her, except for the radar, still twirling slowly over the wheelhouse roof. There was no sign of life in Larsen's gut. Marie. Eliza. *Sofia*. The only animals left were animals of death; the emptiness of total loss, the disappearance of extraneous beings to which he had given parts of himself, a vacuum that bred vacuum. The emptiness of a desire to make the self felt one last time in an act of revenge on those who had taken his life.

The coaster was backing off at two or three knots, already eighty yards away. Larsen swam to the sluggish wreck of his vessel. He had a Lee Enfield .303 in his cabin locker. When they came back, he could take one or two of them with him to Davy Jones.

An answer came, too late.

What he was watching, minus the ramming, was what must have happened to the *Marie S*.

The knocking of the freighter's propeller slowed, then stopped. The higher frequency of *Sofia*'s prop continued, the prop probably pulling the waterlogged vessel underwater against her own anchor.

Suddenly a strong tentacle grabbed Larsen's waist, and he bucked, submerged, swallowing water, then resurfaced. The face of a sea creature with two panicked green eyes and twin scuba tanks stared at him.

The loss of loss. He had to find Long John.

Larsen wasted no time but resumed his crawl, hard towards *Sofia*. The woman followed, but she had somehow held on to the mesh bag with the logbook and it hampered her movements. The fishing boat rocked when they were ten feet off as a bulkhead somewhere in her hull gave way. The fishhold hatch sailed lazily into the dreary sky, propelled by released air. There was only one engine noise now, and when Larsen looked up he saw the coaster's bows moving again, towards them.

As Eliza held with one hand to the gunwale, looking on without hope or comprehension, Larsen slid on to the afterdeck and grabbed his tanks from the submerged dive locker. He searched the rising flotsam by the gunwale for his mask and flippers before realizing that he had pulled off his face mask to hang around his neck. He found only one flipper and tossed it to Eliza, who was swimming now with both hands full. The coaster loomed slowly larger. He stepped towards the foredeck in case Long John had gone back down the hatch – with tanks he could dive into the flooded anchor locker. The water near the wheelhouse erupted soundlessly into 100 tiny fountains, just before a crashing of automatic rifle fire came through the air.

Larsen grabbed at Eliza on his way over the rail. She followed willingly, flipper, mesh bag and logbook wedged stubbornly under her left elbow. He spent all of two seconds at the surface, draining and fitting his face mask and mouthpiece, then sank below the surface. A depth of only five feet would stop all but the heaviest of bullets.

At thirty feet Larsen paused and donned the twin tanks, purging his mouthpiece briefly as he adjusted the airhoses, then took the flipper from Eliza's elbow and fitted it to his foot. Then he resurfaced, risking another couple of seconds there to locate the buoy that marked the wreck of the *Marie S*, and swam towards it. When he had located the buoy line underwater he gathered some slack and cut the line with the diving knife strapped to his leg. Holding the buoy with one hand, he threaded the line through the buoy's plastic mooring grommet and then pulled the buoy underwater, by hauling the end of the mooring line through the loop while using the standing part of the anchored line as leverage.

The marker had too much buoyancy, or he had too little strength to drag the buoy deeper than six or seven feet. He hoped the buoy would be invisible from the freighter's bridge. Those men were not interested in leaving any souvenirs of their passage, and he and the woman needed the buoy now. The buoy connected them with the *Marie S* and intuitively Larsen had realized the dead fishing boat had suddenly become their only chance of survival. Without a buoy, the line to the wrecked boat would sink out of sight.

He rejoined Eliza where she floated, zombielike, at thirty feet. Her lips were corpse-purple, and he could feel the cold thickening his own movements. He indicated that he wanted to 'buddy breathe' from her tanks, each taking a breath from

234

the same mouthpiece before passing it to the other.

The green, cold limbo of undersea surrounded them, and grew chiller as a monstrous shadow blocked the light and a humming penetrated to their very bones. They sank deeper, looking up at the black shapes filling the sea forty feet away. He could count the barnacles on the coaster's keel. She was in need of time in dry dock. Her prop was a bronze spider that whirled sporadically as it ground the freighter back and forth into the *Sofia*'s bowels. Larsen found himself looking away from the obscenity of gratuitous destruction.

Like Marie Riley, he was losing half his body up there. He hoped no one watching from the bridge would spot the orange hint of their submerged buoy.

When he surfaced, cautiously, he caught a glimpse of a grey cliff and heard the chatter of automatic weapons ringing through the air. The guns had the distinctively impossible cyclic rate of an Ingram M10 Maxi: thirty rounds a second. A far-off yell, between bursts.

Long John!

If Silva had survived the first impact, he was done for now. If only –

No time to deal with that.

Sofia's anchor line must have paid out its full 200 fathoms, and the dying vessel and her attacker had both been brought up short a couple of hundred yards away after passing almost over their heads with the current. The men on the ship's bridge were still within easy view. He submerged again in a hurry.

No more time. Larsen's air gauge showed that his own dual tanks held, perhaps, enough air for a bounce dive to the *Marie* and back if he took less than five minutes to make the return trip. Eliza's tanks were getting dangerously low while they both fed their lungs from her mouthpiece.

He'd have to risk it, although the boys on the coaster showed no signs of leaving: they had been happily firing away for the last fifteen minutes. He signalled for Eliza to stay at her depth, took her underwater flashlight – she had ditched his own – and looped it around his wrist, then jackknifed towards the bottom, bare foot flapping ineffectually while his single flipper did all the work.

When he glimpsed *Marie*'s outline on the bottom he headed straight for the wheelhouse roof. He gave the life raft, still strapped in its wooden cradle on the portside of the roof, a quick inspection with Eliza's flashlight. It seemed undamaged. The fibreglass shell encasing the folded nylon raft, as well as a CO_2 canister that would inflate it at the surface, appeared intact. No Maxi holes, anyway: the raft was on the other side of Joe's wheelhouse.

He cut the safety line between raft and boat, tripped the catch, and without any warning found himself being hauled swiftly upward by air still trapped inside the fibreglass shell. He had lost sight of the anchor line that connected him with Eliza.

He tried to slow the ascent, but to little avail. The raft had become their only chance of survival and he could not let it go. Without it they had two choices: quick bullets or slow drowning. All he could do was pull against the current, hoping to drag himself away from the grey death downstream. He used the disappearing wreck to orient himself. At eighty feet, his bad shoulder collided violently with a steel bar, which turned into *Sofia*'s anchor chain as he bumped past it. The chain was taut, almost horizontal with the force of current. *Sofia*, his *Sofia*, had gone down.

His left arm was frozen senseless where the barnacle had torn the drysuit sleeve, and he was ascending too fast. Although it was getting harder to suck air out of his emptying tanks, Larsen breathed rapidly to ensure that air he had swallowed four feet lower did not stay long enough to expand with the decreasing pressure and burst through the wall of his lungs.

Still no sign of the buoy line in his rushing world.

More light shone through his faceplate; then both he and the raft were wallowing helplessly on the surface, the wind cutting at his numb lips.

Larsen floated on his back, low in the water, and looked around for the coaster. She was farther to the north and her profile looked different, because she was stern-to and heading away. The fisherman ripped off his face mask so it would not betray him by reflecting light. The shiny white fibreglass of the raft casing was bad enough.

He kept his nose and mouth above water, ditched his weight belt, inflated the life vest, and floated on his back for five minutes, worrying about Eliza. Would she guess he had lost the anchor line on his way back to the surface, realize that he could not, from the surface, spot the submerged wreck buoy that showed where she was waiting, thirty feet below? It was more likely she would assume he had got into trouble on the wreck. He kicked away from the receding coaster, trying to counteract the tidal current that would be affecting him but not Eliza, dragging the life raft against the wind.

Would she be able to spot him by the time he was out of sight of the freighter and could inflate the raft? The bright orange life rafts were designed to be visible from a ship's bridge over a good four miles. If the freighter was doing ten knots, that meant he would have to wait twenty minutes until the ship was far enough away. If they saw the raft they would come back, and all he and Eliza could do would be to wait there stupidly for the lead to blow them into oblivion.

He peered northward again. The freighter was still clearly visible whenever he came to the top of a swell. Larsen could discern a black figure on the bridge wing. The coaster flew no flag, and no name or home port was painted on the stern.

He had seen ships like her before, in Tripoli and Jounieh and Barranquilla. 'Smuggler' was written all over her unregistered lines. They had taken one hell of a risk bringing her, the mother ship, this far inshore to sink his boat.

Suddenly his alternatives were simple; inflate the raft now, or risk losing Eliza in order to be absolutely certain of saving himself. He jerked the lanyard to release the CO_2 canister.

Nothing happened. Without the raft, they would live four, maybe five hours in their drysuits. He jerked again, once, twice, and it wasn't until the brightly coloured life capsule hissed into recognizable shape that he allowed himself to think how incredibly lucky it was that the raft should still be serviceable after two weeks on the bottom of the Atlantic.

When the raft had blown up to full size he shrugged off his tanks and clambered into it to stand precariously at the opening, scanning endless waves for a black head or the flash of a faceplate, waiting for one of the ship's blood-hungry lookouts to spot the brilliant orange dot astern.

One minute later he was starting a second 360-degree search, squeezing control out of his brain, sick despair in his stomach. Two weeks ago he would have said he liked the sea; now he could feel only black revulsion for each indifferent wave.

Then a seagull cried, although there were no gulls in the air. He spotted her briefly, a dark knob on top of a swell 150 feet away. The coaster was swinging. Fear returned, then subsided; it was heading eastward now, into the shipping lanes.

When he dragged Eliza aboard five minutes later, sobbing and vomiting, the freighter suddenly disappeared into a rain squall as if it had never existed.

The only material evidence they had to prove anything untoward had ever taken place was the mesh bag with the sodden leather logbook that Eliza Blatchford still had looped under her left elbow.

The life raft became their planet.

It was a world made of two nylon doughnuts, one on top of the other. The hole in the doughnut was covered over, on the bottom, with a sheet of nylon for a floor. The floor had baffles underneath that filled with seawater and acted as a keel, slowing their wind drift and keeping the raft upright in tall waves. The top of the raft was covered by a nylon tent that could be zipped shut.

In theory, body heat would keep the temperature inside well above freezing when the canopy was closed. In practice they huddled together on the weather side of the raft and shivered violently, despite the added protection of their drysuits, for the whole of the first day.

The following night they tried to huddle even closer into each other's body heat, digging hands deep between the other's legs without a hint of desire while the bitter cold sapped their strength. Every couple of hours they used the hand pump to keep the doughnut from buckling over the crest of waves as the raft leaked air. The zip lock was not watertight and they took turns bailing and poking their heads out every thirty minutes to look for ships or planes. But the wind had shifted easterly and it seemed to be keeping them too close on Nantucket Shoals to see any seaborne traffic. The overcast sky, moreover, made an air sighting unlikely.

The Atlantic stretched on forever, a water desert that reached to the ends of a flat earth. Lying in damp drysuits in a puddle, they listened to the freezing waves splashing overhead. They felt as if the sea had already taken possession of them and death would be a mere formality. Warmth and dryness had never really existed; they were myths like the rest of civilization. Reality was endless cold and empty horizons. After a while, they stopped expecting to see a ship.

Larsen insisted that they talk, do isometric exercises, and stay awake. At first they could not find a frame of reference to deal with the enormity of what had just happened to them, could not think of anything they wanted to say. The exercise was a sick chore at first but physical want soon gave it more than theoretical interest. Finally they remembered Lifeboat Survival 101 and discussed what they would eat if given the choice of any food or drink in the world.

Eggplant parmigiano with wild rice and endive salad, Boodles gin and tonic with a slice of fresh Jamaica lime. Rare entrecote with cream and mustard sauce, the kind served by his favourite Left Bank brasserie; Larsen could almost see the tall glass of Pimms Number One gin sling that would come with it, beaded icy and stuffed with slivers of cucumber and orange . . . He would have settled gratefully for a cup of lukewarm tapwater.

The salt they lived in had made them thirsty from the start. Dehydration and cold were the enemies now. His training and knowledge of what happened to survivors who let their minds and then bodies succumb to hopelessness forced Larsen to play the frivolous game, but as the day wore on and the wind picked up, his mind began to absorb the facts, and the irreverence of irrelevance grew repugnant.

He could feel sadness sandwiched between emptiness and loss from murder, accumulated in layers like the bottom of a Mayan sacrificial cistern – Joe, Marie, their unborn child, Long John Silva, *Sofia*, all virgins of a sort. He realized he had fallen silent, against the rules, eyes staring into nylon. He noticed Eliza watching him. The track of one fat tear made it easier for the next to grease its way down her cheek.

Larsen said, 'He risked his life to help me out, and I lost it for him. He was that kind of friend. If you didn't see him for five years you could come back out of the blue and he'd risk his life for you again. He was going to go back to Dolores . . .'

The tears were coming faster now, but her face didn't contort into release; sadness had only come to sit on her being and she had become part of it.

'Why?' she finally asked.

'I don't know. I don't even know how they found us. No one knew where we were going – and if that ship was what I think it was, then she didn't follow us here, she would never go inside Nantucket Sound, or even inside territorial waters . . . We could have been tracked by another boat, of course. But I never saw them on radar.

'But they are going to pay, Eliza,' he went on in a low voice. 'If I have to go down to New York and blow up the whole fish market, every brick and every fish warehouse. It has to be the people at Fulton who did this. Nobody can be allowed to get away with it.'

'You'll just get yourself killed,' she said, hugging her knees hard to keep the shivering to tolerable levels.

'My life is about all I have left to lose.'

'Don't give me that shit,' she said, suddenly furious. 'You've got your *life*. Do you understand? I've got mine. Add a little courage, and mix well. What more do you want?'

'My friends. Marie, Joe, Long John.'

'What's the matter with you?' she shouted. 'When I first met you, I figured you for the happy-go-lucky, easygoing type. The debonair lady-killer who never ever ties himself down to anything . . . now you're talking about death and revenge.'

She added, 'We're going to die anyway, if no one finds us soon, aren't we?'

Larsen pretended not to hear her.

'You're sort of right,' he answered, pretending to be thoughtful, but saying anything to get her mind off an accurate assessment of their chances for survival.

'I've spent my life avoiding getting tied down, but I always get stuck. Sofia Mavromikalis, this,' he continued, peeking for her reaction. 'And then, like a fool, I get stubborn, and what my brother diagnoses as paranoia turns into blind anger at being shoved around, at seeing my friends getting shoved around, always by forces outside their control, whether it's the economic system or Vietnam, or the military–industrial system, or fate, whatever made Sofia Mavromikalis die. And now it's the bastards who rig the price of fish.'

He was keeping her mind off the mortuary, anyway.

'I spent my whole damn life reacting to being shoved around by the gods,' he continued bitterly. 'Maybe it's my substitute for religion.' It was only after he said it that he saw it made sense.

'So?' she replied. 'I've spent my whole life committing madly to everything and everybody.'

'Maybe we have something to teach each other,' Larsen said hopefully.

'As long as you know how not to bore me.'

'Look,' he gestured at the raft's taut canopy, 'I put on "The Wreck of the Hesperus" for you, and already you're bored?'

She smiled at that, then abruptly leaned forward and started working the hand pump to conceal a renewed spate of tears.

The temperature plummeted overnight and ice began to crystallize in the folds of orange nylon. There wasn't much chance of fielding so much ice that the raft would capsize but he was worried about the sharp edges rubbing on thin fabric.

When the first nacre of dawn streaked over the waves he took stock of the human damage.

Eliza Blatchford was dozing in fits and starts, getting as much rest as chattering teeth would allow. Her lips were the colour of a blueberry popsicle. Her eyes looked a much deeper green, almost black, and she was deathly pale.

He forced Eliza to wrench her drysuit off to let the limbs breathe outside the neoprene and sodden underclothes. It was an exhausting exercise on the flaccid waterbed that was the raft. The suits were skintight and sticky, and her nude limbs were wrinkled from the constant humidity. He helped her put her suit back on and went through the same exercise on himself. It helped to pass the time.

They told small jokes and took turns watching the horizon. When they repeated the striptease exercise at midday it took twice as long. He didn't have to tell her that he wasn't sure either of them could survive another night of this kind of exposure: he could tell by the terrible jokes that she was already far gone.

'Why did the punk rocker cross the road?'

'I dunno.'

'Because he had a chicken nailed to his face.'

His growing sense of hopelessness was compounded when she dozed off to sleep with her head cradled in his lap.

He took out the logbook, which they had stashed in a flap reserved in the more expensive, yachtman's version of the life raft, for emergency rations, water, and a radio beacon.

Gently separating the sodden pages he had found the ink surprisingly legible, and blessed the modern era of disposable convenience for the indelible ballpoint pen.

Courses, bearings, the arcane spells of navigation were penned neatly in Joe's small, precise hand. Loran, radar sightings. Fish caught, how many boxes, when, where, on what tide. There were even notes on what the fish had been eating, based on what fell out of their stomachs when gutted. Long transcriptions of Morse radio messages taken right off the air. Fuel charges, the albatross around every fisherman's neck. Engine check-ups. And here and there the odd idea, the fish-marketing scheme, a series of exclamation marks that shouted out Marie was pregnant, a sober ritualistic hand that marked the death of his father, a looser script that noted only fourteen months of boat payments to go. The pocket in the back contained Nantucket Shoals sand, and Joe's mortgage forms, the title to the *Marie S*, her federal fishing permits, and the titles to their cars.

But no 'insurance policy'. He searched carefully twice to make sure. Larsen was as helpless as before against an enemy who remained as mysterious and ruthless as ever. And now Silva was dead and *Sofia* was sunk and it had all been a waste of time.

Thirst, hunger, and exposure weakened the will to live. For the second time in as many days Larsen felt he would welcome death when it came.

Halfway through the afternoon Eliza scared the living daylights out of him by sitting up rigid in her sleep, opening her eyes, and pointing at the leeside of their enclosed life raft.

'Look, Lars!' she exclaimed. 'Who are those men?'

He tried to nudge her awake, unsuccessfully.

'What are they fishing for? They want us to come with them. Let's go with them, Lars.' She turned partway towards him, her voice trailing away into mumbling. He had to lean forward to catch the last words. 'Let's go with them, Lars, want to?'

She sagged back all of a sudden and the movement propelled her into consciousness with a fit of trembling and a crack in her voice.

'Who were they?' she asked, trying to focus on Larsen as he cradled her.

'You were dreaming.'

She looked around the empty raft, disbelieving. 'I wasn't asleep.' Her breath steamed into the raft. 'It was so real, Lars . . . Two men in thick, black oilskins,' she went on in a tone that made Larsen's spine cold. 'They had jiglines, they were sitting right there, fishing at the door of the raft. They were telling us to come with them!'

'You were dreaming,' he repeated, feeling a hole in his stomach reamed by her ever-heightening pallor, by this further evidence of how despair and stress were scrambling the signal traffic between body and brain.

Although if you did believe in ghosts, they were floating on prime territory. He and Eliza would only be two more in a long line of mariners who had left their bones on Nantucket Shoals.

*

The east was beginning to darken when Larsen picked out a trawler on the horizon.

He almost missed it: he checked the ocean once, automatically, and was manoeuvring to slide back into the raft when a tiny break in the horizon line caught his eye. The dragger was only just inside their field of vision but appeared to be heading on a course that would take it within a couple of miles of the raft.

As it got nearer Larsen propped himself as best he could on the jellylike floor, hauled off the top of his drysuit, and waved it back and forth in the freezing air.

The boat came up and abeam, two or three miles away. Larsen shouted like a refugee from Bellevue. Blatchford crawled up, leaned on him, and moaned repeatedly under her breath, 'Stop. Oh, stop. Please stop.' But the trawler continued on its course, like a direct insult.

Death breathed affectionately on the back of their necks, and the chill of their smashed hopes made it seem almost warm. Eliza collapsed on the floor of the raft and vomited, harsh, repeatedly, but nothing came out of her retching throat.

Suddenly the trawler changed shape in the twilight. It turned its whaleback bows ten, twenty, ninety degrees, pitching and rolling around until it was heading towards them, a diesel-guzzling, stern-trawling miracle with a strong Portuguese accent. They had been seen, although Larsen refused to let himself believe it until the dragger was alongside.

The *Sao Joao* was from New Bedford, light blue hull with cheerful red-and-yellow trim and a large white cross painted on her bow.

It was pure happenstance that the dragger had tried her luck on the fluke banks inside the shoals at this time of year. It was pure luck she'd done well and filled her holds with flounder or her skipper would have taken her inside Nantucket Sound to try his luck on Horseshoe Shoal instead. It was lucky he hadn't taken the inshore route home anyway, as it was a smoother, safer ride. He had picked them up in a dead spot well northwest of the shipping lanes, where only shing craft ventured, and not many of them at that.

The Portuguese crew smothered them in wool blankets, roiled them near the ship's stove, drowned them in hot nguiça broth and strong brandy. The skipper, whose name was Barbosa, spoke some English, and Larsen learned there had been no *sécurité* alerts put out for any missing boats over the last few days.

No one had missed them yet. No one, at any rate, who would report it to the United States Coast Guard.

He made up a story about wreck diving and collision that frayed just far enough from the truth, how they'd forgotten to tell anyone where their pleasure boat, the, uh, *Sea Robin*, was going. The skipper looked at him with polite disdain that showed he considered this stupidity well within the capabilities of most yachtsmen. Larsen's bearded face rang no bells with newspaper captions. At any rate he asked no more questions. Eliza was already passed out in the skipper's private cabin.

Barbosa insisted that Larsen immediately rest in a deckhand's bunk in the fo'c'sle and turned out the deckhead lights to help him into the arms of Morpheus.

So it wasn't until the following day that Larsen found the body.

CHAPTER EIGHTEEN

The Portuguese loaned them clothes and a '62 Olds jalop in exchange for the expensive drysuits. The six-cylind engine only fired on four but managed to complete th journey from New Bedford to Mallebarre the next evening.

Larsen did not talk during the entire drive, but kept h eyes on the highway trees as they belly-danced to a bitter ar strengthening wind. Eliza spoke once, but he snapped at he then was contrite, and she left him alone afterwards. She ha no need of her witch's genes to sense the reason for his mood

Long John, and more. There was a continuing dearth options to be shuffled and reshuffled like the seven cards a poker hand that would never make a flush. There was als fear, fear of an enemy who remained unknown, inexplicabl and seemingly omnipotent.

And there was the question that had been creeping up o Larsen's consciousness since the raft: how had they bee fingered so unerringly on Asia Rip? Who would have know they'd be visiting *Marie*'s grave?

When they passed the Wareham intersection where Eli had delivered the rental car, she gave him only a rueful smil He still said nothing but Larsen was grateful for the smil it was final confirmation that she no longer suspected him.

When they crossed the Sagamore Bridge they decided th under the circumstances O'Malley's offered the easiest an safest refuge. Larsen got out and shivered behind a blac abandoned barn on the Old King's Highway while Eli stuttered on ahead in the Olds to check for surveillanc spotting none.

They found O'Malley soaking in orange candlelight insi his tub, a huge enamel relic that drank boilerfuls of hot wat at a sitting. He was puffing on a Romeo y Julieta, sipping shot of Glenfiddich, and listening to Bizet's 'L'Arlésienr Suite' through a pair of powerful speakers located on eith side of the sink. He looked like an Irish Caligula among the various Victorian fixtures scattered in the bathroom's penumbra. O'Malley, who prided himself on his hedonistic approach to everyday life, would not have resented the analogy.

He could not hear them come in through the unlocked front door and the cigar went out in a fizz of panic when they came into the bathroom. They looked strange to begin with, Larsen in a week's worth of facial hair, sea boots and a tight duffel coat, the woman smothered in a thick Azorean wool jumper and painter's pants three sizes too large for her.

Eliza looked vulnerable, the rough, oversized clothes emphasizing her delicate build, but O'Malley assumed the same look of uncertainty that had visited Long John Silva's eyes when he recognized Larsen.

If Long John had trusted his own uncertainty, Larsen reflected bitterly, he would be alive today.

In a jungle of mortally cold feelings, two things became warm: Eliza's newfound trust in him, and the satisfaction of killing doubt in Caligula's eyes as they warmed themselves against the bathroom radiator and told O'Malley what had happened to them over the last week.

The police, apparently, had not yet noticed anything amiss in *Sofia*'s departure. So who had been checking the boat?

'Holy Mary . . . I wonder what it could be,' O'Malley muttered to the stogie clamped wetly in his teeth when they had unwound the tale.

'The insurance policy?'

'Yeah. Whatever it is that makes them go to such unbelievable lengths to terminate your contract. It's unlike most organized crime, frankly – they stick to their own, in life as in death, as Shapiro probably told you.' O'Malley reached for the Glenfiddich bottle, handy beside the steaming tub, and cracked the hot water tap, with a deft wrench of his toes, before continuing. 'They're smart enough to realize the Feds won't have much motivation to go after them if they keep homicide within the families. It's kind of an unwritten social law with them.'

'I guess we'll never know, now,' Larsen replied. 'But the

bitch of it is, we're stuck. We don't even know how to tell them we don't have what they want! As if they'd believe us anyway . . .'

'It would be sad,' Eliza Blatchford agreed, words plastered with sarcasm, 'to be practically machine-gunned to death for no good reason.' She shivered, remembering.

'You're sure it's not in the logbook.'

'Yes, dammit. There's nothing in the place I thought it would be in, the pocket he kept important papers in. The rest of it's the usual notations like courses, estimated times of arrival, that kind of thing. *God*, was I stupid,' Larsen finished angrily. 'What an idiotic, murderous, wild-goose chase. And don't tell me, "Don't blame yourself." It's my fault, I don't buy that line.'

'No codes?' O'Malley asked, absently.

'No codes, I must have searched it three times over when we got off the *Sao Joao*, nothing,' the fisherman answered, irritation roughing the words. Then he caught himself. 'Oh only – wait!'

He left the bathroom, walked slowly out to the jalopy and retrieved the logbook.

Fishing-boat skippers like Sciacca carried short-wave radios for emergencies, but they seldom used them, except for emergencies.

Sciacca had been unusual, a perfectionist, in learning Morse code at all, but even he would be unlikely to spend hours of time jotting down radio traffic in Morse. Practice maybe? No.

Some code. So obvious it was deceptive.

He flicked on a reading light in the living-room, reluctant to be disappointed in front of the others.

His own Morse was rusty and he had to ransack his brain for the meaning of some of the grouped dots and dashes.

```
 −.  .  --  -.--  ---  .-.  -.-  ...  -.-.  ..  .-  -.-.
 -.-.  .-  -.-.  ---  ..-.  .-..  ---  ---  .-.  ...--
```

But it was good enough to work out that the messages had nothing to do with normal maritime radio traffic.

248

'New York, Sciacca Co., Third floor, South Street, DEC 300 Computer terminal.'

Had Joe Sciacca written this for his own use? Or was it in the logbook in case something happened to him, an insurance policy for an insurance policy, so to speak?

'Terminal is hooked into stock brokerage and accounting system belonging to three families. Codes to enter system are . . User ID: type "Lupo 1". Password: press "Return" button three times, type "Bacalao". Mode: type "@ DS". First index override code: type "Miseria VTI:5" . . .'

Larsen went into the bathroom.

'You were right, Sage,' he said softly. 'It's here. Coded.'

Eliza whooped.

They crammed the fireplace with driftwood till the flames beat, and drank cocoa with single malt chasers into the early hours of morning.

The Morse was scattered among seven different pages of the thick logbook. Sciacca apparently had filled the code into spaces between older entries to throw off the inquisitive.

Eliza camped by the hearth in what he was coming to recognize as a favourite position, arms locked around her knees, staring into the fire the way Kalahari bushmen did when telling their fortunes.

They were both still exhausted, despite sleeping aboard the dragger, but the mascara of fatigue, like men's clothes, only underlined her good looks, Larsen thought.

O'Malley blew smoke rings with Dunhill and pipe, dangerously stretched out in a silk kimono with purple dragons.

'"This program is untraceable without knowing the codes,"' Larsen translated slowly, using an encyclopaedia for the groupings he had forgotten. '"Program, and codes, shelter private section, of main data bank memory, by overriding index programs. Information includes dates, places, agreement, on price-fixing at Fulton, extortion of dealers, tax fraud, laundered money, hits on three informers, disguised as accidents." Christ.'

'Brilliant,' O'Malley commented, the thick beard wagging shadows in the firelight. 'The Organization enters the 'computer age. Instead of an ancient crackling parchment with cryptic directions such as "when the fourth finger of y broken idol meeteth ye rising moone on Skeletone Rock . . ." Instead, a code that unlocks a program designed t conceal part of its own data from those who don't know th code' – he made Chinese boxes of his hands – 'within th code.'

'Old man Sciacca must have been tricky as hell,' Eliza said 'It's the last place the Fulton people would look – *inside* thei own computer.'

'He must have helped design the program itself,' O'Malle added. 'Or bought off the programmer.'

'Listen to this,' Larsen said excitedly, index finge following another sequence of dots and dashes.

'"Data also specifically outline payoffs to powerfu politicians, judges, cops,"' the fisherman spelled out slowly '"also details on Neapolitans, Corsicans, Koreans, trying t take over fish market for drug traffic."'

He flipped the pages to the next Morse entry.

'My God.'

'Now what?'

'Here he is . . . Lu Guercio. Two words. So it was a name or a nickname or something: "Bobby Mondragone," it says "a.k.a. Lu Guercio." That's what Joe was trying to say that's who must have been behind the sinking. Lu Guercio!'

'The one-eyed man,' Eliza Blatchford added softly.

'I forgot you knew Italian –'

A flash of thick glasses, angled strangely, blinking fro the windows of a Lincoln, a patched eye under a head c white hair marking down numbers in a notebook at the fis market, the other eye sunk under huge lenses, colder tha the chipped ice inside the fish boxes he was counting.

'Son of a bitch!' Larsen said, closing the log with a snap 'I think I know who he is.'

'Then maybe we've got him!' Eliza said excitedly. 'Yo can tell him to lay off or you'll go to the Feds. You can te them to clear your name, or else! Just like in the books!'

'Easy, easy,' O'Malley cautioned.

'It has to be done right,' Larsen said.

'You're trying to light a joint with a stick of dynamite,' O'Malley agreed, pulling a marijuana cigarette from his kimono pocket, a magician loosing a dove.

'First things first,' Larsen added. 'I have to get hold of that data. Maybe Sciacca had a key to his father's office, where the computer terminal is, but I don't.'

'Well, then. You've got to go to New York. I'll come with you,' Eliza insisted.

'No, Eliza. It's too risky.'

'But you said . . .'

'Trust me. I know a place where you can stay, not far from here, where no one will find you, as long as you report to your court officer regularly so the cops don't start looking . . . It's a small boarding-house in the backwoods of Truro that we once used as a safehouse,' Larsen continued soothingly. 'Only local people know about it. It's run by a couple of tough, ancient lesbians. Gertrude Stein vintage. They're both half dead, and one's half blind, but they'll take good care of you.'

Eliza scrambled to her feet, knocking over a mug of cocoa, and stood at the window, her back declaring a frigid fury.

'I see. Keep the little woman out from underfoot. So the big, strong macho man can play cowboy, or Eliot Ness, or James Bond,' she said bitterly. 'Fuck you. I'll go on my own. There are things I can find –'

'Don't be stupid, Eliza!' Larsen retorted. 'I'm the one they want most of all. If they want to – find – you at all, it's only because of your association with me. I'm not letting you put your neck on the line for me, female or no female.'

She kept her nose glued to the frosty pane.

'Why don't you go to the cops? You've got something now.'

'No, I don't. This doesn't clear my name. And if they did *anything*, by the time the clodhopping Feds got around to searching the Fulton office, they'd have cut it right off from the main computer, transferred all the data banks, fancy programs, and all, to a separate, untappable computer. My brother mentioned that organized crime owns at least thirty thousand separate businesses, so they can pick and choose computers . . .'

She glowered.

'You're leaping without looking again, Eliza.'

'Go to hell! You *pushed* me!'

Larsen stifled a surge of irritation. He said gently, 'It makes sense for me to go. I'm used – or I was used, anyway – to dealing with these kinds of people. I'm used to walking down dark alleys where men carry knives. It's got nothing to do with sex, I've got experience.'

She turned around at that, merely looked at him, her eyes voicing what her mouth would not. His alleged experience had not saved John or Marie.

'You notice O'Malley isn't volunteering?' Larsen pointed out.

'I'd be of but little use,' O'Malley agreed wholeheartedly. The Limerick accent was back. 'When are you going?'

He offered Eliza the joint, expelling a thunderhead of sickly sweet smoke at the same time. She took the spliff and drew on it angrily.

'Tomorrow if I can. I want to go to my brother's first, give Per a chance to help me. I have enough information now to really back up my story if he decides to look at it. Jesus, all he has to do is get my boat, and Joe's boat, dived on and inspected, check the fucking bullet holes. He may have become a government man, but I hope he'll give me a break.'

'Be careful, Lars,' O'Malley said, through a yawn like a rattlesnake's. 'You can never trust a lawyer, even if he is your brother; they are specifically trained to play both sides of the game. The ultimate whore, when you consider that they do it for a system of justice that is usually hopelessly biased. I mean, look at the Agee and Snepp decisions . . .'

O'Malley's words came back to Larsen the next evening as he stood in the living-room of Per's house in a three-Volvo subdivision of Brookline, keeping himself casually between his brother and the phone.

It was a sumptuously done room, with a delicate-hued Tang vase under glass in one corner, a Roche-Bobois sofa, a superb copy of an Edvard Munch oil over the mantelpiece.

The painting showed a young girl, wan and bored, lying on a rumpled bed under a closed window. The colours and execution were reminiscent of Bonnard.

Lars knew Per must have had a hand in the decoration: Patty Bailey Larsen's taste, true to her upbringing among Cotacheset's summer set, ran more to shocking pink and china figurines.

'The logbook with the information is in the false drawer in Pa's rolltop desk,' the fisherman said. He had told his brother everything: Fulton, the bullet holes in *Marie*, the ramming of *Sofia*, and it had been like talking to a wall.

'What are you *doing* here?' the lawyer repeated in a disbelieving voice for the fifth time.

The fisherman could almost see the frantic, anxious thoughts spinning around: what if the fugitive had been *seen* near his brother's house? How would it affect his *career*?

Even Per wore that veiled distrust, the look of muted fear the fisherman had come to know so well.

'I want you to listen to me, to help substantiate what I'm telling you.'

'I can only do that once you have given yourself up to the Massachusetts State Police.' The uncompromising tone had the deaf quality of a true bigot.

'You're my brother!' Lars burst out. 'What *happened* to you? Haven't you listened to what I've told you? Don't you believe it? Per?'

Per's face contorted. 'Don't *you* understand? I can't help you till you give yourself up for that very reason: we are related. My enquiries would be disputed as nepotism, I might even be disqualified from the case. And as for the sunken boats: don't *you* realize they only back up the DEA's suspicions? Oh, yes.' The lawyer whirled, paced the room and then thrust his body, prosecutor style, at his brother's face. 'Smuggling! I guess that's how you bought the *Sofia*, how you paid off the mortgage on our house. Isn't it?'

Larsen looked at Per levelly, sadly. 'It's irrelevant. Why don't you at least look at the logbook. I'll bring it up for you . . .'

'I knew it!'

Then, silence. The United States Attorney for Massachusetts stood in his flannel slacks and cashmere pullover, rigid as if it were Larsen's outlaw status itself that was holding him hostage.

'Remember that time all the other kids were laughing at me, in school, when I was caught stealing the flag and they made me sing the football song thirty times in the yard?' The fisherman's voice was low, and soft. 'Remember how you went and challenged every one of them who wouldn't stop making fun of me? Remember?'

'What about it?'

'What happened to that brother?'

'I grew up, Lars. It's time you did, too. Give yourself up,' he urged, stepping closer, putting his hand on Larsen's shoulder, smiling now and looking into his brother's grey eyes in a manner more reminiscent of Dale Carnegie than childhood affection. Larsen forced himself not to twist away.

'You know, Per,' Lars said, 'you're making a big mistake, trading in your strength for the security others sell you. You yourself have become weak. It's the bureaucratic equivalent of Dr Faustus,' he added, trying to prevent his voice from shaking. 'I only wonder who your Mephistopheles is.'

His brother dropped the influence-people hand, looked at the ceiling, studiously bored.

'And if that's what growing up is,' Larsen said, walking towards the door, 'I'll stay a kid, like Peter Pan.'

It was a childish parting shot, but Larsen felt hurt when he left, hurt like a kid.

As he left he noticed two things from the corner of his eye. His brother was edging towards the phone. And the Munch was not a copy.

What in the name of all the gods had happened to his older brother?

Larsen had worked out a plan in case Per proved unco-operative and he was glad of his foresight when he saw the swirling blue lights weaving a net of roadblocks around Brookline five minutes later.

He was out of the danger zone, and no one had seen him

park the car in a smug bourgeois side street near his brother's house. But there would be cruisers sharking around the Southeast Expressway and Route 128 and the Massachusetts Turnpike, so he followed secondary arteries south and west, Routes 109 and 126, heading across a white, skeletal, clapboard New England slowly invaded by fast food, cut-rate gasoline, and money-market funds. He crossed the Rhode Island border around eleven p.m.

At least no one would be looking for this car, a fibreglass Chevy Vega with a loose clutch belonging to Annie Webquitch. Annie was tall, blonde, beautiful and O'Malley's cousin, which hadn't stopped him and Larsen from competing for her favours before she headed off to a nursing job in San Diego and left the keys with O'Malley for safekeeping.

Some safekeeping.

Larsen made six phone calls from different phone booths between Providence and New York.

Two were to Fritzy Vogel. He reached him at two p.m. on the second try.

'Larsy baby.' Through the initial irritation Fritzy sounded surprised to hear from him. 'I'd figured you'd left town.'

'I did. Sorry to get you out of bed.'

A pause.

'She wasn't that great anyway,' Fritzy whispered confidentially. 'One of those great-looking would-be actresses with long legs who only really turn it on for Francis Ford Coppola.'

Telephone hiatus, again.

'Anyway,' he continued in a louder voice, 'I got what you wanted, man. Where do you want to meet?'

'Can't you just tell me now?'

'Are you kidding? On the phone?' Fritzy's years in Beirut had inculcated him with truly Levantine obsessions, spies in every cupboard and taps on every phone.

'Plus,' he continued, 'I've really got a whole bunch of info on these guys. And I'm busy now. So when are you gonna be in New York, buddy?'

'Early this morning.'

'How about dinner tomorrow? I mean today. I know, you

used to like the Normandie, in the thirties, on Eleventh Avenue?'

'Sure, Fritzy. What time suits you?'

'Say, uh, how about nine-thirty. I'm busy till then.'

'Okay,' said Larsen, and hung up, listening to an alarm buzzer sounding faintly in the far recesses of his cerebellum. He thought about it for a minute but failed to detect any dissonance which might have triggered a warning, and tuned off the alarm. It could not have been very serious. After the past two weeks, it would be surprising if he trusted anyone.

Two more calls went to the Truro boarding-house Eliza had checked into that morning. There was no reply – the elderly disciples of Sappho who ran the place went to bed at eight p.m. and it was up to guests to answer the phone, if they felt like it. A wonderful set-up for a lone combi driver to go to ground in as he awaited the arrival of smuggled hashish, but again, Larsen felt inexplicably uncomfortable.

He was getting too involved with Eliza, he thought with half his mind while the other half revelled fatly in the realization. She was distorting his ratiocinations. She was probably fast asleep.

He made another call to Ole to tell him he was all right, to explain what he had been doing, to avoid the old man's questions about his next move. Ole's phone could still easily have a tap or tracer, but the call gave Larsen a childish feeling of false security. His uncle had raved and yelled in Norwegian-peppered English about the stupid police, *ja*, and had not doubted Lars' story for a second. Larsen, fearing the phone tap, had to cut him off in full spate.

The last call he made was at four a.m. to the Pierce Fish Company. He asked to speak to Bobby Mondragone. The name Joe's code had said belonged to the man with the one eye – Lu Guercio.

'Yeah.'

The voice was harsher, the Italian accent sharper than Larsen remembered, or maybe it was the phone connection. Or had he seen a different one-eyed man that night at Fulton Fish Market? Doubt reared its wishy-washy head. The whole thing was so crazy.

256

'Mondragone?'

'Yeah? Who is this?'

It *was* him. Confidence returned.

'My name is Lars Larsen.'

'Who?' the voice said in an even rougher tone.

'Lars Larsen,' the fisherman repeated. 'Don't pretend you don't know who I am, Lu Guercio, I just want to tell you that I have the information you're looking for.'

'I don't know what you talking about. I don't know you! You're wastin' my time.'

'More precisely, Guercio, my lawyer has the information. All about you and the prices and the murders, the ones that are supposed to look like accidents? My lawyer has instructions to give it to my brother, the US Attorney for Massachusetts, if anything happens to me. Even if I die of the flu, or old age.'

'I don't know what you talkin' about,' Mondragone repeated.

'So leave me alone, Guercio. Because I want to do a deal with you. Don't try interfering with me. I'll call you later.'

Larsen had intended to insult the wholesaler by hanging the phone up first, but another click came through the receiver just before he broke connection.

He stood for a moment by the deserted highway feeling fear and chill.

Here he was, playing poker with organized crime. Playing poker and bluffing. The logbook was not in a lawyer's office; it was still at O'Malley's.

But if the bluff worked, he should be able to negotiate with the Organization from a position of strength and safety. If it failed – well, when someone called your bluff he had to show you his hand. That was certainly a whole education you missed if you folded.

The Normandie was founded in the 1930s by a Parisian steward who had worked on the crack French liner of the same name.

It consisted of a dark, oak-panelled room draped with maces, battleaxes, and other B-movie props, along with coats of arms from all the major towns of the French coastal province.

In its prewar heyday, it had been as chic as Chez Jean was now, attracting New York's beau monde as well as travelling celebrities on their way to and from Pier 88, the Compagnie Générale Transatlantique berth at the foot of nearby Forty-eighth Street. Those were the days before 707s when everyone from Greta Garbo and the Prince of Wales on down journeyed by ship, and the ships were glittering, scaled-down working models of European civilization before the pall of Auschwitz, and the models all docked within a square mile of the Normandie.

Now the neighbourhood had filled with cheap Thai restaurants, Korean grocers, Shylocks, numbers operations, and drug peddlers, but enough diehards taxied back night after night to keep its doors from closing permanently.

Larsen found Fritzy in a sombre booth near the back, nursing a Chivas Regal. Tonight he was dressed in a black silk turtleneck, a tightly cut black Armani suit, and desert boots. Fritzy Vogel, Office of Strategic Services, dressed for dangerous spy work on the Riviera.

'*Marhaba*, Lars baby.' His eyes looked everywhere but into Larsen's.

Boeuf en daube was a speciality of the Normandie. Larsen ordered Perrier in response to a new awareness of the quantity of alcohol he had been ingesting recently. Recently, hell. Over the last fifteen years.

Fritzy looked at Larsen's forehead in astonishment, slid his eyes away hastily, and ordered another Chivas. Larsen drinking mineral water instead of hooch meant the Nile was running back into Sudan. Certainties crumbled and all bets were off.

While they waited for their food, the fisherman asked Fritzy what he'd dug up on Lu Guercio and Laparensa.

Given the connections Fritzy and his boss Stangerson had with the New York and Chicago Families they delivered drugs to – Families Shapiro said had links with Fulton – Larsen expected some detailed answers that might have given him more insight into the information apparently locked inside the Organization's computer.

Right now, to extend the poker analogy, it was like pulling a bluff in a variety of seven-card stud he hadn't learned, with a hand he didn't know the value of.

So he wasn't surprised when Fritzy said: 'Not now, buddy!' Another sliding glance and the clatter of forks. 'There's a lot of stuff to tell. We'll go to my car after dinner.'

Fritzy sank two snifters of Courvoisier and didn't complain when Larsen offered to foot the bill. After all, it was Fritzy, this time, who was doing the favour. Vogel put on a leather Gestapo coat, looked with nostrils pinched at the wrinkled Antartex sheepskin Larsen wore over his khakis, and led the way out of the restaurant.

The Korean fruit vendors next door played their white ceramic scales like pianos, bundling perishables against the frost.

Fritzy pointed up Eleventh Avenue, except for the grocery store a deserted hero sandwich of junked autos and litter between two slices of obsolescent commerce. 'The car's there.'

It was a new Ford Thunderbird. Vogel unlocked the rear passenger door with a flourish, then stood aside. The red-carpet treatment, his gesture read.

The fisherman was almost seated when two black shapes hurtled out of a doorway across the sidewalk from the car. One jumped inside the Ford and on top of Larsen before he could slam the door. The other got in the front seat.

Larsen managed to arch his back, jamming his assailant against the car roof but when he looked up the second hood had a silenced .22 revolver levelled at his groin, and Fritzy had got in through the other rear door and was holding a similar weapon at his teeth – Colt Challengers by the look. The Mob's favourite hit piece, a calibre reserved for traitors.

Larsen froze, then let himself be shoved between the monkey on his back – a pyramid of a man with a huge, monstrous, Caliban face – and Fritzy. He cursed himself silently.

He should have known. He should have known when he'd seen Fritzy's clothes. Fritzy *always dressed the part*. And tonight he'd been dressed for spy work, spy work with a Gestapo overtone.

'Hands behind yer neck.'

Larsen found himself holding his breath, wondering if they were going to shoot him now. He tried to look at Fritzy and almost lost an eye in the silencer. He didn't want to look at the man in the front seat. Quite apart from the .22 held rock-steady and pointing at Larsen's gut, the man had a face like a half-empty bottle, something gone from his lips, something human missing in the eyes. A pleasant, boyish White Anglo-Saxon Protestant face with GI Joe blond hair and an off-colour lilt to his way of looking at you that showed he would physically enjoy plugging you right between the eyes and watching your blood and brain-matter decorate the rear window.

Someone came up on the driver's side and got behind the wheel. The stranger did not look behind him. There was a whiff of aftershave. The ruff of a maroon parka hid most of the driver's head from view. The hair on the scalp appeared well groomed, a fancy cut.

'Fritzy,' Larsen said, but Vogel only whispered, 'Shaddup, Lars buddy,' in his best television *Geheime Staatspolizei* voice and rammed the silencer hard, into his ear this time. Trying to impress the boss, as always. But Larsen shut up. It would be just like the flashy smuggler to file down the action on his revolver till the trigger pulled through at the slightest pressure. He'd bet good money the safety wasn't on either.

The driver started the engine, which fired easily despite the cold, and eased out into the deserted avenue, turning his head slightly to watch a side mirror.

The alarm buzzer that had gone off when Larsen had made tonight's appointment started up again, much louder, much too late.

That was it. He had never gone out on the town with Fritzy Vogel in New York during the old days. Beirut, yes, Izmir, Marseille, yes. New York, no.

So how had Fritzy known he liked to eat at the Normandie?

260

Only one person they knew in common had been to the Normandie with Larsen. The thought tried fitting itself to the way the driver held his head as he steered the Thunderbird uptown through staggered lights and sparse traffic. The patterns matched, but it was the smell of Paco Rabanne that threw the final switch.

'Stangerson!' Larsen breathed.

CHAPTER NINETEEN

A rush of smells invaded Larsen's memory as he spoke the name.

The decadent spices of Beirut; sleazy cafés smelling of sewer in the old quarter of Nice, the Greek part of Marseille. The last time he had seen the Englishman had been at Francisco's restaurant in Cartagena, haggling with a 'coronado' over a shipment of cocaine and a plate of peppered fish. The coke had turned out to be the brown heroin that stank of pickles.

'Hello, Larsen,' Joseph Stangerson said quietly. 'I was rather hoping you wouldn't recognize me.' They were stopped at a red light, and Stangerson pulled out a pack of cigarettes, fitted one into his jade holder, and pushed the dashboard lighter. The fisherman knew before tobacco met glowing coil that the smoke would have the distinctive Turkish aroma of his Senior Service brand.

'What's going on?' Larsen asked innocently.

Fritzy said, 'No talking, Larsen,' but Stangerson said, 'Leave him be.'

'What's going on?' Stangerson went on, mimicking rhetorically. 'You have something that belongs to the Fulton Organization, Larsen. Or rather, had. Because you were hiding it, I understand they tried to kill you, as they killed your friend and his wife, in order to bury the information.'

As always, Larsen was struck by the contrast between the delicately coddled Oxford syllables and the substance of what he was enunciating.

'But you're a tough chap to nail,' Stangerson went on, puffing smoke. 'We're still trying to figure out how you and that bitch swam thirty miles to shore in the North Atlantic in November . . . that mother ship was under contract to me, in case you haven't guessed. But I should have known: a case of "I prophesied, if a gallows were on land, this fellow could not drown'', eh, Larsen?'

'But why *you*? What are you doing here? I thought you stayed in Nice.'

'Well, I'm afraid they found whatever it was you were blackmailing them with . . .'

'What? That's impossible,' Larsen blurted out, angrily.

'. . . so now they have to get rid of you because you knew what it was. Potent stuff, I should imagine, though of course I don't ask questions. It's tiresome, but you've got some powerful people very annoyed with you.

'And to answer your second question,' the Englishman continued, passing a bus, 'I live in New York now.'

'But how do you fit into this?' Larsen asked, pretending to lean forward with keen interest but busy checking Fritzy, and GI Joe in front, to see if they were leaving their weapons exposed. They weren't.

GI Joe was still enjoying himself in anticipation of a kill. Why, oh, why hadn't he brought the Heckler and Koch from the hotel?

Stangerson brought his profile to bear on the back seat.

'Did you bring the produce, Vogel?' he asked Fritzy.

Fritzy said, 'Yup.'

Without looking at the Englishman, GI Joe asked, 'Why do we have to fuck around with that stuff? It's a lot surer with a bullet.'

'Because the paymaster for this operation says it's not to look like a homicide,' Stangerson replied sharply, the round vowels dropping like ripe plums among the squashed Brooklyn syllables of GI Joe.

'He likes to kill people the way they lived,' the Englishman added a little dreamily. 'It has a certain philosophical justice to it, rather like a Euripides play . . . The revenge of the gods, eh, Larsen? Only the gods were always ourselves.'

So he was to die, Larsen thought, and he thought of Eliza and felt himself teeter near a cliff of despair, then retreat. It was easy to translate despair into action when you had nothing left to lose. However, there was nothing he could do at the moment.

'Why *you*?' Larsen insisted, a third time. They were

turning left on West Seventy-second Street, under a canopy of Christmas lights, towards the Hudson River marina. Did Stangerson have a boat there?

'Because Fritzy was a nice chap and returned the favour you did him off Jounieh,' Stangerson replied. 'The only trouble was, word got around the Organization that Fritzy was asking questions, the Organization asked questions of the Families, and pretty soon the boss was asking questions of Fritzy. And of course, myself, since I run this operation. You see, the Fulton Oganization and the New York Families co-operate with each other, and we do all our business with the New York Families now, so we were only too happy to co-operate.' He chuckled. 'Fritzy told them what you were up to.'

The Englishman sighed, a sound of boredom. 'And so that's how they found you hanging around Fulton, and that's how we got you tonight, as well as that journalist woman. How kind of you to stash the bitch in our old safehouse in Truro. We've had that place watched ever since you ran from the cops. Expensive, but neat, don't you think?'

The fisherman felt himself go totally cold.

'You've got – that journalist.'

'Sorry, Larsen,' Stangerson said hypocritically. 'Had her. I'm afraid the Organization's had her ticket punched, permanently.'

She had said something about their relationship . . . it had a smell of death about it.

Larsen threw himself insanely at Stangerson but GI Joe had a blackjack in his other hand and he struck the fisherman a hard and beautifully accurate blow on the nape of the neck that knocked Larsen into Fritzy's knees, making constellations blink on the floor of the Ford.

'I'm afraid, old man, that I'm death on your boring love life.'

Larsen felt vomit swell in his throat. He bit back. The automobile had stopped. Perhaps it was the cosh that jostled Larsen's brain enough to finally make the connection.

'You used to call Sofia "the bitch" as well,' he said, his voice bitter, hoarse. 'Could you have . . . did you kill her, too? Did you,' he asked, voice stronger now with the effort, 'stage that accident in Delphi?'

There was a pause, and when Stangerson replied there was a tinge of respect that had not been in his tone before.

'I must remember that you aren't quite as thick as you pretend, Larsen. Not that it matters . . . when did you figure that out?'

'Why, Stangerson? *Why*?' He tried to get off Vogel's lap but GI Joe tapped him again, just hard enough.

'I needed you for the business. You were the best skipper around, you were a professional, you knew these waters. She prevented you from doing your job. I had her taken care of. Nothing personal, you understand . . . simply business. Logic, my friend. Emotions are irrelevant in the cosmic game, eh?'

With Eliza dead, there was only one point left in the cosmic game of life: kill Stangerson. To kill Stangerson he had to play for time.

'That information the Organization wants is hidden. If I die it will come out. Even if it looks like an accident, my lawyer will give it to my brother. He's the US Attorney,' Larsen finished desperately.

'Sorry, Captain Larsen. Nice try.'

Stangerson must have given a signal. GI Joe tapped him again, harder, so that he almost lost consciousness. The right rear fender of his skull was being seriously bent. Fritzy and Caliban on the other side hauled him into a spreadeagle on their knees, and flipped him over. He struggled weakly, expecting a knife in the throat. They had mentioned a death that looked like an accident but you could not trust these people. Fritzy grabbed his beard and pinched his nostrils and Caliban took out a full bottle of bourbon. Jim Beam. Ugh.

'Do it right this time, you bastards,' Larsen heard the Englishman hiss. 'If this one gets snafu'd again you'll be in more trouble than you've ever dreamed.'

Larsen kept his teeth shut but Caliban smashed him in the stomach, forced a brace of long, filthy nails inside Larsen's lips, and ripped. He jammed the bottle inside the lips. The whiskey gurgled into Larsen's throat, choking his air passage, and as he opened his mouth to cough the bottle neck was forced between his front teeth.

There was a strange feel, a strange taste to the bourbon. It was thick with a powdery substance that tasted like bitter parsley. They let him breathe twice, puking, retching, tipping the bottle, he was almost grateful, but he couldn't prevent them from pouring most of the quart down his throat. His strength was coming back despite the singing in his brain, and he rammed his heels through the rear side window on the car, making pretty crystals on the street. The cosh found his temple and he passed out cold, still choking and gagging on the doctored whiskey.

He awoke later. Two minutes later? Ten? He had no way of knowing. The pain in his head precluded thought. They were dragging him out of the Ford. They had driven it under an archway that opened on a river; streetlights, frozen trees on one side, brick buildings on the other. The Hudson, Riverside Park. A tug was pushing a barge up the river: two white range lights, a green starboard running light. The tug looked normal, friendly, like all the friends he had ever had, forever out of reach.

Caliban and GI Joe manhandled him through the arch and down a flight of steps. Above them the Henry Hudson Drive swooped uptown in a single granite impulsion, laden with cars.

The thugs slipped and cursed, leaving concrete for a slope of mud, litter, and dead bushes. His heels bounced independently behind.

'We should just plug him here,' GI Joe gasped, ever hopeful. Caliban grunted in a negative tone. Orders were orders in this man's army.

They came to the bottom of the hill. Just to their left an expanse of granite abutment underpinning the parkway came to an end, becoming, on their right, a series of huge, steel arches, a light blue cathedral of steel and rivets that carried the cars to and from downtown. Beneath the arches, row upon row of train tracks and weeds crept out of a vast, black tunnel under the granite, spreading into the switches and sidings and roundhouses of a freight yard. Only a couple of working lights served as contrast to the sinister expanse under the highway's shadow.

The Penn Central freight yards, Larsen thought inconsequentially. The City of New York was going to turn these into a condominium project, like Fulton. Every part of Manhattan that had a little history was going to be converted into a condominium until the whole city would be one giant playground centred on the cute aspects of yesteryear, a housing project for young professionals with discretionary income . . .

Suddenly the fisherman felt his body go completely numb. Then sounds started to distort, as if his head were inside an aluminium trash barrel. He was still limp from GI Joe's blackjack symphony, and already a little drunk from the effects of the bourbon, but this was different – he could feel his muscles wanting to move faster, faster, faster. His heart was galloping crazily.

They went through a ripped chainlink fence, across frozen puddles on a small baseball diamond, past a cement handball court, and through an iron fence that looked like it had been twisted open by Godzilla. They threw him down five feet of wall into the entrance of the railroad tunnel.

Larsen now felt as if his eyeballs were trying to pop out of their sockets. Sweat was pricking out all over his body . . . He had to move, let off the surcharge of pressure. He got up on his knees, head lolling off the shoulders, but Caliban and GI Joe both leaped down and threw him into a pile of pigeon excrement and litter and worked on him with cosh and fist. Then they started dragging him into the tunnel.

Blackness.

This is the way the world will end, Larsen felt vaguely, this is the way the world will end, not in a T. S. Eliot poem but in an eternal darkness of vast underground tunnels and bomb shelters, an underworld of crumbling concrete, and rusting steel, and train tracks dimly outlined by one or two very lonely spotlights; cold unending hell limned in circles of girders, partitions, alcoves, bunkers, culverts, and braces; a black concrete cathedral built to honour evil and the rats, bats, and other inhuman things that survived here, mutated and oozing pus after the radioactive storms had wiped out the beings that lived in light.

They dragged him deeper into the tunnel for what seemed like miles, his heightened perception making pythons out of every riveted girder. An occasional rectangle of faint light high above was a jalousie through which condemned souls could clutch prison bars with their reddened eyes, a hint of another world where cars still passed regularly bringing Dad home to pork chops, talk shows, and report cards.

Larsen squirmed hard, but he couldn't seem to co-ordinate his legs any more. He had to move but he couldn't. He had to move because otherwise his heart was going to race out of control and loose its moorings, a diesel gone amok without its governor, accelerating on the heat generated by accelerations gone by, making a charnel house of his chest. But if he moved the girders would come in on him. He cowered, trembling, as they dragged him. What had they given him in that whiskey?

Then Caliban dropped his left arm. Normally that would have hurt but his shoulder, his whole body was on some third level of anaesthesia.

'I go now,' European accent, North Italian, Trieste, Yugoslav.

'Come on. I thought you said we gotta drag him further? As far as the windows.'

'No. This is far enough. He will die soon anyway.'

'Coward.'

'Or the track people will take care of him first. One or the other. You must stay here to make sure. The boss said.'

A rustle of ratshit, old Smirnoff bottles, Budweiser cans, yellow newspaper, all projected in the narrow beam of a pencil flashlight Joe flicked on to check his solitude. Caliban had vanished, partisan of the night.

All around them the darkness echoed with the silence of dead space, the drip of run-off water, and, far above their heads, the rattle of cars in another world.

'Mother *fuck*,' said GI Joe, dropping his other arm. Larsen fell heavily in a pile of tumbleweed. The tumbleweed seeds

268

had been brought long ago by a freight headed east from Texas during the war, and had flourished in sunny corners of this eternally arid underworld.

Larsen felt as if he were convulsing, the sweat pouring off in rivers now, but when Joe played with the flashlight again he could see his own fingers were totally still. He finally managed to arch his body off the ground and the whole tunnel collapsed as GI Joe gave him a final cosh, a blow reinforced by the thug's own fear, and walked away at a rapid swish through the tumbleweed. Then Larsen's heart burst its moorings and he vomited thick gall over his chest, puking his heart out, then the shreds of throat, swallowing the puke, choking, gasping, helpless. He could not breathe, he could not move; the world was dark but he could just see the shades of Eliza's lost freckles as he felt consciousness slip slowly out of reach.

Right before complete darkness within darkness, the creatures moved in.

He was becoming aware of light, but it was happening in a sketch within a play within a movie where the colours of sepia and black and shadow blurred and changed of their own accord.

He was stretched out, totally naked, on a bed of black, L-shaped pieces of razor-thin steel. He was trembling violently to the disco beat of his heart, and every time his body convulsed he acquired minute razor slashes all over his back.

Dead and gone to Hades.

GI Joe was stretched out beside him, fully clothed, oozing chocolate blood from a long gash in his face.

The light came from a campfire that combined garbage from a defunct consumer culture with the last molecules of oxygen left from the Third World War. The flames danced, happily pagan. *Their* gods would always survive.

He felt a rib crack into a million splinters as someone kicked him hard in the side. There was a high-pitched giggle to the right. His head rolled over, shifting the bed of razors with a hiss.

Something had happened to his vision, it made everything

seem underwater, but as he became used to the light he could discern blurred people seated in a row to his right.

The fire made caverns of their mouths and pits of their eyes.

If this was Hell, these were the Damned.

'The court will come into session,' a Moses-like voice boomed from behind them.

Larsen's eyes were focusing a little better now. The doctored whiskey and his bucking heart combined to lift him to the mildly intrigued but completely uninvolved plane of observer, spectator, playwright. He would croak eventually from the stuff they had given him, Caliban had said that, but it seemed so irrelevant to this level of consciousness.

The 'court' consisted of:

an incredibly emaciated white man of about thirty-five, or maybe forty-five, with a Marine crewcut, filthy combat fatigues, and eyes that were all white, giggling crazily and endlessly cocking and rechecking the slide mechanism of an oily blue Colt .45;

Central Casting's idea of a railroad tramp, in old homburg, prewar work clothes, a knotted bandanna of gear and brogan shoes. He was shaved, clean – fingering with love a straightedge razor and aiming a grin of brown teeth and pure hatred in Larsen's direction;

a huge, shambling mountain of a man, caked in dirt, clad in five or six different blankets, nervous, braiding and rebraiding his beard or his three-foot ponytail, also caked in dirt;

another emaciated creature, an ancient black tramp with no teeth, dressed in a stained, patched, three-piece suit. He seemed quite normal except for a constant dribble of saliva down his chin, a perpetual trembling of the fingers.

Track people. A sentence drifted into Larsen's tortured mind. John. From New York. Track people: people who don't really believe that being human is where it's at any more.

The 'court' was seated in a semi-circle, in front of the entrance to a square, burned-out concrete blockhouse with

270

the slogan 'KILL JEW' and a swastika spray-painted on the wall.

The thick, southern black voice came from inside the blockhouse.

'These men have been found trespassin'. *Trespassin'*. On the tracks. White honky imperialist assholes invadin' the world of the lumpen proletariat of which we be the seat o' justice.

'Swear on *Playboy*.'

A faded copy of *Playboy*, 1973 vintage, was passed around and sworn on, palms on the cover like a Bible. The décolleté breasts looked apologetic. Razor Man was the only one who seemed not to take the ritual seriously. As he passed the old glossy down, Larsen could see Giggles' arm was stippled with hypodermic punctures.

'Exhibit A.'

GI Joe's silenced .22 was thrown between Larsen and the four seated track people.

'Only heah, we gotta twist, gennuhmen of de jury,' the voice continued. 'The honky imperialist asshole with de clothes on brought de naked honky heah by force.

'Both men, by our laws, are goin' to die.'

Joe had been shivering, harder and harder; he was probably used to violent death but this was right out of his league. All of a sudden he whimpered, jumped to his feet, and tried to run, but his wrists were bound and he was hobbled by the thick rope tied about his ankles. Mountain Man plucked him off his feet with one flick of the rope and hauled him back on to the pile of metal while he screamed insanely and beat his arms.

Very uncouth, a remote section of Larsen's brain commented.

'What's the *matter* with you!' GI Joe screamed. 'What do you guys *want*? I'll give you *money*!'

Larsen would have laughed if he commanded any muscles. GI Joe reminded him of himself in the Fulton Market.

'The prisoner will be silent. Because of this contemp' of court we'll decide his case first. What say you, gennuhmen of de jury? Innocent or guilty?'

'Brother Elijah.'

The old man trembled and drooled even more profusely. 'I don't know, brother,' he whispered, and drops of spittle flew into the firelight.

A snort came from the blockhouse.

'Brother Abraham?'

Mountain Man rumbled, burbled some more, finally rumbled, 'Guilty.' The strain made him unbraid one whole section of mane.

'Brother Cain?'

Giggles turned his thumb downward, majestically, like a Roman emperor.

'Brother Abel?'

The hobo shrugged. 'Why not?'

'Come on, Brother 'Lijah,' coaxed the Moses voice. 'You know this man must die.'

'I – I suppose so,' the old man whimpered. 'Whatever you think, brother.'

Mountain Man and Giggles got up at that point and grabbed GI Joe by the hair and ankles. Stangerson's man was wailing, pleading pathetically, his cries echoing among the bunkers, but they hauled him off the pile of strange metal, through the gap in the jury's ranks where Mountain Man had squatted, and next to the blockhouse door.

There they propped him in a sitting position against the cement. Mountain Man stood back, arms folded like an Apache chief, and looked at the seated man, and GI Joe stared back in horror, words of entreaty subsiding hopelessly on his lips.

He didn't notice Giggles step on to a discarded oil barrel, reach over the blockhouse roof, and delicately, gingerly even, bring down the severed end of a thick electricity cable, copper strands shining through the broken insulation, and snake it gently towards GI Joe's exposed neck.

There was a scream, an explosion of giggles, and GI Joe's roped body went rigid as an iron bar, hair standing straight up and then incredibly the figure bent over backwards, its backbone snapped with a crack as a massive electric shock flipped it five feet into the air, jerking wildly. Mountain Man had to jump out of its flight path. The body crashed into a pair of rusted tracks. There was a smell of roasting meat, of voided bowels, a sound of litter swishing spasmodically as the body convulsed. In the flicker of firelight Larsen could see a swollen tongue protruding between teeth bared in a death grimace. Then silence.

Giggles put the cable lovingly back on the roof, smiling like a born-again Christian, and resumed his seat on the Bench.

'Next,' the voice continued, calm and deep, 'the condemned man's apparent victim. Is the enemy of owah enemy owah friend? A delicate question of law, gennuhmen, for he remains an imperialist interloper asshole.

'Brother Abel.'

'Guilty.' The razor unfolded. No prizes for guessing how Larsen was going to die. Revenge is mine, saith the Lord.

'Brother Cain.'

'Guilty.' The Colt was back in Giggles' right hand. He lowered the gun until the black hole was pointing into Larsen's throat.

'Brother Abraham.'

A rumble. 'Not guilty.' Mountain Man sounded indifferent.

'Brother Elijah?'

'I dunno, brother,' said Saliva Man.

'Come on, boy,' said Giggles. 'Kill the fuzz. Kill the pig. Kill Saigon Sam. Kill the imperialist.' He giggled.

'Don't call me "boy",' croaked Elijah, then he gasped in horror at his own temerity. A string of sputum did yo-yo tricks on his chin.

'Don't listen to the honky. Decide fuh yuhself, Brother 'Lijah.'

'Yeah, well, fuck you, nigger,' Giggles said pleasantly, but in a voice too soft to penetrate the blockhouse.

'Not guilty,' Brother Elijah finally gasped, having decided which way the Moses voice was leaning.

'Then he lives,' the voice said with finality. Apparently the law of the tracks had been bent in Larsen's case. He felt vaguely privileged, the recipient of some unfamiliar honour.

273

A bearded, black face paraded out of the blockhouse, an Old Testament face deformed by skin disease and accentuated by the fire into a caricature of doom. It wore robes of black cloth, black tarpaper, and a fake snakeskin belt with three ice-picks wedged behind the fabric. Incredibly, two huge breasts rolled under the robes.

'Take the body to the pits. Take the reprieved man to the gates. We meet again tomorrow night. *Playboy*.'

Mountain Man began urinating into the campfire and the voices responded from out of a growing gloom:

'*Playboy*.'

'*Playboy*.'

'*Playboy*.'

Larsen vomited helplessly, constantly, bloodily all night, trying to decide if the play was over, if he had tipped the hat-check girl. He still could not move his muscles. Hell now was an effective off-Broadway production about a string of frozen nightmares in shades of black and tan.

Some nightmares were in his head – dreams of drowning, falling, choking, forfeit. Others were more real.

Once a razor blade appeared and started to carve a line around his throat as he lay helpless on the abandoned tracks.

A fog of poisonous breath mingled with a hum, as constant as it was off key. Delicate fingers performed an experimental pass of the blade so the coup de grâce would be accomplished more smoothly. The aesthetics of the straightedge.

The razor froze as a Moses voice whispered out of the blackness.

'No, no, no, no, no, Brother Abel.'

There was a gasp. The blade knicked Larsen's neck, then withdrew.

'He's an interloper,' the Razor Man wheedled, craftily 'He should die. I'll take care of him.'

'The court has ruled,' Moses Voice hissed menacingly. 'On *Playboy*.'

Razor Man laughed. He didn't think much of that religion, apparently. The laugh turned into a surprised cough, a wheeze, then a thud and thrashing, endlessly prolonged. The thrashing slowed and stopped. A sound of dragging receded uptown.

Ice-picks.

Nightmare within nightmare spun out of control within the fisherman's brain, then started to recede. At the same time light began to filter, sparse, into the chinks of the underworld.

The Penn Central police found him at eight in the morning.

CHAPTER TWENTY

'Angel Dust, horse tranquillizer, maybe half an ounce,' said the voice. 'And booze, bourbon by the smell, point eighteen concentration at least. He should have died three times over. Could be a suicide case.'

'Unggh,' came another voice.

'But these track people are unbelievable. This one wasn't anywhere near as bad as some I've seen, but he's been drinking steadily for years all the same. Enlarges the liver, gets it permanently revved up so it oxidizes everything in sight. Incredible . . .' Someone fiddled with the window. 'A little enzyme called cytochrome P450 in the liver, eats drugs up like crazy. We have to give these people sometimes ten times more anaesthetic than normal to put 'em under. Cytochrome P450 is how they couldn't poison Rasputin. In case you didn't know.'

There was a rasp of a match, the smell of Virginia tobacco.

'Not only is he an alcoholic, but he's big. And he has a heart like a horse, so he made it. Someone kicked the shit out of his ribs and head, too. Contusion city.'

'I'm not an alcoholic,' Larsen thought defensively.

The voices faded.

Memory rushed in. Not whole, but whole enough.

He fended it off as long as he could, trying to regain confidence in perceptions distorted by drugs and alcohol. Antiseptic tiled ward. Hispanic words of pain. White walls, clear plastic bags full of nameless fluid. Saline drips. And then a rush into a familiar grey.

If the feelings of sadness that came with the death of Joe Sciacca, of Marie Riley, of John Silva, and of his beloved boat could be stacked up and multiplied tenfold they would never amount to what he was feeling now for Eliza.

She had been the first snowdrops after a Yukon winter. No matter what their future would have been, no matter what each would have learned about the other, no matter that quick temper, so obviously built up like scar tissue around earlier psychic wounds. The initial perception of her had been reinforced in a thousand ways, conscious and subliminal, to build the complex psychological pattern of long-term infatuation. Pattern bred response, the release of amino acids in the brain, depressed frontal lobes, accelerated heartbeat, loss of appetite – love.

But it had been killed. Again. By the same hand. There was something wrong with a system of nature that allowed men to become gods and play with the destinies of others.

Freedom, he had once told O'Malley in the heat of a drunken political discussion, was more than a political ideal. It was a relative order of nature that best allowed an organism to interact as efficiently as it could with its environment. An adaptive mechanism.

Stangerson and Lu Guercio interfered with that order. They had to die. It was that simple.

Afterwards he could face the rationalizations, face the endless void of colours and decide what to do with his own life, assuming he had the choice. Life without Eliza: day without sun, night without stars. A lifetime of tunafish sandwiches without mayonnaise.

Larsen spent most of the day in the crowded ward, weak, unwilling to move. The hospital told him to leave at three that afternoon, sending a squad of credit department enforcers to grill him first. He was made to sign sheafs of forms, using his false name, acting dumb, a track person, making promises to repay the department within forty days for medical costs incurred. They didn't even pretend to believe him. They talked openly about Hill-Burton benefits, about getting the bad debt reimbursed by the city.

The Salvation Army representatives gave him clean duds that were much too small, and Christian advice that came much too pat. His wrists and calves burst out of the plaid vinyl jacket and Truman-era trousers. They gave him pamphlets on demon rum and professed a good will so general that it turned cold in the specific.

He thanked them anyway.

He had left his bags at the Chelsea. That was a mistake, even with the false John Hancock on his passport. Stangerson knew his New York City habits too well. But they would not be looking for him because they thought him dead. Until GI Joe failed to check in.

He spent ten minutes leaning, exhausted, in a doorway up the street from the Chelsea. The walk from the hospital had drained him. No one, at any rate, appeared to be watching the hotel.

Larsen finally persuaded the manager to let him into his room and settled accounts from the wadded cash in his bag. Two neo-punkettes in the lobby were looking at his attire, openly envious. He left immediately.

Feeling sullied by the cheap Sally Ally clothes and by the after effects of horse tranquillizer and bourbon, he took a taxi straight to Brooks Brothers, fifteen minutes before closing time. He hadn't gone eight feet into the store before he was intercepted by two courteous bouncers, tape measures draped around their collars for camouflage, who suggested that he leave, now, if he didn't mind.

Larsen eventually purchased a charcoal, pinstriped, Savile Row three-piece suit, the kind that had been in fashion for forty years and would remain in fashion as long as Harvard was Harvard. He also bought a shirt, a tie, socks and a pair of English shoes made of beautiful, mahogany-brown calf's leather. They made him show his cash before letting him try on the suit, but he left wearing it, transformed, in his own mind at least, into a facsimile of Ferguson Whipple III, with a beard, a purple bruise at the base of his skull, and twenty-five razor nicks on his back. He wished they made clothes for the insides as well; he still felt dirty, through and through. A burglarized soul.

He took another cab from Brooks Brothers, and as it inched through Fifth and Madison traffic, Larsen allowed his eyes to be entertained by the faerie spectacle, the showers of Christmas lights that adorned every priapic office block.

He checked into the United Nations Plaza Hotel, a skyscraper with a wedge divoted off the sides by an architect so it would stand apart from all the other buildings in New

York that took their lines from butane cigarette lighters. A hotel built of mirrors that substituted fast elevators for large staffs. A hostel for the travelling salesmen of international bureaucracies, by and for the under-under secretaries of ILO, UNESCO, WHO.

But Larsen knew it had a swimming pool on the twenty-seventh floor that looked over the East River. He showered in his room, took three aspirins for a bruised head, then went up and bought a skimpy nylon bathing suit from the pool attendant for an inflated price and floated like a spaceman on his back in the warm water for a full hour, looking over the lighted galaxies of New York City. Emptying his mind in the womb warmth of the pool.

He needed to be emptied, cleared out. The sullied feeling could be traced to the after effects of poisonous drugs and alcohol, but it came also from the certainty that he had been betrayed.

His bluff had been called and the enemy had shown his hand in doing so. The fact that he was still around to appreciate the fact that his own brother had marked the cards was a matter of chance alone.

He went back to the insulated, air-conditioned room and tried meditating for the first time since college. He couldn't even recall his mantra, and fell asleep in a quarter lotus on the double bed. The last things he saw were the lighted windows of the greenish glass megalith, burning late as delegates continued the world's longest exercise in indispensable futility.

The next day Larsen stepped out of the UN Plaza into a town as empty and bitter as his general state of mind. Nowhere did winds get funnelled and twisted to blow as cold as they did in New York. Even the bright yellow cabs were faded into a sullen wash and the faces of hurrying commuters looked sallow and repressed. Iron clouds scudded and burst overhead with a speed that suggested bad news behind them. Matrons cracked brittle thighbones as they slipped on sidewalk ice. It had begun to snow.

Larsen bought a scarf and parka at a Madison Avenue ski

shop. The parka was the kind whose hood zipped into a little sphincter for one's nose to breathe through. The scarf would cover even that, and the thirty degrees of frost and twenty knots of wind would explain his lack of face. He took the IRT subway to Brooklyn Bridge and walked as far as the fish market.

It was eleven a.m. and the market was deserted, except for some empty truck trailers and piles of fish guts, smashed boxes, and a lingering stench from the night before. Bony cats and the cruel wind reinforced the loneliness of the place.

Larsen shivered. He was getting a cold. If he had a spirit it would probably be deathly ill, but his body compounded the problem. His mood was lower than it had been in his entire life.

Only one dealership was open, down the street. A broom swung out of the open doorway at regular intervals. The Sciacca Fish Company was locked up and tight and dark. Larsen, reckless in his despondency, strode straightforwardly down the market cobbles and peered through the thick iron bars that locked the Sciacca dealership.

It was a fish house like every other fish house in Fulton, a long, tall, narrow shoebox of brick and concrete, lined with stainless-steel tables and oilskin aprons, piled high with fish boxes, and centred around a set of scales. A large German calendar showed a naked blonde suggestively working the controls of an automatic fish skinner. The floor was cambered to funnel water and fish guts into a single hole in the middle.

Towards the rear, a flight of steep, crooked wooden steps angled up to green-hued windows on the second floor. The office. That was where the computer terminal would be.

To the side of the door there flowed a faint ray of orange light. As Larsen's eyes adjusted to the gloom he picked out the electronic eye of a proximity alarm, a fancy piece of semi-conducted hardware that focused on the slightest movement to set off bells and sirens, presumably bringing cold-eyed people with .22 revolvers out of the brickwork.

The eye was aimed at the iron-barred doorway. There was

no other way in. Even if he could burn his way through the inch-thick bars without arousing suspicion, the alarm would be triggered long before he could shut off the mechanism. And it was the kind of alarm that went off automatically if you tampered with it in any way, shape or form. The Rolls-Royce of burglar catchers. All the big southside mansions on Cape Cod had at least one.

Yet there was no other entrance into the Sciacca offices, unless you carved your own by tunnelling through brick walls from the fish houses next door on either side.

Larsen ambled slowly back towards the subway stop. He could take care of Lu Guercio, anyway. He knew where he worked. Stangerson might be more difficult to find, but knowledge worked both ways: if Stangerson knew Larsen's habits, the fisherman knew the smuggler's. But the system that had killed Eliza would remain intact if he did not obtain the information secreted in the computer.

The wet snow gave up its struggle for crystallization and became cold rain. Car tyres hissed. Larsen walked and tried to think through his sniffles.

It would be too hard even with expert help to tap into a link-up with their main computer. There *had* to be a way into the fish house. Tunnel through brick?

Not if there was a tunnel already there – the gurry hole.

Fish wholesalers in New York and elsewhere used a large chute to dump the massive amounts of water and fish waste they went through daily. The chute typically consisted of a hole one and a half feet wide which communicated directly with the sewers. The Sciacca gurry chute would be no exception. And sewers were accessible, for inspection, maintenance, and repair.

Larsen turned on his heel and went back to the Sciacca dealership.

The chute was roughly two feet wide, covered with a removable iron grate. More important, it lay well behind the entrance, out of range of the proximity detector.

He departed a second time, passing a lone fish market worker, going home, who looked briefly but without suspicion at his bundled face.

The phone book gave him the information he wanted: The Office of Sewer Permits, Division of Environmental Protection. A deep voice said 'Uriko's Boy' would be happy to show him the sewer maps. Uriko's Boy, the voice continued, was at 65 Woit Street.

White Street?

No, Woit. Larsen mentally compensated for the Brooklyn accent and came up with Worth Street. It was a few blocks from where he stood, across City Hall Plaza.

'Uriko's Boy' was a plump piece of city ethnography aggregated around a White Owl cigar. He lived in a dingy eleventh-floor office painted in dirty yellow, with blueprints of cross-sectioned sewer pipes and unflattering caricatures of the mayor tacked up on the walls.

The man found the underground layout of Fulton and photocopied the relevant maps with casual efficiency, patiently explaining the more arcane notations.

Larsen went back to the UN Plaza and studied the chart. It looked almost too straightforward. A four-foot wooden barrel outfall, aiming east to the river from the main four-foot sewer that drained the Fulton Street fish houses, would provide a handy, out-of-the-way entrance point. If you went up the barrel sewer, crossed through the sluices and tunnels of a regulator, you came to the main sewer. There would be some kind of grate preventing rats and other thieves from entering via the various gurry chutes that connected with the sewer, but there were ways to get around even that.

At a cut-rate construction supply house not far from the Chelsea, Larsen purchased portable oxyacetylene equipment, a welder's mask, thick welding gloves, a couple of waterproof flashlights, a tube of quick-setting, all-purpose glue, a two-foot crowbar, and a canvas carrying bag that would hold the lot.

At a nearby yachting-goods outlet he bought a pair of fancy Norwegian rubber boots, a waterproof chart case, and a Zippo lighter with fluid. The lighter had a sailboat engraved on its side.

The best time to burgle the market would be just after dark, around eight or nine p.m., long before fish houses began to open their doors at one or two in the morning.

By three-forty-five p.m. he was back at the UN Plaza.

He ate dinner by the window in his room, watching the horizon fade and be invaded by a million pinpricks of light stretching to the Atlantic. His brain seemed to have finally disconnected from emotion, leaving only a sense of purpose on an empty steppe of mind.

But as he watched the lights of New York come to life, one by one, a strange, wistful feeling of beauty pervaded the steppe. He was looking at visual harmonics, mutually enhanced, for once, by humans and nature.

It had no effect on his sense of purpose, but it accentuated the poignancy of his exclusion from real life.

Outlaw.

The outlaw had turned hunter in the jungles of the secret world, and the hunter was ready. The equipment fitted easily in the huge canvas bag; his Heckler and Koch had a belt holster that was invisible under the parka. At eight-forty-five he put two spare clips in his pocket and left the hotel.

The manhole Larsen had chosen lay buried under accumulated tiers of the Franklin Delano Roosevelt Drive and the Brooklyn Bridge.

It was hidden in a shattered landscape of reinforced concrete, broken asphalt, and rubble from a construction site next door. During working hours, said a sign, the site was used as a parking lot and watched over by a patrol service. At this hour of the night there were no patrolmen in sight.

The landscape led out among the ruins of a destroyed wharf, broken-toothed pilings that went as far as the westernmost pier of the Brooklyn Bridge. The bridge foundation towered like a monster's foot among the layered archaeology of previous monsters, waiting for monsters yet to come.

And everywhere the excrement of consumer America: styrofoam, Coke bottles, plywood, tyres, and nameless plastic mouldings.

Larsen found the manhole right where the maps said it should be, and used his crowbar to lever open the heavy

283

cover. He gave a last look around to make sure he was unobserved and slipped underground, sliding the cover back into place by lifting it on his shoulders.

Immediately he was immersed in the sewer environment: a sickly sweet stink, a constant rush and dripping of liquid, the scurrying of nameless things with atrophied eyes and highly evolved teeth.

Larsen took out a flashlight, clambered down fifteen feet of chipped concrete and rusted brackets, and looked with dismay into the 'four-foot wooden barrel outfall', so clean and direct on the map.

'Barrel sewer – dat's de old kind, tricky,' Uriko's Boy had explained.

It was a black stream, with amorphous pieces swirling out to freedom and the East River. Its sides were a mass of rot and mould, loam and granite poking out where the barrels had crumbled. There was maybe two feet of fetid gas to breathe. In the darkness of the tunnel he could hear the squeaking of rats, louder than the hurrying water. He was grateful that his head cold prevented him from smelling as much as he could have.

Stifling revulsion, claustrophobia and attendant nausea, Larsen dropped into the flow and began wading upstream, back bent double, probing with the flashlight. Here and there, he found his way impeded by dams of rubbish, by large rocks cracking through the floor of the city. He held his breath and cleared debris carefully, just enough to get by, expecting at any minute the rush and crash of a cave-in.

Up ahead, maybe twenty feet, the flashlight glanced off the black water and found new concrete. A steel gate, or rather a sluice, that could be cranked up and down through vertical tracks, to dam or free accumulated waste water. He sloshed up, clambered over it, and found himself in a deep concrete chamber, newly built, but covered in growth, weird and dank. Another sluice up ahead channelled sewage out of two tunnels beyond that, both brick. There was another brick tunnel to his left.

He dug out the photocopies of the sewer maps, sending his flashlight beam swinging, and caught his breath as the light flicked on something alive.

There was a dog looking at him from the next tunnel.

He steadied the flashlight and found it again. It was the size of a toy poodle, but it wasn't a toy poodle. It had red eyes and brown fur and it cheeped as it waddled around and headed back crosstown followed by a long, bare tail.

Rats as big as dogs. So it was true. The mythology of urban civilization was confirmed. If he wasn't careful he'd find himself grappling sewer pythons, rabid gerbils, or baby alligators that had been flushed down the toilets and had grown to monstrous proportions on a taste for garbage.

Larsen turned left. The outflow was shallower here, the going easier.

He counted one, two, three manholes. From the third manhole he began ticking off the house connections above his head. One dumped waste water as he passed beneath, spilling excrement on his shoulders. He retched at the smell, then gave up trying to keep his head clear of the thousand and one drips and runnels of the sewer. The waste had an overtone of fish to it. He was passing under the market, and the shit meant someone was awake.

The Sciacca Fish Company should be the fifth house connection from the third manhole on South Street, on the western side of the sewer. That was assuming every fish house had a sewer connection. But they had to; it would be a sine qua non of obtaining a city permit to sell seafood.

The house connections were all protected by a set of standard one-inch-thick iron bars cemented deeply into the brick-and-mortar outlets of the openings. The fifth hole was no different. The bars were rusted, but they held firm when Larsen tried to pry them loose with the crowbar, bending only slightly in their seats.

Reluctantly he unpacked the tube and nozzle connected to twin oxygen and acetylene gas tanks in his bag. Decaying organic matter always decomposed into methane gas, among other things, and methane gas could accumulate in sewers. A spark could set off an explosion that would turn the tunnel into a low-rent crematorium.

The silver lining in that cloud was the probability he would take half the fish market with him in the explosion.

He put on the welder's goggles, cracked the cylinders, turned the nozzle to 'on', and flicked his lighter. Once, twice, and the nozzle caught in a disconnected jet of white light, but the only flames in the sewer tunnel remained attached to the nozzle. Larsen put on the asbestos gloves, adjusted the jet to a blue heat, and used his lungs again.

The bars were made of low-grade iron and cut easily. When he had finished Larsen put the cutting equipment into his bag, hung the bag from the hot stump of one of the severed bars, took out the rope and the chart case, which he had filled with pens and paper, stuffed them into his parka, and wriggled into the dark opening.

The tunnel was two feet wide and angled up a forty-five-degree slope, but for every two-foot wriggle upward, he slithered back one on the decades worth of accumulated fish guts. The only way he could progress at all was on his stomach, sliding his hands in front through the ooze, wedging his shoulders as he brought his knees up, ignoring the ache on the left and then trying to wedge his toes and knees as he straightened his body again. Larsen, the Human Worm.

He was covered with putrid gurry, his hair was impregnated with gurry, fish oil had seeped to his underwear and inside his boots. He had to wipe it from his eyes.

Ten, then twenty feet. It felt like a mile. The stink was indescribable. He mashed his nose. The tunnel had ended in a wall.

When he switched on the flashlight, he saw it hadn't ended. He must be under the fish-house floor. Three feet overhead was the thin grate of metal with pinpricks in it whose flip side he had spotted earlier, covering the gurry hole. He turned off the flashlight, flopped on to his back, and eeled his shoulders upwards. No light came through the grate, but he eased it open very cautiously anyway. If the Fulton Organization was still outthinking him as consistently as it had to date, they would be sitting comfortably around the gurry hole, smoking and drinking sambuca and waiting to put a slug between his eyes the minute he poked his head out.

He did so. No bullet came. The fish-house air smelled like brochures claimed the Swiss Alps did, rare and pure, compared to the gurry. A faint light came from the doorway, enough to illuminate the German calendar which read, '*Benützen Sie unseren Stockfisch Apparat.*' It was the right place.

Larsen took off his outer garments and piled them next to the hole. If he kept them on he would leave a trail of sewer slime, like a slug. He preferred to leave no tracks at all. He took the P7 from its holster. With gun in one hand and waterproof chart case in the other, he climbed gingerly through the creaking darkness to the office door.

It was locked. Damn! He had expected this, but hoped differently. It meant his visit would not go undetected. He took a piece of paper from the case, covered it with all-purpose glue, and adhered it to the lower right-hand corner of the frosted glass that formed the upper half of the door. He waited for the glue to set, then cracked the glass delicately with the butt of his gun and removed the paper. Only the small shard fell to the floor. He reached in, twisted the nipple on the door handle, opened the door, and stepped inside the office.

The fisherman made personal acquaintance with a series of thick metallic desks, piled slips, sharp-cornered filing cabinets, coffee machines, and desk chairs, before he found it. A tiny spot of green light showed the terminal to be locked in the eternal standby of software existence. As he bumbled by the keyboard he nudged into what looked like an automatic printing machine hooked up next to the terminal. He allowed himself a sliver of flashlight and confirmed that it was indeed a Digital Equipment Corporation line printer.

A real stroke of luck, that. One tap on the print button and he would have a complete transcription of whatever data he wanted, typed out by darting needles of light at one thousand words per minute. It would save him time, and right now his life depended on time.

He surveyed the keyboard. The mute black screen, shaped like a curved square in weightless, unresponsive plastic, was the antithesis of right-angled geometry, of the gears and counterpressures of traditional mechanics. The soft glow of the standby light hinted at a ghost in the machine.

Larsen felt an almost Luddite apprehension as he pressed the command button of the DEC 1300. Here was associative intelligence: primitive, not living because it was incapable of adapting its own program to new circumstances, incapable of reproducing itself. But a form of intelligence nonetheless, in the service of an organization that had murdered four of his friends within the last month. An enemy intelligence, fraught with traps.

He would have to be careful, Larsen thought, watching the screen glow into eerie life.

A little rectangle of light, the cursor, appeared and flicked on and off impatiently. Letters glowed into being.

'SYSTEM C: VT7:VT71/T* PLEASE LOGIN**'

Larsen took out his transcript, and hit the button labelled 'RETURN' as indicated by Joe Sciacca's code.

'USER ID' the screen said, peremptorily.

Larsen consulted the code.

'LUPO 1' he typed out, the letters appearing obediently in the upper left-hand corner of the screen. He again pressed the return key.

'PASSWORD' the computer immediately signalled.

He pressed 'Return' slowly, cybernetic ritualism, and typed 'BACALAO'.

'MODE' read the screen.

'@ DS' Larsen replied, and hit the return key.

'SEARCHING DIRECTORY PLEASE WAIT'

He waited. At least it was a polite computer.

'@ READY.'

'Type MISERIA VT1:5' the instructions Larsen had translated from Morse code commanded. Larsen typed obediently.

'NO SUCH FILE' the computer said, after checking.

'FILE OVER*RIDE' Larsen replied.

'PRIVILEGE VIOLATION' the DEC 1300 countered.

Sciacca's instructions read, 'Type out "@ REQUIEM RETURN".' Larsen spelled out the message via the keyboard and sat back hopefully.

Nothing happened. He checked the code, pressed the return button once more. Nothing happened again. He waited, perplexed, rereading the instructions. Two minutes passed.

Without warning the screen stitched itself rapidly full of ghastly green letters, left to right, up to down, jerking lines out of sight to let new lines in.

Pages' worth. Long lists of what looked like names, places, dates, sums of money, and bank account numbers. Paragraphs of prose, a lot of which seemed to be entries in a microchip journal. Old Gaetano Sciacca had kept right up with the times in his diary habits.

Larsen began to read.

The first part of the hidden computer file obviously dealt with fish prices.

'*12 March. Frank Trapani, representing the New York Families' interest, Sciacca, Johnny Golub, Solomon Steiberg, Peter Jonson, Phil Morrello for the Organization. We met 2 a.m. on top of the bar. Sol and Pete have taken a lot of striped bass orders from the Carolinas: keep a floor price of $1.80. Agreed . . . Market cod, we ordered 2500 pounds. The Westside Jewish group has ordered a lot from the Cape and Gloucester, Meier excepted. Steve Palermo wants to keep the price real low on scup, squid, mussels for some restaurants he's into. Vince says OK if Steve agrees to a higher price later when the shrimp are supposed to come in . . .*'

Larsen read every word, hitting the return key to move the text up so he could read the next line.

'*18 March: weekly dues from the Morrello fish house $1400: not bad for 5 per cent of the take. Money collected by Bill Ferrara, given to Frank Trapani, who I know stashed it in his uncle's bank on Madison Avenue, closed account. Sol says they hide it in dividend fund.*'

After five minutes Larsen began to get a vague impression of a secret city where everyone knew everyone else by sight and name, where contracts went by word of mouth and deals were strictly cash. A world of extended kinship ties, based on Mediterranean peasant groupings, a world where favours asked are returned, loyalties given or withheld replaced the more mundane production quotas, the inter-office memos, the pension plans of ordinary business. A world controlled by the Organization – a myth come to violent life – of which shadowed hints over espresso at Marino's Bar, coded telephone conversations at three in the morning between harried men in offices crammed with fish sale slips and styrofoam coffee cups were the very heartbeat.

Gaetano Sciacca, Larsen realized, had put every illegal deal, payoff, agreement, contract, and rumour that affected the secret world into his hidden computer file. The old man must have stayed late every morning, after the market closed its doors, his fingers tapping away at plastic keys, recording it in minute detail.

The little passwords for midnight phone calls, the schedules for meetings at 'the bar', details of the Flatbush cipher used to readjust the price of fish at short notice.

The data were day-to-day specific, impressionistic in their more general implications, but after ten minutes Larsen began to make sense of the overall picture.

The inner circle of fish dealers at Fulton, Gaetano indicated, formed a price-fixing cartel and the cartel essentially let the supply of fresh fish, as affected by good or bad weather, the time of year, the number of boats fishing, the type and abundance of fish available, determine whether the price of fish would be high or low – *within a spectrum previously set by the cartel*. The computer file showed that no one at Fulton paid fishermen more money, or charged less than the agreed floor and ceiling prices.

He had found it, Larsen realized. Evidence to prove 'the Organization' existed, to substantiate the rumours all fishermen believed but nobody could prove. Even he had not fully believed it, until now, Larsen realized.

And Fulton was the largest market on the East Coast. The fresh fish auctions in Boston and New Bedford might have marginally different prices, but since they relied on New York to either absorb their surplus or send fish up when New England was short, they also took the lead from the floor and ceiling prices agreed upon in Fulton.

Fixed prices!

But according to the file, price fixing wasn't the only scam going at Fulton. There was that 5 per cent rake-off from each house's profits that was essentially rent, paid to the Organization and the New York Families for allowing the dealer to work at Fulton. As Stangerson had said, the Organization and the New York Families worked together, like fingers in a glove. If the dealer didn't pay the 5 per cent his trash wasn't hauled, his fish cutters quit, and his trucks were not unloaded; then they were stolen or burned and he himself was beaten or worse. Everybody paid the 5 per cent before they paid their electricity bills, the computer told Larsen.

Another scam going at Fulton was straightforward theft. Sciacca had a whole separate accounting system for profits made from the rough 10 per cent of gross poundage that was lifted directly off incoming trucks. Truck drivers that objected never came back.

A mosaic of rumours, hearsay, inside information.

'10 July: Tong Seafoods wants to take over the RiccoBono house. The Koreans are willing to pay 5 per cent plus another 7 per cent for the first five years, plus cash up front. They want a stake in parking protection and the union pension. I said OK but the others don't know about letting in Koreans. Zangara says he is a good Catholic and doesn't like them. It's been all Sicilians and Jews up to now. But Tong has already been dealing with the Parensa and the Corsicans so potential allies . . .'

Whatever that meant, but there was the word 'Parensa' again, presumably the person or animal that was mentioned by the voice who had threatened Marie.

As Larsen read on, he saw that payoffs and bribes also had their own accounting column in Sciacca's unique records. Many of the names mentioned were references to nicknames or metropolitan family names that were unfamiliar to Larsen. Some he knew.

'$5000 in consulting fees to Amoriggi Services of Manhattan, for helping us with the Board of Estimate, money in unmarked bills that Tony heard was Costillini's casino rake-off.

'Judge Sheridan got a Christmas present from the Parking

Co., $1000, liquid, delivered by Johnny Zangara, they said cash came from Moe Socks' laundry . . .

'*Sam Kirby, manager of Down Cape Seafood Co-op, 10¢ per box of fish he sends to us instead of Boston this winter. Total $475.*

'*New York Families' turn to be chairman of the Organization: Trapani voted in for two years. Meier's group next . . .*

'*$1000 for Dan Murphy in Boston, Senate, for helping us with customs and Canadian fish (Samuel Beinwitz, Billy Goose, Zangara).*'

Murphy, the fisherman knew, was a Massachusetts state senator, a two-time candidate for governor. He was also known to be a close associate of Per's sponsor, Frank Smith.

Was that how it had worked? Had Per been taking money from organized crime via Smith and Murphy? A federal attorney could write his own ticket, making enough money to buy original Munch paintings: enough perhaps to make it worth turning in his own brother.

Larsen resumed pressing the return key to make new lines appear on the screen. The marching ranks of letters gave no notice. It was just there.

'*$50,000 cash to United States Attorney for Massachusetts swordfish case. Charges dropped against Canadians. 10 per cent to New York Families (Genoveses) via Trapani for the contact . . . Also Zangara.*'

The item was dated two years ago, one year after Per had been named to the post.

Somehow the evidence did not cut as deep as Lars had expected. Perhaps his subconscious had been way ahead of his conscious brain, piecing together inconclusive, subliminal shreds of evidence, chiselling out a dovetail of acceptance for the conscious knowledge to slot into when it came.

Or maybe it just didn't matter so much any more.

When he came to the end of the file he sat still for a minute.

There was a lot of money in Fulton, close to $80 million tax free, the computer said. The kind of golden egg that might prompt men to commit murder unhesitatingly, viciously, repeatedly, on the mere chance that the goose which laid it might be imperilled. And yet –

Larsen sat and stared at the video display terminal. The cursor marking the final line of data blinked steadily.

And yet the information, useful as it might be to a grand jury in policing present practices, would be of limited help in convicting any of the ringleaders.

As soon as the first hint of investigation came out the numbered accounts would be transferred, the phones changed, meeting schedules shifted, codes altered. The patterns of money flow that were the most revealing evidence of wrongdoing were of limited use without corroborating evidence from witnesses. And evidence from a dead man in a stolen computer printout was not conviction material.

Maybe *they* didn't know that.

The cursor blinked hypnotically.

What was it Joe's logbook had said about a takeover by Neapolitans?

Larsen checked his notes again and saw that there were two code words left unused. He typed out the first and found Sciacca's most deadly secret.

As the hidden layer of data was printed out in front of him, the fisherman realized what the men who had killed Eliza, Marie, John, Joe, and three other seamen feared. They were not afraid of the data's getting to the Feds. They were terrified of it getting back to the Organization – and its allies. This part of Sciacca's file read like a confession, testament – or death warrant.

'*For the last five years, I, Gaetano Sciacca, Bobby "Lu Guercio" Mondragone, Guido Orsini, and Kwo have been working so our groups can assume control over major houses in Fulton Fish Market from the Organization and the five New York Families.*

'*Mondragone and Sciacca represent the Neapolitan families, the Parense, which are known together as the Camorra. Orsini represents the Unione Corse, the Corsicans. Kwo represents the Koreans and the Taiwan Tongs they work with. "Guercio" Mondragone is in charge of all the groups since most of the drugs come through the Mediterranean. Most of the cash comes from Naples.*

'We have been steadily replacing owners and managers of the top fish houses in Fulton with our own people. Up to now the Organization and the five Families have been keeping Fulton open territory. They do not want to see drugs here. They refuse to allow competition in the racket and they kept their drug operations separate. Since Funzi was nailed the young men have been running the Organization business. They are more interested in legalized businesses like the fish houses. But they do not allow the Camorra or the Unione Corse to open our own drug operations uptown, or anywhere in New York.

'Two years ago we began smuggling and distributing drugs through the fish houses controlled by Neapolitans. Profits last year were over $55 million from heroin, hashish, cocaine. Drugs were smuggled in the abdominal cavities of fresh fish and distributed to groups that are cut out by the Organization: Blacks from the old Gallo group, the Flying Dragons and Ghost Shadows in Mott Street. A group of Vietnam veterans called the Purple Gang on the West Side and New Jersey. Mendez and the Colombians are very important.

'Our first fish with drugs came from Plymouth, Mass., and Portland, Maine. Smuggled in from Italian, Canadian, and Colombian boats. Kiddo and Violet, Joker and Big Nuts ran the New England operations.'

The confessions grew darker. 'Sonny Tramunti was taken out by Blondie Amalfi on 30 July. No one knows this. Mondragone planned it like an accident because no one must know. We cannot draw attention to ourselves. He was knocked out and put in his car and rolled off the highway. This leaves the Seafine Fish Company controlled by Vic Positano, the sixth for the Parense.

'The real reason Dorilli was shot was he was working with Kwo and found heroin. Mondragone did the cover, as usual. He has planned five hits and all except for Dorilli were ruled misadventures . . .'

There was more, much more, and it all spelled death for the conspirators involved, a death as painful as it was certain if anyone from the Organization or the Families got wind of his information.

He had found 'La Parensa', a.k.a. Camorra.

Larsen went back to mark the previous blocks of data, and hit the print key. The automatic line printer began ripping out sentences across rolls of green printout paper.

He repeated the process for the second block of information.

It was twelve-thirty a.m. He had to get out of there.

The printer finally fell silent. Larsen checked the reams of paper with his flashlight. The information was all present, clearly spelled out. He folded it into the waterproof chart case and hit the command button that pulled the computer terminal in and out of standby mode.

It was only then that he remembered there was a final code word listed in the instructions, a code word he hadn't used. A siren ululating outside told him what it had been for.

The log-out code.

Larsen grabbed the P7 and rushed out of the office and down the steps. There was a shout, faint outside behind a patter of rain. He pulled on his filthy outergarments, stashed the waterproof chart case safely inside his parka, and wiped clean the area next to the gurry hole. Only then did he slip into the hole, pulling the grate over him.

He sledded easily down the gurry chute, braking his slide with the elbows. The water was colder, less smelly, deeper, up to his crotch. He remembered the rain.

Larsen unhooked the bag containing crowbar and cutting torch, dropped it into the current, and started walking as quickly as his hunched-over position and the sewer water would allow. At least the flow was going his way.

It was frightening how quickly the water level was rising. At one point he felt a tight furry bag, about the size of a toy poodle, bump into the small of his back and drift away. Friend Rat, apparently, had met his doom. By the time he got to the regulator sluice the water was kissing Larsen's chest with foul lips.

He clambered over the first sluice. Water roared all through the darkness, gouts of liquid and waste objects flying around the concrete. He aimed his flashlight at the regulator's central chamber and felt butterflies in the stomach.

Rainwater had been funnelling off the city streets and into a myriad of culverts that ran into the sewers, hundreds and thousands of gallons pouring through three tunnels into this set of concrete chambers and through the barrel outfall into the East River. But the outfall would never take the combined volume sluicing into the regulator.

If he did not go *now* he would be trapped and drowned like his rodent pal. The water was perceptibly higher already and there was only one foot of breathing space left in the barrel sewer leading to his manhole.

He plunged into the maelstrom, clambered over the second sluice, slipped, tripped, and was sucked helplessly into the rotting ancient tunnel he had first entered four hours earlier.

Larsen had to fight a renascent wave of claustrophobia as he let himself be carried downstream by the thundering current of rain and waste. The rotten barrel structure was irregular and twice he felt himself pushed below water as the roof dipped.

He kept his arms rigid over his head, scraping the roof, feeling for the vacuum of the manhole.

If he missed it he was dead. The current would sweep him helplessly to the end of the outfall.

His hands met nothing. He kept them extended, grabbing for the brackets he knew were on the left side of the manhole. He missed. His feet, scrabbling downward, could find no purchase on which to erect his body. His right hand met the farther side of the manhole, where concrete shaft met barrel outfall, and held his body there briefly against the current. But friction was not enough to hold him, his grip was going. He grabbed again and hit a bracket, this time almost opening his mouth in relief, gagged, and finally, hand over hand, hauled himself out of the filthy torrent.

CHAPTER TWENTY-ONE

Larsen spent the next two days in his hotel room on the thirty-seventh floor studying the Sciacca printout, or bent over a rented typewriter, occasionally using the phone, sometimes staring out over the giant tombstones of the megalopolis, watching the walking dead reverse Dracula's pattern as they left their suburban coffins in the morning and returned to them when dusk stole into their heated, insulated cubicles in the sky.

The flu Larsen had contracted on the tracks got better as the weather got worse. A circular depression was forming off Cape Hatteras, moving slowly northward, up the coast, sending ahead panicked refugees of grey cloud and sleet. The wind rattled and thudded against the Thermopane of Larsen's eyrie alongside the seat of world government.

Larsen had once paid to be taken on a quick safari through Luangwa Game Park in Zambia, with a couple of rich friends from Beirut. From that brief time he knew that the most dangerous game in the bush was a hunted leopard, wounded by gun-toting bwanas. The leopard didn't just lick his wounds and die; he first circled back to ambush the men who had hurt him.

Larsen had to translate the lesson of the big cat.

Larsen's quarry was above all else a system of privileged information spread by word of mouth only among initiates. Joe Sciacca's father had committed the ultimate crime against that system. He had written it all down, and passed it along to protect his son. The insurance policy. The ultimate weapon.

It was the weapon of the fisherman's revenge, a futile act to satisfy his sense of impotence, his hatred of excessive imbalance. Eliza, Marie, Joe, John. A litany. They had all died because frightened and violent men had deemed them obstacles to power. Revenge, in that context, was an act of nature to restore balance out of excess.

Or did striking back stem simply from an existentialist motivation, the kind he had laughed about with Marie, a desire to fight a basic lack of meaning by scarring the earth with your own gratuitous act?

Rationalizations were irrelevant. The wound alone was real. The fisherman wrote a long letter to Robert 'Lu Guercio' Mondragone, head of a secret Neapolitan grouping within Fulton Fish Market.

Larsen had heard of the Camorra in the natural course of events during his smuggling days in the Mediterranean, but only as a distant myth: Stangerson, at the time, dealt only with middlemen for his US clients, usually the Chicago and New York Families.

Know thine enemy. He looked up 'Camorra' in encyclopaedias loaned by the hotel management.

'*CAMORRA (ku mo' ru), Italian secret criminal association in Naples,*' the encyclopaedia read. '*Of controversial, probably Spanish origin, it first came to light in 1830. Its activities were extended by intimidation, blackmail and bribery until Naples was completely controlled by the group. In 1901 Neapolitan citizens formed an Honest Government league and succeeded in breaking the power of the Camorra, which was finally dissolved in 1911 . . . Up to that time, the Camorra had frequently terrorized Italian immigrants in the United States.*'

No kidding.

A more recent edition said, dryly, that the Camorra (ko mo ru) had been reactivated to fill a political vacuum in southern Italy, had regained its control of Neapolitan political and economic life (especially the black market), and now dominated, with the help of sister organizations in Sicily, the drug traffic in the western Mediterranean.

Amazing what you could learn from an encyclopaedia.

Larsen wrote another letter, this time to Frank Trapani, whom the Sciacca computer file indicated was the *sottocapo* responsible for both keeping the peace at Fulton and representing the five New York Families.

The third letter was to his brother, Per Larsen, United States Attorney for the Commonwealth of Massachusetts.

He sent all the letters by professional courier service, paid for in advance in cash.

Then Larsen pounded out two detailed summaries of information contained in the computer printout. One dealt with the evidence on price fixing, money laundering, tax evasion, and other standard activities within the market. The other dealt exclusively with the Camorra–Unione Corse bid to turn the market into a drug centre and beat the Organization at its own game, in its own territory.

The printout itself he sent by overnight courier service to O'Malley after asking his friend, over the phone, to put it immediately in the hands of a lawyer, with certain specific instructions.

No bluffing this time.

He went outside to telephone Ole from a public booth. The old man demanded a complete history of his more recent activities, the 'where-have-you-been' syndrome of a surrogate parent. They argued, disagreed, but Ole finally accepted his request for help. Then, grumbling, Ole related the news from home. One of the goats had mastitis, and Pariah again had been busted by the dog officer. One more time and he would be 'banished', a quaint custom whereby the dogcatcher took the reprobate hound and let him loose in the next town, for those townspeople to deal with.

Larsen spent the afternoon of the second day in the pool, and again had dinner sent to his room. The menu carried a 'wildlife special' that included bear, caribou, and hippopotamus steaks. Larsen ordered roast brown bear, the perfect repast if you were to believe the tribal superstition that claimed a man automatically acquired the salient characteristics of the relevant cuts of whatever he ate. Larsen hoped he would eat the portion that gave strength and courage, rather than a taste for blueberries.

The deepest part of the circular winter storm was due to strike around midnight. The chorus of wind and sleet was warming up for a final crescendo. It was perfect.

And it was time.

*

Long ago, when Larsen had been eight and his brother ten, their father had taken them for a ride on the Staten Island ferry, and Larsen could still feel the wonder of standing on the stern of the ferry and watching Manhattan's skyline punch out its message to the sky with every arrogant brick and steel girder.

The temperature fell after midnight as the depression passed overhead, sprinkling thick sprays of snow into the clutches of a thirty-knot wind. Even behind a shroud of white lace Larsen thought he remembered the ferryboat terminal, a squat, ugly building that looked as if the god of lavatories had taken a green-tiled institutional restroom, turned it inside out, and wedged it at the very foot of Manhattan Island.

At two-forty a.m. the discarded granite offices of old shipping companies – Cunard, French Lines, United States Lines, North German Lloyd – stood silent in the shadow of uninhabited skyscrapers. Only the ferry terminal, the Coast Guard offices, and the Seaman's Church Institute cast more than token light.

He shook his way out of the blizzard into the warmth of the terminal, went past the barbershop and bar, up the escalator, and through the turnstiles. The round-trip fare had quintupled since Larsen took the ride as a kid. It was twenty-five cents now, still the best and cheapest entertainment in New York City.

Light-green walls, Camel ads, olive-green linoleum. 'No Smoking, No Smoking, No Smoking' in big orange letters. Three sets of garage doors. Rows of wooden benches, empty save for a couple of old Rumanian men in long coats exchanging stuffed grape leaves and memories in their own tongue ('Do you remember Maria from Tirana, the one with the big boobs?'), a black punk with a tape deck that filled the vast room with syncopated, incoherent echoes, a cab driver on his way home from work, and a fat bum with large glasses, knickers, an army jacket three sizes too small, and a plastic flute.

Larsen and his fellow passengers waited fifteen minutes in the cherished solitude of imminent travel. There was a mute thunder and rumble, and the garage doors to the left swung open.

Larsen followed the other five travellers into a cave of chains, drawbridges and up-from-under lighting where the ferryboat had rammed itself into New York.

The *Private Joseph F. Merrill* was a fat, floating pastry of flaking orange paint, dirty decks, and oily warmth. A pastry that smelled of steamed hot dogs and sweet bunker fuel, that made its rumbling, crashing, freezing, sweating, sometimes dangerous run, day in, day out, night in, night out, come hell and black water, through one of the busiest harbours of the world.

The drawbridges clanked up.

A hoot, an acceleration in the rhythm of the rumble – it felt like the ferry would shake itself into pieces – then the cave was left behind and the *Merrill* went into the storm.

Larsen had spelled out appointments in the letters he had sent from the UN Plaza. The appointments were all for three-twenty that morning, at a stand of public phones next to Battery Park.

Assuming everyone showed up.

Larsen thought they would. There were enough facts, in sufficient detail, for each and every recipient of a letter to be very interested in meeting with the sender as soon as possible. The facts had all come from Sciacca's computerized cache.

Trapani, who according to the DEC 1300 was a captain in one of New York's most powerful Families, was the only unknown quantity. But his rank made him a good risk: high enough to be able to negotiate freely for the New York Families as well as the Organization, yet low enough for the invitation not to constitute a case of *lèse majesté*.

As the *Merrill* rolled her way through the blizzard, past the invisible nineteenth-century Disneyland of Ellis Island, the Coast Guard apartments on Governor's Island, and the Statue of Liberty, Larsen familiarized himself with the ferryboat's layout.

The lowest deck was all engine room, a steamy confusion of boilers and condensers. It was off limits to passengers, and in any case too cluttered for his purposes. Next came the open-ended parking deck, three dim lanes separated by hatches and ventilators, companionways and spare anchors, and flanked by two musty, enclosed corridors of windows and benches for the drivers whose cars were chocked outside.

Above that was the main passenger deck, a triple set of wooden pews, chrome snack bars, with an open deck fore and aft. The top deck had the same layout, but the ferry's twin wheelhouses, one on each end of the vessel, took the place of open decks.

Because there were two wheelhouses, allowing helmsmen to steer from either end of the ship, the Staten Island ferry had never turned around in its thirty-odd years of linking two islands.

The ferry crashed into the dolphins of Staten Island Terminal at three-twenty-five a.m. Larsen ran over the drawbridge as soon as it was lowered aboard the ferry and sprinted to the public phones in the waiting-room. He dialled the telephone number he had jotted down from one of the public booths at Battery Park.

A voice – mellifluous, educated, calm – answered on the third ring. Not Lu Guercio. Not the US Attorney, thank the gods; he lacked the self-control to talk with Per right now. Trapani.

'Yes.'

'This is Larsen. Is that Trapani?'

'Yes. You want to play games, Mr Larsen?'

'No. Take the four a.m. ferry to Staten Island.'

Larsen hung up and ran down the long horseshoe-shaped corridor back to the ferry. Uncle Ole was standing uncertainly by the drawbridge, one hand clutching a long duffel bag, the other in the pocket of his New Deal coat. A dented porkpie hat was jammed on to his head to keep the snow off.

Larsen surprised himself by hugging the old man. There was aquavit on Ole's breath, but not overmuch, considering he'd spent the last eight hours driving through a storm down the New England Thruway, across Long Island, and over the Verrazano-Narrows Bridge to the ferry terminal.

Larsen took his uncle to the automobile parking deck and

showed him what he would have to do. The old man smoked nervously, one hand scratching his crotch, and said little while Larsen explained. Most of the talking and arguing had been done over the phone.

But then he extricated his left hand from the pocket of his coat, where it had been fondling a quart of Aalborg, took both the fisherman's hands in his own gnarled claws, and looked rheumily into Larsen's eyes.

'I still think you're wrong about Per. He, like you, is my son,' the old man said in his distinctive singsong.

'You *vill* find out. But ve vill stand up to these bad men dat killed your woman. She was good. I talked with her. There is no other way . . . I believe you too . . .'

There were tears in Ole's eyes.

'Like Finland,' his nephew said, hoping the old man had not forgotten the lessons he had learned in a winter war over four decades ago.

'*Ja*, like Finland. Like Hitler's var, too. Only ve must remember our history. These men, dey are like Swedes, tricky. It will not be easy.'

Larsen twisted his nose, hoping the old man was not too drunk. They walked together on to the ferry.

The *Merrill* rumbled, shook and rolled back into thinning snow, her softly lit windows only making the waves blacker. Through the blizzard, the towers and bridges of Manhattan were distant, blurred, like a castle in a child's toy that had been shaken up and down so the tiny white crystals would swirl and give a feel of winter.

Larsen had been worried about the Manhattan side of his plan. The ferry's crew made sure all passengers went ashore to pay their quarter if they wanted to make the journey back. Larsen would have no problem leaving the ferry, but he did not want Per to see Ole.

At four a.m. the crew was sick of the night shift and tired of standing in an Arctic storm to handle gates and make sure passengers didn't try to lean over icy railings to watch the pretty waves. Their check consisted of a perfunctory walk down the lower decks.

Larsen and his uncle waited until they could hear cars

drive off, a couple of very early commuters. After five minutes they felt two, no, three, cars roll aboard the ferry, drawbridge clapping under the tyres.

Then Larsen got up from the bench he had been crouched behind, walked silently down the dim, deserted top deck and down the stairs to the main passenger level. He sneaked through the open doors of the companionway with their sign that read 'upper deck closed'. Coast Guard regulations prohibited locking the doors. As if anyone gave a damn at this time of night anyway.

There were two men at this level, separate as only the early hours of morning could make them. One looked like an insurance salesman. Short back and sides, inside and out, a plastic attaché case, rubber overshoes. The other was a Hassidic rabbi. The rabbi proceeded to conform to stereotype by eating a bagel.

He found his appointed travellers on the car deck, grouped uncertainly around a black Cadillac Seville with smoked windows, and cursed himself for not realizing they might bring a car with them. Larsen observed the men briefly from the shelter of a bulkhead at the end of the deck. They must have all taken a ride together from the phone booths, unless they had also brought the blue Dodge van and the Toyota lined up on deck in front of the Cadillac.

Per was leaning stiff against a ventilator, Lu Guercio was pacing steadily, up and down, white hair flapping in the little whirls of wind coming through the opening in the bow. He held his head in the curious way Larsen had first noticed when he was attacked in Front Street, tilted in two dimensions, favouring the one eye that could see.

That made the third man Trapani: moderately tall, late thirties, dark hair, sitting on the hood of the Cadillac. Trapani might drive the classic mobster's automobile but he looked like a well-to-do lawyer. Probably was.

Larsen had told them to come alone and maybe they had.

The fisherman walked casually down the deck towards the group. His heart was pumping faster – at least one of those men had blown away seven people on the stark possibility that silencing them would prevent discovery of the Sciacca

304

file – but his mind kept repeating the names of his friends and he walked a little more firmly in response.

'*Dodge City showdown*.' The thought came unexpectedly and his chuckle was more so. Living on the edge brought you closer to the truth of humour: every joke was a brief leap into nothing before you again hammered a reality together out of the void.

Trapani wore a three-piece business suit: his coat was probably in the Cadillac. The others had nondescript city overcoats that could conceal antitank weapons, if necessary.

Per Larsen, United States Attorney for the Commonwealth of Massachusetts, threw himself off the ventilator when he saw his brother, stalked towards him, and planted his frame in Lars' path?

'What in God's name are you playing at, Lars?'

The tone was furious and the eyes were angry but they both had a cast of real fear. It was the first time Lars had ever seen his brother scared.

'Do you know who these guys are? Do you know what you are *doing* with your pathetic little blackmail?'

Lars tried to step away but his brother matched his step.

'I don't know where you got the information you did, nor do I care, but there is no way you can prove it, kid brother. You're playing with the real world. Professionals, not amateurs. And professionals play hard ball. Give these guys what they want and go back to play with your little boats: you can't *prove* anything!

'I'm an attorney, Lars,' Per added more quickly, one hand plucking obsessively at the skin of his forehead. 'I know. You have no proof.'

'The fact that you are here, *brother*,' Lars said, even more quietly, 'is all the proof I need. Now get out of my way.'

He didn't feel like a younger brother any more. He felt much too tired, much older. The sibling bond was broken, the subconscious well of respect, trust, and obedience to the firstborn was dry. His brother felt it and was silent.

Lu Guercio had stopped his pacing and aimed the one clear bottle bottom of his glasses towards the fisherman. The Neapolitan stood, squat and square in a prizefighter's stance, both hands jammed in his pockets.

Trapani got up coolly from the Cadillac and lit a long cigarette with a steady hand, a curiously theatrical gesture. He had strong eyes, a wide forehead, and two truly magnificent eyebrows. He put the gold lighter away and said, 'Larsen? You write an *interesting* letter.

'Men have, shall we say, disappeared,' Trapani went on, 'throughout history, for far, far less.'

Lu Guercio said nothing, but the eyes missed not a single detail.

Per, trailing behind, said, 'My brother here is way out of his depth. He has agreed to return the stolen information.' Per's voice was cracked, unsure.

'Shut up,' Larsen said quietly without looking at his brother. Staring at Trapani, he continued, 'I'm disappointed, Frank. Empty threats, words. I've bluffed some, myself, throughout this business, but not this time.

'This time,' he turned to include Lu Guercio, 'I have everything Gaetano Sciacca recorded about thirty years of working for the Organization. Or your uncle's Family, Trapani. As a lieutenant, and as the head of a fish house, he knew everything about price fixing, tax evasion, money laundering. It's all in the hands of lawyers.' Larsen suddenly felt self-conscious. These men had all heard this kind of spiel before.

He forced himself to look as if uncertainty or nervousness were total strangers to him. 'If I suddenly died of cancer tomorrow the information would be in the hands of a real US Attorney, not your tame one here, a Justice Department official in Washington, before the week is out. You'd better hope I'm in good health.'

The man looked at him levelly, then brought his right hand up to smooth the long hairs of his right eyebrow with the second and third fingers. It was a reflex action, almost subconscious, like Per's plucking of the forehead, Larsen thought. The thought gave him confidence. Beneath all those layers of cool, Trapani was concerned.

'The fact that all you gentlemen kept this somewhat inconvenient appointment is proof enough that the few facts

I put in your invitations were accurate,' Larsen continued, giving each a look in turn, as politicians did.

The squat man with the strange glasses remained silent, but he shifted restlessly from foot to foot, hands still locked in coat pockets, eyes now fixed on the *sottocapo*.

'I am not very much interested in your so-called evidence about the fish market,' Trapani replied, finally. 'It is inconvenient, your letter made that plain, but the evidence of a corpse is not admissible . . . no jury would convict on that basis.'

He sucked on his cigarette. 'You mentioned something else.' His eyes stabbed at the one-eyed fish dealer. 'Please hurry. I had to go to a disco instead of going to sleep so I could keep this ridiculous appointment. I have to work in the morning.'

Larsen bent his right hand towards the inside pocket of his parka. He could feel the tension rise, and smiled in what he hoped was a comforting fashion. These men would always be wary of inside pockets and hands that went into them. He slowly pulled out two sheafs of typewritten papers from the pocket.

If the letter he had sent to the Family man had been an *hors d'oeuvre* of information compiled from Gaetano Sciacca's computer file, this was the main course. The nub of the ambush.

'These are for you, Trapani,' Larsen said. 'The information came from a hidden data cell within your own computer. The same DEC 1300 that services your own Wall Street brokering house.

'As I spelled out in the letter, it concerns the attempted takeover of the Organization's traditional, neutral fish market' – Larsen noticed the *sottocapo* wince every time he used the word 'Organization' – 'by a drug ring. Directly against the Organization's orders. The drug ring is led by the Naples Camorra and the French *milieu*, the Unione Corse, but it includes Chinese and Korean Tongs, Black gangs, Puerto Ricans. It is against the Organization, against the New York Families. Lu Guercio, here, is the head of the ring.'

Trapani took the pages impatiently.

It amazed Larsen how the normal world, as represented by the *Private Joseph F. Merrill*, rolling securely through a blizzard, could continue functioning while such strange business was at hand.

'I transcribed a lot of the information, but the computer printout itself is in the hands of lawyers. Don't try to call that bluff, because this time,' he glanced at Per Larsen, 'it's not a bluff. Take my word for it. Or don't, and find out the hard way.'

Lu Guercio had levered his gaze away from Trapani, and Larsen felt his eyeballs freeze in the coldness of the look the Neapolitan gave him. It was a light blue loss of temperature that stated the world was peopled only with flies to squash, or pull the wings off of. A fish eye.

Lu Guercio spoke at last, clearing his throat in preamble.

'It's bullshit, Frank.' The voice was harsh, unemotional. 'Gaetano made that up, completely. To blackmail us. He was a fucking scum –'

Trapani dismissed him with a gesture of his free hand, and moved nearer a light on the deckhead to read the closely typed pages. The one-eyed man shut up and made a truncated movement, as if he wanted to raise both hands in a rude gesture, but could not.

The ferry started pitching a little, and the sound of engines was loud from a ventilator on the parking deck. A crew member came out of the engine-room hatchway, watched them curiously for a moment, and went into the passenger accommodation. The same fat bum who had been on the last trip with Larsen walked unsteadily out from under the lifeboat, lurched in their direction, then sat down suddenly, clumsily, on the spare anchor and tried a trill on his plastic flute. He was unsuccessful. Even at fifty feet you could see his expression of surprise and disgust. He tried again.

A lot of bums paid a quarter to hide out on the ferry as Larsen had done, stay warm, dry, moving. It gave their lives an illusion of progression. So what if they always ended up where they started . . .

Trapani said, 'There are details here you might want to talk about, Bobby.'

His voice was calm, friendly. Larsen found himself wondering if he wasn't way off in left field.

'The Tramunti killing, for example,' he continued, without looking at Lu Guercio or taking his eyes off the typed pages.

'What killing? Tramunti died in a car accident. Everybody knows that . . .' The Neopolitan hunched away from the other men, leaving himself facing Trapani: 'I don't know what's going on, *amico mio*, but I ask you not to fall for his trick. Someone's trying to split the Organization. The Families on one side, us on the other. It's so obvious.'

Trapani took a couple of steps down the deck, still reading, as if to get away from the smaller man's influence, and went on absently. 'He was killed so one of the Neapolitans could take over a fish house? This came from Sciacca's computer? I find it hard to believe . . .'

'It's bull,' Lu Guercio snarled.

'I'll give you the codes,' Larsen offered, desperately. He was being cut out here, made a target. This was not according to plan. 'You can look for yourself.'

The *sottocapo* continued reading, puffing almost girlishly at his cigarette, not swallowing the smoke. The minutes dragged by as if each second were reluctant to miss the dénouement of this weird little act. Trapani dropped the butt and ground it delicately into the deck with a tasselled Italian shoe. Then he said to Lu Guercio, 'You're going to pay for this.'

'Shit!' Lu Guercio yelled, wiggling his shoulders, but he kept his hands in his jacket. Larsen could see Trapani was also aware of how the lack of hand gestures contradicted the Neapolitan's anger. 'It's lies, lies, lies! Lies! I've proved how loyal I am to the Organization how many times? How many times have I washed my hands with blood for your Family, Frank?' The Camorra man was pacing again in agitation. 'I know you young guys don't like that, you want it legal now, *ma e' importante! Per rimanere un'uomo di onore —*'

His jaw snapped shut.

'*Un'uomo di onore*,' Trapani repeated softly. 'A man of

honour. You betray yourself, Bobby. That's the Camorra's phrase, not my Family's.'

'So what?' yelled the Neapolitan, but the Organization man was looking at the fisherman.

'That's why you wanted him along, isn't it? So that I would believe you through his reaction. You know we trust people more than computers. You're an intelligent man, Larsen.'

'What am I supposed to do? Blush?'

'Well, I believe you,' Trapani said, and the eyebrows were combed again. 'The facts, as they say, speak for themselves. I will have them checked out, of course, but they explain a lot of questions we have had over the last couple of years. *Non e' vero, Guercio?*'

Lu Guercio complained, 'It's *your* fault, Frank. The Families and the Organization together want everything for themselves. Drugs, fish, everything. It's not fair,' he whined, 'if you'd just let us take a cut, Frank?'

Trapani made a gesture of sharp dismissal.

'We will talk later, among family –' Lu Guercio began.

'We will *not* talk later,' Trapani screamed out of the blue. 'You and your friends from Naples will find out what it means to go against the business! The Organization has team players; that's what we are, it's what we have to be. It's like football,' he spoke more softly. 'You screw up, you get thrown off the team. Like the Cowboys,' Trapani mused fondly. 'You sell the plays to the Eagles, you don't play with the Cowboys any more . . .'

Without turning away from the fish dealer he said, 'What do you want from me, Larsen?'

'Three or four things.'

'You don't ask for much, do you? I will not be blackmailed.'

'Wait. Just a favour. Lu Guercio and his people killed four friends of mine and framed me for murder. I want them punished, legally if possible.'

'And if that's not possible?' asked the *sottocapo*.

'I want them punished.'

'They will be punished. I wouldn't worry about that.'

Trapani, fishing for his cigarette case, had now totally cut out the Neapolitan.

'I also want somebody to take the rap for killing Marie Riley.'

'Who?'

'Gaetano Sciacca's daughter-in-law. A friend of mine. Lu Guercio's people killed her with my knife, so as to put me on the run. I guess they figured if I was on the run, I wouldn't find Old Man Sciacca's file. So now I'm wanted for murder.'

'Why should I do you a favour like that?' The question was put in a neutral, disinterested tone.

'So I don't send the printout to the FBI. I know,' Larsen said, as Trapani started to interject, 'I know it's not great conviction material. I know you don't like being blackmailed. But we both know it would seriously screw up your Fulton operation if the Justice Department got hold of it because they would be watching you and your people so closely that you couldn't even fart without being recorded on an FBI tape.'

Trapani took a drag at his cigarette and threw it away with only a fraction burned. He turned towards the stern of the boat, turned back.

'Okay. I guess we can do that. That's why your brother, the US Attorney for Massachusetts, is here, right? I think Peter will go along with that. We'll find out who did the hit, anyway, and we'll funnel some evidence back through Peter's office. We might even buy you a confession,' he said, boasting a little. 'It's not hard.

'I guess you know Peter's a – an associate of ours, although how you figured that out . . .' Trapani said, smiling a crocodile smile.

Lars Larsen's older brother actually had a small grin perched on his own lips.

'That's the third thing I was going to ask you –'

'You fucking *scumbag*!'

Lu Guercio was looking at the fisherman, not talking loudly.

'I should kill you now.' Very, very slowly, he brought his hands out of his pockets and raised them, empty into thin air.

Trapani gave him some attention for the first time in three minutes.

Then the back of the blue van slammed open and two men stood framed in the doorway, each cradling the blunt black box of an Ingram M10 machine gun. The Ingrams were silenced. Both men wore blue jeans and dark sweaters. One was a young Chinaman, wearing yellow spectacles; the other was Joseph Stangerson.

'But perhaps I won't,' Lu Guercio continued softly, still eyeballing Larsen. The one-eyed man stepped backward, away from the field of fire.

'Perhaps I will only kill my young Sicilian friend here,' he continued, 'along with his tame US Attorney. Perhaps I will let you go – if you give me the printout. The original. And the codes, so I can kill Gaetano's file for good, you no-good, interfering *pezzo di merda*,' Lu Guercio added, unable to control the venom.

Trapani was combing his eyebrows. Per Larsen looked as if he'd been freeze-dried like a coffee crystal.

The theatre inside Larsen where fear should have held centre stage only registered mild audience reaction at this new turn of events.

'You're with the Camorra people?' he asked Stangerson, who was smiling politely behind his Ingram. 'I just figured you for a coincidence.'

The Englishman shrugged. 'The Lebanese, the Corsicans, and especially the Camorra have taken over most of the drug trade in the Med. They supply me, they're the hottest new show in town, and suddenly – I don't have any choice but to play with the Camorra if I want to keep living in the style to which I have become accustomed.'

The one-eyed man jerked impatiently.

'Get in the van,' he interrupted, talking to Larsen.

'No,' said Larsen.

'Move,' the Neapolitan yelled.

'Go ahead, shoot me,' the fisherman said calmly. 'Why wait? Whether I get the information or not, you've got to kill me anyway. And my brother, and Trapani. We'd remember too much.'

'There *is* a reason,' Lu Guercio said slowly, taking a snub-nosed pistol out of his coat. It almost disappeared in his large hand. 'You. *Get* it.'

Stangerson bent so slowly it seemed insolent, into the depths of the Dodge, then inched back towards the door, hauling a large, full potato sack that stank of old fish and was marked 'New Brunswick Fish Meal Co. Ltd. 100 lbs.' The Neapolitan fumed. Stangerson folded the machine gun's shoulder stock so he could aim it easily with one hand, like a pistol, then kneeled down and ripped off the baling twine that fastened it and folded down the top of the sack.

Larsen felt the blood drain entirely from his face. His heart simulated thrombosis. Somewhere deep in his gut there stirred a new embryo of hope that came because –

Eliza–

Eliza was alive. Her mouth was taped shut and her eyes were closed, but Larsen could see a pulse hammer blue in her temple.

Once again, hope was renewed. Once again, fear came in its wake. Once more he had something to lose.

'Get in, *cazzo*,' Lu Guercio hissed. He sidled towards the fisherman and held the pistol steadily at his head.

'No,' Larsen repeated stubbornly, knowing his face had gone pale as chalk, hoping the pallor would not detract from whatever performance he had to play.

'I will let you both live. I will give you running time, if you do not believe me.' The fish eye was trying to look paternal and failing miserably. 'I need the printout that much. It is my life that is at stake.' The .38 waved at Trapani, rather unprofessional.

'Show me she is alive, unharmed,' Larsen said hastily, thinking faster, harder than he ever had in his life, under odds he had never met before, shoving back a wall of fear with the sheer frequency of his brain waves.

Which lifeboat was Ole hiding under? The bum, still trying to figure out how to play his flute, oblivious to the small drama being performed next to him, had left the shelter of the portside boat, Larsen remembered. Presumably he had left when Ole showed up on the starboard side. He hoped so, because now it was Eliza's life on the line.

'I want to know she's unhurt. She could be paralysed, a vegetable.' Larsen shouted, 'You said you'd *killed* her,' letting panic creep into his voice.

'You always were a dumb bastard, but you never used to be weak,' Stangerson said, the Oxford accent leaking contempt.

'Fuck that,' Lu Guercio said.

'No. We need his co-operation, for the time being.' There was a ring of authority to Stangerson's words now, and Larsen wondered, far from idly, who now wore the pants in the Camorra drug-smuggling clique. Maybe Stangerson was gunning (in a manner of speaking) for the top.

The smuggler dragged the sack over the van's bumper, letting Eliza's heels crash on to the deck.

'I want to *see* her,' Larsen cried and lunged forward, hoping he wouldn't get plugged then and there. One squeeze on an Ingram trigger and he would be partitioned like India and almost as messily. Trapani was only smoothing one eyebrow now. Definitely a cool bastard.

Larsen dragged the girl halfway out of the sack, away from the van, trying to pull her at a speed halfway between foolish anxiety and attempted escape. He felt a surge of fury when he saw she was freezing, blue lips, nothing on but a T-shirt. She looked absurdly young. He quelled the fury immediately. No time, *no!*

Neither of the men with the Ingrams was going to move, as he'd hoped. Stangerson stepped out of the van and crab-walked sideways, lithely, to keep the fisherman within a broad field of fire, closer to him so the machine gun would not hit his boss by mistake, because Lu Guercio had moved with Larsen, keeping the .38 aimed towards the fisherman's head, but his good eye dropped once to Eliza's left breast, peeking out of the rucked-up T-shirt.

Larsen bunched his muscles, pretending to concentrate on the girl's white face, then released them in a surge of adrenalin, throwing himself backward into Lu Guercio's legs, grabbing behind him for the P7 concealed at his back, and screaming, 'Now Ole!'

He heard a burst of bullets that ricocheted off the metal bulkhead behind them, filling the air with twenty pieces of lead that bounced around the car deck at 1100 feet per second. The only reason the Ingram slugs weren't scissoring a 'cut-out-the-coupon' line across his stomach was that he was beneath the one-eyed Neapolitan. He was trying to dig the P7 from his belt holster, but their combined weight was making it impossible. He grasped Lu Guercio's throat and pulled sideways, hauling the one-eyed man off swiftly enough to keep him from aiming his .38, got a grip on his own pistol and pulled it out of the holster into his palm and through in an expert movement that had the Heckler and Koch levelled on the Chinaman's chest before the man realized Larsen had rolled out from under his boss. But Lu Guercio had the reflexes of a cat and was rolling back to bring the .38 to bear; Larsen put a bullet in the Oriental's chest and dropped sideways just before Lu Guercio pulled the trigger, the .38 bullet scoring a deep gash across Larsen's forearm.

There was another boom and Larsen saw Lu Guercio's head snap backward, the thick glasses flying off in pale imitation of the Neapolitan's brain pan now dribbling, a squashed peach, fore and aft down the car deck. A glass eye bounced grotesquely.

Trapani's fancy shoes were all Larsen could see of the mobster. The rest of his body was trying to weld itself to the Cadillac's oil pan.

Stangerson had disappeared, leaving a pool of red on the corrugated iron where Ole, presumably, had plugged him with the Krag-Jorgensen. Larsen couldn't see him any more but the fat bum with the plastic flute had given up music for martial arts and let off two rapid shots from a snub-nose revolver, two huge Magnum '*booms*' aiming under the van before a silent wall of lead picked him up and flung him bodily eight feet backward, the entire front of his body spouting into squashy fountains of blood and intestine and stomach lining.

Another huge report.

Larsen dropped to the deck over Eliza's prone body, the Heckler and Koch levelled in both hands, and fired once into

315

the general darkness under the van. A long shadow grunted, rolled, and the Ingram pivoted towards Larsen, bullets clanging closer, closer, the wind of their passage ruffling his hair. The fisherman let off a second shot, then a third, and the Ingram jerked, ripping up into the van's floor. The shape rolled again, faster, and came to awkward rest against the chock under the automobile's front left tyre and was still.

Everything was still, except for the *Merrill*, always shaking and rolling her way to Manhattan Island.

Keeping the P7 aimed with one hand, Larsen crawled carefully under the van and slid the Ingram out of a thickening pool of blood. He did the same with the Chinaman's weapon. The yellow sunglasses, a conceit of life, looked sad and silly next to all that death.

'Not business,' Larsen said in a casual tone towards Stangerson's body. 'Just personal.'

Only then did Larsen turn, slowly, and look at the pale, partially naked body that lay, half in, half out of a stinking fish meal sack. The body was motionless. Blood was spattered scarlet all over the sack.

The green eyes were open now, green eyes with a dark corona. The eyelid on one of them dropped, slow, and rose again. An invisible tear was carving tracks through the fish-meal dust on her cheek.

Larsen groaned and fell to his knees, feeling as if he were six years old, that vulnerable because of this woman.

'You're okay?' he whispered. He couldn't seem to talk any louder.

The long neck heaved as she gulped, shuddered, and nodded.

The fisherman prayed silently at her temple then rose again, leaving her bound, gagged, helpless, and surveyed the carnage of the automobile deck.

A couple of crewmen were peering in sheer terror around the stern bulkhead.

Trapani was on his feet again, unscathed, leaning into the Cadillac, trying to get a mobile radiotelephone to work. It would be difficult inside the all-steel ferry. Typical business executive, Larsen thought. Couldn't even be bothered to check the bodyguard who had given his life for his boss. Although there wasn't much left of the 'bum' to check.

At least Larsen assumed he had been Trapani's bodyguard. He must have had the Battery Park rendezvous point staked out, and followed the fisherman to the ferry.

Then he saw Ole kneeling over Per, the old Krag-Jorgensen rifle lying on the deck by his side, next to the duffel bag it had been concealed in. Lars' brother had taken two ricocheted slugs in the side, and the saliva oozing down the attorney's smooth-shaven cheek was pink instead of clear.

The eyes were already lacklustre, but they moved to take in the fisherman. Larsen was not conscious of standing up, walking, till he was next to his brother. He took out his jackknife and cut open the attorney's coat, jacket, waistcoat, and shirt in one clean slice.

His uncle was ripping up his own soiled shirt for use as a bandage, tears coursing down the eroded cheeks.

'Easy, Per boy, easy, boy, easy,' the old man kept repeating.

'Is – it – serious – ?' Per gasped, little pink bubbles popping out of his words. His eyes were wide open like a kid's.

The fisherman shook his head. 'You'll be okay,' he tried to say.

Per didn't seem to believe him. He must be able to feel the air passing in and out of his perforated chest.

'Poor – li'l – brother.'

The fisherman took off his sheepskin coat and put it over the dying man.

'Why, Per?' Lars finally managed to say. 'Why'd you do it? Why'd you betray me? The only reason I wanted you here was so you could prove you didn't.'

'You suspected all along?' Lars nodded. 'How'd you – find out?'

Lars shook his head, watching the face gain pallor, the same face, well remembered, yet different from what he had idolized through all the years that made a person what he was.

'No one else knew that I had found the wreck of *Marie*
Eliza never published her story, and the people she or my
crew might have talked to would be unlikely to talk to anyone
connected to the Camorra. But when that smuggling ship
sank *Sofia* there, they knew exactly where we were. And I
had told you the position. You were the only one who knew
. . . who could have told.

'Of course, I wasn't sure . . . I didn't want to believe it,'
Lars murmured. 'But no one else knew,' he went on, 'that
I hadn't given the information to a lawyer when I came down
here this time. I told Lu Guercio a lawyer had it, but that was
a bluff.

'Yet they tried to kill me anyway, which would be stupid
unless they knew the information really wasn't in a lawyer'
hands. They *knew* the information was in safe hands,' Lars
continued sadly, 'because I had told you where it was. So you
told them it was in safe hands. Yours.'

'They went through Worcester,' Per Larsen gasped
'They asked me where you had gone – I – I owed them – but
they never said – they'd – *kill* – you. Threats.' Per tried to
raise his head and fell back, coughing. 'Please, Lars.'

Larsen adjusted the coat over his brother. 'Easy, man
Easy.'

Per licked pinkish froth from his lips. 'When your boat –
left – figured you'd gone back, to the wreck,' he whispered
'Said they just wanted . . . stop you . . . told them . . . Asia
Rip.'

They were a quarter mile from the dock. The ferry was
slowing. A plump man in an officer's cap was walking over
tremulously with a First Aid kit. Red lights winked on the
Battery Park bulkhead.

'We have this Congressional seat pretty much guaranteed
through Frank Smith.' Trapani was standing behind them
He had approached, silent as a ghost, hands in his hip
pockets, pants still with a knife-edge crease in them. 'Pete
was helping us set up legal gambling in Massachusetts.'

'But – mistake!' Per whispered. Lars had to lower his
ear to Per's mouth. His brother moaned. 'Should have
known . . .'

'They must have gone through Mazzie, Family channels in Worcester, without asking us,' the *sottocapo* said. 'He really isn't a Camorra man – he isn't Mondragone's. The Camorra, I think, tricked him. We were paying him a lot of money,' Trapani explained.

'Why, Per?' Larsen asked, knowing Per would know the question remained the same.

'Hardball – game – li'l brother. You'll learn, we'll show 'em.' But the eyes registered surprise and looked over the fisherman's shoulder, Larsen looked behind him but there was only Trapani.

He heard his brother mutter something like 'Pa', or maybe he was trying to say 'Patty', and when he looked back down the head had fallen aside, blood flowing from nose and mouth, and Per's eyes stared blankly at the void.

Ole was sobbing grotesquely, his false teeth sucking loose with every harsh breath, holding on to his nephew's hand.

Larsen staggered up and went to kneel by Eliza. He took out his jackknife again and cut the thick packaging tapes that held her. She was everything pure, fresh, and sweet, not only in the fetid, freezing harbour but in the rest of a sorry world, and cutting her loose would satisfy the only need he had left in that tragicomedy.

Her lips moved clumsily, framing 'Lars'. Her tongue darted in a pink reflex to rescue a drop of spit.

The fairytale towers of New York reached for emergent stars. The snow had almost stopped but still Manhattan blurred and melted in the square archway of the ferry's bow.

'Lars.'

'What, Eliza?'

'Lars.'

She touched his cheeks wonderingly.

'You're crying, too,' she said.

The *Joseph F. Merrill* slowed and lined up to enter her berth.

Fontana Paperbacks: Fiction

Fontana is a leading paperback publisher of both non-fiction, popular and academic, and fiction. Below are some recent fiction titles.

- ☐ HEAVEN Virginia Andrews £2.75
- ☐ THURSDAY'S CHILD Helen Forrester £1.95
- ☐ THE EXILE Peter Essex £2.75
- ☐ BANNISTER'S CHART Antony Trew £2.50
- ☐ WHERE LOVE RULES Elizabeth Nell Dubus £2.95
- ☐ THE LANDOWER LEGACY Victoria Holt £2.95
- ☐ WILD ABOUT HARRY Paul Pickering £2.50
- ☐ FIELD OF BLOOD Gerald Seymour £2.75
- ☐ KING'S CROFT Christine Marion Fraser £2.95
- ☐ THE MORNING TIDE Audrey Howard £2.95
- ☐ THE HUNT FOR RED OCTOBER Tom Clancy £2.95
- ☐ PROFIT WITHOUT HONOUR Tom Keene £2.95
- ☐ RIDE A PALE HORSE Helen MacInnes £2.75

You can buy Fontana paperbacks at your local bookshop or newsagent. Or you can order them from Fontana Paperbacks, Cash Sales Department, Box 29, Douglas, Isle of Man. Please send a cheque, postal or money order (not currency) worth the purchase price plus 15p per book for postage (maximum postage is £3.00 for orders within the UK).

NAME (Block letters) _____

ADDRESS _____

_____

While every effort is made to keep prices low, it is sometimes necessary to increase them at short notice. Fontana Paperbacks reserve the right to show new retail prices on covers which may differ from those previously advertised in the text or elsewhere.